BLOOD ALLIANCE SERIES
GHASTELY BITTEN
ROYALLY BITTEN
REGALLY BITTEN
REBEL BITTEN
KINGLY BITTEN
CRUELLY BITTEN

REGALLY BITTEN

Lexi C. Foss

Editing by: Outthink Editing, LLC

Proofreading by: Allison Irwin, Barb Jack, Jean Bachen, Joy Giachino, Katie Schmahl, & Loves2ReadRomance

Cover Art and Design by Tairelei (https://www.instagram.com/tairelei/)

Crest Illustration: Nathan Hansen

Interior Character Art: Manuela Serra

Interior Character Photography: Wander Aguiar

Interior Character Models: Wayne, Evan, & Patrick

Published by: Ninja Newt Publishing, LLC

Print Edition

ISBN: 978-1-950694-27-3

AI Disclaimer: This book does not contain any elements of AI content. All art was designed by real artists, and all of the words were written by the author.

To Katie, for loving this trio of lycans as much as I do and for your amazing friendship and incredible support. I appreciate you more than you know!

To Matt, for your love, patience, and companionship and for your willingness to go on adventures all over the world with me and my laptop.

And to the readers, for giving me a chance to try new things. I really hope you enjoy the lycans. They bite.

REGALLY BITTEN

A Blood Alliance Novel

Dear Reader,

My writing style is very "prolific," meaning I tend to have the next three to six books planned in a series while writing a current one. This was definitely the case with *Regally Bitten*. I had my hero and heroine lined up, the "bad guy" picked out, and an initial outline in my head.

But a strange thing happened during *Royally Bitten*.

That "bad guy" I'd selected for *Regally Bitten*? Yeah, he started talking to me. And I couldn't stop listening.

So I really hope you enjoy Edon's book, as he well and truly took over.

This is a ménage romance between lycans.

There are harsh moments.

It's riddled with dystopian darkness.

And a hell of a lot of orgasms.

Some important story elements to consider:
✔ Arranged Mating
✔ Dubious Consent

✔ MM Content, MF Content, MMF Content, MFM Content
✔ Heroine & Heroes are not virgins
✔ Primal Play
✔ Hero is forced to "share" heroine publicly (with his Enforcer)
✔ Death of tertiary characters (this world is brutal and ruled by vampires; humans are toys…)

*Once upon a time, humankind ruled the world while vampires and
lycans lived in secret.
This is no longer that time.*

Luna

An arranged marriage? F*ck. This.
I'm an alpha female. I choose my future. Not society. Not
my father. And certainly not *him*.

Silas

I didn't survive just to be cast aside as a low level lycan. I'm
more powerful than they realize. More determined. More
intelligent. And far more worthy of her than anyone else.

Edon

Duty—a word I loathe.

I'm the future Clemente Clan Alpha. There are rules.
There are responsibilities. There can be no love. No free
will.

But the heart wants what the heart wants, and right now, I
desire them both.

*Welcome to the Clemente Clan.
Be careful. We Bite.*

Once upon a time, humankind ruled the world while lycans and vampires lived in secret.

This is no longer that time.

Welcome to the future where the superior bloodlines make the rules.

Proceed at your own risk.

THE BLOOD ALLIANCE

International law supersedes all national governance and will be maintained by the Blood Alliance—a global council of equal parts lycan and vampire.

All resources are to be distributed evenly between lycan and vampire, including territory and blood. Societal standing and wealth, however, will be at the discretion of the individual packs and houses.

To kill, harm, or provoke a superior being is punishable by immediate death. All disputes must be presented to the Blood Alliance for final judgment.

Sexual relationships between lycans and vampires are strictly prohibited. However, business partnerships, where fruitful and appropriate, are permitted.

Humans are hereby classified as property and do not carry any legal rights. Each will be tagged through a sorting system based on merit, intelligence, bloodline, ability, and beauty. Prioritization to be established at birth and finalized on Blood Day.

Twelve mortals per year will be selected to compete for immortal blood status at the discretion of the Blood Alliance. From this twelve, two will be bitten by immortality. The others will die. To create a lycan or vampire outside of this process is unlawful and punishable by immediate death.

All other laws are at the discretion of the packs and royals but must not defy the Blood Alliance.

LYCAN FAMILY CREST

Twenty-two years of promises wrapped up in lies.

Win the Immortal Cup, they'd said. *And join us in immortality.* The images that had followed were ones of wealth, excitement, and a life of indulgence.

Those images depicted the worst kind of deception.

As I writhed on the ground, growling in pain through my "welcome" to immortality, I couldn't help but wish I'd died instead.

Because what lay ahead was a fate worse than death.

Edon—my torturer—crouched before me, his expression bored. "It'll pass." The crowd around us chuckled.

His father, Alpha Walter, snorted. "This year's crop was shit."

"Clearly," Edon agreed, standing. "Can we finish this now?"

It's not done yet? Fuck.

"Part of the fun is seeing how long the new ones last in limbo," the alpha replied, his tone filled with disgust. "But clearly he's not long for this world."

"An omega," someone else jeered.

I wanted to snarl at the word, prove him wrong, but the pain had me groaning instead. Too many weeks without food, battling for my life, had weakened me to this degraded state where I could hardly move.

But I'd won.

And for what?

Torture.

Edon sighed. "He had a lot of promise." He ran his fingers through my matted hair, down my jaw, the touch surprisingly intimate from a male. "Shall I end him or finish it?"

"Up to you, son. These are the decisions an alpha must make for the clan." He whistled, the sound piercing my skull and shooting stars off behind my eyes. And then he howled. Others joined in, including Edon, and energy shimmered through the air.

Shifting.

I felt the magic crawl over my skin, enticing me to follow suit, but something blocked my ability, causing me to growl low and feral.

Edon's brows rose. "Well, well." He tilted his head, still in human form as his clan circled and sniffed, their muzzles terrifyingly large. "Perhaps there's hope for you yet, Silas."

My lips curled, a defensive instinct shuddering down my spine.

Edon's palm circled my throat, his obsidian pupils ringed with inky embers. "Challenging the son of an alpha is a dangerous move. And ballsy as fuck." He squeezed, but I didn't give an inch.

If he wanted to kill me, fine. I'd been through hell and back, only to find out I'd fought for a life that didn't exist. Not here. Not with the Clemente Clan.

The excitement rose in the crowd, the decision of my life weighing in the palm of their future alpha.

And then he struck.

His fangs sank deep into my neck, the power rippling over my skin and connecting to his earlier bite.

My moan turned into something deeper, starker, more animalistic, as my bones shifted into something *other*.

Edon watched, his palm shifting to my nape, his gaze cold and merciless.

I hated him.

Feared him.

Wanted to *be* him.

All in the span of seconds as my body transitioned into its new form.

More howls.

My own joining the fray.

My instincts heightened.

Scents and sights I never knew existed.

And then strong human fingers ran through my stark white fur, Edon's forehead pressing to mine. "Welcome to Clemente Clan, Silas."

Several Weeks Later...

BE USEFUL, they told me. *Guard the perimeter.*

In other words, they didn't want me to disturb the precious mating ceremony between my sire—the alpha heir—and his intended from Ernest Clan.

Fine.

I'd prowl around out here, memorize the scents, listen to the secrets from afar, and plan. Because I couldn't continue on as the pariah in the Clemente Clan. The only turned wolf in over two decades. A half-blood to them all.

No.

I didn't survive all this bullshit just to be exiled.

Nothing in this world was what they promised us. *Nothing.*

I hated it here. Loathed my new life as a lycan. And while I respected that it could be a hell of a lot worse, it could also be better. There had to be something else out there, some other way for us all to live in harmony.

A low growl had my ears twitching toward the woods that bordered the party, my eyes finding a tall female with elfin features standing near the forest edge.

Her clenched fists displayed her discomfort, her focus on a male towering over her.

"You will behave," the alpha wolf snarled. "Yield to him, Luna. Or else."

With those tender words, he entered the festivities, leaving her snarling in his wake.

The alpha's intended, I realized. Her stature depicted her strength and defiance, marking her as distinctly different from all the other females I'd seen around her. I also recognized her name as the one whispered amongst the Clemente Clan, their curiosity at what she would look like a hot topic among the males.

Beautiful, I thought. *Beautiful and pissed.*

It intrigued me. I clearly wasn't the only one dissatisfied with my circumstances.

Her focus shifted to me, sensing my presence in the woods. I held her gaze, my instincts refusing to bow to another.

She snorted in reply, the sound carrying along the breeze.

Rather than come after me as most alpha wolves would be inclined to do, she flipped her long dark hair over her shoulder and returned to the party, deigning me as insignificant.

Just like everyone else.

My fur ruffled in irritation.

Someday these wolves would take me seriously.

I just had to figure out my place in this new world. Because one thing I knew for certain—I didn't belong at the bottom.

CHAPTER 1
LUNA

Fuck. This. Shit.

I couldn't decide whom I wanted to punch more—my father or the Clemente Clan Alpha, Walter.

Probably both.

My mother squeezed my hand. Again. A polite reminder to keep my mouth shut and accept my fate. Just like she did all those years ago. And wasn't she a happy pup?

I almost snorted. All of this was complete and utter bullshit. I wanted to pick my future mate, not have one assigned to me. Especially not a prick like Edon. He looked just like his father, with those sinfully dark eyes, nearly black hair, and arrogant smirk.

Walter had quite a reputation for fucking his harem to death. His poor *mate* was usually forced to watch or participate. And she appeared just as broken as many of the females in this clan.

My future, I growled to myself. *Not fucking happening*. I'd break Edon's dick before he touched me with it. And I let him see that with a glance.

His eyebrow arched, intrigue flashing in his pupils.

Of course he wanted to play.

All males did.

But I had a plan, one that guaranteed he'd deny me tonight. Then I'd be on my way back to Ernest Clan. Oh, my father would be pissed. He'd probably try to sell me off to the highest bidder. I would deal with that when the time came, just as I planned to handle tonight's little ritual.

Alphas were possessive.

And I intended to use that to my advantage.

My father introduced me to some royal vampire and his new toy. I barely listened. The politics in this world sucked. It was all most people knew, but my mentor growing up spoke of an old time, one where females had more rights. Where we chose our own mates. Where we hid from vampires and humans.

What I wouldn't give to have been born in *that* century.

Alas, no. I was stuck here with these assholes who expected me to bow, curtsy, and maintain polite conversation, as if I weren't an alpha female. Forcing me to deny all my instincts, to accept my place as beneath the males of the pack even though I could easily slaughter most of them.

It churned my stomach.

Conversation flowed around me. Formalities shoved down my throat. Until, finally, the ceremony began.

I couldn't wait to get this over with.

And from the looks of it, neither could my intended mate. Only, he was looking forward to something very different from what I had in mind, something that would not be happening once he realized my secret.

Hums of approval haunted the air, the wolves eager for the show to start. Only a handful of royal vampires remained, mostly the ones intrigued by the lycan rituals. I wasn't surprised to see Jace among them. He was notorious for taking wolves to bed. A dangerous proposition for a bloodsucker, but he struck me as someone who could handle himself.

He stood with two other royals, their eyes glittering in the night.

I ignored them in preference for the surrounding alphas, their expressions hungry and expectant as they formed a crescent near the altar beneath the full moon.

Next month when this happened, it would be to complete the mating bond.

But I wouldn't be here to see it. Because I had no intention of seeing this through.

Edon stepped to the front, his black button-down shirt undone at the collar. Unlike me, he was permitted to wear clothing for this event. I would be expected to approach him naked, to show him everything I had to offer.

Because all alpha males cared about was fucking.

And he would want to make sure I met his physical needs.

My lips curled. *Oh, won't you be shocked.*

Chants began, my parents taking their position on either side of the aisle. Wolves and vampires alike dotted the audience, everyone in human form.

I stood at the end, allowing my mother to remove my dress and heels.

No undergarments—not because of any requirements, but because I preferred it that way. Easier to shift when I wore minimal clothes.

I rolled my shoulders, confident in my appearance. Our clan undressed in front of each other all the time; some didn't even bother with clothes. But it was a little weird to walk down along the path between foreign lycans.

Clemente Clan had a different vibe. The air here was

different, too, the texture resembling a sultry kiss against my pale skin. I rather preferred the icy planes back home. *Former-day Russia,* my advisor once called it. Clemente Clan was in the southern United States. All foreign terms in this new world, but I knew all about the old one. Something that would infuriate my parents if they knew, which was why it'd been my little secret with Claudette and my brother, Logan.

"May I present Luna of Ernest Clan," my father said, his tone filled with pride as we approached the Alpha of Clemente Clan and his heir apparent.

Yes, I hope you're so proud of yourself for forcing me to mate a man I don't know, I thought. *Such excellent parenting.*

Edon met my gaze and held it, the challenge in his dark depths clear. He expected me to bow. I narrowed my eyes instead.

I bow to no one.

My mother's nails bit into my forearm, causing me to flinch.

My father cleared his throat.

I could practically hear Logan scolding me as well. *Don't be an idiot, Luna,* he would say. *Play it cool.*

He was probably the only one I'd ever listen to, his advice usually sound.

Fine, I thought to them all. *Fine.*

I would bow. Only because this would be our first and last meeting.

My knees bent, my head lowering. It felt so wrong. So ridiculous. And I couldn't help peeking up at him as I did it, which earned me a surprised look from the alpha heir.

"You're going to have your hands full with this one, son," Walter commented.

"I can see that," he replied dryly.

Pricks, I thought, righting myself after my half-assed attempt at a curtsy or whatever the fuck that'd been.

Edon stepped forward, his eyes roaming over me as if he were appraising a piece of meat. Which, I supposed, was accurate considering our predicament.

My parents moved to allow him to circle me. An inspection. If he approved, we would become betrothed. If he didn't, I'd be sent home with a very angry alpha father.

But I'd been on the receiving end of his wrath many times.

I knew what he would do.

And I didn't fucking care.

A life as a rogue lycan would be better than a forced mating to a monster inside the Clemente Clan.

Edon drew his finger down my arm, the heat of his chest caressing my back. "What's wrong, little wolf?" he breathed into my ear. "Afraid?"

"No," I replied, turning to face him, much to the shock of the audience.

Intended mates were meant to remain absolutely still during the alpha male's inspection. My mother had gone over the rules a thousand times, and her sigh behind me said how she felt about my disobedience.

Anger colored the familial bonds, my father's annoyance palpable.

It gave me pause only because I knew it wouldn't be me he punished later for this, but my mother. I felt it writhing in his intentions, distorting the air with a violent promise that had my eyes dropping to the sliver of tan skin peeking at me from Edon's unfastened collar.

He hadn't moved, perhaps unsure of how to handle my outright rudeness. Should he castigate me before the masses? Or should he allow it to slide since I wasn't yet his to throttle?

A hint of unease trickled down my spine. He merely continued to stare, as if waiting for me to do something else.

When I didn't, he continued his perusal, his touch tracing along my skin. No one spoke. The audience waiting for his decision. This could take minutes or hours. He could choose to fuck me right here, just to test the merchandise. He could send me to my knees. He could ask me anything he wanted to know and I had to answer.

It was all so one-sided.

Whatever the alpha male wanted, he received. Fuck what the female wanted.

Edon's palm slid up to my nape, the act a gesture of dominance that prickled goose bumps along my arms. I hated him. Wanted to snarl at him, to fight him, to tell him to back the fuck off, but I felt my father's tension through the bond. One more outburst and my mother would pay. Severely.

Then he really wasn't going to like what was coming next.

I'd already done the unthinkable. He just didn't know it yet.

But Edon suspected it. I could tell by the way his nostrils flared, the way his pupils tapered into points as I boldly met his gaze again.

His lip curled. Not necessarily into a snarl, but into a smirk.

He leaned in to brush his mouth over mine in a chaste kiss, one that resulted in growls of approval from the audience.

They wanted a show.

They wanted him to mount me.

I could feel it in the wind. In the way the hairs along

my neck danced in warning. This pack was cruel. They didn't believe in equality.

But then again, none of the clans did. Not anymore.

Edon's nose ran along my cheek to my ear and down the column of my throat. Scenting. Searching for the anomaly I knew his wolf senses had picked up on. He continued to trek downward between the valley of my breasts, along my flat stomach, to the apex between my thighs.

He looked up at me from his knees, the obsidian pools of his irises swirling with warning. He most likely knew now. Surely he smelled the evidence of the male I allowed to fuck me this morning.

His growl confirmed he did.

Only, it wasn't the menacing sound I expected but one underlined in heat and hunger. The kind of sound a wolf made when he desired his mate.

This is wrong, I thought, confusion settling over me.

Alpha males were possessive. And the rituals required my virginity. Something I'd given away not even twenty-four hours ago, wanting to be certain he knew.

And he did.

I saw it in the way he watched me.

His tongue slid from his lips, tasting me deeply, leaving me absolutely no doubt of his knowledge. Because I had purposely not showered afterward. I *wanted* him to know.

Another lick had my knees going weak.

This can't be happening.

He should be raging. Ranting. Threatening to kill whoever defiled my body. Demanding my parents take me away at once. Not—

Teeth met my flesh, causing me to cry out in surprise. The lycans in the audience rumbled in excitement, enjoying the very primal display of ownership.

The bastard had just *marked* me.

Right on the damn thigh.

And the way he gazed up at me showed his pleasure at doing so. He slowly stood, his well-over-six-foot height dwarfing my five-foot-five frame. His fingers clasped my chin, holding me in place as he brushed his bloody lips over mine. I fought the urge to growl, not in warning but in need.

Then his tongue slid inside, forcing me to experience the intoxicating mix of my own arousal tinged with coppery sweetness.

Bastard, I thought at him.

He smiled against my mouth. "Welcome to Clemente Clan, little mate," he said, loud enough for everyone to hear.

A spiritual cuff wrapped itself around my neck, banding my heart, as the reality of his actions and words settled into the air.

He'd bitten me and claimed me vocally.

The ceremony was already complete, the betrothed bonds well enforced.

He'd severed my ties to Ernest Clan with that bite against my thigh, and I'd been so shocked I'd not even felt my familial ties shatter.

But I did now.

Especially as I looked at my mother, noting the slight mist in her gaze. And then my brother. He stood in the front row, his hair the same color as mine, his eyes a bright blue. He appeared as unfazed as everyone else in the audience, but sadness radiated from him, a sadness I felt deep in my heart.

Goodbye, he was saying. A word he already spoke to me last night when leaving me with his final bit of advice to behave and to keep my head high.

"You may be his, but you're still an alpha female, Luna. Never forget it."

His parting statement wrapped around my soul, attempting to ground me as despair threatened to rip me apart.

I was no longer one of Ernest Clan, but the betrothed alpha to the Clemente heir.

Astonishment mingled with horror inside me. I'd been so certain this wouldn't happen. No alpha in his right mind would accept damaged goods.

My head swung in his direction, his fingers still lightly tracing my jaw. I gaped openly at him as the howls thundered around us, the next phase of tonight's rituals expected to commence.

Edon smiled, his lips dipping to my ear. "I prefer my women experienced, little mate. Makes fucking all the more exciting."

My heart leapt into my throat. My defilement had the opposite impact of what I'd anticipated. It'd made me even more desirable in his eyes.

And now…

Now his pack expected us to go consummate the bond. For him to fuck me all night. Either before them all or in the privacy of his quarters. It was his choice, not mine.

Wolves weren't shy. We were primal beings. But the idea of being intimate with him in front of all his pack had my head swimming with doubt.

I wasn't really experienced.

This morning's stupid affair had only lasted a few minutes.

And I'd hated it.

But being with Edon? That would be so much worse. He'd bite me again, only much harder than before. He'd take me any way he wanted, over and over again, even if I cried. Fuck, he might even *want* me to cry.

This wasn't supposed to happen at all.

His eyes tracked every thought as they spun through my mind, his lips curling deviously. So much intrigue. So much desire.

This is going to hurt.

I really *fucked this up.*

CHAPTER 2
EDON

Luna of Ernest Clan was not what I expected. Not in the slightest.

The females of Clemente were always willing, sometimes a little too willing. But Luna, she reeked of defiance. And I found the harsh scent intoxicating.

She'd even gone as far as to fuck another wolf this morning.

Clever and deceitful, little mate.

If I hadn't been buried deep inside another pussy just last night, I might have cared more. However, it struck me as a double standard to expect my intended to come to me as a virgin. And I meant what I said—I preferred my partners experienced.

I also preferred them to be excited participants in the act. Fucking an unwilling female held no value to me whatsoever. While I adored the chase, I wanted my prey to *desire* her eventual capture.

Ah, but Luna, she possessed no yearning to be here at all. It was written in the defiant lines of her shoulders, the fury highlighting her honey-brown eyes, and the overall air of resistance that permeated her aura.

"Come," I demanded, my palm at her nape as I led her away from the chaos of the ceremony.

My father wouldn't be happy.

He intended me to fuck her publicly in front of the clan.

But as the rising alpha, I chose my actions. Not him. The bastard could indulge in his sick proclivities himself. I would not be sharing my mate the way he shared my mother and his other females—humans and otherwise.

Luna remained brittle beneath my touch, but her legs followed my direction.

The alpha female in her wanted to rebel. The woman in her knew better. Because if she tried, I'd put her in her place so fast her head would spin. And I really didn't want to do that. Not here.

In the privacy of my quarters, maybe.

Two sentries stepped out of my way as I approached, their heads bowed in reverence.

I ignored them, guiding Luna through the front house, into the royal courtyards, and up to the log cabin I called my own. It was smaller than my father's, which sat on the opposite acre of this massive property. Ample woods separated our estates, a necessity due to our conflicting natures.

He was the current alpha.

I was the one destined to take his place.

That sometimes led to complications—complications that I always won of late, much to his obvious chagrin.

Luna glanced at the weeping willows outside my home, causing me to pause.

We were completely alone out here, no one daring enough to enter my property without sufficient permission or cause. And the majority of the clan was busy celebrating anyway.

Alpha transitions happened once every three hundred years or so, making the next month a rare time for lycans. It was also the first one to occur for Clemente Clan in the new world.

Things felt new.

Fresh.

Exciting.

Which meant they were all too busy enjoying themselves to bother with us. They expected me to fuck my betrothed. As most of them had seen me in the throes of passion before, it wouldn't intrigue them much now.

My father had wanted me to break her in front of the masses, but he'd just have to deal with my choice to do so privately. Figuratively speaking, anyway.

Luna swallowed, her tension palpable.

I released her and took a step back, giving her the space she clearly desired. "We're alone here."

She blinked, confusion marring her pretty face.

No, not pretty.

Beautiful.

Unmated alpha females weren't allowed to attend political events, like Blood Day or the Immortal Cup ceremonies. Those were reserved for clan alphas and their respective mates. But I'd anticipated her features after meeting her parents several years ago. She had her mother's caramel-colored eyes and her father's brown hair. Her alabaster skin matched them both—a trademark from her region of the world—but her curves were all her own.

Lithe, athletic legs.

Supple waist.

Fantastic tits.

And a scowl that made my heart race.

Oh, this was going to be fun.

"Why?" she demanded, seeming to have found her confidence once more.

"Why what?" I countered, knowing exactly what she meant but desiring her to say it. To admit that she purposely fucked another male this morning just to piss me off.

Luna growled, the sound primal and sexy as hell. "I'm not a virgin."

I smiled. "Neither am I, sweetheart."

"Being a virgin is a requirement for potential female mates."

"Perhaps I don't care about the *requirements*," I countered, meaning it. If I wanted a docile wolf, I'd have taken one of the omegas in our clan as a mate. No, I preferred an alpha female, someone who could fight me when I needed it, and this one more than fit the bill.

There were three others in existence as backups, should I require one.

But my father and Niko were old friends. This pact between our two clans was created the day of her birth.

She'd always been mine.

Just as I'd always been hers.

No amount of fucking around was going to belittle that point.

Her pupils flared in the moonlight, her stance defensive. "I won't yield to you."

I tilted my head forward, deeply amused. "Oh, you will. And you'll beg me to fuck you, too."

She snorted. "Not a chance in hell."

I laughed outright and shook my head. "All right, little mate. Let's play." I unbuttoned my shirt, not wanting to ruin it in the dirt, folded it, and placed it on the doorstep. Her nostrils flared as I unfastened my trousers.

She thought I meant to fuck her.

Poor darling wolf was in for one hell of a shock.

I kicked my shoes and socks off with my pants, leaving me as naked as her. "Do your worst," I invited her.

Her gaze snapped upward from my package, her cheeks flushing. "*What?*"

"Attack me, little mate. Show me what you can do." The pack wanted me to deflower her. Well, that was already done. So I'd taste her in other ways. Starting with her ability to keep up.

"I..." She licked her lips, her confusion adorable. "What?"

"If you don't want to fight, then we'll fuck," I replied, trying to goad her. "It's one or the other. Lady's choice."

"You want me to fight you?"

"Yes. You claim you won't yield. Prove it." I arched a brow. "Unless this is you already yielding, in which case, I'd prefer to take you from behind." She had a delectable ass that would feel perfect against my groin as I thrust into her—

Luna's fist narrowly missed my face, her punch astonishingly accurate and powerful. I felt it in the air that whistled by my cheek as I dodged her.

Impressive.

She followed up with another hook that almost landed in my gut.

I hadn't expected to have to work hard to avoid her hits, but she proved to be quite the little boxer as she came at me full force, making me sidestep and jump to evade being hit.

At this rate, she'd be exhausted in minutes.

But I rather enjoyed watching her tits bounce with each move.

And I always did enjoy a little physical sparring before fucking.

I caught her next throw, deftly twirling her in my arms to bring her back to my front, and clamped my opposite arm around her. "Boxing is fun, but can you wrestle?" I wondered aloud.

She responded by dropping into a leg sweep that nearly sent me to my ass, and followed it with a kick to my shin.

I growled, turned on and furious at the same time.

Most would heed that as a warning.

Not Luna.

She came at me again, not even winded, and I realized this little thing might actually make me work for it.

This time when she tried to punch me in the face, I caught her wrist and twisted it, putting her on the ground. She yelped in response, cradling her arm as I stood over her. "I'm impressed," I admitted. "But I'm the alpha of this clan, not you."

I took a step back and startled as she leapt at me like a wild cat, tackling me to the ground. Her hands tried to find my throat, her nails turning into claws. The scent of blood tinged the air as she drew those sharp talons across my skin, her intention to maim clear.

Fuck.

Protective instincts overcame me, forcing me to fight back. I grabbed her forearms, using a pressure point to loosen her grip, and grappled over the ground in an effort to restrain her. But she thwarted several of my moves deftly, confirming that she wasn't just smart, but also fast. And strong, too.

It took far too many minutes to finally get her on her back in a position she couldn't escape from. My hips and thighs pinned hers, one of my hands holding her wrists above her head while the other clamped down hard around her throat. "*Yield*," I demanded, the snarl in my tone one I rarely had to use with my wolves.

"Fuck you," she snapped, not even fazed by her inferior position.

"Poor choice of words," I said, pressing my very aroused cock into her slick folds. Not inside. Just against. Enough to demonstrate my dominance and warn her of my intent should she push me too far.

She bit her lower lip, her cheeks flushed in glorious fury. And when I tried to hold her gaze, she looked away.

The first sign of submission.

And a very telling one.

While her body might be wet and willing beneath mine, her mind was nowhere near ready. If I took her now, I would only confirm to her that I was a monster. As we had several centuries ahead of us, I preferred not to start off on the wrong paw.

I sighed, shaking my head. "I really hope you enjoyed whatever pup you allowed between your legs, little mate, because it's the last time someone other than me will ever please you." I released her and leapt off her before she could get another swipe in.

She sprung expertly to her feet, assuming the fighting position. "I didn't yield."

I grinned, amused by her determination. "No. Not with your words, anyway. But your body definitely did." I glanced pointedly at my slick cock, and then back at her. "I should make you suck it off. Just to prove my point."

Although, I strongly suspected she'd bite me instead. Her clenching jaw verified that to be an accurate assessment. It should have pissed me off. Instead, all it did was please me greatly.

I'd definitely chosen right with this one.

The wolves of my experience were just so damn

submissive. I desired a female with fight. One who wasn't afraid to challenge me.

Like Luna did now with her eyes.

I grabbed her chin and wrapped my opposite arm around her back when she tried to strike me again. I'd gone easy on her, and I allowed her to feel that in the way I held her now. She couldn't squirm, could barely even breathe. That was how hard I held her as I took in every detail of her beautiful face.

"No one will touch you here," I said softly. "Not when they all know you're mine." It served as a warning while also confirming her security in the pack. Because she didn't need to fear anyone. But she also couldn't fuck anyone but me.

"Let go of me," she demanded, a note of fear finally tinging that sweet voice of hers.

I ignored her request while making her hold my gaze. "Don't worry, little mate. I'll never force you, and there is plenty of willing pussy on these grounds."

I allowed that to sink in, compelling her to see the truth of my statement. Then I released her with a shove, sending her back several steps so she couldn't physically retaliate.

"I strongly suggest you consider our circumstances, Luna. You're here because I require an heir. And I will have one." Because I had no doubt she would one day succumb to me. They always did. "What you have to decide is whether you want to end up alone after fulfilling your purpose or be by my side. Because I mean it. None of my wolves will touch you. Ever."

"While you can fuck whoever you want," she replied, giving a harsh laugh. "Yes, I'm very aware of society's rules, *Alpha*."

So disrespectful.

So fucking hot.

My cock pulsed, eager to put her on her back again. But I refrained, instead staring her down with one of my infamous *alpha* glares. "Keep me satisfied and maybe I won't desire anyone else." Cruel words, but true. Lycan society encouraged the males to take a harem, even when mated. But the females, no. Once mated, they were to remain faithful.

Those who weren't died. Badly.

Luna had to know that.

She laughed, but it lacked humor. And she slowly shook her head. "Go fuck whoever you want, *Alpha.*"

I narrowed my gaze, displeased with her easy dismissal. Most in my position would have already mounted her and forced her submission. I offered to play first.

Still, she denied me.

Even with her body ripe and willing.

"Fine," I replied. "This is my house. Pick whatever bed you want. Just not mine. I may have company later."

I didn't wait for a reply, my inner wolf raging at me to either fuck or run. And I chose the latter.

Her arousal was even more potent as I shifted, my nose picking up the trace of liquid heat rolling down her inner thighs. It took considerable effort to back away and not pounce on the one my wolf recognized as his intended.

She didn't want me. Not yet.

I darted toward the tree line, a growl vibrating in my throat.

The bolder females of the pack would track me down, demand I allow them to satisfy the lust burning inside me.

And maybe I'd let them.

I wasn't mated yet. Nor did I have a mate who wanted me. So why shouldn't I indulge in another?

Luna's snarl gave me pause just inside the tree line, her dark head bowing as she fell to her knees.

"*Fuck,*" she growled. "Fuck. Fuck. Fuck!"

My lips pulled back at her display of rage. It seemed my intended did care. She cared *very* much. But there was also a note of cunning in her scent, a plan taking root in that mind of hers. A mind I very much wanted to get to know.

What are you thinking, little mate? I wondered, an image of her trying to escape our grounds flashing behind my eyes. Was that telegraphed through our subtle link? Or something else entirely?

Regardless, it intrigued me.

I rather hoped she would try to run.

Because I always did enjoy a good chase.

CHAPTER 3

SILAS

THIS TASK IS BULLSHIT, I THOUGHT, KICKING A STONE WITH my paw.

Every day, they sent me out here to "guard" the perimeter. Right. Because the nearest territory was hundreds of miles away in each direction, which meant there were other patrols out there doing the same thing and stopping anything that could get this close.

They'll probably send me there next. The only reason I'd been allowed to stay this close to the heart of the pack was because of my supposed need for training. Not that anyone had bothered to explain a damn thing to me.

No.

All they did was tell me to patrol. Like maybe I could learn something by sniffing grass and dirt in wolf form. I snorted. *Right.*

The only scent I continued to pick up out here was a sweet orange blossom aroma that belonged to Edon's intended mate. She seemed to enjoy running the perimeter. Alone.

Everyone stayed clear of her, including me. But I couldn't help wondering what she was up to out here.

I trailed her scent along the creek, following at a distance. As we were on the boundaries, it still qualified as me doing my job. It just gave me something a little more exciting to do.

Something about her intrigued me. She smelled different from the pack, but my interest went deeper than that. Her presence boasted a hint of pride that the other women around here seemed to lack. Perhaps because Luna was an alpha—a rare designation for female lycans.

Hmm, no, it was the way she moved so gracefully through the bayou, her long legs dancing across the ground with liquid ease.

I nearly approached her twice this week, just to make myself known, but I sensed that would break a myriad of rules.

For one, I was the omega of the pack. A new wolf. A weakling.

At least in the eyes of everyone else.

But I certainly didn't feel all that *weak*. If anything, I felt restless. Like I needed to be doing something more important than wandering—

Death.

My nose twitched.

Another breeze ruffled my fur with the foul stench, stirring my instincts to high alert.

Where is it coming from?

I tracked a pungent tendril through the creek and to the other side. These lands still belonged to Clemente Clan but were just outside of the primary grounds housing the pack hierarchy.

And something was very off.

My lips pulled back in a low snarl, the reek of violence

unsettling my insides. Something or someone had died out here in the worst kind of way.

Torture.

Innards.

Blood.

I lifted my muzzle, scenting for the source.

There. I bounded through the moss-covered trees, my pads silent over the grass-covered stones below.

A corpse lay demolished in the grass.

The head rested a few feet away, leaving a nasty stump of a neck behind.

Vampire.

Pack scent rioted with the stench of decay, naming the clear murderer as someone from Clemente Clan. But who would do this? It broke one of the most sacred laws among the Blood Alliance—no exterminating of immortal life without higher order.

And this vampire's death clearly wasn't sanctioned.

Unless Walter approved it.

Or whomever this vampire belonged to.

But then again a whole ceremony would have been performed.

No. Definitely an unsanctioned kill.

I lifted my head back in a howl to alert my fellow sentries, uncertain of how else to proceed since no one had actually given me details on proper protocol.

What is it? a deep voice asked in my head, causing me to stumble on my four legs.

What the hell? I thought, glancing this way and that. No one in Clemente Clan had telepathic abilities that I knew of. Or maybe they did. Because how the fuck would I know? No one told me shit.

Silas, the voice growled. *Report.*

Who is this? I demanded, spinning again, confused as fuck and slightly paranoid that I might be hearing things.

Edon, your alpha, came the voice, a hint of irritation underlining his now recognizably arrogant tone. *Report.*

How are you in my head? I asked. *Wait, can all of us do this?*

Oh, fuck. That would be bad. Very, very bad. I didn't want anyone in my head. A lot of private and very rebellious thoughts formed up there, thoughts that, if voiced out loud, could get me killed.

Like my interest in Luna's exquisite scent.

And my overall hatred for this new life.

A long-suffering sigh that didn't belong to me—in my own fucking head—caused my fur to stand on end.

Calm down, Silas. I made you. It's the link between a sire and his progeny. It exists within the pack psyche but can only be accessed by us. Now can you tell me what the fuck is going on over there?

It was the most the alpha heir had said to me since he turned me all those weeks ago. And yet this link had existed the entire time?

Fuck.

And what the hell is a pack psyche?

Silas, he growled. *Focus before I come out there myself.*

The threat in his tone had me swallowing a whimper. I did not want to see him out here. Or really at all. Especially after the hell he inflicted on me during the change.

Edon was not a kind lycan. That, I knew for certain. Even if he seemed to be allowing his mate to roam freely over the grounds.

Silas! You are severely testing my patience, something I strongly encourage you not to do.

I sat several feet away from the corpse, grimacing even in wolf form. *There's a dead vampire on the outskirts of the property, and it reeks of pack.*

Silence.

Edon? I wasn't sure if he heard me or not.

I'm on my way. Don't let anyone fucking touch the scene, or I'll have your hide.

I growled in response to the threat, hating him even more. But as the sounds of paws approaching tickled my ears, I took guard as he demanded. I shifted back into my human form, something that hurt the first several times I'd done it, but now felt second nature, and stood with my arms crossed.

Three wolves with silky white coats appeared, all males, all purebreds in the pack—meaning they were born as lycans. As long as one parent had a wolf gene, the child was born a lycan. Hence the need for the breeding farms.

Where Willow is being held, I thought, flinching. She'd been part of my class, one of my best friends. On Blood Day, the Magistrate sent her to the breeding farms to create either more humans or more lycans.

I really hoped it was the former.

At least Rae is okay, I consoled myself, thinking of my other best friend. It'd been a welcome shock seeing her at the alpha ceremonies. When I heard Kylan, the infamous harem-slaying royal, had taken her as a mate, I'd worried about her well-being. But she'd seemed fine. Happy, even.

Well, that makes one of us, I thought as the approaching wolves shifted into human form.

"What'd you do?" the stockiest of them demanded. What was his name? Edwin? Ethan? Goliath?

Fuck if I knew.

None of them wanted to be friends with the human turned lycan, so I'd returned the favor.

"I asked you a question, mutt," Goliath—he looked like a Goliath, anyway—growled.

"I found a dead vampire," I drawled, stating the obvious.

Three matching unamused expressions stared back at me.

"Edon says not to touch him until he gets here," I added.

That seemed to grab their interest.

"Edon, huh?" The redheaded one scratched the stubble along his jaw. "Do we take orders from Edon yet, Barry?"

"No, we don't, Glenn," the third—Barry—replied, his lanky body the least threatening of the trio.

"Didn't think so." Glenn smiled, the expression one of evil intent.

This is going to end badly, I sighed to myself. "He may not be your alpha yet, but he's the heir. Best to do what he says."

Glenn's gaze lit up with wicked determination. "Nah, I didn't hear any orders, mutt. I think we'll do whatever the fuck we want. Isn't that right, boys?"

"Yep," the minions beside him said in unison.

Part of me wanted to welcome them to their funeral with open arms and allow them to do whatever the hell they wanted. But the obedient part of me—one beat into me over years of submission in the university—caused me to fold my arms and stand my ground in front of the corpse. "No."

I didn't elaborate.

Didn't lay down a threat.

Just merely enforced the fact that they would not be fucking with this vampire corpse until Edon gave his approval.

Barry chuckled, shaking his head. "Allow me."

I saw his punch as it formed, noted the way his body

angled for a fight before he even took a step. And I deftly dodged the throw while landing one of my own against the flat planes of his abdomen.

"Oomph," he breathed, hunching over from the strike I knew would leave him winded for at least thirty seconds.

Unfortunately, my instinctual reaction caused his buddies to charge me at once.

I caught Glenn's fist, twisted his arm, and sent him to his knees. Which left my right side open for Goliath's brutal attack.

One crack to my ribs, the other to my back, in quick succession, sent me tumbling back. But I'd endured much, much worse. I'd survived the fucking Immortal Cup. I knew how this worked, and I used his temporary victory to my advantage.

Because he didn't try to hit me again.

He merely stood there smirking like a dumbass, assuming I wouldn't get back up.

The disbelief in his gaze was a gorgeous sight as I kicked out my legs not even seconds later, landing on my feet, and sent my palm into his nose.

Crunch.

My other hand slammed into his sternum.

Snap.

And my knee sailed into his side.

Pop.

His howl as he fell to the ground was music to my ears.

Movement in my peripheral vision had me kicking out sideways into Glenn's abdomen, then my fist crashed into his skull with a deafening blow. He whimpered, falling on top of his friend, as Barry stood and held out his hands in defeat.

I narrowed my gaze at him. "Are we done?"

"Yes," a low voice snarled from the woods.

Edon.

He strode forward on two feet, shirtless, and in a pair of jeans that slung low across his hips. An indication that the bastard had jogged here on two legs instead of shifting into the faster form of four.

In other words, the jackass had taken his time on purpose.

"What happened?" he demanded, taking in the scene of his two wounded wolves and Barry's contrite stance.

"Just fucking around, boss," the idiot said.

Yeah, fucking around, my ass, I thought.

Edon arched a brow at me. *Care to say that out loud.*

I folded my arms instead, staring him down.

A beat of silence passed.

Snitching wasn't my thing. Besides, it was pretty damn obvious what happened. They attacked; I defended. *No one touched the body,* I added mentally. *Your Highness.*

Edon snorted. "Barry, get the jackass twins back to central. I'll deal with you all later. Silas, you stay."

Woof woof, I thought. Oh, it was entirely stupid to challenge an alpha. I knew that. But I had nothing to lose other than my life, and that could only be taken with due cause. Edon would sooner throw me to the rogues of the world, a place where I suspected I might actually be happier.

Maybe then I could find an old bed to sleep on instead of curling up under a random tree on the ground.

Although, likely not.

But a wolf could dream.

Dumb, Dumber, and Dipshit all took their leave, hobbling away under the careful eye of their future alpha. When he glanced back at me, I said nothing. If he thought I intended to apologize for putting those assholes in their places, then he had another think coming.

"They threatened to touch the corpse, didn't they?" he asked once they were too far to hear.

I didn't confirm or deny it, just continued to stare at him.

"Defying an alpha is a dangerous game," he warned.

"Try telling those three idiots that," I suggested.

"Those three idiots, as you call them, are purebreds and far higher in the pack than you."

Like I didn't know that. It was why they lived on the main grounds. Why they had a roof over their heads when I didn't. Why they could talk to someone of Edon's status while I was expected to bow and grovel.

Well, fuck that.

Edon took my measure, his smoldering irises running over each exposed inch of my skin. Nudity never bothered me. I'd spent many, many years being appraised by immortals, evaluated for my looks, my agility, my intelligence. I knew where I stood on every measure. My becoming a lycan just heightened all those attributes. Whereas wolves like the idiot trio never had to fight for anything in their lives. They were born into their positions. Just like Edon.

I *made* mine.

I fought for it.

And I would continue fighting until my dying breath.

Edon smirked. "You held your own, mutt. Earned a little respect. Try to hold on to it, yeah?" His focus shifted to the dead vamp, his amusement dying as he took in the severely abused torso, bite marks, and twisted ligaments.

He began to prowl in earnest while his words replayed through my mind.

He saw the fight.

Why else would he comment on me holding my own?

Unless he determined it from the broken pile of males he stumbled across.

But no.

I suspected he'd watched the whole damn thing unfold as some sort of fucked-up test.

"You told me to guard the body on purpose," I said out loud.

"Of course I did," he replied, crouching by the shaved head of the former bloodsucker. "You're my only progeny. I had to see if I could trust you." His knowing gaze flicked upward, a hint of respect in his depths. "Your loyalty may one day be rewarded. Something to keep in mind."

I swallowed the dubious sound threatening to crawl out of my throat.

"What do you smell?" he asked, his attention again on the scene.

"Dead vampire and pack."

Edon shook his head. "I mean, do you smell anything else? Anything that can help us determine who engaged in this unsanctioned kill?"

I scented the air again, frowning. "All I smell is collective pack, but I've not learned everyone's signature traits yet."

"It smells like collective pack to me, too," he agreed, frowning. "Which means someone purposely covered their tracks." He grabbed the chin of the vampire, tilted it to the side this way and that. "He's one of Silvano's. A higher-ranking official, but not a sovereign or a regent. Just an upper-level wannabe diplomat."

Edon stood, glancing around, his nostrils flaring.

"I need you to bury the body," he continued. "Maybe near one of the bordering creeks."

My brow furrowed. *What?* "Shouldn't we tell someone?" This seemed like something the Goddess would want to know about. The royal vampire, Silvano, would probably appreciate a heads-up as well.

He faced me. "And if we did, what would happen?" His tone lacked his usual arrogance and instead infused a note of curiosity.

Another test, I realized.

I considered the query carefully, recalling all my years of political study.

And frowned.

"They'd demand an eye for an eye." Edon neither confirmed nor denied it, his mostly black eyes holding mine, waiting for me to continue. "Which you'd be forced to accept," I added, thinking out loud. "And the omega member of the pack would be sacrificed—me."

"So I suggest you bury the body, *Omega*," Edon replied.

I scowled. There was the pompous prick I loved to hate.

But he was right.

Because what else could I do?

My lips nearly parted on a reply of acceptance, when the hint of orange blossoms teased my nose. *Luna*.

Her light brown eyes flashed from the trees a few yards away, her white coat a stark difference from the moss and ivy decorating the landscape.

If Edon noticed her presence, he didn't show it. She studied the scene openly, not at all afraid of me for catching her in the act.

Did she realize I followed her as well?

That I adored the way her paws—

"Silas?" Edon interjected.

Right. Alpha demand. Not the best idea to lust after his female either.

I cleared my throat. "I'll, uh, get to work." I glanced at the tree line once more, but Luna was already gone.

What are you up to? I wondered, not for the first time today.

Edon smirked, his hand falling to his jeans as he unbuttoned them. "I have a little wolf to catch, so I'm going for a run," he murmured, sliding the fabric down his toned legs. "Hold on to these for me," he added, handing them to me. "I'll be back for them."

I wanted to growl an unsavory reply, but the magic of his shift held my tongue captive in my suddenly dry mouth.

It was beautiful. Graceful. The most amazingly perfect shift I'd ever seen, and I'd observed several over the last few weeks on these grounds. He was just so liquid, so practiced, so fucking smooth.

Would I one day look like that? Doubtful. My bones still crunched. His just seemed to slide into their natural place as if he should always exist in this giant wolf form.

Edon shook out his coat, stretching.

No, *preening.*

He knew I was admiring him.

And he liked it.

I could tell by the cocky twinkle in his gaze.

He nudged me then with his nose, pushing me not so gently toward the body at my side. His nip to my arm seemed to be a warning.

Hurry up, he said into my head. *I'll be back in an hour.*

And with that, he took off through the woods—in the direction of Luna's orange-blossom scent.

CHAPTER 4
LUNA

I ran across the grounds, trying to put as much distance as possible between me and Edon. The progeny noticing me was fine. The alpha, not so much. I'd avoided him for the better part of a week, and I wanted to keep it that way.

Ugh.

My damn nose always got me into trouble. However, the scent had drawn me toward the perimeter, where I'd watched in shock as the new lycan took on three full-blooded males while Edon watched from the sidelines. I'd thought for sure that the alpha would intervene and beat the young wolf into submission.

He didn't.

Instead, he leaned against a tree and watched in amusement.

The others were too caught up in their own testosterone to see him. But I caught the sexy tilt of his mouth as it quirked up at the show.

Then it was gone just as fast as it had appeared when

he stepped forward. The three purebreds cowered. The young one did not. And that only drew me into the action more, my curiosity forcing me to step forward to hear every word.

The newbie's cocksure attitude shocked me, but not nearly as much as Edon's reaction. He'd *allowed* it.

My father never would have tolerated that kind of lip. He'd have flogged the fur right off the disobedient wolf.

A nip at my heel had me whirling midstride, a snarl on my lips that died as Edon towered over me.

Oh, dear forest above, he's fast.

And stealthy, too, because I hadn't even felt him gaining on me, much less being close enough to bite.

I swallowed, uncertain. Was he angry with me for spying? I wasn't officially pack yet, shouldn't be privy to any political matters. But his stature seemed calm, not aggressive. If anything, he appeared agreeable.

We hadn't spoken since that first night, and I'd pretty much been doing my own thing ever since. He began to circle me, appraising every inch of my wolf form. It was hard not to cower to his much bigger size.

If anyone questioned his alpha status, they just needed to ask this guy to shift, because *wow*.

Even I could admire the breadth of his shoulders, his strong thighs, and sleek, white coat. Perfection in wolf form. And the low rumble coming from his chest said he felt the same about me.

Another nip to my hind leg had me spinning again, a growl catching in my throat. He jumped to follow, his teeth snagging my rump—not hard, but playfully.

I didn't understand what he was doing.

We just kept dancing in circles, his teeth touching my coat, my legs whirling me around, until finally I lunged at him. I didn't like this dizzy game.

His masculine growl had my blood running cold until he tried to pin me with his jaw against my nape.

Oh. Hell. No.

I leapt away from him, only to find my much smaller form beneath his, grappling for purchase on the ground. I had half a mind to shift just to demand him to explain himself, but his muzzle against my neck forced me to fight back.

Round and round we went, sparring in wolf form beneath the willow trees.

He never snarled.

But I sure as hell did.

Especially when I pinned him with my jaws around his scruff. Only, he flipped me off him with a shake and pounced again.

It was ridiculous.

And… admittedly fun.

He's playing, I realized with a shock that landed me on my rump beneath him again.

His mouth closed over my flank, sending me skidding away once more, this time at a dead run through the underbrush. He gave chase, his strides longer, more knowing, but I refused to give up.

I ran with everything inside me.

Fast.

Hard.

Sprinting over the earth at breakneck speeds.

It felt amazing. Free. Exciting.

And every time his teeth skimmed my hide, I pushed myself to pick up the pace even more.

Edon's paws were silent, his presence behind me so invisible I thought I'd lost him.

Until he landed on me once more.

We tumbled and rolled from the impact, cascading us

down a hill to the bank of a nearby river. Edon clamped down on my scruff to keep me from falling over the ledge, then gently pulled me back.

I blinked several times, dazed.

Then something soft and soothing ran over my muzzle. Edon's tongue.

I made to back away, but a growl from him held me captive as he licked me again. It stung a little, telling me I'd scraped my nose on something—likely during the tumbleweed fall down that hill—and Edon was *cleaning* the wound.

I flinched at the sensation of his tongue slicking across my fur. It didn't feel bad, just intimate. And I didn't want to be intimate with him.

Except the wolf inside me had very different feelings on that front. She was practically preening beneath his touch, urging me to lean into his side to beg for more.

Disagreeing with my animalistic soul went against my instincts, stirring a discomfort inside that I wanted to relieve.

But I refused to give in to Edon or any other alpha.

I wanted to be in charge of my life. To be free to make my own fucking choices. Not have to submit to an alpha for direction.

Edon rumbled, the sound one of pleasure and happiness, and my damn wolf almost purred in response.

I needed to shift back into my human form where *my* brain ruled. But I couldn't. *She* refused to budge.

Gah. Damn alpha hormones!

I swore he chuckled, as though he knew all about my internal struggle. And maybe he did. The mark on my thigh denoted me as his regardless of how my heart or mind felt. That meant our mating bond had begun. It would only be a matter of time before he owned every piece of me.

While I would own exactly none of him.

As was proven by his behavior this past week. I had no idea where he slept, but it wasn't in his bed. Not that I cared. If anything, it'd been a relief.

But it certainly painted a picture of what life here would become.

Me—alone—raising a pup while he fucked and played and ruled.

Edon nuzzled my nose, his obsidian eyes glowing with curiosity. Maybe he wasn't as entrenched in my head as I feared. He rolled into me, his warmth a blanket of security that set my fur on edge.

I didn't need his protection.

His adoration.

His attention.

I didn't *want* any of it.

Except my wolf seemed quite content to accept it all. She bathed in his energy, reveling in the power he possessed, his strength, his agility.

The water flowed before us, rippling over the rocks, flowing toward the ocean south of us. I'd studied the geography extensively prior to arriving, had spent the last week pacing the grounds to acquaint myself with the perimeters.

I'd originally pegged the newbie as the weakest link. After watching his performance today, I wasn't so sure.

But I could take him.

He wasn't an alpha, just a male. My training and strength and years as a wolf far outnumbered his. It wouldn't be hard. I just had to find the right time to catch him off guard, subdue him, and run.

Given how much freedom this pack had allowed me, it'd probably take at least a day for them to realize I was gone.

Edon even longer if he continued to avoid his home at night.

He stood and stretched beside me, drawing my gaze to the athletic lines of his form, the sexy masculinity of his coat, and the breadth of his shoulders.

He was a big wolf. In every way.

The image of him nude in human form flashed behind my eyes unbidden, reminding me of his muscular build and the way his abdomen tapered into an impressive V at the waist. Which seemed to point to his most masculine part. And yeah, I could begrudgingly admit it was well proportioned.

He nudged me with his nose, causing my eyes to lift to his. Amusement and hunger shone brightly in those ebony orbs—a promise of passion to come.

"And you'll beg me to fuck you, too."

His words seemed to hum across the air, engraving themselves in the moment and vowing to come to fruition.

Such arrogance.

But he was an alpha lycan. They were *all* arrogant.

And if it were up to my wolf, he'd probably win.

I laid my head back down, my way of displaying boredom and disinterest. It earned me a low sound in response, one brought on by the back of his throat. A growl of intention.

Not happening, I thought, conveying it with my body posture, refusing to look at him.

Silence fell between us.

My fur danced in anticipation, waiting for him to pounce again, to engage me in another game. But seconds rolled by into minutes. Until finally I looked back to find him gone.

He'd left me without a word.

An act I saw fitting because I intended to do the same to him. And soon.

CHAPTER 5
EDON

Well, at least Luna's wolf liked me.

The woman beneath, however, clearly did not.

That was fine. After that beautiful display of speed, I could wait. Because winning her over would be worth the chase.

Someone above had crafted my ideal female. Feisty, sexy, athletic, and fierce. Just sensing her had heated my blood. And then her shock at my wanting to play had amused me deeply.

Did the Ernest Clan not engage in such affairs? Because we Clementes enjoyed our sparring. Well, we used to, anyway.

My father's way of ruling our people was more self-serving than caring. From what my grandfather told me, it wasn't always like this. And it didn't have to stay this way unless I wanted it to. Which remained to be seen.

I trotted along the grounds, scenting for anything suspicious along the way. The Alpha Trials were well underway, and my father seemed hell-bent on putting me through the wringer. If I failed, he would continue to rule for another year until we could restart the process.

Some alphas required almost a decade to complete the ascension.

I planned to do it in one.

This year.

So I welcomed whatever damage he wanted to send my way. Even if it came in the form of a dead vampire.

It had to be a test to see how I chose to handle the situation.

As far as I could tell, I only had one option. Pack first. Always. And fuck bullshit politics. I would not sacrifice my only progeny over a corpse. Especially as he was proving to be useful.

Most of my kind looked down upon the mutts, claiming them to be half-breeds since they weren't born lycan. But I saw it from a different angle—Silas grew up fighting for his life. That did something to a man. It strengthened his resolve, made him harder, faster, and smarter. Nothing was given to him on a golden platter, unlike the idiots who questioned my authority earlier. They were all pompous pack royals, sitting neatly beneath the alpha line and awaiting their futures in glorified enforcer roles.

While Silas, he had no role.

He was one of a kind since all the previous mortals turned lycans were dead in our clan. Mostly because my father had sired them. The last one in our territory was turned just over two decades ago. I'd been a wee pup, but old enough to witness what happened to the female who won the Immortal Cup that year.

My father turned her.

Then gave her to his buddies as a present.

The next time I saw her was during the burial my

grandfather organized in her honor. He'd forced me to attend, saying I needed to know how to properly respect the dead. When I asked after my father, wondering at his lack of attendance, I was told that times had changed.

"Your father leads in a different time and manner than I once did," he'd said that day. *"That's evidenced now by this poor girl's treatment."*

I thought of her as I came upon Silas sitting naked on a log with my pants folded neatly at his side. The stench of death had lessened, but I pinpointed the grave several yards away. Silas had probably shifted to dig the hole in his wolf form. Which explained his now wet hair—he'd gone for a wash in the creek after.

Because he didn't have a home.

Or a shower.

No one would provide him with shelter here, yet his presence was required on the grounds. I suspected my father intended to use him somehow in the Alpha Trials.

Let's go for a run, I told Silas, meeting his wary gaze. I'd grab my pants later. *Shift.*

I didn't wait for him to comply, just jumped over the log he sat on and took a path away from the main grounds, deeper into the marshlands beyond. Wolves didn't live out here, mostly because we preferred to be together.

But there were times when some of us needed an escape—especially me. I'd actually spent the last few nights out here, away from the expectations of the pack to clear my head. That was how I'd been so close to Silas when he'd howled in alarm.

I just needed space.

From my packmates.

From my father.

From the trials ahead.

From Luna.

There were certain demands that I'd yet to meet, much to my father's fury. When he found out that I'd left Luna alone after the mating ritual, he'd struck me. Hard. But I wasn't like him. I wouldn't force an unwilling female into bed. And rather than hit him back, I'd walked away telling him to mind his position. Because we both knew that in a fight, he'd lose, the traditions be damned.

My grandfather had met me around the back of the house, where he'd suggested I take a few days away. Given the growing anxieties of the pack and Luna's chilly welcome, I'd agreed.

Silas's scent grew stronger as he caught up to me, his transition to wolf form taking longer than it should. *Have you been eating and sleeping regularly?* I wondered.

He didn't answer right away, but his mind did with a series of images outlined in his memories.

His first nights—cold and alone.

Sleeping under a tree in wolf form.

Learning to hunt on his own after several days without real food.

Bathing in the creek when he realized he wouldn't be given access to normal showers.

Stealing a roll from the mating ceremony, then throwing it up when the rich quality hit his stomach.

I sighed. *I've severely neglected you.* Mostly to protect him. My father wanted me to kill Silas, not turn him. I'd considered it after observing Silas's initial transition, but the fight in his gaze when he glowered at me that night had me making another choice. Watching him today confirmed my decision as the right one.

But if I'd showed him any favors before the pack, they'd definitely use Silas against me in the trials.

So we would have to be very discreet.

I'm fine, Silas said after a beat, unwilling to voice the

real thought in his head. Which I translated to be, *No shit,* based on the firing images of his fist meeting my jaw.

If I were in human form, I would have smirked in amusement. I liked this newbie. He had an impressive set of balls on him. His fighting style wasn't half-bad either.

The trials are a difficult time for an alpha heir. With my father leading them, I suspect they'll be close to unbearable. I picked up our pace to a slight run that Silas held with ease. At least his athleticism had remained in spite of the poor nourishment. Definitely a fighter. *I think the vampire was the first test.*

Silas followed me in silence, his mind racing with images of the body and the surroundings. He'd taken stock of every detail, every scent, and all the potential clues.

With each passing second, this male amazed me more.

Most of the wolves my age were like Glenn and his idiot minions. Silas was different, his approach thorough and not impulsive.

My grandfather would probably like him.

If it's a test, then you failed, Silas said, surprising me. *The Blood Alliance favors order, and you broke the Goddess's cardinal rule by covering up the murder.*

My ears flicked in irritation. *You think I should have reported it?*

Yes. He glanced at me. *I mean, I'm thankful you didn't. But I won't be surprised if the dead vamp resurfaces in the next few weeks, thereby forcing your hand.*

Then maybe we need to hide it better, I thought.

The river would carry the remains to the ocean, where the body will eventually decompose in the waves.

A solid plan, one that would distort the evidence. It would also make it impossible for anyone in the pack to stumble across the remains. I should have suggested it earlier rather than tell him to bury it, but I'd been distracted by Luna's lingering scent. My desire to chase had overridden reason.

I'll handle it, I told him.

Silas tripped beside me, his shock evident in the tense lines of his limbs. He'd obviously expected me to demand he do it, but I had another task in mind for him.

I need you to keep an eye on things for me, report back anything and everything that piques your curiosity. If something doesn't feel right, I want to know about it. If you see pack members acting suspiciously, tell me. I slowed my run and ducked beneath a low willow tree toward a path no one but me ever traveled.

We were over a mile from the outskirts of the pack's central zone. Very few bothered to venture this far, the home grounds spanning thirty miles of well-kept acres of land. This area was a pit in comparison.

But it held a secret.

One my grandfather had gifted me a decade ago.

An escape.

Sure, Silas replied, sounding about as thrilled as a pup getting his first bath.

It's not a task to take lightly, Omega. There could be great reward in it for you if you perform well. Having the respect of the clan alpha carried a lot of weight. And considering I planned a complete overhaul of my father's staff, it would be wise for Silas to remain on my good side.

Of course, I hadn't exactly given the newbie cause to trust me.

Nor did I really trust him.

Our sire link, however, provided a unique opportunity. One I intended to exploit for my benefit.

It's not like I have anything better to do, Silas muttered, his tone edging the line of disrespectful.

My father would put him in his place with a harsh bite to the nape. Or worse. He believed in ruling with an iron fist, his preference for cruelty well known in Clemente Clan. His advisors approved, as did the elder families of the pack.

Families like the one Glenn came from.

Those were the males my father forced me to befriend, the ones he wanted to influence my upbringing and opinions.

My grandfather had other ideas.

He taught me about the old ways, customs long dead, thanks to societal laws today. He taught me the value of respect.

If my father ever found out, he'd oust my grandfather and force him to live with the rogues in no man's land.

Fortunately, my father was too busy lording over his kingdom to notice. If anything, he seemed thrilled to not have to deal with me.

Until now.

The rules forced him to interact with me for the Alpha Trials.

And he'd been very clear about his disappointment thus far.

I think Luna is up to something, Silas said, startling me once more.

What do you mean?

She keeps scouting the boundaries, like she's considering the best escape route. Silas sounded nervous. *I've watched her cross over a few times just to see if anyone would stop her.*

I snorted. *Of course she is.* I suspected it after the mating ceremony, and even more so today when I found her creeping near the perimeter.

She's an alpha female, I added. *Independence is ingrained in her. I'm actually surprised she hasn't run yet.*

You're not mad. Not a question, but a statement.

No. I'm intrigued. I hope she runs. Because then I could

catch her. And that would be so incredibly fun. *Keep an eye on her. If she makes a break for it, let me know.*

And then what?

I slowed to a walk, transforming into my human form as I moved. My bones lengthened, the magic of my lycan soul giving way to the male within. And then I rolled my shoulders, cracking my neck and popping my joints into place. "And then I'll chase her," I replied out loud, eyeing the property ahead.

Silas remained in his wolf form, likely because shifting took too much out of him and he didn't want me to see just how weak he'd become from all his transformations today.

Smart wolf.

Showing weakness to the alpha was the fastest way to being dominated.

"This cabin is mine," I told him, nodding to the small wooden lodge ahead. "It's a bit archaic and uses solar technology to keep the utilities fresh, but I keep it well stocked with supplies." I looked down at him. "And there's an extra bed inside that's rarely used."

A hopeful note graced the air, one I only caught because I'd been waiting for it. Silas hid it in the next breath, his stance becoming bored as he searched the area with his nose.

"You can crash here, but don't tell anyone." Not that I expected anyone to notice. My nose never picked up on any pack out here. It was why I used it as a refuge. Only my grandfather seemed to know about it. "Whatever you find inside is fair game. Including the food." Which I'd try to keep as refreshed for him as I could. If he was going to help me, then I needed him in top shape.

I also sort of wanted to see what kind of lycan he'd become under the right circumstances, because he was already proving to be stronger and faster than half the purebreds back at the main camp.

Why are you doing this? he asked, sounding hesitant.

Because it's the right thing to do, I admitted. *Also, I need an ally, and no one will suspect me of working with you in the Alpha Trials.* The clan all thought I'd left Silas to fend for himself, just like my father would have done.

And, in truth, I had. Not necessarily because I didn't care, but because I'd been a little preoccupied with the upcoming ascension.

That changed today.

How do you know you can trust me to help? he asked, his tone incredulous.

"I don't," I replied out loud.

Seems like a risk.

"It is," I agreed.

He remained quiet for a beat, then stood and shook out his fur. *Is there a shower in there?*

"Yes."

All right, he replied. *A favor for a favor.*

If that was the way he wanted to look at it, then that worked for me. "Then I'll let you get acquainted while I go retrieve my pants and handle our headless friend." I didn't bother with a goodbye. If Silas needed me, he could tap into my head.

Although, I suspected he wouldn't.

Silas struck me as a wolf who relied only on himself to survive. It was something we had in common.

Because while I desired his assistance, I wouldn't depend on it.

The only one who could win these trials was me. But I'd use every advantage I could to pass, including the sire bond to Silas.

CHAPTER 6
LUNA

I COULDN'T ESCAPE EDON'S SCENT. HE RETURNED TO HIS home two days ago—a few hours after our frolic—and only left twice to handle pack business.

I hated it.

His presence overwhelmed me, taunted my lady bits, and left me in a writhing pile of need in my sheets.

And the bastard knew, too.

It was written all over his amused expression as I entered the living room. He sat lounging in a pair of jeans that he wore like a king, his chest bare, his abs defined, his package—

Stop, I demanded, focusing on the kitchen and not the very virile wolf on the leather couch.

"There's coffee in the pot," he called. "Just brewed it."

Of course he did. Because he sensed me waking up from the dream his nearness caused.

Or, more likely, my fantasies came from his unwanted bite the other night. I healed almost instantly, but his claim thrived inside me, heating my veins and forcing me to walk down the path of fate. My wolf was attuned to him, curious, hungry, and intrigued.

I forced her to heel every time he walked into the room. But we all knew he'd win me over eventually. Probably around the time I went into heat.

He stood behind me now, his stealthy moves barely perceptible to my senses, but I *felt* his warmth. Like a liquid caress down my spine that culminated between my thighs.

"Do you want to go for a run?" he asked, his voice deep, seductive, and far too dominant.

I pointedly poured a cup of coffee—something I meant to do upon entering but couldn't because my hormones held me frozen in the middle of the room like a damn idiot.

Hatred at being here rippled through me, the ire overriding my need.

My family hadn't even said goodbye after the ceremony. Not that I expected them to. I was raised for this purpose and this purpose alone. It was my brother who had taught me how to fight, who had made sure I was prepared for the trials that lay ahead. Unlike my father, Logan actually cared if I survived. My mother, she would probably care, too, if my father hadn't degraded her to omega status.

I saw similar notes of that treatment here in Clemente Clan. Edon's mother barely looked up from the ground, the alpha female so sickeningly submissive to Walter that I could hardly stand looking at her.

And the other females were either omegas or betas, all with their tails between their legs when it came to the males of the grounds.

It was wrong and yet far too common. Our society saw men as the betters and women as serving a single-minded purpose—to provide pleasure and pups.

Well, I wouldn't be doing either of those things if I had my way.

Edon could kiss my alpha ass.

As if he heard me, he pressed his groin into my ass as he grasped my hips, his lips falling to my ear. "You realize fighting me only makes me want you more, right?"

A growl rumbled in my chest. I tried to swallow the noise around a mouthful of scalding coffee, but it was already too late. We both heard it.

He chuckled and pressed a kiss to my neck—the gesture both seductive and holding a hint of command that I loathed. "Run with me later."

So we'd escalated from a request stage to a demand stage. I set my cup down and turned in his arms. Big mistake because it put my back to the counter and gave him an opportunity to cage me between his impressively muscled arms. He gripped the counter on either side, his body angling over mine, crowding me.

"It's a run," he said before I could even comment. "I'm not asking you to fuck, even though we both know you want to. I just want—"

"I do not want to fuck you," I bit out.

His lips curled. "No?" He leaned in to run his nose along my cheekbone and then down my neck, the light caress scattering goose bumps down my arms. I shivered, and not because I was cold. "Mmm, your scent determines that to be a lie."

"It's my wolf." My voice came out gravely, underlined in both frustration and yearning, and I hated the sultry quality to it. "You forced the mating bond. My wolf is responding."

"Forced?" he repeated, drawing back slightly, his eyebrow arching. "I forced nothing."

"Oh?" I feigned a look of surprise. "So you didn't bite

me the other night in a claiming ceremony? Huh. Didn't realize I dreamed that." I tried to return to my coffee, but his knee lodging between mine held me before him, captive.

"You were mine whether I bit you or not. Be thankful I didn't do more." The threat in his tone had my hackles rising.

"Thankful. Right." I snorted. "Okay. Thank you, Edon, for not raping me. *Yet*."

His obsidian gaze narrowed. "Most wolves beg me to fuck them."

"I'm not most wolves."

"No, you're not. You're my intended. But something you seem to be ignoring, little mate, is that I had no choice in this either."

"You had more of one than I did," I argued. "*You* could have denied me."

"And what? Subjected you to whatever punishment Niko desired? You realize he would have killed you, right?"

"He would have been pissed, but not enough to kill me."

"No?" He laughed, but it lacked humor. "You really don't know how our politics work if you believe that for a second. My father would have demanded your life for such disrespect, and Niko would have given it to honor the clan ties. Because he would have had no use for you after my rejection."

I opened my mouth to argue that point, then closed it. I knew my father would have beat me for defying his orders. That wouldn't have been anything new. It was Edon's comment about Walter that gave me pause. I'd never considered his reaction or what he'd demand, and given what little I'd observed of him over the last week in

Clemente territory, I was inclined to believe Edon's summarization.

Oh, I would have fought it, but with that many angry wolves? I wouldn't have stood a chance.

"Ah, you see it, don't you?" Edon taunted, his tone holding a hint of menace. "You thought fucking another wolf would save you from a life by my side, but all it did was guarantee it." He leaned in so close that his breath fanned my lips as he added, "You're not the only one who enjoys defiance, little mate."

I shuddered beneath him, conflicted.

He wasn't anything like I envisioned. Alpha, yes. But he didn't demand my compliance the way my father would command it from my mother. Instead, Edon seemed to want to coax it from me, like we were playing some sort of game. Only, I didn't understand the rules of this battle between us.

"You weren't the only one forced during the ceremony," he continued, his mouth brushing mine with each word. "Yes, I could have rejected you and chosen to do this all over again in a year with another intended mate. But my pack needs a regime change. I will not fail them."

His words surprised me almost as much as the desire pooling in my belly. His nearness, his touch, and his lips so close to mine were all fucking with my head.

I needed space.

To breathe.

To *run.*

He nipped my lower lip, not harshly, just a sweet little taste. A taunt. A promise of what could be, if I allowed it.

Only my wolf was already possessed by his claiming bite. It would never truly be consensual when I submitted, and we both knew it.

I swallowed and closed my eyes.

What did he mean by his pack needing a regime change? Did Edon plan to rule them differently? I wanted to ask, to request he clarify his intentions, but my jaw wouldn't loosen. If I gave in to those queries, I risked giving in to him. And I refused. I'd rather live a life as a rogue than as a glorified alpha pet.

"Edon?" a feminine voice called from the entryway, disturbing the moment.

"Mmm, since you don't seem to want to run, then I guess I'll go play." He pressed a quick kiss to my lips before he pushed away to meet the intruder in the hallway. "Bianca," he greeted, the licentious tone in his voice causing my stomach to clench. There was no question as to what those two intended to do.

And as she came into view, I could see why.

The blonde, curvy beta oozed sex.

"Bianca, have you met Luna yet?" The way he asked it told me he knew we hadn't met yet. He was escalating the stakes of our game by introducing me to one of his mistresses—because I had no doubt there were several throughout the clan. All alphas had a harem of humans and wolves. Edon would be no different.

It was part of the psychological madness that broke alpha females. We were a possessive breed, and to share our mates with others went against our natural instincts.

I didn't even claim Edon as mine yet, and my wolf already wanted to shred Bianca to pieces. Especially as her arm slid around his waist in a knowing caress that spoke of their intimate familiarity. That he leaned down to kiss her on her perfect blonde head only infuriated me more.

"I've seen her exploring," Bianca replied, a note of disinterest in her tone. "She's not very friendly," she added in a loud whisper.

Edon chuckled. "No. She's really not."

Fuck you both, I thought, turning around to dump my coffee in the sink.

If Edon wanted to taunt me, so be it. He wouldn't win.

I turned around with a serene smile, meeting his gaze without hesitation. "I'll give you both some privacy and go for a run." I pulled my shirt over my head, unfastened my shorts, and shimmied out of them while focusing solely on him.

His smile died at the sight of my naked breasts, his eyes traveling lower to the well-groomed thatch of hair between my thighs.

He would be able to smell my arousal, the way my body naturally responded to his. Maybe it would fuel his time with *Bianca.*

I refused to even think about it.

"You two have fun now," I added, smirking at his conflicted expression.

His arm blocked my exit, his hand curling around my hip to tug me into him as his mouth descended over mine.

Bianca growled in annoyance, which, for some reason, only made me want to kiss him back to piss her off more.

I didn't even know the female, and I hated her on sight.

Mostly because she had the audacity to walk into Edon's house without knocking, knowing that he had me here. Her boldness spoke of her confidence, of her desire to throw our mating bond off balance, and I found myself wanting to return the favor in kind.

Because even if Edon entertained a harem, it would never compare to what we would have together.

So I allowed his tongue to slide inside my mouth to explore and pressed my body into his at the same time. He rumbled low in his throat in approval, his hips angling toward mine as he deepened the kiss.

It wasn't my first time embracing a male like this, but it was the first time I *reacted* to it.

What began as a hint of fun and revenge turned into something primal. Hot. Overwhelming.

My wolf stretched inside me, roaring to life and taking over my instincts. I slid my arms around his neck, pressing my breasts flush to his bare chest. He growled in response, his groin hot against mine.

Fuck. This was far too arousing, far too *right*. I'd meant to play with him, but now I couldn't release him. I wanted more. To feel his prowess, his dominance, his skill in the bedroom.

He kissed me with the same vigor, his tongue skillfully mastering mine into submission as his palm spanned my lower back.

I wanted to climb him like a tree, find out what else he could offer me.

Until his lips left mine to travel to my ear. "Thank you, Luna. Bianca will handle the rest. I wouldn't want to *force* you, after all."

My blood went cold, my arms freezing around his neck.

His amused chuckle soured my stomach.

Bastard, I thought, livid.

My nails bit into his nape, drawing blood, marking him as *mine*, before I released him completely. His nostrils flared, his amusement dying.

"Enjoy your playtime," I said, hating myself for the yearning in my voice.

Bianca practically purred beside him, her fingers trailing over his chest—a chest I'd just vacated—all the way down to his belt.

I refused to stay here to observe what happened next,

to hear him fuck her in the home we were destined to share.

But it gave me a nice dose of reality regarding my new life, one I would not accept.

I'd spent the last several days testing the boundaries. I knew where to go. How to run. And it seemed Bianca had just provided me with the distraction I needed to keep Edon off my tail.

He wanted to fuck her? Fine. I hoped he enjoyed it. Because I wouldn't be returning to find out.

I shifted in front of him and bolted from the house.

No more Clemente Clan.

No more Edon.

No more fate.

I chose my rules, my life, my destiny. Not anyone else.

Fuck all of you.

CHAPTER 7
SILAS

It took me several minutes to orient myself as I stirred to awareness.

A mattress, not leaves, cushioned my back. Instead of tree branches, wood beams decorated the ceiling above me. And an open window beside me graced my senses with fresh forest air.

My eyes stung with an emotion I didn't want to acknowledge. *Relief.*

Fuck, I couldn't remember the last time I slept in a bed. Intellectually, I understood it'd only been a few months since my time at the university. But that all felt like several lifetimes ago, between the fight for immortality and my transition to Clemente Clan life.

Everything inside me ached. Not from physical strain, just from the pain of existing. I had killed so many people, all in a game meant to entertain others. My reward? Being turned into a lycan and essentially exiled from the pack just for being alive.

You could be Willow, my subconscious whispered, causing me to flinch.

Being forced to fuck humans or lycans for the rest of my brief life was definitely worse. As were several dozen other avenues available to humans in this world. Hell, I could have been picked for a moon chase.

I groaned at the thought, digging my palms into my eyes.

Fuck. I'd be expected to participate in a moon chase one of these days. Would I be able to hunt and kill my old kind? Doubtful.

I rolled to my side, my stomach churning from both the motion and the thoughts running rampant through my mind.

Eating a full meal last night had not been a wise decision. I'd barely kept half of it down afterward. Everything was so rich. So crisp. Not at all like the food from my previous life, or even my new one.

Raw fish from the streams hadn't been my favorite, either, but at least they mostly stayed down. The meat from Edon's fridge was too flavorful for my taste buds.

Yet the wolf in me craved more.

It was so fucked up having this creature inside me dictating my wants and needs above my common sense.

With a deep growl, I forced myself out of the soft bed. I had no idea what time it was, nor did I really care. But it felt like I'd been sleeping for days, not hours.

I frowned at my appearance in the mirror. *Maybe I did sleep for days.* Because I looked a hell of a lot better than I did last night, or whenever I'd lain down.

The hollows beneath my eyes were gone.

My hair still resembled a blond mop of locks, the shaggy strands hitting just below my ears. *I really need a haircut.*

There are scissors in the kitchen, a cool male voice replied, giving me pause.

Are you always in my head? I demanded, feeling slightly violated by this whole sire-progeny bond bullshit.

Yes. He didn't elaborate. Not that I expected him to. The alpha hadn't proven to be all that chatty, just authoritative.

And maybe a tiny bit sympathetic—a trait that left me conflicted. I didn't want to like him. However, I couldn't deny feeling a hint of gratitude for giving me a place to rest.

I blew out a breath and consoled myself with a hot shower. The water beat against my back, giving me a brief glimpse of heaven.

I'd practically lost myself the first time I stepped into this marble enclosure, my body so thankful for a proper cleanse. Now I just indulged in it because I wasn't sure if I'd be allowed to take another again. Who knew when Edon would change his mind about the arrangements? They were definitely temporary.

He wanted me to keep an eye out for him.

Fine.

I'd do it because there was nothing else to do out here. And also because I appreciated the shower.

It took effort to leave the soap and water behind, but I managed in favor of the scissors Edon mentioned. Then I stared at my reflection once more. I had no idea where to start or how I would reach the back.

"Fuck it," I said, giving it my best shot. It wasn't like I had anyone to impress.

Thirty minutes later, I appeared almost human again. Minus the feral glint in my blue eyes where the wolf peeked out. I'd seen my reflection in the water numerous times, knew what I looked like, but it seemed even more real now as I stood here before the mirror.

You've missed two days of rounds, Omega, Edon said,

intruding on my thoughts once more. *There are whispers about it floating around. Go make an appearance to shut them up before someone tells me to look for you.*

Two days?

You needed the sleep was his reply.

Shit. No wonder I felt better.

Pushing away from the sink, I ventured into the kitchen to snag another piece of the too-savory meat. It nearly made me gag as I chewed and swallowed, but the wolf in me grinned. I chugged some sweet orange liquid after it, grimacing the entire time, and wandered out into the midafternoon sun.

The solar panels Edon mentioned were high up in the trees, their wires looping down the trunk like a vine to feed into the cabin. From what I gathered, the water came from a nearby well. Something about the system pumped it into the home and through a filter. I actually liked the taste of it.

Closing my eyes, I focused on calling my wolf to the surface—something that came to me surprisingly naturally now. The transition shifted over me, reforming my bones and lowering me to the ground onto four paws. It wasn't as sleek as Edon's. Not even close. But it felt right for me, and that was all that mattered.

With a shake of my fur, I bounded off in the direction of the main grounds. Hopefully, an appearance was all they needed. If anyone demanded an explanation, I'd just tell them I fell asleep out in the marshlands.

But something told me no one would care enough to ask.

I was the pack omega. The newbie. The grunt.

I only existed because of a game that left me on the clan's doorstep.

Most would say I was lucky to be alive.

Today, for the first time, I sort of agreed.

A rusty scent caught my nose, causing me to pause mid-run. Vampire. But that didn't make any sense. We were hundreds of miles from the nearest vampire territories. I knew my geography, understood Clemente Clan's position on the globe, including the heart of the capital. Vampires shouldn't be anywhere near here.

So why did a dead one appear the other day?

And now this one?

I sniffed, tracking the source. Unlike the first visitor, this one permeated the air with life. His scent didn't match any of the visitors from the mating ritual, and the blood lacked the rich quality of a royal.

Was it a rogue of some kind? A vampire without a liege?

The trail took me deeper into the marshlands, away from Edon's cabin and the clan headquarters. All that existed out here was swamp and wildlife. Why would he choose to muck through—

A bolt of white in my peripheral vision caused me to spin on my haunches.

My instincts triggered the chase before I could register that I was running, my paws bounding over the earth toward whatever had caught my eye.

Several yards later, the scent of orange blossoms hit my nostrils, causing them to flare. *Luna.*

I knew that little she-wolf was going to make a run for it!

By the looks of it, she was heading south, likely with the ocean in mind. Where she intended to go from there was anyone's guess. But I didn't plan to let her get that far.

My predator drive honed in on her sprinting form, pushing me to a speed that sent shivers of delight down my legs. It felt good to run this fast. Really good.

Luna was quick.

But my strides were longer.

I caught her back leg with my jaws, yanking her to the side. She whirled on a snarl, her jaws going for my throat without preamble.

Fuck.

I dodged her, then found myself in a ball of rolling fluff as my wolf took over my reactions. Subduing her became my primary objective, the inclination laced tightly with survival.

She was wild.

Fierce.

Furious.

But no matter how agilely or swiftly she moved, she couldn't get a hold on my throat. I refused. And when I saw an opening to go for *her* neck, I took it, slamming her into the ground beneath me.

It happened in a matter of seconds that felt like minutes.

She stilled on a growl, her defeat written into the lines of her form.

And then she began to shift.

I jumped backward, confused.

Until she attacked me again—on two legs.

The woman was fucking crazy!

But then I realized why she'd done it.

If I left a mark on her with my teeth, Edon would have my balls in a vise.

Damn. I was almost impressed by her wit. Except I was more focused on turning human as well, something that happened faster than ever before.

She took off in a dead run instead of hitting me while I was vulnerable.

And I gave chase.

Two legs felt natural to me, my athleticism in this form

superior to my performance on four paws. I caught her in seconds, tackling her to the grass once more.

She pushed and shoved, sending us sprawling until I seized her around the waist and yanked her under me.

Her resulting snarl vibrated against my chest as her fist sailed toward my jaw. I captured it just in time, pushing it to the ground, then did the same with her other hand. Which left her writhing beneath me in an effort to throw me off her.

"Stop," I growled.

She didn't.

Her legs squirmed, trying to gain the upper hand, and I knew exactly what she intended, so I pressed my groin into her sex, belatedly realizing how bad an idea that was. I'd just wanted to stop her from kneeing me in the jewels.

Instead, I'd aligned my hardening length right against her slick folds.

She immediately stilled.

I took a moment just to breathe, my heart racing in my chest.

Her light brown eyes held mine, her pupils enlarged in a mixture of fright and something else. Something darker.

"Do it," she said. "Dominate me to completion."

It was a dare that held a touch of a plea that I didn't understand.

"I don't…" I swallowed, my blood running far too hot for my liking. This position stirred chaos in my mind. A primal part of me—the wolf—wanted to fuck her. *Hard.* While my human side knew that would be wrong.

And yet I couldn't let her up.

She'd just run again. I could see it in the stubborn set of her jaw.

"Coward," she taunted.

My eyebrows rose. "You're calling me a coward for not raping you? That's charming."

Her teeth sank into my lower lip before I realized she'd moved, her bite deep and drawing blood.

"*Fuck.*" I yanked my mouth away from hers, cursing again at the resulting sting of the open wound.

She grinned up at me, my blood tainting her lips.

"You're insane," I accused, half-crazed myself by the feral sight of her. *What is wrong with me?* It was the wolf inside. Instincts overriding reasons. I pushed it back down, needing my head clear.

But Luna rubbed her soaked pussy against my length, a low mewl of yearning emanating from her chest.

"You don't even know my name," I marveled.

"Silas," she hissed. "Newbie. Dominant. Male."

The broken speech confused me. Then I realized the wolf had completely stolen her senses. Because it was a pair of black irises that stared up at me now, not light brown. "Luna…"

"Take me," she begged, pressing against me once more.

"No." I rolled off of her, then jumped up onto my heels as she came after me in a haze of brown hair and white skin.

Her nails slashed across my chest, her knees came at my groin, and her fist attempted another hit at my face. I caught her and whirled her into my arms, forcing her back to my front. She tried to stomp on my foot and kicked back at my calves.

It fucking hurt.

"Stop this, Luna."

"Never." She completely lost it in my arms, fighting for her life—and clearly coming for mine.

Her one goal seemed to be to kill me, leaving me no

choice but to defend myself once more. I blocked hits and kicks, dodged her claws, and tried to find a way to subdue her that didn't end up with us on the ground again.

Hurting her would be a mistake. On some base level, I understood that. But years and years of fighting for my life came to the forefront, taking over my vision and painting it in red.

I hadn't survived this long to be taken down by an angry little alpha wolf.

And I'd killed men twice her size in battle several times over.

"Luna," I snarled, demanding her submission, demanding she cease this before I *really* fought her.

She didn't heed the warning, her lithe form dancing around me in a wave of violence that called to my inner animal.

"Yield, little alpha," I demanded, giving her one last chance to do the right thing.

"Fuck you," she seethed, her claws swiping across my cheek and leaving a burn in their wake.

Primal need vibrated through my veins, stirring a reaction from within I couldn't repress. I had her on her back in a second flat, her hands clasped above her head, my other palm at her throat. "*Yield,*" my wolf roared.

And she did.

Oh, how she did.

Her nostrils flared, her eyes resembling obsidian pools of lust, her mouth glowing with traces of my blood.

I licked it off on instinct, earning me a growl of approval from the female beneath me. Her lips parted, her tongue touching mine.

My chest rumbled. *More.*

Part of me acknowledged how utterly fucked up this

was, but the sensation of pliant female wolf overrode my sanity.

I needed to *taste* her.

To dominate her.

To *win* her.

My mouth sealed over hers, the kiss brutal in its damnation and perfection. She hungrily met me move for move, her arousal sweetening her natural orange scent as we devoured one another.

Blood.

Growls.

Bites.

Licks.

It went on, the embrace one of the most erotic experiences of my life, and we weren't even fucking yet. Not in earnest. Just our mouths mating in a forbidden kiss.

I released her hands, needing and wanting to feel every inch of her.

Her fingers clawed into my hair, holding me to her as she returned the passion, her other hand raking nails down my back, marking me.

It was so fucking primal.

So fucking wrong.

Yet so fucking right.

"We can't do this," some weak part of me managed to say. But for the life of me, I couldn't remember why.

"We can do whatever we want," Luna replied, the sultry quality of her voice sending me cascading over the edge into a world of sensation and alpha female.

She had me by the balls.

Whatever she wanted, I'd do, if it meant I could continue tasting the heaven she offered. The bliss. The alluring escape from reality.

I wanted it all.

And I found it in the form of a wolf who wasn't mine…

CHAPTER 8
EDON

I couldn't take my eyes off the sight before me, my lips parted in absolute awe.

Primal energy radiated off Luna and Silas, their erotic aroma seducing my senses and stroking the ire burning inside. An intoxicating combination that left me frozen beside a nearby tree.

Silas had shouted Luna's name repeatedly in his mind, sending me running here to find them engaged in a battle between their wolves—in human form.

I didn't catch all of it, but the predatory nature of their duel told me everything I needed to know.

Neither of them was thinking with their heads. Only their instincts.

Silas had caught Luna.

Now she wanted to submit to the stronger wolf, to feel him dominate her in the most basic way—through the art of fucking.

It was why I had wanted to chase her. I'd wanted to be the wolf on top of her. But Silas had beaten me to it.

Yet something held him back.

And rather than take advantage of the moment to subdue them both, I leaned against the tree stump and watched him fuck her mouth with his tongue.

I should have been furious.

I wasn't.

Well, no, I *was*.

But this was also really fucking *hot*.

They were both naked, sweaty, and tainted with Silas's blood. How far would my progeny go with this? All the way? Or would that hesitation get the best of him?

Luna had all but lost herself to her wolf, her body writhing up against him, her long, sexy legs wrapping around his waist in an effort to move him along. Yet Silas didn't give her what she craved. He controlled the kiss, his hands roaming over her in tantalizing strokes that only seemed to turn her on more.

His mind told me how badly he wanted this, how he longed to sink inside her slick heat and propel himself into oblivion. Deep down he knew it was wrong; I sensed it in his thoughts. But his wolf refused to acknowledge it, too eager to rut against the willing female beneath him.

Silas showed remarkable strength in pushing the urge down, satisfying himself with licking Luna instead. He started at her neck, pausing to circle her thundering pulse before continuing a path downward to her breasts.

Her fingers threaded through his thick blond hair, holding her to him as she mewled in pleasure beneath his wicked mouth. An image of him doing the same to me flashed behind my eyes, giving me pause.

And as he trailed his mouth along her abdomen, I imagined it was my body he caressed with his tongue.

Holy fuck, I thought to myself, my balls squeezing tight at the exquisite fantasy. Which only deepened as I added Luna—placing her at this tree—watching Silas licking and sucking all the way down to my cock. Her little fingers would disappear between her thighs, pumping in and out in response, her moans music to our ears.

Moans that I heard now as Silas licked her deep, in the place only meant for me.

And still I couldn't move, too fascinated by the show in the field and the strange ideas populating my mind.

Silas on his knees before me, taking my cock deep into his throat before passing me to Luna, who sat eagerly waiting for me to fuck her mouth.

Just as that vision ended, a new one of me inside Luna appeared, pumping her sweet cunt full of my cream—cream that Silas licked from her like he licked her now, before she returned the favor by sucking him off to completion.

I shuddered, my dick harder than it'd ever been.

Luna's cries of satisfaction blended with Silas's groans, his face soaked by her eager pussy. The entire scene played out before my eyes, her climax a scream that echoed off the trees, causing the birds to fly.

And she soared with them, her body vibrating beautifully beneath Silas.

Another man.

One I created.

One who *owed* me his life.

Yet he defiled that partnership by taking *my* female. And he continued to do so with abandon, bringing her to another earth-shattering orgasm I felt to my very bones.

I wanted to destroy them both. To rip them limb from limb. But, at the same time, I wanted to fuck them.

It didn't make any sense, this riot of sensation, this anger, this *need*. I couldn't tell what I craved more—retribution or Silas's mouth around my cock. And Luna, oh, darling Luna, I wanted to mount her more than I'd ever desired mounting another woman.

It'd been over a week since her arrival, and we'd barely spent a moment together other than the first night and our little run the other day. I'd avoided her, spending time with my grandfather instead. I needed to prepare for the trials. He was the only one willing to help me.

But now I regretted more than ever not going to her, not forcing her to yield the way she did for Silas now.

It was his name leaving her mouth as she screamed a third time.

I growled in response. A low, feral sound, one that had her stilling beneath Silas. He lifted his head, looking for the source. Rather than let him see me, I ducked behind the tree, not ready yet to discipline them for their actions.

Because I'd end up either killing them or fucking them both.

I ran a hand over my face, my cock straining at my zipper. *What the hell is wrong with me?* It shouldn't even be a decision. Silas needed to die for betraying me—his sire—in such a way. And Luna, she needed to be brought to heel.

Yet I still couldn't move.

My blood hummed hot, desire tightening my groin, my base urge telling me to run out there and *join* them, not punish them.

I shook my head. Dazed. Confused. Way too turned on for my own good.

I should have taken Bianca up on her offer to fuck this afternoon, should have let her go to her knees like a good little wolf and take my cock between those plump fuck-me lips.

But I couldn't.

It felt wrong.

Oh, goading Luna had been fun. At least until she ran

off. Not that I blamed her. I'd been an ass, but her comments about rape and forcing the bond had truly pissed me off.

Women usually adored me, but Luna acted as if it would be a hardship, even when her body clearly desired mine.

It infuriated me, left me frustrated, and some twisted part of me had wanted to hurt her right back.

Which obviously fucking backfired because I'd left her all hot and bothered with a desire to run. And now all my threats of her not finding a wolf to fuck her were blown out the window by my own damn progeny.

How did this happen?

No, better question.

Why did I let *this happen?*

I stole a deep breath, needing this insanity to end. Whether I fucked them or killed them remained to be seen. I couldn't just stand here like a pansy ass and allow this to continue.

But when I finally stepped into the clearing, they were both gone.

Silas's scent led back to the home I generously lent to him, while Luna's went toward the main properties.

They'd split up, leaving me with a choice of whom to follow first.

It was easier than I expected. I chose Silas. Because I owned him. And he was about to find out what it meant to demolish the trust between progeny and sire.

Maybe after I dealt with him, this urge to chase Luna down and fuck her into submission would subside.

Maybe, but not likely.

I was the alpha here. Not her. Not Silas. *Me.*

It was time for both of them to realize that.

It was time for them to *kneel.*

CHAPTER 9
SILAS

Fuck. Where did I just do? How could I let that happen?

I paced the interior of the cabin—lost.

Edon knew.

I *felt* his knowledge deep inside, the fiery energy burning and coming right for me. But I was helpless to run. Like he'd placed a shackle on my leg, forcing me to stay here, to wait for him.

I was a dead wolf. I knew it in every fiber of my being. There was no excuse in the world that would save me now. Not that I even had one.

Fighting had left me aroused.

And Luna. *Fuck.* I couldn't say no, didn't want to deny her. Part of me wondered if it was her intention all along to put me in this position, to distract her very irate intended mate.

But I caught the fear in her gaze when his growl echoed over us. She ran faster than I did, her terror leaving a pungent scent behind.

What would he do to her? Was he there right now?

Punishing her?

No.

No, he wasn't.

Because I could feel him here.

Could sense him lurking in the shadows of the room, debating my fate.

I shivered, uncertain of what to do. Should I try to fight? To plead my case?

He surrounded me with his dominance, his power a palpable presence that weighed on my spine, demanding submission. Yet my legs locked in rebellion, my abdomen tightening beneath the intensity.

"You touched something that didn't belong to you," he said, his voice low, a rasp of sound that sent a chill down my spine.

I swallowed. "I know." Not the right response. I should have apologized, should have promised it wouldn't happen again.

But both statements would have been lies.

I neither regretted it nor could vow not to repeat it. Because something had happened between Luna and me, some sort of intense pull, and it was far from done. I wanted to taste her again. To fuck her. To *own* her.

It was completely insane.

I barely knew her.

Yet my wolf desired her. Not as a mate, but as a prize. And he refused to be denied.

Edon circled me, the shadows of the room keeping his presence concealed. However, I *felt* him moving, eyeing me as one did its prey.

The setting sun outside seemed to be an omen of what was to come—the end of a day, the end of a life.

"How did she taste?" Edon asked softly, the words

holding a lethal edge to them. Almost as if he were daring me to reply.

If I was going to die, I'd go out with my spine intact. "Like oranges."

"Mmm." Edon stood behind me now, his hum a vibration against the back of my neck. "And did you enjoy it?"

"Yes."

I waited for the blow to come, waited for a threat, *something*.

Silence fell between us. If the warmth of his skin didn't bathe my own, I'd have thought he left. Awareness teased my senses, a new scent arising.

No. It'd been there since Edon arrived.

A dark, addictive flavor. The cologne of the forest, a predator in his prime, evaluating his target—me.

Only, it wasn't violence radiating from him, but something harsher. *Savage need.*

My heart skipped a beat, then sent my pulse racing, pumping blood to the one part of me I couldn't allow to react.

But something about Edon's masculinity appealed to me. His dominance was a trait to be revered. Respected. Acknowledged.

It took significant effort to keep my head upright when all I wanted to do was bow. To go to my knees before him. To acknowledge him as the bigger wolf.

"You clearly took oral training in university." His words were a breath against my ear, his chest a threatening flame brushing my back.

My mouth went dry, my body reacting to his nearness in a way I never would have anticipated.

It's because of the fight and subsequent fuckery, I told myself. *You're aroused because of Luna.*

Are you? Edon's voice taunted. "Did you only learn how to please females in your classes?" he asked, his hand gripping my hip. "Or did you learn how to pleasure males as well?"

Oh, fuck. I wasn't the only one aroused. No wonder he radiated heat. His cock was just as hard as mine and touching the cleft of my ass.

I licked my lips, the words stuck in my throat.

Silas, he growled into my mind. *My patience will only go so far.*

Yes, I admitted with a tremble. *Yes, I learned how to pleasure males in addition to women.* I wanted to be completely prepared for whatever life threw at me.

Never in my wildest dreams did I expect it to be an aroused alpha lycan.

Nor would I have guessed my instinctual reaction to that predicament to be a favorable one.

But my dick stood proud, my skin tight with yearning, my stomach clenched with a readiness that required satisfaction.

Luna might have started it. But some sick and twisted part of me wanted Edon to finish it.

"Kneel," he demanded.

A war battled inside me, my pride telling me to remain upright while my wolf *begged* me to obey.

I gave in to my wolf, my knees buckling.

Edon placed his palm on my head, his fingers lightly running through my hair as he circled to stand before me.

I'd been in this position before—being presented with a lycan's cock to suck. Humans learned all manner of *skills* at the universities. Oral sex was one I perfected and achieved high marks in, on both males and females.

His grasp in my hair tightened, pulling my scalp and forcing me to look up at him.

A black whirlpool of fury mingled with arousal stared down at me.

I couldn't tell if he wanted to fuck me or kill me, as he seemed to be walking a fine ledge between the two.

He tensed his grip even more, his opposite hand going to my throat. "I should kill you for your blatant disrespect."

My throat bobbed beneath his palm, causing him to squeeze a little harder. I could still breathe, but barely. And while it should have scared the shit out of me, all I felt was a tingle deep inside. A yearning building between my legs.

It was so fucking messed up.

How could I be attracted to this asshole?

I never had a preference either way when it came to sex, but I never saw myself being into a power-exchange situation.

"I should kill you," he repeated. "But I find myself more intrigued by your oral skills. Luna seemed to enjoy them. And now I wonder how I'll feel about them. Do you think you'll please me enough to change my mind about your life, Silas? Or will it just make me want to kill you more?"

His words should have sickened me, should have left me feeling fearful of my future. But all they evoked was a sense of challenge, a desire to prove myself to him, to blow his fucking mind. Because this? This I could do. And I would do it well. "Fuck my mouth and find out."

Edon's resulting smile was all wolf. Hungry, wild, and barely restrained. "Open up, Silas."

The dare in his voice had me grasping his hips and tugging him forward.

He wanted to dominate me? He'd have to work harder.

Because I knew how to bring a man to his knees. I'd done it before, and I would do it again now.

I took him deep, the way I liked it, and groaned at the

masculine taste of him. Fuck, my wolf senses intensified this just like they did with Luna, providing me with a new experience despite my years of training.

He reminded me of the forest, the fresh leaves mingled with life. So different from Luna's oranges, yet their combination of flavors created the perfect mix on my tongue. I wanted more. Much, much more.

And so I took it, swallowing him to the back of my throat while sucking at the same time.

"*Fuck*," Edon breathed, his grip tightening in my hair to a painful degree.

I dug my nails into his flesh in response, forcing him to stay in place as I devoured him with my mouth. His thighs tensed, the power in his body rippling around me in a violent wave. My balls ached, my body primed from what felt like hours of foreplay with Luna, and now Edon.

It was overwhelming to the point of pain.

But the taste of him drove me onward, his cock threatening my gag reflex as he attempted to control the rhythm.

It wasn't kind.

It wasn't easy.

It was an intoxicating blend of alpha brutality, unadulterated lust, and anger, all wrapped up in a culmination of grunts and merciless thrusts.

I slid one hand to cup his sack, squeezing it in warning as he forced himself even deeper, trying to make me take his well-endowed cock all the way to the end.

My silent reprimand only intensified his energy, his need to put me severely beneath him taking over. But I held my ground, accepting only what I could while also driving him mad with my tongue.

His harsh exhales and pants told me I was winning, that he couldn't hold out on me much longer.

He wanted this almost as much as I did, perhaps even more.

"Swallow it," he growled, the words heating my veins and causing my cock to weep with want, begging to be touched.

But I focused on him.

His shaft.

The salty pre-cum teasing my tongue.

His guttural sounds as he drew closer to the climax he craved.

Each primal shift of his hips, lodging him to the point where I could no longer breathe.

I accepted it all, fighting back with my mouth in the only way I knew how—by forcing him closer to that edge with each suck, nip, and lick.

He cursed, his face contorting into beautiful lines of aroused agony. He didn't want to like this, didn't want to need it, but he couldn't seem to help himself. His dick pulsed, signaling his pending release, and then exploded down my throat.

"Silas," he hissed, his nails clawing at my scalp, his opposite hand around my nape, forcing me to take every inch as he came over and over again.

My own grip tightened, indicating to him that I couldn't breathe.

But he didn't seem to care, too lost in his oblivion to notice.

Or maybe it was on purpose.

Maybe he wanted me to die like this, on my knees, with his cock buried in my throat.

The idea of it angered me, had me forcing him backward with a shove that seemed to stun him from his orgasmic bliss.

He released me long enough to catch a breath, then

wrapped a hand around my throat, dragged me up to my feet, and pushed me up against a wall. I gasped at the sudden move, my back protesting the savage treatment.

His eyes resembled smoldering black orbs, his jaw so tight I thought it might break. But then his mouth landed on mine. Not gracefully. Not kindly. But ruthlessly. As if he didn't want to kiss me but couldn't stop himself.

And my tongue responded in kind.

Because I didn't want to kiss him either. Didn't want to be anywhere near him. And yet my fucking dick practically begged me to touch him, to stroke him once more, to do *something*.

As if he heard the plea, he aligned his groin with mine, his damp skin—from my mouth—heaven against my aching flesh.

I couldn't stop myself from pressing into him, seeking friction, heat, *relief.*

His teeth sank into my lower lip, drawing blood.

I bit him right back, earning me a snarl from the beast.

My hands grasped him just as cruelly, my nails digging in just as much as his, my need to fight him harsh and apparent. And still we kissed as if we were old, angry lovers fighting through a haze of violence.

I hated him.

Wanted him.

Loathed him.

Desired him.

And his responding growls told me he felt the same.

It wasn't unheard of for alphas and royals to pick harem members of the same sex—most enjoying a good degradation.

But this went deeper.

This wasn't about Edon needing to humiliate or tame me. I sensed it in his movements, his mind, his snarls, his strokes, his kiss, his general handling, that this went beyond societal platitudes and games.

We were connected on a bizarre level, his turning me into a wolf binding us in a forbidden dance that left us starved.

"Jack yourself off," he said, his hand moving to my throat. "Do it now."

Fuck off, I wanted to say, but I couldn't, my palm already moving toward my swollen flesh. I hissed at the first pump, my back bowing off the wall and directly into the wall of male before me.

He didn't kiss me again but watched each of my strokes with a hungry gleam that only turned me on more.

I'd never felt anything like this, all my previous experiences almost clinical in comparison. We weren't allowed to engage in sexual activities outside of classes, not that I'd ever desired anyone enough to try. Rae and Willow were my best friends, not my fuck buddies. And none of the men in my courses ever intrigued me, despite the sexual things we had to do to each other in our classes.

But Edon… he made my blood *burn.*

And Luna, fuck, her scent drove me crazy.

It had to be my wolf, all the new sensations stirring a riot of insatiable yearning.

The pressure built in my gut, causing me to strengthen my grip and increase my movements. If he told me to stop, I'd kill him. Or worse, I would disobey him.

I needed this, earned it, fucking *required* it.

My sack practically twisted in its fury to find release, my lower abdomen threatening to explode beneath the onslaught of the exquisite eroticism of the moment.

Edon's gaze lifted to mine, holding me captive, his grasp squeezing, endangering my airway.

And forcing me to erupt.

My groan vibrated beneath his palm, coming out as a choked sound that left me panting against the wall in a cold sweat. Ropes of semen decorated his abdomen, my arousal marking him in a way it shouldn't.

However, it gave me a brief moment of joy to claim something that didn't belong to me. To name the alpha as *mine*.

He must have known, must have seen the glimmer of pleasure in my eyes, because he mercilessly propelled me to my knees with a single demand. "Lick me clean."

A shudder of annoyance rocked my spine. Not because of the task—which was indeed degrading—but the idea of removing my scent from his skin.

This is so fucked up. He couldn't be mine, nor did I *want* him to be mine.

Ever.

And I proved it to myself by doing exactly what he dictated, laving every inch of his torso to remove the evidence of my arousal from his skin.

He remained in a towering position above me for so long I thought he might command me to suck him off again. His cock strained toward my mouth as if in agreement. His body hot and hard and clearly in need.

I didn't dare meet his gaze. If I did, we'd repeat this entire dance. And I wasn't sure I'd survive another throat fucking from him today. Anger radiated heavily from him, mingled with a lethal intent.

He wanted me dead for touching Luna.

I couldn't blame him. Alphas were possessive.

But he also seemed to be struggling with something deeper—this bizarre connection between us.

In the end, it was the connection that won.

He released me without a word or a strike and left as quietly as he'd arrived.

I remained motionless on my knees in his wake, unable to speak or move.

Because my fate still hung in the balance.

He'd merely spared it for another day, to be handled whenever he saw fit.

Somehow, that was almost worse.

CHAPTER 10
LUNA

Edon's house reeked of beta bitch. My jaw clenched in response, any and all residual guilt riding my wolf gone in an instant.

I shouldn't have submitted to Silas. It was stupid. Really, *really* fucking stupid. Not that I had much choice. He was a hell of a lot stronger than I expected, his prowess very uncommon for a newbie. Most humans resembled pups after a change, at least from what I'd heard. I'd not met any, as it was extremely rare, but Silas struck me as far more extraordinary than usual.

Unfortunately, he was now a dead wolf walking, thanks to me, and was probably being punished right now, hence Edon's prolonged absence.

Fuck.

Okay, maybe some guilt remained.

I buried my head in my hands, hiding in my room and dreading Edon's return.

He *knew*. His growl shook the ground beneath me out in the marsh, heightening the sensations in my core to a dangerous level.

Because I'd thrived from the chase, my body reacting unspeakably to the adrenaline that coursed through my system. That, coupled with Edon's assaulting kiss not even an hour before, and I'd been hopeless to my need.

Oh, and Silas's tongue. Holy hell, that man's tongue could win wars. He had me coming faster than my hands ever had, leaving me hot and needy and screaming for more.

Until Edon's growl rumbled the earth.

It sounded an awful lot like the one echoing through the home now.

I swallowed. *Shit.* He was back. I felt his anger in the air, thick and intoxicating and overwhelming.

He didn't knock on my door. He opened it.

I nearly drowned in the furious dark pools of his eyes.

"Did you enjoy your run?" he asked, his voice deceptively calm.

"Did you enjoy your playtime?" I countered, noting his healthy glow.

His lips curled. "Oh, you have no idea. Best head of my life. You'll have a lot to live up to."

A growl built in my throat, my blood heating while my stomach constricted. How could he be so blatant about fucking another woman's mouth?

I nearly snorted. As if I had the right to be pissed. I just ran back from having another wolf's tongue between my thighs.

And Edon had just come from delivering punishment. I smelled Silas all over him. Whatever punishment he'd received, it wasn't good. It was also all my fault.

My shoulders fell, leaving behind a defeated feeling. It was a sensation I hated. A weakness. But I couldn't help it. My actions had led to the death sentence of another wolf, someone who, for all intents and purposes, didn't deserve that fate.

"What? No offer to prove me wrong?" Edon taunted.

"You look pretty well satisfied," I muttered, nodding at his well-endowed, yet clearly appeased, groin. "If you need more, then go fuck yourself."

A feral sound came from his chest, sending a shiver down my spine. "Careful, Luna. Or next time I'll make *you* watch while I fuck someone else."

I swallowed. The way he said it made it sound like a promise, not a potential situation. My father forced my mother to observe his activities over the years, each one breaking her more.

"What? No fiery comeback?" He waited. "Don't tell me your defiance is gone already."

I said nothing. He wanted my submission. Instead, I gave him my silence.

"Your ground privileges are officially revoked. The next time you want to run, you'll have to ask. If I catch you outside the boundaries of the village without my express permission, I will punish you. Do you understand?"

I met his gaze. Did I understand? "Yes." Would I comply? Fuck no.

The tilt of his lips said he knew, too.

And that he would enjoy administering whatever punishment he had in mind.

Fine.

It didn't scare me.

He had no idea what sorts of punishments I grew up enduring. I was so incredibly well versed in the art that he would have to be extremely creative to even consider impressing me.

So good luck to him.

Edon left without another comment, the air thick with promise and sex in his wake.

I wanted to vomit.

Today, I tried and failed to escape.

Tomorrow, I would try again.

And the next day.

And the day after.

Until I either died trying or succeeded.

Edon thought I'd given up? Hardly. I was just getting started.

I WOKE TO BLISSFUL SILENCE.

Either Edon stupidly expected me to obey his command or he had a trap waiting for me.

Regardless, I was going for a run. No one grounded me. Especially not him.

Pulling on a pair of jeans and a tank top, I decided to take a walk through home base first and see what they were saying. Because if Edon informed them of my little house arrest, then I needed to know whom to evade.

It would also give me a cover if he asked where I went today. *Oh, you know, around.*

Only, the second I set foot on the main property of Clemente Clan's headquarters, I regretted it.

Bianca stood with a group of friends, her face positively glowing as she spoke—loudly—about the things Edon did to her last night.

You went to her? Again? I thought, irritated beyond measure. It was so illogical, so completely unfair given that I'd shared an erotic session with his progeny, but to know he went to this bitch in his aggression-filled hormonal state pissed me off to no end.

Which was how I justified my fist meeting her face.

Twice.

It all happened so fast, my reaction to hearing her gloating—in front of me—about fucking *my* mate, that I couldn't pull my wolf back in time before striking out.

That she smelled like Edon only made it worse.

Mine, my wolf growled, sending my fist into the bitch's jaw a third time.

"*Enough,*" a male voice snapped, one underlined in authority.

One that belonged to an alpha.

Walter.

My knees bent without preamble, my head bowing in a submission I felt down to my very bones. *Survival,* my wolf whispered. Something that didn't happen with Edon. Because somewhere deep down I knew he wouldn't hurt me, unlike the alpha approaching me now.

Walter would gladly flog me, rape me, beat me to a pulp. I felt it in his intentions with every step, his interest in breaking whom he saw as the strongest female in his pack —a female who needed to learn how to properly heel.

The back of his hand met the side of my head, the strike sending me to the ground on a whimper. "You do not have authority here, Luna of Ernest Clan," he said in a deceptively calm voice.

His foot connected with my midsection next, causing me to curl in on myself in protection, years of my father's similar treatment flashing behind my eyes.

I can do this.

It only hurts for a little while.

Go to the happy place.

Think about sparring with Logan.

Don't—

His next strike came to my back, shooting pain up my spine.

"Gentlemen, who wants to help me teach the little wolf a lesson?" he asked, the licentious notes in his voice sending ice through my veins.

Because I knew what he was proposing.

I'd seen my father do the same to my mother for misbehaving, had to watch her gang rape firsthand. It wasn't meant for her pleasure but my father's. And as he oversaw the treatment, he didn't care about those seeking their own ecstasy through the use of her body.

He'd even fucked another woman beside her just to prove his point.

It'd made me so sick, stunned me so harshly, that Logan had to hold me all night to keep me warm. He promised that when he took over, things would be different, that he wouldn't treat our people with such disrespect.

But now that I wasn't there, who knew what vile things my father would implant in Logan's mind?

A crowd formed, hungry male testosterone filling the air.

Violence seemed to rain down upon me in the form of jabs, kicks, touches I didn't want to feel.

It all blended together, the chaos a cloud in my mind.

This can't break me, I pleaded with myself. *You've been beaten before. You've been drowned. You've lived outside in subzero elements for days. You can do this. You can do this. You can—*

A furious growl rumbled the ground, one that seemed to shake the foundations of my heart and broke through the cruel fog circling my aching body.

"*Mine,*" the voice said. "You will not touch what is mine."

"She's a disobedient little bitch who needs to be taught

a lesson," Walter replied, a belt in his hand that appeared to be tinged with blood.

My blood.

I didn't remember him hitting me, couldn't even feel the remnants of any slash, but I felt certain he'd struck me more than once.

"And you will not be the one delivering that lesson."

"Like hell I won't," the alpha growled.

Edon caught his father's rising wrist, twisting it so harshly the bone threatened to snap. "You have no authority over my mate. If I want her beaten, she will be beaten. If I want her raped, she will be raped. But you will not dictate the punishment. *I* will."

He shoved the alpha back with a force that elicited gasps from the crowd. So much power. So much command.

An alpha in his prime.

The rising heir.

I saw it now in his stance, in the way his muscles bunched across his bare back. Even in nothing but a pair of jeans—no shoes—he stood with an authority few others would ever possess.

This male *required* dominance.

And if I wasn't already on the ground, I'd be kneeling at his feet beneath the aura of superiority rolling off him in waves.

Edon turned, his eyes pools of black that brought the majority of the crowd to their knees with a single glance.

No one would challenge him.

Not here.

Not ever.

"Luna is *mine*," he said, his tone carrying across the village, and probably into the surrounding areas as well. "If anyone would like to fight me for the right to touch my property, I stand well prepared." He stared down every male in attendance who remained standing until each of them bowed their heads. And then he returned to Walter, who had stood with an ambience of fury that chilled the atmosphere around us. "Your days are numbered, Alpha Incumbent. I bow to you no longer. Do not touch Luna again without my permission, or I will make you regret it, *old man.*"

Edon didn't wait for a response; he scooped me off the ground and carried me through the throng of bowing wolves.

No one stopped us.

No one said a word.

Not even the furious alpha in our wake.

I buried my head against Edon's neck, my face wet with tears I hadn't realized I'd shed. Just the fear of those men touching me had destroyed my confidence, the helpless realization of my fate, and the knowledge that I couldn't fight them all off.

They wouldn't have killed me.

They would have subdued me and made it hurt so much worse.

Edon brushed a finger along my spine, his touch burning through the fabric of my shirt. Just a tender stroke, a notion of comfort, that somehow hurt even more.

I'd lost my shit over a female for bragging about him, for fucking him when he didn't truly belong to me. I couldn't even imagine what he had done to Silas.

The jealousy inside me had burned so hot, forcing my wolf to the surface.

And this was just the beginning.

Edon would always take other females, likely even in front of me. How would I stomach it if I couldn't even handle it now?

The scent of his home drew my eyes upward to the familiar beams above, his legs having moved so quickly that I didn't even realize we were here until he slammed the door shut with his heel.

I expected him to drop me in my room or on the couch, but instead he took me to his bedroom.

Punishment, I realized. He had to do something, to put me in my place for behaving the way I did, and this was where he planned to do it.

Would he make me blow him? Fuck him? Use a belt against my skin the way his father had? Strangle me? Burn me?

Lycans healed quickly, especially purebreds like me. Which meant I could withstand all sorts of torture before passing out, and I'd almost always wake up as good as new without scars.

I opened my mouth to explain, to voice an apology, to say *something*, but my throat refused me. It was too tight. I could barely even breathe.

He set me on the mattress. "Lift your arms," he demanded.

I complied only because I didn't know what else to do, and I whimpered as he peeled off the remains of my bloody shirt. He guided me downward onto my side, and my legs automatically curled into my abdomen.

This was going to hurt.

I needed to find my happy place, to think of the few moments I enjoyed in my childhood, to think about Logan and Claudette and all our lessons together about the old world. To pretend I lived there. With them. In harmony. Without tyranny. In a place—

Agony sliced through my ribs, causing me to cry out.

Edon held me down, his fingers prodding my tender skin, his expression livid.

It took me a moment to realize he wasn't inflicting pain on purpose but was trying to assess my wounds.

"I'm going to fucking kill him," he gritted out, slowly rolling me to my other side to better examine my back. It hurt like a son of a bitch, my entire body tingling beneath his touch. He cursed, the sound harsh enough to make me flinch. "Don't move."

As if I could.

My body ached from the two kicks. Wait, hadn't there been more than two? *Yes.* Walter had a bloody belt. But I couldn't remember what he'd done with it. I'd retreated into—

Ice stabbed my arm, forcing a scream from my throat, but a stern hand forced me to stay put. The room began to spin a little, painting my vision in a drunk-like sensation. I tried to shake it off, tried to focus on the shifting wall, but couldn't.

Was this Edon's punishment?

To make me delirious?

To fuck with my mind?

"I'm not going to punish you, Luna," he said softly, a warm cloth sliding over my back and causing me to hiss.

"*Fuck...*" It stung. No, it *burned.*

And, wait, had I said something out loud? Or had he read my mind?

"Shh." He combed my hair away from my face, his palm sliding to the back of my neck. "The pain medicine will kick in soon to provide some relief. It won't last long with how rapidly our bodies consume drugs, but it should give you a little bit of comfort while your insides heal."

Another swipe of the cloth had me clenching the bedsheets, my lips parting on a groan that turned into a plea for him to stop.

I hated this show of weakness.

Hated more how I craved his touch.

"I need to clean the wounds," he explained, his cloth returning. Or maybe it was a new one. I couldn't tell. The stench of antibiotics made my stomach heave, my skin screaming beneath the healing salve.

Until another wave of dizziness hit me.

I blinked rapidly, trying to clear the dots from my vision.

"Pain medicine." The two words were a breath near my ear, his touch turning into a caress against my back. My eyes drooped closed, the sensation easing me into a cocoon of warmth I longed to live in forever.

Then a second prick had my eyes flashing open in concern, only to be soothed by a low growl from Edon.

Mate, my wolf acknowledged, at peace with his touch, the way he took care of me, the manner in which he protected me from others.

His warm body curled around mine in the bed, pulling me gently back into him. *Sleep*, my mind whispered.

Or maybe that was Edon.

Mmm, but I didn't want to sleep just yet.

My tongue felt too funny. Thick. Dry. Like I'd licked a lot of sandpaper.

Odd.

I twitched my nose, the scents swirling around us confusing me.

I smelled only Edon.

And another masculine scent, one that reminded me of cypress trees. I rather liked the calming nature of it but didn't know where it came from.

"My grandfather," Edon whispered, either due to somehow reading my mind or possibly because he'd deciphered my sniffing. "That's where I was last night, little mate. Bianca was showboating because I turned her down. She's jealous of you."

I frowned. He might have turned her down last night, but he definitely spent yesterday with her.

"Did I?" he asked softly, his lips caressing my neck. "I said someone sucked me off, but I didn't say it was her."

I didn't understand.

I also didn't know how he was in my head, how he heard my thoughts. Unless I was voicing them out loud? I did feel pretty weird. Dizzy. Like I was on the verge of a dream without sleeping.

"It's the medication." He kissed my temple, his arm draping across my chest while his other slid beneath my head. "Rest, little mate. You'll wake up as good as new. I promise."

Why is he being so nice to me? I wondered, suspicious. This wasn't how alphas treated their mates. Not in a very long time, anyway.

Claudette whispered of a different time, one where females and males chose each other for life, their faithfulness to one another the heart of the mating bond.

Now males were encouraged to cheat and females demanded to endure.

Logan once said he preferred the world Claudette spoke of in our studies.

I did, too.

But I wouldn't be able to find that here. Or anywhere, really. The old world no longer existed. Only this new society controlled by the Blood Alliance.

I closed my eyes, Claudette's words a low murmur in my mind. *"Everyone deserves a choice. Everyone deserves their very own Jolene Mason."*

She loved once.

A male named Jolene. Claudette spoke of him often,

about how choices matter. In the end, his heart went with another, but hers always belonged to him. Which was why she never mated.

"What did you say?" Edon asked, his breath a warmth against my skin.

I shook my head, not sure what he meant. I hadn't said a word. Or maybe I had. But what would it matter at this point?

Dreams didn't exist here.

And love was a figment of the old world.

"Give me a chance, Luna," Edon murmured. "I just may surprise you."

"You already have." The words slurred in my mouth, sounding drunk with sleep.

He nuzzled my throat, the gesture far more alleviating than I wanted to admit.

But it lulled me into a false sense of safety.

One that followed me into my dreams, where I envisioned a world that didn't exist. A fantasy future based on a past I didn't know but wished I did.

CHAPTER 11
EDON

LUNA SLEPT SOUNDLY IN MY BED, HER LITHE FORM CURLED around one of my pillows. She hadn't moved much in the last two days, but her body appeared to be fully healed. *Finally.*

I swept her hair back to place a kiss against her temple and ventured into my living room, where Silas stood waiting.

I'd called him here through the sire link, much to his annoyance.

He was dressed similarly to me in a pair of jeans, his blond hair damp from his run, his skin glistening with a sheen of sweat that seemed to define his muscles even more.

Silas arched a brow, his skepticism written in that single expression alone. But I also heard it in his thoughts, his uncertainty underlined with a begrudging satisfaction at my demanding his presence.

Is he going to kill me? Or fuck me? he wondered, causing my lips to quirk.

"I haven't decided yet." A lie, of course. If I wanted to

kill him, he'd already be dead. It was the fucking-him part I hadn't quite figured out. Because I wanted to. I just didn't think it would be right.

Of course, I'd already taken advantage of his mouth. Why not push him all the way?

"I hate that you're always in my head," he said flatly.

"Better get used to it." I would always be there unless one of us died. And if he looked deep enough, he'd realize the link went both ways. "I need you to watch Luna for me."

His lips parted, drawing my attention to his mouth.

Which reminded me of the other night and how skillfully he took my cock.

Mmm, yes, I wanted to do that again.

"*What?*" He gave a laugh. "You're fucking with me."

"Not even close," I said, taking a step toward him. He held his ground, something that only intrigued me more. "You're the only one I can trust with Luna." Because I had a permanent link to him that I could access regardless of the distance. "Just don't touch her."

Without my permission, I wanted to add, surprising myself. An image of Silas going down on Luna flashed behind my eyes, causing my blood to boil—in a good way. I shook it off, forcing myself to focus on the task at hand.

"Can you do that, Silas? Can you watch without touching?"

His nostrils flared, challenge written into his features. "You're setting me up for failure before I've even begun."

"This isn't a test."

"Everything in this fucking world is a test," he retorted, his anger warm and hot. I wanted to play in it, to stoke it higher, to see how far I could press before he exploded.

If it wasn't, he'd have an actual friend do this, Silas added, speaking to himself.

"I don't have friends." Nor did I need them. "My last *friend*—a term I use loosely—died just after my thirteenth birthday. My father called him a distraction. Said I didn't need one of those and sliced the kid in half in front of the clan. Didn't have a whole lot of offers for friendship after that."

Silas's eyes widened a fraction, the only indication that my words had alarmed him.

"Look, I need to go speak to my grandfather," I continued, uncertain of why I felt the need to explain myself, but did so anyway. "And I need someone I can trust —someone I *own*—to guard Luna. You are that someone, Silas. I'm not asking you for a favor. I'm not testing you. I'm giving you a task as your alpha and sire. You will stay here and protect my mate until I return. Should anyone disturb my home or you or Luna, you will alert me. Do you understand?"

He lifted a shoulder. "Fine."

Oh, his defiance goaded my inner wolf. I wanted to bend him over and fuck him into submission. But I didn't have time.

And it would wake up Luna.

"We're going to have a chat later about obedience," I said, stepping away from him. "And it'll probably end with you on your knees again."

Hunger flashed in his gaze before he could conceal it. "You're the alpha."

"And you're my omega," I returned, amused. "Behave."

Silas barked into my mind as I left, causing me to chuckle as I took off at a jog toward my grandfather's estate.

The insanity of what had happened to Luna left me feeling on edge, but a few minutes with Silas had cooled me off enough to run the grounds without trying to kill anyone. That would change if anyone stepped in my way. Especially if it was one of the jackasses who joined my father in his little circle of punishment the other day.

One of the older members of the clan, Barry's father, had found me in the woods and alerted me of my father's intentions. I'd taken off running before he finished, arriving just as two of the wolves—Glenn and his idiot of a brother—started taking off their pants.

It didn't take a genius to understand their plan.

They were going to gang-rape Luna into submission.

Over my dead body, I thought, my bare feet pounding over the earth, my blood pumping full of rage yet again.

If that had been another of my father's little tests, I'd failed, and I didn't give a fuck. Luna was mine. No one touched her except me. The others might crave a broken female in the bedroom, but I did not. Her fire was one of my favorite traits about her, and the pack had snuffed it out, leaving her cold and disturbingly distant in my arms.

Luna had clearly been abused before, as she knew how to retreat into her mind.

I'd seen that look so many times on my mother's face. These days, she wore it permanently. She didn't even acknowledge my presence when I visited her now, so broken and alone.

That would not happen to Luna.

I refused to allow it.

Silas's uncertainty trickled through our connection, causing my run to slow to a jog as I navigated through his thoughts for the cause.

Hunger. He'd been about to eat when I called him to the house. Not wanting to sprint on a full stomach, he'd returned the items to the fridge and took off toward his fate. Which, apparently, he thought would include his very public death.

The man sure did hide his fear well, because I hadn't caught an inkling of it on him, just cocky, irritated male. But his mind painted a very different scene.

Help yourself to whatever food you need, I thought at him. *And I want to know when Luna is awake.*

Annoyance darkened our link. *Sure.*

I smirked. *Don't sound too thankful, Silas, or I may be inclined to do something ungracious in the future.*

Like fuck my mouth? he drawled. *Or should I consider that a gracious act?*

Oh, the pair of balls on that man nearly rivaled my own. *Keep talking, progeny. I'm considering this foreplay.*

Probably best you don't flirt with me too much, Sire. *There's a gorgeous alpha female in the other room.*

I stopped jogging.

Like, flat-out froze.

And he must have sensed my sudden pause, because he added, *I'm not going to touch her.*

You better not. Except my earlier intrigue returned, causing me to wonder what would happen if I walked in on another sexual interlude between them. My blood heated once more, the idea arousing as fuck.

Hurry back, Silas said, sounding bored. *Or I'm eating all of your food.*

I snorted. *Go for it.* He needed it more than I did. His lean, muscular form could use a hint of bulk, something I knew he had more of prior to the Immortal Cup and recruitment into Clemente Clan.

He'd get it back.

I returned to my run and smiled when I found my grandfather waiting on his old porch, his shoulder braced against a pole at the top of the stairs. "Trouble in paradise?" he drawled, likely having sensed my hesitation about a mile ago when talking to Silas.

"Errant progeny," I replied, walking up the stairs and past him into the house.

"I can't wait to meet him."

"I know." I'd already told my grandfather a few things about Silas, mostly in regard to his fighting skills and defiance. "I'm pretty sure you're going to disown me for him."

My grandfather chuckled and shut the door behind us before collapsing into his favorite recliner. "It's about time you had some competition for my affection."

I snorted and took over the couch. "Are you kidding? I can't wait to be rid of you, old man."

"Yeah, yeah. That's why you've been to see me practically every day since your mate arrived, right?" He gave me a knowing look. "What'd she do now?"

Nothing like cutting directly to the point of my visit. "She attacked Bianca." And, according to Barry's father, the bitch deserved it for goading an alpha female so publicly. Luna's possessive reaction should have pleased me, but the violent aftermath of the incident severely tainted my pleasure. "My father attempted to beat Luna into submission as a result."

My grandfather whistled. "A ballsy move to touch another alpha's female."

"I think we both know he has no respect for me or my pending claim to his territory." Things had been tense with my father for years, and I strongly suspected he wanted me dead. Fortunately, he wasn't strong enough to do it. Nor could he face the political repercussions of assassinating his only heir.

"You need allies," my grandfather said for the thousandth time. "Walter did one hell of a job alienating you, to the point where it's almost a sure thing you're going to fail these trials."

"Gee, thanks for the vote of confidence," I drawled, irritated.

"You need Luna on your side. And that boy Silas. And anyone else you can get to help you. Because whatever Walter has planned, it's going to be bad."

"It already is bad," I corrected him, thinking of the vampire I had to cut up into pieces before depositing him in the ocean. My grandfather had confirmed it was definitely the start of my Alpha Trials and that Silas's idea to get rid of the evidence was a sound one.

"He's only just begun."

I know, I thought, leaning forward with my elbows on my knees. "I didn't come here to discuss the trials, Gramps. I need to ask you about something else."

"Yeah?" He cocked his head in that curious way he favored, the one that made him look like a young pup despite being close to seven hundred years old with white hair and wrinkled skin. He was one of the oldest lycans in existence, most dying around the six- or seven-hundred-year mark. But not my grandfather. He was a stubborn old bastard, much to my father's chagrin.

The pack gave him his space out of respect, while my father avoided him entirely.

"Well?" my grandfather prompted. "I'm not getting any younger over here."

My lips quirked. He always seemed to know what I was thinking. But I doubted he could anticipate what I wanted to know now. "Who's Claudette?"

Luna had murmured about the woman in her drug-induced daze, saying something about her lessons and the history of the world. Most of it I already knew, having learned much from my grandfather about the old times, but then Luna said something utterly fascinating.

"Everyone deserves a choice," I repeated her words now, my eyes narrowing at him. "Everyone deserves their very own Jolene Mason."

Strange words from a woman who had never met my grandfather.

Even stranger for her to use his full given name, not the pack alpha designation he'd gone by for the last few centuries.

And the mist that entered his gaze told me I'd struck a chord.

There was a story here.

A long one.

CHAPTER 12
SILAS

Eggs and spinach.

Two items I grew up eating that somehow managed to taste far too rich now.

My lycan palate was too intense for my stomach. I couldn't seem to eat anything without it churning inside me. Even now, my breakfast threatened to expel itself all over Edon's granite counters.

So much for my promise to eat all his food.

I force-fed myself another bite, grimacing as I swallowed. "Ugh," I groaned, setting my fork down and bowing my head. "I fucking hate this."

The hairs along the back of my neck flickered to life, alerting me of an approaching presence. But I relaxed as I scented the familiar orange blossoms of Luna's scent.

She's awake, I told Edon, since he demanded I inform him.

Good. No touching.

I rolled my eyes and didn't bother with a reply. Instead, I glanced over my shoulder and admired her sleepy approach. She'd thrown on a shirt too big for her frame, one that hit her at her knees. *She's wearing your shirt,* I thought at Edon, then paused in confusion as to why I felt the need to share that detail.

Yeah? How does she look in it?

Hot, I admitted, once more surprised by my easy candor with the alpha male.

It was probably a result of having his cock shoved down my throat. Sort of erased any and all formalities between us. That I kind of wanted to do it again, well, I didn't quite know how to feel about that yet.

"You're alive," Luna whispered, her eyes widening a fraction.

"For now," I replied, standing. "Do you want any eggs? I made too many." Not true. I just didn't want to eat any more.

The way her nostrils flared in disgust told me her answer before she voiced it. "No. I'll make something more appetizing."

I frowned. "It's eggs and spinach. A staple."

"It's bland and boring," she countered, going through the cabinets with the ease of someone who knew her way around the kitchen. Specifically, *this* kitchen.

Which, yeah, made sense. She was Edon's mate.

What is she doing? Edon asked.

Get your ass back here and find out, I thought back at him.

His amusement touched my mind, leaving behind a caress that heated my blood. *Oh, Silas. You're an expert in respecting your betters, aren't you?*

I snorted. *You seemed pretty satisfied with my* respect *the other night.*

He growled, the sound hungry and aroused. *Are you flirting with me?*

No. I'm stating a fact. We both know you enjoyed it. Don't deny it.

I wouldn't dream of it, he replied, his voice silky and warm and deep. *Careful or I'll demand a repeat.*

I hope you do. I regretted the thought immediately, my hands gripping the countertop as I closed my mind. He wasn't supposed to hear that, but his resulting silence told me he had. *Fuck. Ignore me. I'm just irritated.* Understatement of the fucking century. I wasn't just irritated but also frustrated, and confused by the riot raging in my head.

I pressed my forehead to the cool marble, trying to thwart the headache.

And failing because Edon was back in my mind again.

Don't touch Luna until I return. His command only pissed me off more.

"I already said I wouldn't," I grumbled out loud and in my head.

"Wouldn't what?" Luna asked, drawing my attention to her curvy ass. She'd bent over to retrieve something in the fridge, presenting me with her delicious backside. The shirt had ridden up to the bottom of her rounded cheeks.

No underwear.

Fuck.

Edon said something back to me, but I ignored him in favor of the female before me. "Edon won't leave me alone," I said in an effort to explain my show of mental insanity. "It's this damn sire bond."

"Ah, the psyche. I assume you're the only one he can access other than me right now, not that he's tried opening our door. Which means he's probably smarter than I give him credit for." She finally stood up again, in her arms an array of items that had my brow furrowing. "It's not a common bond, you know. Your sire bond, I mean. Most lycans are born, not made." Her light brown eyes met mine. "It's not something I'll ever be allowed to experience."

"Trust me, you should be grateful. Edon is a pain in the ass."

Her lips curled. "You're not afraid of him at all, are you?"

Was I? "Not really." I couldn't exactly say why. Maybe because I trusted him on a naïve level, thanks to the sire bond. Or perhaps because he'd never been particularly cruel to me. Even on the day of my turning, he gave me relief by not extending the pain. Much to his father's disapproval—a stark emotion I'd sensed, more than witnessed, in the air that day.

"I'm not either," she replied as she broke an egg into a mixing bowl. She added several more while chewing on her lower lip. "I should fear him," she continued softly. "He's more powerful than Walter. I can feel it in his aura, the way he takes charge, but some part of me refuses to retreat the way I should."

"Maybe because you're his mate." I folded my arms on the counter, leaning forward a bit on my stool to observe her choices in ingredients. "He can't hurt you."

She snorted. "Clearly, you've not been around a lot of alpha pairings. I mean, you've seen Walter's mate, right? She's utterly broken. It's what Edon has grown up around, what he likely intends to do to me. Yet..." She trailed off, her brown eyes lifting to mine. "He saved me from Walter the other night. Or I think it was the other night. Honestly, the drugs Edon gave me sort of fucked with my concept of time."

"What are you talking about?" I asked, confused. "What happened?"

"You weren't there?" she countered, then shook her head. "Right. You're probably not allowed in the main village as a newbie." She cocked her head. "Wait, how are you here right now?"

"Edon told me to guard you," I admitted. "He's worried about packmates using you against him in the Alpha Trials." Which, I suspected, had something to do with whatever she'd just mentioned about Walter. What had happened to her while I was out wandering the boundaries?

"And he chose you to protect me?" She sounded so surprised that I growled, my earlier irritation returning in spades.

"I may be a *newbie*, but I'm not weak, Luna." Something she knew firsthand. "I kicked your ass just the other day, didn't I?"

She bristled, her wolf prowling beneath the surface. "First of all, yes, you did. And I want a rematch. Secondly, that wasn't what I meant, jackass." She flipped her long hair over her shoulder and returned to her odd mixture of flour, eggs, and milk. The addition of cinnamon had my nostrils flaring.

When she didn't continue, I prompted her with, "What did you mean?"

"That it isn't common for an alpha to talk to a newbie, let alone to interact with one. And asking you over to his house? Especially after the other day? Yeah, that's definitely not normal. You should be dead for touching me, not sitting calmly in the alpha's kitchen watching over me while I make pancakes."

"You sound disappointed," I drawled, cocking my head. "Wishing he would have killed me?" I wondered out loud, grinning. "Should I remind you that you begged me to fuck you and not the other way around?"

I didn't know why I said it. Maybe because I wanted to talk about what the hell happened between us. Or maybe because a dark part of me wanted to know how she felt about it all. To find out if she wanted to explore the forbidden dance we'd started and not come close to finishing.

A dangerous topic.

One I should divert us away from.

And yet, I didn't. Instead, I waited and watched as she stopped stirring her mixture.

"I did not beg you," she said, her soft voice underlined in steel.

"You did."

"I did not," she said through gritted teeth. "I was… the fight… my wolf… I did not *beg*."

I chuckled. "Whatever you say, little moon." The nickname fell from my lips unbidden, a whisper from the animal prowling beneath my skin. Once said, I couldn't retract it. Nor did I want to. It suited her, and it served as the first nickname I'd ever given a person.

"*Little moon?*" she repeated, a growl in her tone. "Really?"

"Says the one calling me *newbie*," I pointed out.

"That's not an endearment, *Silas*. It's a title. It's who you *are*."

I smiled. "*Luna.*" I drew her name out across my tongue, teasing her. "Means 'moon,' yeah? And you're smaller than me. So I could argue it's what you are as well."

"It's not appropriate for anyone to give the alpha's mate a pet name."

"Should have thought about that before begging me to fuck you." I really should stop baiting her, but the resulting snarl from her lips humored me greatly. It'd been far too long since I had someone to verbally spar with, and Edon didn't count. He didn't *spar*; he commanded.

Very unlike Rae and Willow, who fired back insults at me without even flinching. They were the reason I survived my university years. But, somehow, bickering with Luna felt different. More intimate.

Not because of the oral sex.

I knew Rae just as well as I knew Luna in that department, having tasted them both between their thighs. Although, my experience with Rae was purely clinical in a university class setting, and she faked her enthusiasm. While Luna, well, that had been a moment of heat and passion and unlike anything I'd ever expected. So perhaps that added the heated flare to our sparring, the one buzzing through my blood as she growled in response to my taunting.

A splatter of goop hit me on the forehead, drawing me from my thoughts. "What the hell?"

"That's for saying I *begged* when we both know I didn't," Luna replied, already refocused on her disgusting-looking batter. "I commanded it. There's a difference."

I reached across the counter to snag a towel and used it to wipe off my head. "Seriously? A food fight?" I snorted. "No wonder I bested you so easily."

"I'll have you know that I'd just sprinted about fifteen miles, and I was tired."

"Whatever helps you feel better." We both knew I would dominate her even fully rested. She was smaller, faster, and definitely athletic, but I had the drive and determination to survive instilled in me from years of fighting for my life. Luna, for all intents and purposes, had lived a pampered existence in comparison. As evidenced by the ease with which she started assembling her pancakes on the griddle.

She hummed a little melody under her breath as she worked, forgetting all about me at the bar behind her.

It was oddly relaxing. I barely knew the female, but something about the homey element of the moment placated my inner wolf. Provided me with an insight into what life could be like as a lycan.

Not with her, but with a wolf of my own.

If I was ever allowed such an experience. If ones even existed here.

I had to get out from under Edon first. Along with a million other tasks, like figuring out where the fuck I belonged in this clan.

"Your stress is ruining my usually peaceful cooking experience," Luna said softly as she flipped a round pancake onto the growing stack. "Is it because of what happened the other day?"

I cleared my throat. "No. That was fine. I'm—"

"Fine?" she repeated, glancing back at me with an arched brow. "I was more than *fine*, thank you."

My lips twitched. "As I recall, you didn't perform at all. So I wouldn't know, would I?"

She set her spatula down and faced me fully, planting her palms on the counter. "You want another taste, newbie? Is that what has your fur in a twist over there?"

"Maybe I do," I replied, teasing her a little. Edon would probably have my balls if he knew, but hey, he wanted me to watch without touching. He said nothing about goading her or engaging in a little healthy banter.

Besides, this was the most conversation I'd indulged in with anyone in months.

Fuck if I was going to stop now.

Luna's gaze narrowed. "You must have a death wish, wolf."

"Or nothing to lose." I shrugged. "I have no family. No friends." Minus Rae and Willow, but they weren't exactly here. And I wasn't sure if Willow was even still alive. Just the thought spoiled the moment, darkening my spirit and forcing the rest from my lips without thought. "I have no real clan. I'm just a mutt without a home, the property of an alpha who only needs me until he's done with his trials, and then I'll be on my own again. Back to the status quo without any regard for my feelings or needs. Just a new lycan struggling to survive in this hell."

Whatever amusement I'd felt from my banter with Luna died a withering death at the end of my summarization. It really was quite depressing. And the glimmer in her eyes said she agreed.

"It didn't use to be like this," Luna whispered, her voice low, cautious. "Lycans used to value family. Pack hierarchy was about respect, not dictatorship. Alpha females could choose, and mates were revered, not treated as toys to be used and tossed aside." She swallowed, her gaze lowering. "We're all in hell, Silas. Only those at the top seem to benefit in this new world."

"New world," I repeated, confused. "It's year one hundred seventeen." I knew because I'd competed in the one hundred seventeenth Immortal Cup.

"Yes. Year one hundred seventeen of the new world," she explained. "I mean, you know the vampires and lycans are far older, right?"

"Of course." Some of the royals, like Rae's mate, Kylan, were over three thousand years old. "But I've never heard it called the 'new world' before."

"Haven't you ever wondered what the world was like one hundred and eighteen years ago? What about two hundred years ago?"

I frowned. "Everyone knows what it was like—plague and famine. The Blood Alliance cured the nations of their violent wars and instilled rule and order."

Her smile was sad. "That's the university talking, the society you were forced to accept. But tell me, is lycan life what you dreamed of, Silas? Is this everything you wanted and more?"

I almost laughed but couldn't, my throat constricting with emotion. She'd hit a somewhat sensitive subject for me. "No. Everything they promised me was a lie."

"Exactly," she replied. "They indoctrinate humans in society's ideology, feed them false expectations to keep them controlled, all for the false honor of winning the Immortal Cup. But as you see now, it's not all that fulfilling, is it? And you, Silas, have it better than most."

I swallowed, considering her words, and watched as she turned to check on her food.

Here I sat at the counter in an alpha's kitchen, somewhat healthy and well fed, which, according to Luna, was rare. Yet I'd never felt more alone than I did lately, lying by myself at night, wondering what I had to live for next.

It was always about the Immortal Cup, to achieve immortality. And now that I had, I didn't know what to dream of anymore.

Because all those dreams of the future? They were littered with lies.

Yet, as Luna said, I had it better than most.

"Do you know how Yao is faring?" I wondered aloud, speaking of the male who came in second at the Immortal Cup. He went to Jace Region to become a vampire.

Every year, the vampires and lycans took turns taking the final two candidates and gifting them immortality. My year had been Walter's and Jace's turn.

Walter had first pick and chose me.

"I don't." She sounded apologetic. "Most winners disappear after the Immortal Cup, the majority of them not making it through their first year. Especially in lycan clans." She turned off the burner with a sigh. "But he's probably okay. Vampires like adding to their ranks, while lycans can do so the old-fashioned way. Mutts—no offense —tend to be more expendable as a result."

And that was exactly how I felt. *Expendable.* "Well, as you said, I have it better than most."

"I think we both do," Luna replied, placing a plate piled high with pancakes in front of me. "Edon's not…"

"Like the others?" I offered.

"So it seems," she murmured, reaching into the fridge again. "I mean, he let you live."

"For now."

She smiled as she returned with a bottle of maple syrup. "There's nothing temporary about it if he let you stay here alone with me."

"Maybe." I palmed the back of my neck, blowing out a breath. "Honestly, I struggle to understand him."

"Me, too." She picked up my uneaten food and scraped it into the trash. "All right, enough about Edon. How about a lesson in being a wolf?"

I cocked a brow. "Pretty sure I have the wolf thing down now, but thanks."

She laughed. "Sweets, you're not even close to mastering the lycan thing. Trust me."

"Did I or did I not kick your ass the other day?" I countered. "And *sweets*?"

"Do you prefer 'big wolf'?" She blinked her eyes innocently at me. "'Cause I can improvise on the whole nickname front. And maybe you won because I wanted you to."

"You tried to kill me."

She shrugged. "And now I want to feed you. Are you interested in the lesson or not?"

Considering no one else wanted to teach me anything, I wasn't about to say no. "I'm all ears, little moon."

She smirked. "Good. Lesson number one on being a lycan? You need to please your taste buds. And when we're done, I'm fixing your hair—that'll be lesson number two. Now open up, Silas."

Her words heated my blood with the memory of Edon saying those exact same words to me for an entirely different reason.

I swallowed thickly, unable to deny her despite the sickness I knew would follow.

Because I wanted to give in to her, to experience, just for a few moments, what it might feel like to be taken care of by another. Especially one as beautiful as Luna.

No, she wasn't mine.

But just for a moment, I allowed myself to pretend and parted my lips for her.

CHAPTER 13
EDON

Silas's satisfaction warmed the sire bond. *What are you doing?* I wondered.

Eating a pancake, he replied. *And it's fucking decadent.*

You made pancakes?

Luna made pancakes.

I grinned. *She cooks?* That news caused my lips to quirk up at the corners.

"Silas?" my grandfather asked, his gaze knowing.

"Luna made him pancakes." It should have bothered me that she cooked for him and not for me, but oddly, it didn't. I actually liked the idea of them taking care of each other.

"Claudette probably taught her," my grandfather mused, smiling. "She used to be a wicked chef before, well, everything."

"And now she's a mentor in Ernest Clan," I replied, recalling the details my grandfather had just given me. "Whose primary purpose is to train and ready the future leadership for an uprising." Only, according to my grandfather, Claudette's primary objective was Luna's brother, Logan. But it seemed she'd educated them both. "And your job is to mentor me," I added, arching a brow. "That about sum it up?"

"It's not like I provided all those history lessons for fun, kid," he said, smiling.

"I never thought you did," I admitted. I just hadn't realized the full extent of it until now. He provided me with historical contexts to persuade me to the revolutionary side. To enlighten me about another way of life. To recruit me into a new alliance among those who desired change. "You were just waiting for me to ascend before you explained every detail."

"And I still am," he admitted. "We've only just begun, but the plans have been in the making for over a century."

"Why wait so long? Why not rebel at the beginning?"

"Several did. And they all died." He paused to let that sink in. "We suspect those in power now planned their takeover for many, many years."

"And now you're doing the same." Through the art of "mentoring" the incoming leadership, at least in select clans. That wouldn't be as easy to accomplish in vampire society since they didn't procreate or die. Lycans, however, required regime changes because we constantly aged. I was on the rise as the new alpha, and my future son would replace me in a few hundred years.

"Yes. We're moving all the pieces into play but still have at least another decade before we truly begin."

I whistled low, shaking my head. "What about the vampires?" I wondered out loud.

"There are those in power today on our side."

"Which ones?"

He smiled. "Can't give you that information just yet, son."

I narrowed my gaze. "Don't trust me, old man?" I

knew he did, or he wouldn't have spent the last two decades advising me in this way. I just enjoyed ribbing him.

"Nah, just not my place to elaborate. But you'll find out soon enough." He crossed one ankle over his opposite knee. "There will always be diversity in the class systems amongst vampires and lycans, but I'm not alone in my belief that our superiority also comes with great responsibility. We have a duty to protect those beneath us."

"You mean humans."

"I mean everyone. Take your Luna, for example. You protected her against your father, and you're doing so again now by having Silas stand sentry at your home."

"That's different." And I highly doubted Luna would appreciate my grandfather claiming her to be beneath me, even if it was true.

"Is it? She's in your care as your mate, and you've chosen to fulfill your duty of offering protection. Without it, she'd probably be in a bed somewhere having her dignity and alpha tendencies fucked right out of her."

The stark words caused me to flinch.

Which resulted in a smile from my grandfather. "You're the alpha this clan needs, Edon. Your reaction just now proves it. Because your father? He'd have smirked with enthusiasm at the very idea of breaking that girl's pride. You grimaced."

"Because it's wrong."

"Exactly. Alpha females are a prized species and very rare. Without them, alpha males can't be conceived. But rather than respect what few remain, lycans like your father have chosen to destroy their morale and disrespect the sanctity of the mating bond. You've seen what that does to a wolf, Edon. Your mother is Luna's future, if you choose to follow in your father's footsteps."

Just the idea of it turned my stomach. "I won't do that

to Luna." Oh, I'd bring her to heel, yes. But not like that. Never like that.

"I know. But others will try to demand you do it anyway because that's the world we live in now." His smile was sad. "Your grandmother was one love of my existence. What we had was very special. Unique, too. And deeply revered. Something we'll talk more about someday soon. But I'll tell you now, if another wolf even looked at me the wrong way, your grandmama would have dealt with the problem swiftly and efficiently."

"Like Luna did with Bianca," I mused.

"Yes. Alpha females are as possessive as their males, or they used to be."

"I don't understand why that changed." Or why males would want to break such pride in their females. Luna's fire was what drew me to her, what made her irresistible to my wolf. Her defiance resembled foreplay.

My grandfather rubbed the silver stubble dotting his jaw. "Breaking the sacred mating bonds essentially disrupts wolf loyalty and restructures all the pack dynamics. If the alpha isn't being true to his mate, then the betas feel they need to follow suit with their own mates, and so on."

"Right, but why?" I interjected. "Why would lycans choose to do that to begin with?"

"They didn't choose to, Silas. Those in power did. The alphas making up the Blood Alliance today—or the majority, anyway—created this new way of life to stir dissension among the packs. To break the loyalties that used to be part of our core foundation."

"Okay, but why the hell would anyone want that?" I pressed, flabbergasted.

"Control," he answered simply. "We're pack animals. We fight for our own. But if you disable that mentality, destroy the bonds that tie us together, we begin to fight for ourselves, not as a unit. So you give the wolves someone to protect and cherish—an alpha—and that alpha reaps all the rewards and benefits. But to maintain that absolute power? He has to ensure that he always remains on top, number one, with no ties or loyalties to anyone else. Otherwise, what happens?"

"Events like the other day happen," I said, following his train of thought.

"Yes. You chose your mate over the orders of the current pack alpha."

"So he's probably furious." Which I'd felt, of course. I just didn't give a shit. Luna had been my only concern. "I failed his loyalty trial."

"In his eyes? Absolutely. In mine? You passed with flying colors."

"Except it's not you I need to be impressing," I pointed out, running my fingers through my hair. The more I pissed off my father, the harder my trials were going to be. "He's definitely going to use Luna against me."

"Which is why you need to bring that girl to your side sooner rather than later."

I snorted. "Easier said than done."

"Stubborn?"

"You have no idea." But I adored that trait about her.

"Well, you better figure her out soon because your father is definitely not going by the book with his tests, and I wouldn't put anything past him at this point. Including potentially having you killed just so he can remain in power for another century or so."

I scoffed at that. "Not even he is that stupid." It would be a clear violation of lycan politics. "The pack would riot."

"Would they?" he countered. "Because from what I've seen, he's created an heir and isolated him from everyone else, thereby ensuring that pack loyalty falls in his favor." He shrugged, the gesture far too nonchalant. "Just an observation."

His words sounded more like a warning, one underlined in a bad omen.

Because he was right.

My father had always treated me as an outsider, pretty much scaring off anyone and everyone who thought to ally with me.

Which meant Silas was in far more danger than I originally realized because our sire bond practically guaranteed his loyalty.

And I'd left him at my house with my only other liability—Luna.

I stood. "I have to go."

"You're a good man, Edon," my grandfather called after me.

"We'll see," I muttered, jogging down the stairs.

Tapping into my link to Silas, I asked, *Everything okay?*

Yeah, he replied, but his voice sounded off.

What are you two doing? I wondered, taking off at a sprint toward my house.

She's, uh, cutting my hair.

My eyebrows rose. Luna had already fed him, and now she was grooming him? Who knew the alpha female could be so maternal? *I'm on my way back.*

Okay.

Don't let your guard down.

His sardonic snort came back at me, the male essentially telling me to fuck off. Because yeah, he'd probably spent his entire life on alert. Humans were not treated well in this world. However, my grandfather said it wasn't always this way.

The more I learned from him, the more I questioned

our ridiculous customs. Particularly surrounding the Alpha Trials. It was clear to everyone, including my father, that I was the strongest wolf in the clan. Why the fuck did I need to prove myself?

I entered the village, seeing it with a fresh perspective. The luxury of the cabins, the males lounging about like kings rather than hardworking lycans, and wondered what the peripheries of my region looked like right now. Oh, I'd visited them, but only with my father's entourage. And something told me the outsiders put on a show for him.

A show I wanted to see through.

A show I wanted to end.

My time was nearing. I just had to survive the next few weeks, then I could enact change. I would start by replacing everyone in this village. These lycans weren't my friends or allies; they belonged to my father's pack. And he had made it clear from the beginning that I didn't belong. Had killed the only male strong enough to befriend me. Then the others gave me a wide berth, afraid to contradict the alpha incumbent.

That was a mistake.

One I would rectify very, very soon.

CHAPTER 14

LUNA

"Sit still," I demanded, my scissors poised far too close to Silas's forehead for him to be squirming like that.

"I can shave myself," he muttered.

"Yeah?" His caveman look said otherwise. "Your haircut and facial scruff remind me of a shaggy dog, Silas."

He scoffed low in his throat. "I just trimmed them."

"I know." I could see the frayed, uneven ends all over his damn head. "Stop moving." I straddled his thigh, needing to get a closer look at his "trim."

"Do you even know what you're doing?" he demanded.

"Better than you do, apparently." I'd already lathered his hair with water from the bathroom sink. Now I just needed him to sit on the stool beside it like a good little wolf and let me work.

However, he wasn't very little.

No, Silas was all man at well over six feet with a muscular build that dwarfed most purebred wolves. Except maybe Edon. I suspected they were close to even, with Edon having just a little more bulk on him due to his upbringing. But Silas would catch up to him if he ate properly.

And wouldn't that be a sight to behold? Two sexy-as-fuck males with alpha tendencies.

Silas might be the youngest, the newbie, but I smelled the dominance in him. It was almost as strong as Edon's.

"Look at me," I said softly, needing to judge the hair length on either side of his head.

Bright blue eyes met mine. *So beautiful,* I thought, lost for a moment in his stare.

I cleared my throat, forcing myself to refocus on the task at hand.

Admiring Silas's physique and handsome face could only earn me trouble, and we'd already gotten into enough together. Not that I wouldn't turn down a repeat if our situation was different. Because that wolf's tongue…

My thighs threatened to clench, which was a problem given my position.

Stop thinking about it.

Only, I couldn't. It was all I had thought about since finding him in the kitchen. Pancakes didn't help, and neither, it seemed, did this distraction.

If anything, I'd only made it worse.

"Luna," he murmured, arching a brow.

"Uh…" I licked my lips. "Yeah, looks even." Or at least I hoped it did, because my focus was shot.

Fix the chin scruff next, I told myself. *That'll help.*

It didn't.

If anything, being that close to his mouth only heightened my arousal, something he had to smell. He was a wolf, after all, and my legs were spread not two feet away from his face.

Fortunately, he didn't tease me. He just sat ramrod straight with his hands fisted at his sides.

But I felt the heat coming off him.

He wasn't completely immune either.

Maybe we both should have put on more clothes—him a shirt, and me, well, I should have put on some pants. Because I was bare under Edon's shirt, something Silas had to know since I was straddling his jean-clad thigh.

Just finish it, I coached myself. *Quickly.*

I turned to grab one of the blades I had found in Edon's bathroom, my balance wavering. Silas caught my hips, holding me steady as I righted myself. "Sorry," I said. "Sink was farther away than I thought."

"No problem." He sounded gruff, if a bit hoarse. No sign of the teasing male from the kitchen. This one was holding on to his control with everything he owned, and my nearness only made it worse.

"I'm almost done," I said in an effort to console us both. His jaw didn't need much, just a subtle smoothing. He must have been using a jagged knife to do this before, because it left his chin fuzz rather uneven.

"Sure." He released me, his touch leaving behind a burn I wanted to explore but couldn't.

The forbidden nature of touching him was almost like a drug, my fingers moving to places they shouldn't, all under the guise of fixing his hair and scruff. He knew, too. I could see it in his eyes, the irises turning to liquid fire, and in the way his muscles seemed to clench and tense beneath every stroke.

"What was that the other day?" he finally asked, a touch of hesitation in his voice. "I know we shouldn't talk about it, but…"

I need to know were the final words of that statement. I understood because I felt the same way.

"My wolf was in fight-or-flight mode. You won her over. She submitted." Pretty standard in the lycan community, but it had never happened to me before. None of the males in Ernest Clan desired me, my fate promised to another at birth. The only reason Volk had done the deed when I asked was because of our friendship, but neither of us had enjoyed it.

My experience with Silas was different.

He actually made me come.

And would have again had Edon not interfered.

"Is it always like that?" Silas cleared his throat. "I mean, the submission and wanting-to-fuck thing."

At least he'd stopped claiming I begged him. But I almost preferred the prior teasing to this serious discussion.

Because thinking about it clearly, without humor, stirred a craving inside me to do it again. To finish what we started.

"It happens," I replied, referring to his submission and fucking clarification. "But the wolves have to be mutually attracted to one another."

He frowned, making it difficult for me to shave around the edges of his full lips. Not that talking helped all that much either.

"But our wolves had just met," he said, those bright eyes lifting to mine.

"We've been sniffing around each other quite a bit, Silas." I pressed a thumb to his mouth to keep him from replying and focused on trimming the hairs just above and below his lips. "I know you followed me around. I could smell your curiosity." It hadn't bothered me, just put a damper on my escape plans. "I knew we would fight. Actually, I chose you as the weak link because of your newbie status." My eyes found his once more. "Obviously, I underestimated you."

An understatement.

He'd defeated me without breaking a sweat. And all while taking care not to harm me.

"You impressed me," I admitted softly, finishing the job along his jaw and releasing his mouth. "You impressed my wolf."

"It… it was intense."

"Yes." I smiled. "That part is normal, from what I hear. But you were the first to ever, well, taste me like that." I grimaced a little at how innocent I sounded. It wasn't like orgasms were unfamiliar territory for me. Just the whole receiving-one-from-someone-else thing—that was new. "You're, uh, talented."

He chuckled, the sound low and tempting. "Talented, huh?"

I swallowed. "Yeah. You, uh, yeah." I shook my head, my skin heating. "We shouldn't talk about it anymore." Or I was going to give in to the urge to experience it all over again, and wouldn't that be a catastrophe in the making.

"Oh, I don't know; I find it a fascinating conversation," a male voice drawled from the hallway. "Please continue, little mate. Tell us all about how Silas made you feel beneath his tongue."

My hands froze against Silas's chin, my heart leaping into my throat.

Silas didn't appear surprised at all. Either he'd sensed the alpha's arrival or he didn't care. I couldn't tell. But probably the former.

I hadn't heard or scented Edon's approach, something I attributed to his stealthy alpha ways and the fact that his cologne was a permanent fixture inside his house.

He stepped into the entryway to lean against the door frame. "Well, Luna? Tell us about his talent. Or would you prefer my summary? I did watch it all unfold, after all."

"Edon…" My throat resembled sandpaper, his name

rough on the air. No amount of swallowing or coughing would clear it, the sensation latching on and refusing to let go. And all the while, he stood there with an eyebrow arched, his expression otherwise unreadable, as he no doubt smelled the arousal permeating the small room.

I couldn't hide it.

And neither could Silas.

"I was just cutting his hair," I said, explaining our proximity. I set the blade down, nearly finished anyway. "He looked like a shaggy dog."

"A shaggy dog with a talented tongue," Edon returned, evidently not letting that part go. "Which isn't at all what I asked about, little mate. I want to hear about what you did then and how he made you feel. If you're really descriptive, maybe I'll allow him to do it again, something I know you're both craving. Right, Silas?"

Silas didn't appear nearly as rattled as me, his gaze meeting the fuming alpha's without even blinking. "Yes."

His lack of a denial shocked the hell out of me.

As did the growl in his chest while he stared Edon down.

"Mmm," the alpha murmured. "Your turn, Luna. Tell me how it felt. Tell me if you want to experience it again." He didn't break his focus from Silas as he spoke, but his tone resembled a demand, not a request.

I couldn't speak, the violent intensity in the room too thick for me to form a coherent thought, let alone a sentence. The palpable energy raised the hairs along the back of my neck and tightened my belly. Something was happening, a war of dominance, a claim, but I couldn't define the prize.

It wasn't me, exactly. But it revolved around me, tantalizing my every nerve and lighting my bloodstream on fire.

You're stronger than this, I whispered to myself. *Don't let him dominate you.*

Except that wasn't my problem at all. I could stand up to Edon every day of the week. But right now?

Yeah, right now, I didn't *want* to defy him.

And that was a very telling problem.

"I don't think she wants a repeat performance, Silas," Edon said slowly, his eyes narrowing. "But I know you do. So what should we do about that?"

He pushed off the doorjamb to join us in the small space. It was a decent-sized guest bath with a full tub and double sinks, but two virile males and little old me made for quite the crowded area.

I took a step back, hoping to put some distance between us, but Silas's palms landed on my hips and held me in place over his thigh. He hadn't stopped looking at Edon, the two of them seeming to communicate on an entirely different level.

The sire bond, I realized, swallowing. I'd never actually witnessed a proper one before. My father inherited a winner from the Immortal Cup when I was a little girl. I never met her because the woman didn't survive her turning.

But Silas had more than survived his own.

"Hmm, still so quiet," Edon mused. "I suppose we can rely on your body to tell us what you want, little mate." He moved even closer, placing his bare chest a hairsbreadth away from my arm and effectively trapping me between him and Silas.

I felt captured.

Overwhelmed.

And really fucking *hot*.

Both males exuded heat like it was their job, and I seemed to be absorbing it through every pore. I nearly panted in response, my body on fire beneath Silas's hands. His thumbs were drawing little circles against the shirt, as if to provide a semblance of calm.

It did nothing to slow my racing heart.

Or to quell to the growing need slicking my thighs.

They can smell it.

They know.

And Edon's grin confirmed it.

"I want to know how wet she is," he murmured. "Silas?"

The warmth on my hip shifted south as Silas drew his touch down my thigh and then upward beneath the shirt. His blue eyes slid to mine as he slipped a finger through my damp folds. I shuddered, my hands going to his shoulders to keep myself upright.

This was all so unexpected. So insane. And so undeniably arousing.

Why was Edon okay with this?

How could he allow another male—his own progeny—to touch me this way?

Was it all a ploy? Would he turn on us in the next moment? Punish Silas for touching me? Punish me for allowing it? What—

Oh, fuck… That little brush against my clit nearly had my knees buckling.

"She's practically weeping," Silas replied, his voice low and steady and grounding me in the moment. Only to be derailed by two of his fingers penetrating me deep without warning.

I moaned, my nails biting into his bare skin.

Again, I nearly demanded.

And as if he heard me, he repeated the action.

"She smells fucking amazing." Edon's voice was so close, drawing me back to them both, confusing my senses, and sending waves of hot and cold shocks up and down my body. "I want to taste her."

Silas withdrew his touch, eliciting a whimper from my throat.

And then he lifted his hand for Edon.

My lips parted as Edon took Silas's fingers into his mouth—deep—and sucked my arousal right off the other man's skin.

Oh.

My.

God.

That had to be the hottest thing I'd ever seen.

And the groan they both released?

Holy fuck. I squeezed my legs, seeking friction, only to be thwarted by Silas's muscular thigh.

"Delicious," Edon murmured.

"I know," Silas agreed, his blue eyes inflamed with need as he studied my expression. "She screams beautifully, too."

This was surreal.

Two males and me in a bathroom filled with testosterone and *need*.

"Kiss her for me, Silas," Edon whispered. "Fuck her mouth with your tongue."

Silas grinned. "Gladly."

I wasn't given time to agree.

Wasn't given time to even comprehend.

Silas's fingers were already in my hair, pulling me to him with a ferocity that left me no choice but to obey.

And I melted into him.

Because that tongue was so fucking wicked. The man excelled in kissing. I already knew this from my first experience, but this time blew my mind all over again. The way he nibbled my lower lip, the way he took charge, the way he tugged on my hair to angle my head to where he desired me most.

I moaned, the sound one I couldn't swallow even if I tried.

And then I felt Edon behind me.

His warmth a brand against my back as he drew his fingers lightly down my sides to the hem of my shirt. I shivered as he began to lift it, exposing my body to them both inch by inch.

Silas released me, allowing Edon to tug the fabric over my head, and then his mouth was back on mine again. The movements so seamless I knew they were communicating mentally, but I couldn't bring myself to feel left out. Not when Edon dropped a kiss to my shoulder, then on the back of my neck, while Silas owned my lips.

I'm going to die, I thought. *And I'm okay with that if this is how I go out.*

Because holy *wow*, this was the most intense experience of my very short life.

Two hot, dominant males touching, stroking, licking, and nipping.

And then I was kissing Edon.

It all happened so quickly, his fingers replacing Silas's to tug my head back toward him. My neck protested the sharp shift, but my body wept in gratitude, especially as Silas began to lick a path down my breasts.

Oh...

He pulled my nipple into his mouth, igniting my bloodstream with another heady flood of lust. I needed more. I needed him to go lower. I needed *friction*.

A plea broke from my lips, one Edon swallowed before dominating me with his mouth.

So much harsher than Silas.

The hint of violence in Edon's kiss blended with the

soft nibbles against my breasts, the light strokes along my thighs.

Edon was definitely the alpha.

But Silas... he held his own. Those nips against my skin as he kissed along my chest weren't kind; they were markings of his own.

I shivered, overheated, overstimulated, overwhelmed, by them both.

Until Edon released me.

His mouth hovering over mine.

His grip tight in my hair.

"I know Silas can suck cock, but can you?" Edon's words were a whisper against my lips, and they shook me to my core.

He couldn't mean...? When he mentioned receiving the best head of his life, he wasn't talking about...?

I blinked several times.

And Edon smiled in response. "You enjoyed his oral ministrations so much that I decided to try them for myself. He's quite skilled." He canted his head, those obsidian pools holding so many secrets—including the one he'd just given me. "I want to see you on your knees, Luna. I want to watch you please Silas as he pleased me. Will you kneel for us, little mate? Will you take his cock between those beautiful lips and swallow his seed?"

Oh, fuck...

Just the notion of the two of them together had me nearly coming on the spot. And the idea that Edon wanted to watch me suck Silas off?

Dear God Almighty.

Silas swirled his tongue against my nipple, drawing my focus to where he gazed up at me from my breasts. Yearning tinged with understanding in his beautiful eyes.

We both knew Edon was the one in charge.

We were both at his mercy.

But that wouldn't stop us from *enjoying* the alpha's demands.

"Luna?" Edon whispered, his lips brushing my ear. "You enjoyed his tongue between your thighs, didn't you?"

I nodded, my voice still nonexistent despite all the moans that seemed to be leaving my mouth.

"Don't you want to taste him? To feel him come down your pretty little throat?"

My legs tensed, another groan working its way past my lips.

Silas leaned back away from my chest in response, one blond eyebrow arching. "Now's your chance to prove you're more than fine, little moon."

I couldn't believe this was happening.

That Edon seemed to be okay with it.

But of course he was. He'd just admitted that Silas had sucked him off the other day. And while I would have killed Bianca for admitting such a thing, the image of Silas going down on Edon provoked a completely different response from me. Still lethal, still violent, but in an entirely erotic kind of way.

My only regret was not having been there to fucking watch.

Because these two together? They would set the bedroom on fucking fire.

I knew because the entire bathroom felt as if it'd gone up in flames.

My hands met Silas's chest, his hard muscles flexing beneath my palms. I'd never gone down on a male—my chastity something my father required these last twenty-two years of my life—but I knew the general idea of how to perform the act.

And something told me Silas would be a hell of a lot more patient than Edon.

As if sensing my thought, Edon nipped the pulse of my neck, then laved the tender skin with his tongue. "Such a good little mate," he praised. "Mmm, I just may reward you. If you please us enough."

His words should have pissed me off, but instead they provided the opposite impact. I took them as a challenge. I wanted to blow both their minds not to earn a reward but to earn their mutual respect.

I was an alpha female for a reason.

I didn't bend over and take it.

I fought.

And I won.

My fingers traced the lines of Silas's rigid abdomen as I went to my knees before him. The look in his eyes encouraged me to proceed, telling me without words that he wanted this, too. I allowed him to see the alpha inside me, the wolf who was about to destroy his world in the best way.

Arousal deepened his gaze to an oceanic blue. "Keep looking at me like that, Luna. And don't stop. Not even when I hit the back of your throat."

That wouldn't be a problem.

Because I wanted to watch him fall apart, to gain the upper hand, and to dominate *him*.

The curl of his lips said he knew it, too. And what's more, he approved.

"Now, little mate," Edon said, applying pressure to my shoulders. "Taste him. Suck him. Fuck him with that pretty mouth. And swallow."

CHAPTER 15
SILAS

Don't hurt her, Edon warned.

I met his burning gaze. *Says the male forcing her to suck me off.*

Does she look forced to you? he asked, a taunting note to his words. *You can smell her arousal as well as I can. She wants this.*

She wants to eat me alive, I replied, noting the challenge in her eyes. *Topping from the bottom.*

An alpha female through and through, he agreed, running his fingers through her hair.

I swallowed as Luna slowly drew my zipper down, her body perfectly positioned between my sprawled legs. She licked her lips, her expression hungry, and tugged down my jeans. My dick sprung forward, eager to meet her mouth. She wasted no time, her tongue memorizing my shaft in a way that had my balls aching for another stroke, another taste, another *lick.*

"Fuck," I breathed, my head falling back on a wave of euphoria. Luna put all my previous experience to shame, and she'd barely even started. It helped that I actually desired this.

My courses at the university were all forced. Rae typically volunteered to be my partner, mostly because she knew I'd go easy on her. Unlike in my male-on-male studies, which tended to be a bit more violent.

And still had nothing on Edon.

Lust pooled in his obsidian depths, his cheeks flushing as he watched Luna move her mouth up and down over my cock. Her eyes were all mine, her focus on my face incredibly alluring as she fought to take even more of me into her throat.

I was gone to her and her ministrations, unable to focus on anything else.

Until Edon's mouth settled over mine.

He'd moved so silently, so quickly, that I hadn't sensed him coming for me until he thrust his tongue between my lips.

My muscles tightened.

My hands curling into fists.

I didn't know what to do beneath all the sensations. Fire burned deep inside me, stirring a maelstrom in my groin that hardened my dick even more. It almost hurt. I could barely breathe, my brain fracturing beneath the onslaught.

Mmm, I can feel your pleasure through our sire bond, Edon whispered in my thoughts. *It's making me so fucking hard.*

One of his hands cupped the back of my neck while the other remained on Luna's head, urging her to go deeper. Always in charge. Always dominant. And at the moment, I didn't care. I would do whatever he wanted so long as this didn't stop.

My spine tingled, my thighs flexing, just the thought of him demanding that Luna release me leaving me cold and restless.

What if that was the purpose?

What if—

Shh, he murmured, cutting off my concerns. *I wouldn't dream of allowing this to end too soon.*

Why are you doing this? I asked, my body strung tight as a bow ready to release.

"Because I can," he growled against my mouth. "Because I want to. Because I enjoy seeing Luna down on her knees." He glanced at her, his cheek brushing mine. "Look at her, Silas. Look how beautiful she is with your cock in her mouth."

I shuddered, his words, coupled with the sight, nearly undoing me. Her pupils were blown wide, her cheeks flushed with excitement.

"Did you enjoy watching me kiss him, little mate?" Edon continued, his voice low. He stroked his fingers through her hair, his opposite palm still against the back of my neck.

She swallowed around my shaft, sending a jolt of electricity through my veins. And then she moaned in approval—a moan I rivaled with my own groan. The intensity of her mouth and Edon's warm tones heightened my senses, destroying my ability to move, to think, to inhale, to *be.*

Molten energy caressed my veins, rocking me to the core of my existence. Luna's little noises didn't help, nor did her slight gags as she took me too far. But she didn't stop. If anything, it urged her onward, and all the while, she held my gaze, that look in her eyes enough to demolish a saint's resolve.

I cupped her jaw, my fingers grazing the side of her head near Edon's palm. He brushed the tips of my blunt nails, the touch sending a shock through my system.

This was an experience I never could have anticipated.

Two alpha lycans, both watching me with predatory gleams.

Luna hungry for my cum.

Edon desiring my submission.

I couldn't resist the pull, couldn't back down from the way they made me feel.

"I'm close." My voice was hoarse.

"Good," Edon whispered. Between Luna's mouth and Edon's lips brushing my ear, I could hardly see straight. "Come for us, Silas. Come hard."

"*Fuck.*" The demand shoved me off the cliff, my orgasm a harsh assault that jolted me from my head to my toes. I nearly fell, but Edon was there, his hard body cradling my back, his hands on my shoulders.

And Luna.

Fuck, Luna.

She stared up at me with such heat, such vigor, as she accepted my seed down her pretty little throat. Every. Single. Drop. And her greedy mouth sucked for more, her fingers digging into my thighs.

I quivered, my pulse racing, my vision coming in and out as I panted between them.

Edon massaged my tensing muscles, his hands a brand against my bare skin. And then he gripped my chin, forced my head back, and took my mouth once more.

His snarl shook my very spirit, the possession in that sound one I didn't understand. He drew blood, his teeth skating across my lips before devouring me with his tongue.

I couldn't react fast enough, my moves one step behind. It left me bewildered, hot, and ready to fuck all over again.

Luna seemed eager to oblige, her lips moving up and down, her hands growing bolder and exploring my torso, my hips, the tops of my thighs.

Edon smiled against my mouth, the expression tinged with cruelty. "That's enough, Luna." He reached over me to grab a fistful of her hair and tugged her away from my groin.

She made a noise of protest, her pupils so enlarged I couldn't see the light brown of her irises. Long lashes fluttered as she blinked.

"Watching that made me thirsty," Edon murmured, his voice low. "Luna, clean up the mess you made of my guest bath. When you're done, you can join us in the kitchen. If you want."

Confusion settled over her features. A confusion I shared.

Trust me, Edon whispered into my mind. *She needs this lesson.*

"Now, Silas," he said out loud, releasing me.

He stepped toward the door, his expression expectant.

Clearing my throat, I stood, uncertain of what else to do. Luna gazed up at me, a flurry of emotions traversing her beautiful face. Shock. Hurt. Annoyance.

I didn't like any of them, but a growl from Edon had me taking a step toward him.

What was I supposed to do? Demand we pleasure his mate? Demand another orgasm? Push Luna onto all fours and fuck her the way I craved?

"Silas," Edon hissed, the alpha in him yanking at the sire bond.

I left the room without looking back at Luna, but I *felt* her disappointment, her fury, and most importantly, her unfulfilled need.

Why did you do that? I demanded, following him down the hall while I buttoned up my jeans.

He led me to the kitchen, silent until he opened the fridge. *She left you in the same position earlier this week, did she not?*

Because you showed up, I pointed out.

Maybe. He retrieved two bottles and set them on the counter. *But she still left you hard as a rock and unfulfilled. Now she knows how it feels.*

I snorted and took a seat on one of the three barstools surrounding his kitchen island. *So you're teaching her a lesson in delayed gratification?*

No, her lesson is about behavior. She's an alpha female. If she wants more, she can demand it. And when she does, she'll learn that I'm more than happy to reciprocate.

I considered his objective as he found a bottle opener from the drawer. *You're giving her control.*

To an extent, yes.

This male was nothing like the alphas I had read about in my studies. They all took what they wanted, everyone else be damned. But Edon wanted his mate to have a choice, and for whatever reason, he'd included me in that choice.

"What? No argument to the contrary?" he taunted, passing me one of the drinks.

"Not sure I can argue," I admitted, sniffing the pungent liquid. *Beer.* Not something I'd ever indulged in, but I was aware of the substance. Lycans enjoyed alcohol, especially when playing with humans.

"And here I thought you'd always have a comeback," he mused, leaning on the marble slab of the kitchen island. "Still think this is all a test?"

"Yes." I just couldn't figure out if I'd passed or failed.

He nursed his beer for a long moment, clasping the neck between two strong fingers, then set it to the side. "My father doesn't want me to ascend, and the way I see it, I have two liabilities." He arched a brow. "Care to guess who those liabilities are?"

Wasn't hard to follow that implication, but it didn't

make much sense. "Why would he consider me a liability? I'm just a mutt."

His gaze narrowed. "Maybe, but you're *my* mutt. And I protect those that rely on me."

"I don't rely on you," I countered, narrowing my gaze right back at him. "I rely only on myself."

"Which I can admire, but you're out of your depth here, Silas. It's why you're going to stay at my house—*this* house—until further notice." He picked up his beer again, eyeing me as he took a swig. *And drink that. It's not cheap,* he added mentally.

It smells foul, I muttered, forcing myself to sip from the rim. *Tastes like shit, too.*

"Fine." He focused on the hallway. "Luna!"

A feminine snarl rumbled, preceding her entry. "*What?*" she demanded, hands on her hips. She'd thrown on Edon's shirt again, but it didn't hide her nipples protruding through the fabric.

She was all pissed-off, aroused female, and fuck if that didn't make me rock hard again.

"Finish Silas's beer," he said, gesturing at the drink. "I don't want to waste it."

"Why don't you finish it?" she countered. "Try tasting it, Edon. Suck it all up and swallow. I hear it's fun." With that flippant remark, she stalked off, leaving him smirking in her wake.

"Oh, I adore her." He finished his beer and picked up mine. "If neither of you is going to accept my gift, then I'll enjoy it myself." He licked the rim, his gaze holding mine. "You're staying here."

"I didn't argue to the contrary, did I?" Turning down shelter and protection seemed like a pretty stupid thing to argue about, even if it did infringe on my independence. But I could still look out for myself under his roof.

"No, you didn't." He sounded satisfied, a tone that oddly provided a sense of relief. I liked knowing I'd pleased him. Which was strange because I usually didn't care about anyone other than myself and those closest to me. I supposed he qualified for the latter, being my maker and all.

His throat worked as he swallowed, drawing my attention to the thick cords of muscle along his neck and shoulders. While we were roughly the same height, he definitely outweighed me. That explained why the jeans I found in his room were just a little too big for me in the thighs and waist. I still wore them today because they were in better condition than my sole pair. If Edon had noticed, he didn't seem to care. He had told me I could help myself to anything in his cabin. It seemed he'd meant it.

"I don't want you to run alone either," he said after a bout of silence. "That applies to you both, I mean. I'd rather you both sort of stick together."

"Is that why you had her acquaint her mouth with my cock?" I wondered out loud, arching a brow. "To help us *bond?*"

He chuckled. "No. That was purely for my enjoyment." He set the half-finished bottle to the side and placed his palms on the countertop, leaning forward. "Watching her suck you off was hot as fuck. Maybe next time you can watch her do it to me, or maybe she'll watch as I come down your throat. What do you prefer, Silas?" His gaze dropped to my lips. "Because I'm eager to try both."

And I was hard again.

Really, *really* hard.

Because both those scenarios? Yeah, they both aroused me. Which was so utterly fucked up, but here we were.

Luna chose that moment to join us, fury and lust riding

the air around her. "The bathroom is swept up," she said, her tone as cold as ice. Yet it did nothing to alter the temperature of the room, the heat brewing between me and Edon resembling a churning tornado of temptation waiting to suck us all down to hell. "Anything else you need me to do, Your Royal Fucking Highness?" she asked.

I couldn't look at her, Edon's gaze captivating mine, but I suspected she was glowering at him.

"Yes," he said, his tone laced with command. "I'm famished, Silas. You?"

Catching the innuendo underlying those words, I smiled. It seemed we were moving on to the next stage of his *lesson*. "I could eat."

Edon broke our connection to glance at Luna. "Come feed us, little mate."

Her cheeks blossomed into the most delectable shades of red. "Are you fucking serious?" She glanced between us in utter disbelief, her fury seductive as hell. "Yeah, you both can go fuck yourselves."

She turned on her heel, only to freeze at Edon's growl. It was low and menacing and reverberated through the room in a way only an alpha could.

"Get over here," he demanded. "Now."

Luna bristled but didn't move a step in either direction.

"You can run if you want, but we'll catch you," he warned. "And you know what will happen when we pounce." He waited a beat, watched as she stole a calming breath, and smiled. "What's it going to be, Luna? Are you going to behave for us or make us work for it?"

CHAPTER 16
LUNA

Trapped.

That was how I felt.

Both males watched me with predatory expressions, awaiting my decision. And something told me that, regardless of what choice I made, I was about to be devoured—by both of them.

I'd been so pissed after Edon and Silas left me in that bathroom all hot and bothered. My first time going down on a male, and he couldn't even say *Thank you*. No, instead he left with the alpha who'd commanded me to my knees.

I wasn't a toy but a lycan. An *alpha* lycan. And Edon was treating me like some omega bitch in heat.

Probably because I was acting like one.

But hell, these two males were messing with my head. I couldn't think straight around so much testosterone. There was something acutely unfulfilled between me and Silas—a dominance that had yet to be established.

And Edon... So much between us was definitely unfinished.

The alpha in question lifted one arrogant brow. "Luna?"

Run or play chef.

Except something told me it wasn't food they wanted to eat, but me. Which meant he was giving me the choice to accept it or play hard to get.

After the hell he just put me through in the bathroom? There was only one real option. "Come get me."

The words were tossed over my shoulder, my legs already moving.

Growls sounded behind me—Silas and Edon leaping from the kitchen to give chase.

The shirt flew over my head as I fell into a shift, my wolf ready and waiting, and bolted from the house into the surrounding courtyard.

I knew exactly where I wanted to go—the river's edge where Edon had chased me before. It was secluded and peaceful. And perfect for the activity I had in mind.

Because I was done playing submissive to these two males.

They wanted me to suck their cocks? Fine. But they were going to fucking return the favor.

My paws pounded over the earth, the silence behind me unnerving. I knew they were close, could feel the presence of their dominance gliding across my fur, but they moved with a precision and skill that seduced me even more.

Especially Silas.

Not only should I be able to best him in a race, but I should also be able to sense him. However, he was just as stealthy as his maker.

It sent a thrill down my spine, had my wolf preening in response. No one in Ernest Clan had ever appealed to me like this, not even Volk. And he'd been the only one I could stomach touching me before.

But now… *now* I desired a lot more than touching.

I blamed the mating bond. It had changed me on a level, exciting my hormones into a frenzy only the alpha could tame. Except that didn't quite explain Silas.

Mmm, maybe it was the sire bond confusing my wolf, forcing me to yearn for them both.

Or perhaps I'd finally found two males worthy of my attention.

One of them nipped my back leg. I responded by pushing myself even harder, my need to reach the river a palpable presence in my mind.

They could have me there.

But only if they agreed to my terms.

A low growl vibrated my spine, teeth clamping on my scruff to pull me to the ground. I rolled with it, allowing the much bigger body to nearly pin me—and used my back paws to kick him off.

Only to have a second, even larger male on top of me.

I squirmed, then whined, my goal of reaching the riverbank so close yet so far.

Edon merely tilted his head above me, his muzzle so much bigger than my own. He nudged my head, forcing me to reveal my neck.

Surrender, he was saying.

I wanted to, but not here. I wanted the water. The tranquility. The peace.

And somehow he knew, because he let me go with a soft growl of patience. It said he knew I was his, that I could run wherever I wanted and he'd still have me, so if I wanted to play, he'd play.

I was on my feet in a second, sprinting again.

This time he allowed me to hear his presence as he ran alongside Silas, their pursuit a wave of heat at my back.

They had me and they knew it. This run represented foreplay, a way of drawing out my eventual capture. Anticipation heightened, our pants music in the wind, and finally I reached my desired location.

Edon circled me one way while Silas moved in the opposite direction, their prowls sexy as fuck. No wonder they were drawn to each other. Sexual energy oozed from them both, leaving me in a puddle of need between them.

I shifted back into human form, my thighs already soaked with my expectation. Acceptance formed on my lips, a plea to have them both, when howls sounded in the distance, causing Edon to still.

He listened intently, as did Silas, as a wave of warnings littered the air.

Ice drizzled through my veins, severely damaging my aroused state.

That was the sound of a furious alpha male—Edon's father. It was underlined in a demand for blood. For retribution.

Edon and Silas seemed to be communicating, their eyes locked on one another.

And then the alpha heir took off, leaving us by the stream.

Silas shifted, his expression grim. "He told us to stay here."

"I gathered that by his departure," I replied, noting Edon's speed. "He's fast." Like, really, really fast. He'd clearly been toying with me and indulging in my pace, because holy fuck, that wolf could run.

"Yeah, he is." Silas palmed the back of his neck. "Luna..."

I swallowed, meeting his wary gaze. "Yeah?"

"Something's wrong," he said, his voice hoarse. "Like, really fucking wrong."

The hairs along my arms danced, my stomach churning.

He wasn't talking about us or what had been about to happen. No. He meant with the pack.

"I know," I whispered. "I feel it, too." A depraved sickness, a calling for death.

And I suspected one of us was the target of that call.

CHAPTER 17
EDON

BIANCA.

Her vacant blue eyes stared up at the tree above, while the rest of her body lay several feet away.

Someone had *chewed* through her neck. A horrible way to die that required strength and skill to accomplish.

And Luna's scent was all over the scene.

My teeth clenched as I stayed just out of sight, careful to keep my scent from the others. Not even my father had sensed me yet—a testament to my growing gifts and his weakening ones.

Fury emanated from the pack, words being exchanged that made my blood boil. They'd already taken a vote, not giving a damn that their alpha heir—me—wasn't in attendance. If I had any question as to pack loyalty before, I had my answers now. Everyone standing in this clearing was allied to my father. And it would be in my best interest to remember that.

"Where's your son?" one of them demanded.

My father howled again, the call meant for my ears.

But I didn't move, too furious to take a step.

This was a fucking setup. But I couldn't say a damn word because I was Luna's alibi. Not exactly a winning case, even with Silas on my side. Because everyone would see it as me protecting my mate and progeny. And going against a pack vote would render my relationships irreparable, which was the last thing I needed right now.

The pack demands retribution, I told Silas after describing the scene.

But she's innocent.

That's not the point, I replied. *My father's making me choose between the pack decision and my mate. It's his fucked-up way of forcing me to prove my loyalty to Clemente Clan.*

Failure was not an option here. If I chose Luna, the pack might very well try to kill me.

And you can't choose Luna? Silas asked, his mental voice holding a note of incredulity.

I sighed. The male might be an impressive wolf, but he was still so new to pack politics. Luna would at least understand this. I hoped she would, anyway.

The pack has already voted, I explained. *If I ignore the vote, I risk a mutiny.* Which, I suspected, was my father's goal.

That doesn't make any sense, he growled. *We know she didn't do this.*

I palmed the back of my neck, eyeing the restless wolves a few yards away from me. If I didn't make an appearance soon, they'd go looking for me. Or worse, they might accuse me of being an accomplice to the crime. I wouldn't put it past my father to try.

Let me explain this another way, I said, focusing on both Silas and the antsy wolves. *Luna's new. She has no allies here. However, Bianca had several. Those who knew her want revenge, and they don't care about innocence, not after witnessing Luna punch her the other day.*

So they won't even bother figuring out who did this.

In their minds, Luna is already guilty. And my saying otherwise will just make me look like a male protecting his mate. This trial was designed to hurt one of my perceived weaknesses—Luna. My grandfather had warned me that this would happen. I just never expected it to be so blatantly obvious.

I don't have a choice, Silas, I whispered, stepping into the clearing with a bored expression. I'd already phased back into human form, leaving me naked. But anyone who mistook my nudity for vulnerability would have one hell of a wake-up call.

"Seems my female has been busy," I said, eyeing the remains with disinterest. "I suppose Bianca shouldn't have run her mouth with falsehoods." Because the last time I'd touched her—aside from the casual hug or in taunting Luna—was well before the mating ceremony.

"Are you implying Bianca deserved her fate?" my father demanded.

I lifted a shoulder. "I'm saying it's probably not wise to provoke an alpha female in the middle of a mating moon. The same could be said about a mating alpha male." Except I seemed rather at ease in sharing my intended with Silas. But that was a matter for another day.

Some of the pack members growled. I ignored them, feigning nonchalance.

"That said, I suppose I need to have a word with Luna." I folded my arms. "Unless you question my ability to punish my mate?"

"Considering you interrupted my last one? Yes, son. Yes, I do." My father looked around at his buddies, who all grunted in agreement. "You'll punish her publicly or I'll kill her myself."

I snorted. "You can't kill my mate."

"Can't I?" he countered. "It'll delay your ascension by

a decade or two, but I'm sure more alpha females will be available soon. We can always ask Ernest Clan to produce another as well. I'm certain Niko would happily oblige after we inform him of his daughter's shortcomings."

Yeah, and he would most certainly take out his frustrations on his wife in the interim as well. *No, thanks.* "I'm not interested in waiting, old man." I chose the words with care, making sure he heard my growl on the final two. His time was at an end whether he acknowledged it or not.

"We don't need to rush this, Edon. I'm more than fit to continue running things," he replied, sounding as nonchalant as I had moments ago. "Pretty sure the pack would agree, too."

Of course they would. Because he'd made sure of it.

Which meant I had no choice.

I either punished Luna publicly or risked her death and my standing in the pack. Neither consequence was negotiable on my part.

The sooner I took over this hell, the sooner I improved it.

And Luna didn't deserve to die for something she'd clearly not done.

But looking at the lycans surrounding Bianca, I knew with all my being that no one would believe her innocence. Not even if Silas vouched for her whereabouts as well. If anything, it'd probably result in his death in addition to Luna's.

I fucking hate you, I told my father with a glance. It was too brief for anyone else to see, but his lips quirked up in response.

This was another of his damn trials.

A test.

And I only had one option.

"Fine." It took considerable effort not to growl that single word. "Prepare the ring. I'll find Luna."

I didn't give my father a chance to argue, my feet already moving. *Silas, I need you for another task...*

CHAPTER 18
SILAS

"Absolutely not," I growled, the second Edon appeared. He'd thrown on a pair of jeans, leaving me and Luna stark naked before him. Not that I cared. I was too focused on the insane plan he'd spoke into my head not even ten minutes ago.

"It wasn't a request, Silas." He didn't even look at me, his dark gaze on Luna. "They're calling for your blood."

"I know," she replied, her arms wrapped around herself. She hadn't stopped shaking since the howls began, her mind already processing what the pack wanted before I even had a chance to speak.

Still, I'd relayed every word from Edon, including the *task* he'd given me. A task I'd snorted at in my head and refused, but the alpha chose not to hear me.

"I won't do it," I said again, standing my ground. I could handle a lot. Not this.

Edon turned on me then, his palm around my throat in a flash as he shoved me up against a tree. "The alternative is far worse, Silas. If you care about her at all, you'll do as I say."

"Bullshit," I retorted, livid and not at all frightened by the stronger wolf before me. "She's innocent. I'm not going to fucking—"

"It's fine," Luna cut in, her breath shuddering out of her in defeat. "I accept the punishment." She captured Edon's gaze, a hint of a fighter lurking in her caramel-colored depths. "But I *am* innocent."

"I know," he replied, his grip on my throat lessening in severity without releasing me. "But I still have to do this."

She nodded, her arms still tightly folded around herself as though she were cold.

I gaped back and forth between them. "Why the hell are you just accepting this?" Lycans and vampires were supposed to have rights. They were the superior species. This punishment shit was for humans and humans alone.

"There's still so much about our society you need to learn." Edon's palm flexed, his expression intensifying. "You will do what I say, Silas, or things will get very bad for you both."

I scoffed at the threat. "I can take a punishment." Or several. I'd more than held my own in my twenty-two years of life. This would be no different.

"Perhaps you can, but what about Luna?" Edon snapped. "If you refuse, someone else will take your place. Perhaps more. And then how will you feel, Silas? Because they'll make you watch as they shred her apart, and you'll know all along that you could have helped prevent her mutilation by completing this one fucking task."

"What you're asking me to do—"

"No, what I'm *telling* you to do, Silas. This isn't a fucking request. I need you to help me protect what dignity Luna will have left after this." He released me with a shove. "This is happening. Otherwise, she dies."

Luna shuddered visibly.

And Edon grabbed her arm. "Let's go."

I stared after them, my jaw on the ground.

For two decades, I learned all about the glamorous lives of lycans and vampires. Especially those of the alphas and royals. Yet never once did anyone talk about this—the thirst for punishments, for keeping fellow lycans in line, for brutalizing each other into submission.

Because that was what this was at the core: a way to break Luna's psyche and force her to bow to her male betters.

The alpha heir didn't want to do this.

However, he was going to anyway.

Because his world required it.

There is no better life, I realized, gazing up at the trees above me. *It was all a lie.*

We have a chance to change it, Edon said softly. *But I can't do anything until I ascend.*

Which required him to have a proper mate—Luna.

And it seemed his father was hell-bent on removing that requirement, leading me to wonder, *Do you think he orchestrated Bianca's death and framed Luna?*

Of course he did, he replied. *This is all a fucked-up test, and if I don't punish Luna, he'll kill her and delay my trials. I need to beat him at his own game.*

I swallowed, my fists clenching at my sides. *So you need me.*

Yes.

No elaboration. Just that single-word reply. It served as a concession of sorts. Edon could command me all he wanted, but at the end of the day, he required my acquiescence for this to work. Denying his demands only made his job harder. It would also end up hurting Luna even more.

"Fuck," I muttered, running my fingers through my

hair. "*Fuck.*" It would be so easy to run, to hide from what was about to happen, but I couldn't. Some stupid part of me felt an obligation to stay, not just for Edon but also for Luna.

Loyalty. A dangerous emotion. Which was crazy because I barely knew them, yet some inherent part of me felt indebted to them both. No, not necessarily indebted, but something else. Something stronger.

It reminded me of how I regarded Rae and Willow, only even more intense.

My wolf. I blinked. *It's my wolf.*

You have less than five minutes to make a decision, Edon warned. *As soon as we reach the ring, I'm calling for you.*

He didn't mean mentally, but in a howl. And if I ignored that command, I'd be hunted. That much I understood. Running, I supposed, was never truly an option. To ignore the call of an alpha went against the grain, something I felt deep inside. My wolf would never allow it.

And Edon knew it.

I sensed it through our bond, his assurance that I wouldn't let him down.

Whatever this was between us seemed to grow by the second, leashing me to him in a way I both craved and loathed. I fought him because I could, but some part of me would always enjoy submitting, too.

It confused me.

Enthralled me.

Anchored me.

There was never a choice.

I would do as he demanded because he commanded it. And what I hated most of all was that I'd probably enjoy it because my compliance would please him.

"So fucked up," I grumbled to myself, my feet already moving toward the main camp. I could feel Edon's tug, his need for me to obey, to do what he required, and my body responded in kind.

But it wasn't just about Edon.

I felt Luna, too.

She'd somehow found a link to my veins, heating my blood in a way no one else ever had. I shook my head, refusing the connection. Except it fired again, drawing me nearer, forcing me to submit to them both.

Two alphas.

And me—a mutt.

I didn't know what we were doing, had just sort of gone along for the run earlier when Edon chased Luna. Not because he told me to, but because I wanted to. And that only baffled me more. It was as if my inner wolf, not my mind, drove my instincts, leaving me with no alternative but to follow along.

A howl pierced the night.

Not from Edon, but from Luna. It was agonized and sounded all wrong. Pained. Destroyed. Followed by cries of approval and excitement. *The pack.*

Chaos thrived through the sire bond.

What's wrong? I demanded.

No response.

My walk turned into a sprint as I pounded barefoot over the earth, unfazed by the rocks and dirt beneath my heels. Branches scratched my arms, my sides, my exposed thighs—I had left my jeans at Edon's house before our little run through the woods.

What's happening? I asked again, running as fast as my legs allowed. I was just outside of the main village, the snarls of the pack growing louder with each step. They were near the location where the initial mating ceremony took place. That seemed to be where all official pack matters happened, right in the heart of the territory, surrounded by the cabins owned by Clemente Clan elite.

Edon, I said as I neared one of the larger lodges.

No response.

I ignored the call from my wolf, suppressing the urge to shift. It would take too much time and energy, and I needed to be ready for—

I froze just outside the punishment ring.

Luna lay curled in a ball in the middle of violence, while Edon stood just off to the side and watched as the pack descended upon her. He didn't pay me a glance, his expression bored, his body language nonchalant. But I *felt* his anger through the bond.

Why aren't you stopping them? They're going to kill her!

She's fine, he replied, his mental voice a low growl. But he held up his hand, causing a few of the wolves to still. A warning rumble from his throat caught the attention of the others and earned him a death glare from his father.

"You prefer her death?" Walter asked from across the crowd. "Because I'll happily arrange it." He took a step forward, only for Edon to shake his head.

"No. I merely wish to propose an alternative." There wasn't a hint of anger or annoyance in his tone, even though I felt it raging through our connection. If Edon could, I suspected he'd kill his father right now. Instead, he said, "One of Luna's biggest flaws is her inability to heel."

"A flaw I attempted to remedy the other night before you stopped me," his father replied. "One your pack is willing to solve for you right now if you allow them to continue." He gestured to the salivating males, their lewd stares on Luna's petite frame.

Walter must have orchestrated this harsh reception at the main camp. Because it hadn't been part of Edon's preliminary plan at all, a fact I somehow just understood as if I were connected to my sire's mind.

He hadn't stopped the initial attack, because he knew it would make him appear weak. He also knew his wolves needed to expunge some of their anger to feel satisfied. Which would allow him to better recommend and facilitate Luna's punishment.

I blinked, startled by all that knowledge. Whether he pushed it into me or if I'd stumbled upon it in error, I didn't know. But I felt the veracity of it in my bones.

Edon had a plan.

Everything he did was done with a purpose in mind. Just like this.

"I don't think your method will break her penchant for dominance," Edon said, tucking his hands into his pockets. "But I have one that might." He let that hang in the air, piquing the curiosity of his pack as they glanced between the alpha incumbent and the alpha heir.

Walter folded his burly arms over his bare chest and smiled. "And what, *Alpha Heir*, do you suggest?" he asked, the incredulity in his tone a clear insult.

"Make the mutt fuck her." Edon waved a hand in my direction. "I can't imagine anything more degrading than allowing a mutt's cock inside me. Wouldn't you agree, Father?"

It took significant strength to force my gaze to lower as the focus of the pack fell upon me. I wanted to stare them all down in challenge, to dare them to consider me beneath them, but my defiance would only make this worse. And I understood what Edon was doing. He wanted to belittle Luna's position in the pack by having a newbie defile her.

"Are you sure he can even perform?" Walter drawled.

The hairs along the back of my neck sprung up as the urge to attack hit me square in the gut.

Easy, Edon whispered into my mind. *They assume you're weak. I want them to hold on to that assumption until the time is right.*

I fought the urge to frown, his words not at all what I expected to hear.

"There's only one way to find out," he said out loud, addressing his father's concerns regarding my ability to fuck. "Even if he can't, I imagine submitting to the mutt will put Luna firmly in her place."

His father stroked his chin, a movement I caught in my periphery, as I hadn't yet lifted my gaze from the ground out of fear that I might accidentally challenge one of these jackasses with a glower. The pack collectively would be impossible to beat. But some of these idiots without backup? Yeah, I'd hold my own just fine. And I'd enjoy it, too.

"I can smell her fear," one of the lycans said, a grin in his voice. "I say we make the mutt put on a show, see what he can do."

"I bet he can't last more than ten seconds in that pussy," another said.

Someone snorted. "Nah, I'd give it at least thirty."

"Really? I'm going for a minute. He's not even hard yet."

And then the betting began.

The need for blood had morphed into a pit of ribbing and lecherous expectations surrounding my sexual prowess.

"Don't the humans study this shit, though?" an intelligent male questioned. "What were his scores?"

"Fuck if I know" was the response.

Edon remained silent, but I felt his relief through the

connection. A relief I did not share. He wasn't the one who had to perform for these assholes. They weren't just asking me to fuck, but to essentially rape Luna. She knew, of course. Had already told me it would be fine.

"I mean, it's not like we weren't going to... you know..." had been her quiet statement shortly before Edon arrived.

That didn't make it right.

That didn't make it *okay* either.

She remained tucked in her little ball, her body trembling, her face hidden. There were scratches along her back from where some of the pack had clawed her and a few marks on her sides that likely came from shoes or maybe fists.

This is so fucking wrong, I thought, not for the first time.

There's no alternative was Edon's reply.

The conversation continued to flow around me, the pack growing more eager by the second as they entertained themselves with the thought of my taking Luna. Most voted in the low minutes. Others in the seconds.

If I was going to do this, I'd go long just so none of those assholes won.

Except then I'd be prolonging Luna's torment.

I resisted the urge to grab my hair and tug on it, my attention still fixed on the ground. The lycans had started circling me, taking my measure, weighing my abilities based on my appearance.

It was ludicrous.

I couldn't believe I'd fought in the Immortal Cup just to endure such treatment. They considered me a lesser being solely because I was not born a lycan. But the trials of my life placed me far above them all. And one day, I'd prove it.

"All right, son. We'll try it your way," Walter said, his tone holding a begrudging lilt.

It was then that I realized why Edon had chosen this method—he knew the pack would approve. He essentially used his father's techniques against him by exploiting the clan's thirst for degradation.

Because it wasn't just Luna they were embarrassing, but also me.

"But I want him to fuck her ass," Walter added, causing the world to still around me. "He doesn't deserve to experience alpha pussy."

Luna seemed to freeze, her tension palpable.

What Walter demanded was even more invasive somehow; it was also something I'd never done. And I suspected Luna was the same.

"No," Edon growled, the sound charging the energy in the air. "I've not taken her ass yet. It's mine. He'll take her pussy instead."

His father smiled. "Taking her virgin ass would be an even better punishment."

"As I stated the other day, she's my mate and I decide how best to punish her, and this is my decision." His attention fell to me. "If you touch her ass, I'll kill you."

"Noted," I whispered, my throat dry from the war of wills happening before me.

How Edon expected me to perform under these conditions was beyond me. And the resulting snickers from the crowd said they all agreed. Some even went as far as to comment on my lack of arousal. Apparently, they didn't understand why raping a female might not appeal to me.

Luna will prefer you to anyone else in this pack, Edon murmured, his mental voice different from the harsh tone he'd used only seconds ago when threatening my life. *Remember that when you slide inside her sweet heat. Remember the chase, how she drew us down to that stream with the intent to have us both. The way she submitted to you in the field. Her wolf desires you, Silas.*

"On your knees, Luna," Edon said, the command in his voice a slap against my senses. "It seems the mutt needs some motivation to perform. Use your mouth to help him out."

CHAPTER 19
EDON

It'd taken physical restraint not to react when the pack had assaulted Luna upon arrival, and it took even more restraint not to react now as she struggled to rise.

Any hint of concern or soft treatment on my part would only worsen this experience. My father's eyes were on me, his irritation over my taking control of the situation evident in the harsh lines of his mouth.

But there were little things I could do—like grab a fistful of Luna's hair to yank her upright. To the audience, it looked like I'd grown impatient. In reality, I was lending her my strength as I positioned myself behind her. She stiffened when her back hit my legs, a reaction that pleased the crowd.

I gently drew my thumb along the sensitive skin behind her ear, my fingers still woven into her hair in what hopefully resembled a painful grip. She didn't outwardly relax, but her weight sank into my thighs as she used the support I offered.

That inherent trust went straight to my cock. She understood what I was trying to do without my having to voice it, and it seemed Silas did as well. His approval warmed the bond, his mind not missing a single detail despite his focus being on the ground.

Ignore everyone around us and focus solely on her mouth, I whispered to him. It was my job to protect them, to allow them a hint of peace under the guise of punishment. And I would succeed if Silas let me, if he followed my words and just gave in to the pleasure of the moment.

I circled Luna's throat with the hand not in her hair, making a show of my dominance while secretly angling her in a way that could obscure the motions of my thumb. Her pulse thundered beneath my touch, something I sought to ease with slow, hypnotic circles.

I hoped she felt the similarities of this moment to the one we'd shared earlier when I stood behind her while she sucked Silas off. I needed to bring her back to that experience, to remind her of the chase, and remove everyone around us.

A difficult feat.

Fortunately, I had her wolf on my side. A wolf I'd left unsatisfied earlier with the promise for more. And now I would give it to her.

In the form of Silas's cock.

"Motivate him, Luna," I demanded, my voice far more cruel than my touch. "Show everyone here how eager you are to submit to your better."

She growled even as she complied, her tongue drawing a path along Silas's growing erection as she boldly met his gaze.

Something passed between them.

An understanding.

One I felt connected to even as I stood on the outside.

"That doesn't look very submissive to me," my father pointed out.

I didn't stop tracing her pulse, my touch light even as I infused a harsh edge into my response. "She's on her knees before a mutt with his cock pressed up against her lips. I wouldn't necessarily call that very alpha-like."

"More whore-like," Glenn put in helpfully.

"We need a new pack slut with Bianca gone," Barry added. "Should we consider this an audition?"

"Are you kidding? I won't want her mouth anywhere near my dick after this."

The ribbing continued, derogatory statements about Luna's actions and Silas's position within the pack blending into a haze of disgust around us. I felt my little mate's tension and sensed my progeny's annoyance, providing me with a much bigger task of helping them both perform under less-than-welcome conditions.

Because if Silas couldn't get it up and fuck Luna, my father would intervene. Something I sensed he was eager to do, even now.

Tell me about her tongue, I said to Silas. *Tell me how it feels.*

Forced, he growled back at me.

You accused me of that earlier today, but as I recall, she quite eagerly sucked you off. I hummed into his mind, the sound low and soothing. *Tell me how it felt to come down her throat. To feel her swallow around your dick as it pulsed inside her mouth.*

He groaned, out loud and through the link. *Edon...*

Just think how good her pussy is going to feel clamped down around you, Silas. Pure heaven and something I've not even felt yet. God, I want every detail. Every fucking sensation. And why did even thinking about that turn me on? Hearing about Silas's pleasure as he fucked the woman destined to be mine should piss me off, not cause my dick to harden painfully in my pants.

But fuck, I wanted to watch him.

I wanted to hear their shared pants, smell their arousal,

and connect with my progeny as he took my mate's sweet, hot cunt from behind.

Silas must have heard me, because he groaned again, his shaft fully engorged and parting Luna's beautiful lips. He thrust deep inside just as he'd done in my home only hours before. She flinched at the intrusion, but a swipe of my thumb against her pulse seemed to reassure her once more, and she swallowed him to the best of her ability— which was fucking impressive and a skill destined to be admired.

Shit. I could feel him beneath my hand, his head lodged so fucking deep that I doubted she could breathe. His hands flexed at his sides, uncertain, his abdominal muscles clenching with restraint. The wolves around us thought he was about to come already, their jeers threatening to spoil the moment.

But I understood his tension.

He wasn't about to explode.

No. Silas craved dominance. He wanted to grab Luna and force his cock even deeper into her pretty little throat, but my hands were in his way. And while he might feel comfortable dominating her, he couldn't challenge me.

I nearly smiled.

The two of them were perfection, their unspoken battle for command a fucking aphrodisiac to my senses.

I yanked Luna backward, my gaze meeting Silas's briefly as his lips curled into the faintest hint of a snarl that he forcibly swallowed.

"Present your cunt for the mutt," I demanded, pushing Luna to the ground onto all fours. Everyone else would have seen it as a shove, but my hand around her throat helped ease her into the fall, giving her the notice she needed to catch herself on her palms.

My father was too busy laughing at what someone had

said to notice my movements, something I'd taken full advantage of in the moment.

I smacked Luna's ass, my hand positioned in a way to make a loud sound without causing much pain. "Spread" was all I said.

And she did.

She spread those beautiful thighs, not just for me but for Silas as well. And fuck if that wasn't burning me up inside in the best way.

Every detail, I reminded him as he knelt behind her. "Don't touch her ass," I made sure to say out loud. It was for my father's benefit after his outrageous demand. I hadn't protected her for myself, which she had to know since I'd yet to take her in any manner. But I wasn't sure how she felt about anal and refused to find out in front of these jackasses.

"Understood," Silas replied, his voice thick with a variety of emotions—emotions I felt through our sire link.

Anger.

Excitement.

Challenge.

Annoyance.

Lust.

Is she wet? I asked softly, watching as he positioned himself near her entrance.

Yes, he admitted, his throat working as he swallowed. *Fuck. Yes.*

Good. It seemed my positioning tactics had worked. Or maybe exhibitionism appealed to my little wolf. Perhaps it was a mixture of both. *Slide in slowly. Pretend you're nervous.*

Another swallow. *I won't hurt her.*

I know. That was why I'd chosen him for this task.

And maybe, just maybe, I'd also wanted this. Why else would I have allowed him to chase her with me this afternoon? It wasn't so I could just fuck her in front of him.

No. We'd been in that together. The three of us. Dancing some sort of erotic dance. One I intended to continue now.

Shit, she's tight, Edon. My head barely fits. Sweat beaded across his brow, his teeth snagging his lip. Around us, the wolves tittered, expecting him to blow his load in a single thrust. I tuned them out to the best of my ability, focusing on my mate and progeny and on their joining below.

A mental groan through the link had my balls tightening, Silas losing himself to the sensation of her constricting sheath. His words all jammed together as he described the intensity, the heat, the overwhelming urge to shove his hips forward to fuck her to the hilt. And then he gave in, bottoming out against her on a growl that I felt to my very bones.

Fuck, she's perfect, he told me.

Those three words should have spiked envy within me, and they did to an extent, but not for the reasons they should. I wanted to join them, to lick Luna's sweet cunt while Silas drove into her, and then force him to return the favor. I wanted to fuck her ass while he took her pussy, to kiss him while he moaned, to drag my teeth along her neck and truly claim her as mine before allowing him to lap up the wound with his skilled tongue.

My blood heated with every passing second, a thousand ideas slamming into me one after another, and not all of them were mine.

Because I wasn't the only one who wanted to play.

Silas's yearnings grew hotter by the second, his mouth craving my cock, his ass flexing as if expecting me to join, and I felt the stirrings of both of their arousals warming my insides.

How does she feel? I asked him.

Slick. Hot. She's squeezing me so, so good. He thrust deep, hitting a spot that made her gasp. Not in pain, but in pleasant surprise, although I doubted many of my brethren knew the difference. *Fuck...*

Silas started thinking about his university courses, angling himself in a manner that maximized the experience for them both while also helping him last longer. I nearly smiled, but something about his calculative mind only excited me more.

How would it feel to be inside him and hear his thoughts? To listen as Luna joined us on her knees, taking him into her mouth, sucking him to completion and then licking him clean.

My dick throbbed against my zipper, begging me to join them, to give in to the urges and ignore everyone else.

But they were relying on me to keep them safe, to protect them from the masses. Which meant I had a role to play in this fucked-up trial. Hmm, although maybe I could find a way to indulge both roles—alpha and lover.

I circled them and pretended to evaluate the discipline of my mate. Luna's face was hidden beneath her hair, adding to the effect of her humiliation. I crouched before her, threaded my fingers through her gorgeous strands, and tilted her head upward to study her features.

Ruby-red lips—swollen from Silas's cock.

Pink cheeks.

Blown-out pupils.

Stunning.

"You seem to be enjoying yourself," I murmured, my voice meant only for her.

But of course, my father heard it. "Then how is this effective?" he demanded.

His comment caused some of the amusement among the crowd to die.

But I had them all right where I wanted them.

"I can't imagine a more degrading experience than to not only allow a mutt to fuck me but to enjoy it, too." I stroked my thumb across her lips. "Make her come, Omega. Assuming you can last that long."

That uplifted all the spirits, everyone laughing at my dry tone and cruel suggestions. Shame colored Luna's expression just long enough for everyone to see, leaving them all with the belief that my method of belittling her was working.

Silas, however, took my words as a challenge, his determination thriving through the bond. He read between the lines and understood that I didn't desire Luna's pleasure for the enjoyment of the pack.

Providing Luna with relief allowed us to give her a semblance of strength, a way for her to hold on to the moment and choose to give in to the sensations Silas stirred now with his skilled penetrations.

I released her and stood, taking on my assessing role once more. Arousal stirred in the air, not just from the couple rutting on the ground but from the others in attendance. My father was among them, his eyes falling hungrily on Luna as she moaned.

A myriad of crude comments followed.

They called her a whore.

A slut.

Belittled her place in the pack.

Claimed she loved the feel of lesser males filling her and said she didn't deserve the status of alpha female.

I watched each slur slap my darling mate across her pretty face, Silas's job becoming more difficult by the second. But it was the commentary regarding what came next that forced my hand. The wolves were getting too carried away, making assumptions about who might taste her after Silas finished, and it left me no choice but to intervene. I had to bring Luna back and help her ignore everything around us before I lost the feisty female inside of her.

And most importantly, I had to make sure no one else could touch her afterward.

I could share her with Silas. Everyone else? Not a fucking chance.

"Mmm, I love you like this, Luna." I knelt before her again, blocking her face from the view of others and traced her mouth with the tip of my finger. "On all fours, being fucked by another wolf of my choosing," I continued. "It's making me want to see how well you multitask." I pinched her chin between my fingers, forcing her gaze upward. "I want your mouth."

Those words were met with collective sounds of entertainment, but I ignored them all, my focus on the beautiful alpha before me.

Trust me, I told her with my eyes. *Let me help guide you through this, to give you an act of power.*

I needed her to understand what I was giving her. So many males used oral sex as a way to dominate their women, but I always understood the power in bringing a female to her knees. Feeding her my cock gave her all the control, and the flare of her nostrils said she knew it.

Oh, I would benefit.

But she'd thrive in the moment of it, knowing she'd brought an alpha male to his knees with a flick of her tongue.

I witnessed the fire in her gaze when she sucked Silas off, the way she was hell-bent on destroying his sense of being. And I was telling her with my gaze now that I'd give her the same opportunity.

Silas groaned, his cock lodged deep inside her, his fingers working that sweet little bundle of nerves between her legs as he stroked that spot deep within her. *She's clenching around me. Fuck, Edon, I won't last if she keeps that up.*

Don't you dare come, I warned. *Keep fucking her until I say otherwise.*

He cursed, my demand hitting him in a place he couldn't ignore.

I arched a brow at Luna, asking her without words for permission. If she said no, I'd laugh it off with a harsh comment and find another way to exhaust her. It wouldn't be easy, but I refused to allow anyone else inside her.

Her nostrils flared, her cheeks darkening to a deep rose.

And she parted her lips. "Yes." Barely audible, spoken on a breath, but enough for me to continue.

I drew down my zipper, the top button of my jeans already undone, and hissed as my dick fell within inches of that beautiful mouth. Her tongue licked the head, her eyes holding mine, and I nearly came from that look alone.

No fear.

No mortification.

Just pure feminine lust.

I wrapped one hand around the back of her neck, the other sliding into her hair to position her where I wanted. Her honey-brown irises seemed to pulse, her desire a palpable presence that ate through the last vestiges of doubt in my mind.

Do it, she seemed to be saying. *I dare you.*

Careful who you taunt, I thought back at her, my lips curling.

I'm not afraid of you, her look said, and fuck if that didn't make me even harder.

Silas shifted his grip on her hip, angling his thrusts in a manner that stirred little mewling sounds from her throat that I quickly silenced by thrusting into the damp cavern of her mouth. She swallowed around me, a growl rumbling in my chest in response, one Silas mimicked on a groan.

This wasn't my first time sharing a female with another male. Yet it *felt* like the first time. The intensity shrouded our surroundings in a haze of sound and musk, the lycans eager to join in, but I kept them all at bay.

Silas and Luna were mine. They just didn't know it yet.

Edon, Silas groaned. *Fuck... Luna...* His broken thoughts joined my own as the luscious woman in question ran her teeth along my shaft.

I know, I agreed. *I know.*

She was a goddess, her body seemingly made for us both, and wow, could she multitask. I watched her push back against Silas, urging him to fuck her harder as she punished me with her mouth.

So good.

So perfect.

So... fuck...

Silas's thoughts melded with mine, our heightened need an intoxicating mix that drove us both to the edge that much faster and seemed to spur Luna on as well. Her body tightened, her eyes glazing over on the verge of oblivion as a scream vibrated my dick.

Luna came apart between us, her face glowing on the wave of her orgasm. Silas growled low in his throat, his torso pulled taut as he fought the urge to follow her. I hadn't given permission yet, and that small part of him that I owned forced him to submit, to wait for my command.

Now, I told him. *And don't hold back.*

I wanted to see all of him, to witness his explosion, to *feel* it as if it were my own.

He didn't disappoint, his snarl a feral sound that sang to my wolf, forcing me to pick up my own pace between Luna's lips. She received me eagerly, her hooded gaze holding mine with a lazy ease as she sucked and nipped and licked.

Whoever taught her to suck cock deserved a medal.

Because the woman knew exactly how I liked it, drove me to the near edge of madness while milking Silas's seed with her hot little cunt.

He was still coming, his forehead pressed against my hand in her hair, placing him in a submissive position that appealed to my wolf. The positions of their heads so close to my groin inspired an entirely new idea, one where I took turns fucking each of their mouths as they waited enthusiastically on their knees to see who would receive my seed first.

But I had to finish the current trial before I could engage in such a fantasy.

And so Luna won this round, my ecstasy erupting down her slender throat on a final pump of my hips. She drank me eagerly, her eyes closing as if indulging in a sweet treat.

Silas groaned again, my rapture cascading hot energy through our connection and coercing a final shudder from him. My name intertwined with Luna's in his mind, his bliss complete.

Until the sounds of expectation chilled the air around us.

My father was already preparing, his fucked-up mind twisting Luna's punishment into something so much worse.

No. I refuse.

I tightened my grip on Luna's neck, guiding myself between her lips to a dangerous point near the back of her throat.

Round eyes flashed up to mine, the mist of her oblivion bleeding into uncertainty as I stared down at her.

She'd finished swallowing.

I should be pulling back.

Instead, I pushed in even more while pretending to shudder through a second climax. She gagged, her pupils dilating, her hands lifting to my thighs as if to push me off her.

Trust me, I wanted to say.

What are you doing? Silas demanded, noting the tension along her spine. He started to shift, but a mental command from me froze him in place. *Why?*

I need to knock her out, I explained, my grasp turning to cement as Luna tried in earnest to shove me away. *Don't let her move.*

Silas clearly didn't approve, but he obeyed.

Claws pierced my skin, Luna trying to fight her way out from between us as terror took hold of her. I hated doing this to her, hated the look of fury mingled with betrayal that she gave me now, but I held her anyway.

Some wolves might want to play with an unconscious female.

Most—my father included—wouldn't.

I supposed they could always wait for her to wake up, but she'd be gone before that happened.

Luna's choked whimper hurt my heart, her eyes growing glassy from the lack of oxygen. Until, finally, she went limp. I gave it another few seconds to make sure she wasn't faking it, listened for her pulse to slow, and shook off my pretend orgasmic state with a low growl of relief.

And then I let her go.

She collapsed, unmoving.

Silas shifted back onto his knees, his spent cock heavy against his thigh. He didn't look up, his gaze on Luna.

I stood to zip up my pants, ignoring the urge to check on my mate. Already her pulse had returned to normal, telling me she was fine. Which, unfortunately, meant I didn't have a lot of time to finish this act. If she stirred too soon, the pack would descend upon her.

And then I would be forced to defend her.

Rolling my shoulders, I glanced down at Luna and Silas with a detached expression and shrugged. "She's an excellent multitasker." I glanced at my father. "Better than Bianca, too."

He narrowed his gaze. "It's cruel to speak ill of the dead."

While I agreed, it took considerable effort not to retort, *It's also cruel to kill a lycan for the sake of a trial.* Which was exactly what had happened here.

I had no idea how my father managed to coat Bianca's remains in Luna's scent, but he clearly orchestrated all of this. Some of the pack members knew, too. I could see it in the satisfaction gleaming from their gazes. They hadn't cared about Bianca at all, just wanted a reason to incite retribution to see how I fared with the challenge.

Or maybe they didn't know and they just enjoyed the show anyway.

The fact that I couldn't tell the difference bothered me.

"Take my mate back to my cabin, Omega," I demanded, not looking at Silas but at my father. *Wait for me there*, I added mentally to my progeny.

Silas bent to scoop her up into his arms and paused at my father's growled, "We're not done."

"On the contrary, we're very done." I glanced at Silas.

"Why are you still here? You obey me, not him." *Take her quickly. I'll handle this.*

My father snarled low and menacing. "You're forgetting your place, *son*."

"No, I'm ascending to my place, *old man*," I replied, aware of Silas doing exactly as I commanded. He moved quickly, lifting Luna and bolting from the ring.

No one stopped him, all of their focus on the two alphas squaring off in the ring.

I captured and held my father's gaze, refusing to give an inch. If he wanted to throw down, I was ready. The pack might back him, or maybe they wouldn't. I'd satisfied the punishment requirements, degraded my female, just as they necessitated. I'd done everything right and won their favor in the process. At least mostly.

And the look on my father's face said he understood that, too.

I smiled. "You'll have to do better than that to break me, Father."

His jaw ticked, his mind working through his options. All of them pointed to walking away, and we both knew it. But I couldn't deny the hint of relief that slithered down my spine as he gave a subtle nod of consent before leaving the circle.

Several of my packmates patted me on the back, their pride a sickness I wouldn't allow to infect me. That they felt fulfilled by my actions against Luna said so much.

This was not a world I wanted to indulge. It was one I wanted to change. And soon, *very* soon, I would be in a position to do so.

CHAPTER 20
LUNA

Deep male voices filtered in and out of my conscious. I couldn't understand them, my mind blinking in and out of awareness.

Something warm slid between my legs, sending tingles up and down my spine. Lips caressed my neck. More words. A damp cloth against my back. Another kiss to my jaw. Someone combing fingers through my hair.

It all provided the most intensely sensual dream of my existence—surrounded by heat, alpha wolf, and protective strokes.

I sighed into the male wall behind me, stretching against him, and smiled as he kissed my temple. "You're safe," he whispered.

I know.

Yet, a memory nagged at me. One where I wasn't safe at all, but horrified. I chased the image in my mind, trying to find the source and truth of it, and gasped, my hand flying to my throat.

"It's okay, Luna." I recognized that low voice, that scent, that *male.*

Edon.

My eyes flew open to find him lying beside me, his dark eyes glimmering in the low lighting of his bedroom. I glanced over my shoulder and found Silas to be the source of heat at my back, his palm a brand against my hip. He'd been the one to claim I was safe.

Liar.

Edon had suffocated me with his cock, leaving me vulnerable and alone and so fucking cold. I clutched my neck, surprised my throat didn't ache from him nearly killing me.

"*Why?*" I demanded, my voice coming out in a growl that vibrated my chest as I met the alpha's gaze.

"To keep the others away from you," he replied, lifting his palm to my hand and gently peeling it away from my skin. "I could feel my father planning to prolong your punishment at my expense. So I took away the object of his desire. *You.*"

I blinked, surprised not only by his explanation but also by his lack of hesitation in explaining himself. My fingers curled into a fist, the memory too fresh beneath his touch, even while my mind reasoned that he'd done the right thing.

Well, no. The *right* thing would have been to declare my innocence and not allow any of that bullshit to occur. But sometimes circumstances prevent even the most moral of people from completing the appropriate action.

And I knew what would have happened if Edon refused to punish me. *He* would have received a correction far worse, likely in the form of my death—an act that would allow his father to prolong the ascension process.

My shoulders sagged as I huffed out a breath, hating this life more than ever.

Except Edon hadn't reacted at all how a normal alpha

usually would. For one, he'd attempted to protect me. Most would have thrown his mate to the wolves—literally—and just stood around to make sure no one killed her. Instead, Edon had Silas defile me, which would appear horrible to the onlookers. But to me... I looked over my shoulder again, meeting those bright blue eyes.

Yeah, I, uh, hadn't exactly minded.

"Are you all right?" he asked softly, his thumb tracing my hip bone.

Edon leaned in to kiss my neck again, his nose skimming my jaw.

"Y-yes," I stammered, swallowing. *What's happening? Why are they—*

I jolted as Edon nipped my pulse, drawing my focus back to him. He was only an inch or so away, with one arm tucked under his head and his opposite hand resting along his side. "Tell Silas you don't hate him."

My brow furrowed. "What?"

"He's worried you hate him for fucking you. Tell him you don't."

"Maybe I do." I didn't, but that wasn't the point.

Edon's lips curled. "Please, little mate. Put Silas out of his misery. He's giving me a headache." The growl behind me only seemed to amuse Edon more. Damn alpha male.

"The only person I should hate in this situation is you," I replied, trying to knock that arrogant smirk off his too-alluring mouth. Alas, my words only worsened it, his teeth flashing now as he full-on smiled at me.

"Would an apology fix it?" The teasing quality of his voice told me he wasn't exactly offering, but playing.

"You choked me."

"I did."

"And you don't feel bad about that?" I pressed.

He lifted a bare shoulder—because yes, he was naked.

Of course he was fucking naked. And it seemed Silas was, too.

"Choking you beat the alternative," the alpha replied, his tone as unapologetic as ever. He lifted his hand to draw his finger down my throat, to my sternum, and lower to my belly button. "Do you want us to make you feel better, little mate?" His gaze darkened with the words. "I think Silas would like that."

"Silas has his own voice," the male behind me replied.

"Then why don't you use it?" Edon countered, looking over my shoulder at his progeny. "Talk to Luna. She's awake and very alert." He punctuated his words by drawing his thumb upward to my breast. Electricity hummed in my veins as a result of that touch, my body hyperaware of being sandwiched between two virile male wolves. They practically radiated heat, their scents commingling with mine and bathing me in lust and sex.

I shivered, which invited him to stroke me again. Only, this time he pinched my nipple. I hissed, arching into Silas, and then gasped as Edon lowered his mouth to kiss my abused breast.

Fuck... This... I don't...

I closed my eyes, then opened them again, conflicted.

"I'm sorry," Silas whispered, his lips against my ear. "I didn't... I hope I didn't hurt you."

Hurt me? I nearly laughed. Except nothing about it was remotely humorous. I'd only been with one other wolf, and he'd lasted all of a few minutes. Mostly because we were on a timeline, but I certainly hadn't enjoyed the experience.

Silas, however, made me feel things. Tingly things. Sexy things. He'd helped me forget the pack and their cruelty, had erased the reason for our joining, and had given me pleasure.

Because Edon had told him to.

Oh…

"You didn't want…" I swallowed, closing my eyes.

"Of course I didn't," he replied. "Who could possibly desire a situation like that?"

Shit. The punishment had been just as horrible for him, perhaps even worse with all the things his pack had said about him, the way they'd betted on his sexual prowess, the degrading comments about mutt cock, and the way Edon had forced him to perform by using the sire bond. I understood why he did, had oddly been a bit thankful for the consideration, but I hadn't taken Silas's wants or desires into account.

Actually, I hadn't thought much about his desires at all. Not when I demanded he fuck me out in that field, or again when I went to my knees in the bathroom. I'd just assumed he wanted it.

"I should be apologizing to you," I realized out loud, rotating to my back to stare up at him. He was perched on one elbow, his other hand following my motion to stay on my hip. "I'm sorry, Silas. I haven't taken your feelings into account at all, too caught up in my own shit to pay attention to much else. Which isn't an excuse. It's, well, the truth."

His brow furrowed. "Why the hell are you apologizing to me? I just raped you on Edon's command."

The alpha growled a low warning. "Careful."

"What? At least admit what we did to her." Silas narrowed his gaze at the alpha male. "None of that was consensual."

"Nothing in this world is ever fucking consensual," Edon countered. "It's all manufactured and organized by those in control."

Silas snorted. "Says the future Alpha of the Clemente Clan."

"You say that like it was my choice."

"And you think being the omega of a lycan clan was mine? That I wanted to go into the Immortal Cup and kill all those people? Some of whom I've known all my life?"

I gaped back and forth between them, shocked by Silas's fury and the ease with which he expelled those words at the alpha who had created him. But what startled me more was Edon's reaction. My father would have lashed out and put the newbie in his place, perhaps even killed him.

But not Edon.

No. He merely sighed and shook his head. "No, Silas. I don't. Just as turning you into a lycan wasn't my choice. But here we are. So either we fight about it—a fight you will lose—or we work together and see what we can do about building a more positive future in the clan."

Silas gaped at him. "How?"

"By listening to our elders," Edon replied cryptically. His gaze fell to me then, the ebony in his irises swirling with dark brown flecks. "Was all of it nonconsensual? Did we rape you, Luna?"

My throat went dry as I slowly shook my head. Because no, it wasn't rape. Was Silas technically forced to fuck me? Yes. But I'd wanted him already, and it wasn't exactly a hardship to receive him. And Edon had offered me a choice with his gaze, asking if he could take my mouth. I'd understood he was trying to give me back a semblance of power by offering me a distraction.

"Your father would have killed me," I added out loud. "I much preferred your method."

"That doesn't exactly make it right," Silas muttered.

"No, it doesn't," I agreed, lifting my hand to palm his

cheek. "But as far as punishments go, I didn't mind this one. I… It wasn't nonconsensual. At least not on my part. It would have happened down by the water. Right?"

Except I didn't know if Silas participated in that chase voluntarily or because Edon had made him. I didn't even know if he was here now because he desired it or if he was following orders.

I frowned. "Did you not…? I mean, do you not…?" I couldn't find the words. So I looked at Edon. "Are you forcing him?"

A startled laugh came from the alpha, the sound low and sexy and causing the hairs along my arms to dance on end. "No, little mate. I may have a bit of sway, but his reactions are all his own."

From what I'd observed, I wasn't so sure about that. "You made him fuck me."

He glanced between us, a frown forming between his eyes. "Are you looking for an apology? Because I don't have one to give. Would I have preferred this all happened under other circumstances? Yes. Do I regret how it all has gone down? Also yes. But what alternative did we have? Oh, I mean, I suppose I could have let the pack continue beating you, Luna, before fucking you." He narrowed his gaze at Silas. "Which, by the way, Silas, would have been rape because she wouldn't have wanted it. Unlike how she felt about you."

Edon paused, his expression hardening.

I wasn't quite sure how to respond to that, and by Silas's silence, I suspected he wasn't either. Fortunately—or perhaps, unfortunately—Edon wasn't finished.

"You both can talk to me all night about choices, or lack thereof. Because I get it. Trust me. I have a father who is hell-bent on making me fail these Alpha Trials, and I suspect he won't shy away from killing me. But rather than complain about it, I'm facing it, because that's the only way we can enact change in this world." He gazed down at me with a knowing gleam. "Surely you understand, Luna. What with Claudette's teachings and all."

My lips parted. "You know about Claudette?" *How?* And why wasn't he livid? She preached about the old times, constantly telling me not to give up the fight and giving me every reason to live. All words that could have gotten her killed if my father had overheard them.

"Yes."

"How?" I demanded. Had I mentioned her in my sleep? After the drugs the other night? In passing and just forgotten?

And then a more disturbing thought hit me. *What if there are spies in Ernest Clan? Has something—*

"Jolene Mason," Edon said, confusing me even more.

"What about him?" I asked, my throat as dry as sandpaper. Jolene wasn't a man I knew personally, but I knew all about him from Claudette. He was a legend among lycans, the male she once loved who ended up with another, and he was one of the strongest alphas in history. At least until the new world.

A fire lit in Edon's gaze, one I recognized as pride. "Jolene's my grandfather."

CHAPTER 21

SILAS

I HAD CLEARLY MISSED SOME SORT OF HISTORY LESSON, because I had no idea who they were talking about. But whatever Edon had just revealed seemed to shock the hell out of Luna. My hand instinctively tightened on her hip, my need to protect her an overwhelming urge I didn't quite know how to dispel.

Claudette was her mentor at Ernest Clan, Edon explained, taking pity on my confusion. *She's a very old friend of my grandfather's. From before the new world.*

What does that mean? I asked, confused by his phrasing.

"They remember what the world was like before Blood Day ever existed. When the Alpha Trials were a time of pride between father and son, when mating actually meant something, and when humans had certain rights." Edon met my gaze. "It's illegal to speak of such things, Silas. But my grandfather has taught me all about the prior world, and I believe Claudette has bestowed the same lessons upon Luna."

"She did," Luna whispered. "Every night. To me and Logan."

Edon nodded. "Well. Then maybe you know me better than you think."

Respect shone bright in her gaze, her lips curling. "That's why you treat Silas as you do. You respect the old customs of the sire bond."

He snorted. "I'm trying, but he's not making it easy on me."

My eyebrows shot up. "Lying right here."

"Trust me, we know." His dark eyes captured mine. "But are you here because I demanded it or because you want to be?"

"You know why I'm here."

"But Luna doesn't." He gestured with his chin. "She seems to think I'm forcing you to lie there. Am I?"

He already knew the answer, so I looked at Luna as I said, "No. I demanded he let me stay so I could check on you and make sure you were all right." I cupped her cheek, needing her to see my sincerity. "I want to be here, Luna."

"But he made you…?" She trailed off, biting her lip.

Yeah. That. "As he said, there wasn't a better alternative." I ran my thumb over her bottom lip, tugging it from her teeth. "I would have chosen a much different setting for the experience, but it happened. And now, I just need to know you're okay."

She swallowed. "I'm okay."

"Good." I bent to brush my mouth against hers. "Next time, I promise it'll be better."

"Next time?" Luna repeated, sounding hopeful.

I smiled against her lips. "Assuming Edon allows it."

The wolf in question wrapped his palm around the back of my neck and squeezed. I lifted my gaze to his, not at all apologetic. While I respected that she was his mate, he'd brought me into this fucked-up game, and I wouldn't turn down another chance to play with her. Nor would I allow her to go on thinking Edon had forced me to touch her. As if I could ever consider such an activity a hardship.

Edon grinned and pulled me into him, his mouth capturing mine. I jolted in surprise, then melted into the embrace. Because fuck, the man knew how to kiss. He oozed dominance, skill, and pure masculine need. It was so different from the femininity of Luna's touch, so much more virile, but equally addictive.

His tongue owned my own, demanding I submit. But I didn't. I kissed him right back, matching his pace, and threaded my fingers through his hair to hold on. Luna squirmed between us, her little gasp an intoxicating addition to the experience. And when her arousal scented the air, we both broke apart to stare down at her, hungry for a taste.

"Mmm, I think she likes watching us," Edon murmured, stretching out beside her on his elbow, his opposite hand sliding down my arm to my hand. "But I want to focus on her. Silas?" He placed my palm on the top of her thigh, his gaze on her face.

"I think she's more than earned our joint attention, yes," I agreed, mimicking Edon's pose on her other side and staring down at her.

Indulging the two of them came so naturally, my movements instinctual and so very, very right. I leaned down to kiss her again, this time sliding my tongue between her lips.

She clutched my shoulder as if needing to hold on for the ride, and maybe she did. Because as soon as I finished kissing her, Edon took over and told me through the sire bond to cup the wet space between her thighs. She jerked beneath my touch and then moaned long and loud into Edon's mouth.

A rush of wetness met my exploring fingers, making it

easy to slip through her slick folds to her entrance and dip inside. She squeezed me in the same way she had my cock, and fuck if the sensual memory of that alone wasn't enough to make me come again.

But this wasn't about me.

This was about Luna.

And for once, I was in complete agreement with Edon's intentions. He drew his lips down her neck to her breasts, allowing me the opportunity to kiss her again. I set a lazy rhythm with my tongue against hers, reveling in the sensation and addictive flavor that was all Luna. "I could do this for hours," I admitted on a breath.

She hadn't let go of my shoulder, her other hand in Edon's hair as he continued suckling her rosy peaks. Mutual appreciation permeated the air, the three of us exuding our own erotic scents that seemed to intermingle and bond to one another. It created the most enthralling mixture, one I wanted to roll in and wear on my coat for the rest of my days.

Edon growled in approval.

Luna sighed.

And I gave in to the urge to kiss her harder, to heighten her arousing perfume for my personal gratification.

She satisfied my craving in spades, as did Edon. I groaned, so fucking hard for them both that I could hardly see straight. But the thought of pleasing her grounded me, two of my fingers lodged deep inside her and stroking that place I knew females enjoyed. Her hips rose in response, little mewling sounds of excitement pouring from her mouth to mine as she crested the edge of an orgasm that wasn't quite ready to rise.

Luna quivered, sweat breaking out across her skin. I nuzzled her cheek and throat, adoring her scent and the racing pulse at her neck.

"More," she whispered. "Please. More."

"Needy little thing," Edon teased, kissing a path down her abdomen to where my hand played below. I shifted to allow him access to her sweet bundle of nerves and smiled as her back bowed off the bed.

My lips captured her scream as her world unraveled. Her slick channel tightened so hard around my fingers I thought she might break them. The memory of her doing that to my shaft had me moaning into her mouth.

Fuck, you're killing me, Edon whispered. *I want this to be about her.*

I do, too, I replied. *But fuck. Her pussy is like liquid heaven, Edon.*

Mmm, I know. I want to lick every inch of her. He punctuated the point by drawing his tongue down to my fingers and back up again, his groan of approval an intensely palpable sound.

Luna's nails dug into my neck, her teeth skimming my lip in a silent demand to strengthen our embrace. *Still topping from the bottom,* I mused, giving in to her because I wanted to. And maybe because I enjoyed her dominance just a little.

Edon's amusement trickled through the bond, his mind focused on the task of making her scream again. I removed my hand and allowed him to take over, my palm skimming a damp trail up her abdomen to her tits. I drew a pattern against each of her nipples, saturating her skin in her arousal, and then lowered my head to lick her clean.

She didn't release my nape, her razor-like claws digging into the base of my scalp and keeping me right where she desired. I growled a low warning in reply, my wolf rising to the surface to take on her sexual challenge.

And my teeth sank into her breast.

"Fuck," she breathed, arching beautifully beneath me.

Did you just mark my mate? Edon asked, a hint of something dark in his tone.

I stilled. *I... yes.* It'd been such a natural move, my inner beast responding to the supple female beneath my mouth. Luna shuddered, her chest rising and falling in quick succession, her lithe form shaking in ecstasy and not distress.

My canines were lodged in her, unmoving. Because I'd frozen in place beneath Edon's comment. Tension lined our link, the alpha rising.

Had I pushed him too far?

I tried to apologize, but the words wouldn't form, not even in a thought.

Because I had *wanted* to bite her. And her response said she'd enjoyed it. But maybe she was too lost to the sensations to realize the gravity of what I'd just done?

Edon lifted his head, eliciting a complaint from Luna's parted lips.

Until she caught the dark gleam of his gaze.

It took considerable effort for me to release her, to shift backward enough to yield. My eyes just automatically dropped, my wolf bowing to his superior.

I swallowed, uncertain and still unable to voice the words I needed to say.

"Edon," Luna whispered, her hand still on my nape.

He said nothing, his superiority a heavy presence between us. Seconds ticked by, my heart threatening to halt in my chest. I didn't know if I should run, roll over, or beg for forgiveness. Yet all I could fucking do was lie here with my palm splayed against Luna's abdomen and my head angled a few inches away from her chest.

Edon leaned down to taste the holes I'd created on her breast, his mouth closing over her skin.

Luna practically came off the bed, a surprised scream

parting her lips as he slid his canines into the same bite. I didn't move, too conflicted and aroused by the sight. Edon rose once more, grabbed me by the throat, and yanked me to him on a snarl.

I jerked as his teeth sank into my lower lip, the bite a punishment and a claim. My blood heated, my lower abdomen tightening. *Fuck.*

Mine, he groaned into my mind. *Both of you are mine.*

CHAPTER 22
LUNA

I couldn't hear a damn thing over the pounding in my ears. The way Edon held Silas now, I couldn't tell if he wanted to kill him, eat him, or fuck him.

It had taken me a moment in my lust-dazed mind to realize what had happened—Silas had bitten me. He'd demanded my submission the way an alpha male did a mate, something Edon had to take as a challenge.

This whole thing was so fucking confusing. Especially the way I *felt* after Silas sank his teeth into my skin. Peace, safety, and a healthy dose of desire had knocked me into a cloud of intense yearning. I'd wanted to give in to him, my wolf already submitting before the true alpha in the room growled. Then my wolf had gone weak in the knees, leaving me breathless between both males.

Were they going to fight or fuck?

I still didn't know.

Not even as Edon bit Silas, eliciting a sharp sound from them both.

And then they were kissing almost violently, their tongues sparring with each other in a war for dominance.

Edon won, his teeth drawing blood—blood that he licked up and swallowed before going in for more.

It was so damn intense, yet sensual, and incredibly arousing.

I released Silas, my hand dipping between my thighs while my other palmed my breast. This was too much. I needed relief. And I needed it now.

Only, both my wrists were pinned above my head in a second as Edon stared down at me. I whimpered and then moaned as Silas's tongue slid through my damp heat.

Oh, wow…

How did they do that? They moved so fast, and— *Fuck!* Silas's mouth sealed over my clit so intensely I couldn't hold back my scream.

Edon took my mouth, his kiss not nearly as harsh as the one he'd given Silas. But still showcasing his control. "Tell us what you want, little mate," he whispered. "Our hands? Our mouths? Our cocks? Tell us how to please you."

Energy hummed through my veins, setting my spirit on fire with an intense *need* that only these men could satisfy. How had I ended up here? A mewling, squirming mess beneath two virile males. I never even wanted to join Clemente Clan, and now I had two reasons to stay.

"Luna," Edon pressed, his lips whispering over mine. "What do you want, sweetheart?"

Everything.

Pleasure.

Fucking.

My hips lifted to meet Silas's mouth, my nipples tightening into impossibly hard peaks. Never had I felt this way, not even beneath my own touch. And I'd already come twice today. These two played my body with an ease that was as unsettling as it was addictive.

Edon growled, the sound a low warning, the alpha demanding a response.

But I had none to give.

I didn't know how to articulate my desire. It was all too new, too overwhelming, for me to wrap my head around. My wolf preened, soaking up the sexual tension and bathing in the heat.

Teeth snagged my lower lip, biting gently in reprimand for ignoring the alpha above me. His dark eyes held mine as Silas slid two fingers into me, scissoring in a way that sent a shudder down my limbs.

Somehow, I was even more turned on than moments ago. My body shook with a craving I couldn't vocalize. Couldn't—

"How many lovers have you taken?" Edon asked softly, his palm circling my throat. "Where have you taken them?"

I swallowed, my vision blinking in and out of focus beneath the onslaught of Silas's tongue and strokes deep inside. Edon's pupils engulfed his irises, his handsome face so close to mine. He wanted to know about my experience, but I didn't know why. Maybe to make sure he didn't push me too far? No. Alphas didn't care about such things. They pillaged and raped without thought.

But not this one, my wolf whispered.

Mmm, Edon was proving to be an anomaly. I just wasn't sure how to trust him after everything I'd learned. Except he had a similar mentor, it seemed.

"Luna." He nipped me again, clearing my vision enough to see the stern lines of his forehead, the knowing gleam in his eyes, and the slight smirk playing over his lips as he pulled back to study me. "I need to know what we can do to you, little mate."

Permission, I translated, somewhat stunned by the realization. The alpha wanted me to lay down the rules so they could play within the boundaries I created.

"You're not at all what I expected," I admitted, palming his cheek and pulling him down for another kiss— one he allowed me to take more than he actually gave. "My experience is limited. But I'm open to, um, exploring."

Another kiss. This one deeper. Domineering. Laced with excitement. "I need more, Luna. How many have been inside you? And where?"

I swallowed, my breath shortening as Silas did something particularly sinful with his tongue. If he kept that up, I would—

He stopped, his exhale hot against my damp skin. "Answer him," he said, whether because he wanted the answer as well or because Edon demanded it through the link, I didn't know. But hearing the command in his tone, coupled with the look from the alpha, I could hardly refuse them.

"Only two, including Silas," I whispered. "And the first was only once—the day of our ceremony."

A glimmer of amusement brightened Edon's gaze. "To deter me from taking you."

"Y-yes."

"And how did that work out for you?" he mused as Silas chuckled against my heated flesh. I gasped as his teeth skimmed my clit and then latched on with a renewed vigor that cascaded waves of pleasure through my being.

"Fuck," I breathed, grabbing the bedsheets on one side while my opposite hand curled around Edon's neck. "So good…" I tried to pull him down to kiss me, but he remained there, observing me.

"Does that mean you don't disapprove of my choice in keeping you?" he wondered aloud, a dark smile in his eyes. "Or would you still prefer I send you home? To be punished by your father?"

"Edon…"

"No. I want an answer, little mate. Tell me how you feel right now, with Silas tonguing your sweet cunt and my palm upon your breast. Would you give it all up? Do you long for another? For the one who fucked you first?"

I nearly laughed at the notion of desiring Volk over Edon and Silas, but I caught the predatory gleam in my alpha mate's gaze. His wolf drove these questions more than the man did, his need to know where my desire lay a key detail to satisfy the lycan alpha hovering above me.

My nails bit into his neck, my eyes narrowing. "Fuck me and I'll tell you who I prefer."

That earned me a growl. "Oh, Luna, you're playing a dangerous game."

"Afraid you won't measure up to the challenge?" I asked, feeling far bolder than I should. Especially when beneath a powerful alpha male. But I couldn't help provoking him, my need to battle one I refused to suppress.

Silas slid his caress to my lower abdomen and kissed a path up to my breast before settling at my side. His blue eyes glowed with approval, his lips—glistening with my arousal—curled at the sides. "Your penchant for topping from the bottom is admirable, little moon." He kissed my cheek and lifted his gaze to the alpha. "She's ready."

"Little moon?" Edon repeated, leaning in to capture Silas's mouth in a long, devastating kiss. "Mmm, you taste amazing."

"I taste like Luna."

"I know." He kissed him again, causing my heart to

skip several beats. They were so close, their joined arousals intoxicating and elevating my own to incredible heights. I squeezed my thighs, seeking friction, only to have them parted as Edon positioned himself between them. The head of his cock nudged my entrance and slid inside with expert ease without breaking his embrace with Silas. Their tongues dueled, Edon's cock elongated, and my pussy wept with unrestrained *need*.

I tightened my hold on Edon's neck, my other arm going around Silas, in this odd embrace of ecstasy. Edon grasped my hips, anchoring himself deep inside me, his size overwhelming and so very *alpha*.

I groaned, my head falling back as I strove to accommodate him, and then gasped as he began to move.

Really, *really* move.

Hard.

Harsh.

Thrusts.

His grip turned bruising, forcing me to take him, as his mouth dropped to my neck. Silas's mouth moved to mine, kissing me soundly, swallowing my whimpers as Edon set a brutal pace.

Mating, I realized. *A male wolf taking his mate.*

I had no choice but to accept it.

And worse, I *wanted* to.

My hips rose to meet his, my instincts taking over, and my kiss with Silas melted from soothing to something feral. He palmed my breast, tweaked my nipple, and palmed me again. And then Edon was kissing me, his tongue dominating and forceful, reminding me of his cock below. Silas moved, his mouth sliding along my shoulder, to Edon and back.

So much sensation.

Intense.

Hot.

Erotic as hell.

Silas kissed me again, then Edon captured my mouth, and then Silas claimed my lips once more. And all the while, an inferno built inside my lower abdomen that begged to be unleashed.

Their touches turned molten, Edon's shaft a brand, his body shifting in a way that stroked my clit even as he met that aching spot deep inside.

And Silas.

Fuck, he was everywhere. His hands, fingers, tongue, and lips. I swore he kissed Edon, too. Licked him. Nipped him. Adding to the insanity of the moment, blending it all together into a tornado of *feeling*.

This… I never could have anticipated *this*.

Teeth scraped my skin, growls rent the air, and heat unlike anything I'd ever felt singed the atmosphere around us.

I moaned both of their names, uncertain of whom I touched, but knew I held them both.

And then I was kissing Silas again, his mouth grounding me as Edon took me to new heights below. God, he could move. So much strength and power, his wolf inching along the surface as he dominated me in the oldest of manners.

I raked my nails down his back, claiming him.

"More," I demanded, arching into him and teetering on the brink of an explosion that would likely destroy me. But I didn't care. I wanted this—wanted them—even if just for tonight.

Or maybe longer.

Something to evaluate later.

Because holy wow, they were kissing again.

My orgasm erupted, shrouding my vision in black and stirring a loud, erotic sound from my throat. I shook beneath the onslaught, my limbs tensing and vibrating, my breaths coming in pants, and through it all, I felt them licking and sucking and stroking.

Edon shifted his weight, leaving me empty, and then Silas was there.

I arched beneath him, groaning as he set a slightly softer pace, easing me through the pleasure and kissing me soundly. Edon knelt beside us, stroking himself lazily with one hand while drawing his opposite palm down Silas's spine.

My breath hitched as I realized his intent.

Silas grinned, glancing up at Edon. "I'm not afraid of you."

"You should be," the alpha replied.

"Maybe," he agreed. "But I'm not."

"Mmm. Another challenge." He tsked. "What am I going to do with the two of you?"

"Fuck us?" I suggested, my voice raspy and well used.

"Oh, that I will definitely be doing. And soon, little mate, it'll be you in the middle. But as Silas is the one with more experience, I'll take his ass first." He punctuated his statement by doing something that made Silas jolt above me.

Readying him, I suspected. *Oh, sweet mother of lycans…*

I'd seen this done before, but never for pleasure. Males did this to harm. Yet Silas seemed accepting, his expression expectant in a hungry way, not a scared one.

His mouth sealed over mine, drawing me back to him, to his cock, to his movements, to his expert touch. I quivered, my body still reeling from the oblivion of moments ago. There was no way I could come again—or so I thought—but his knowing strokes fought to prove me wrong.

Fuck.

This was insane.

How could I possibly fall apart again? Wolves were known for their stamina and sexual prowess, but this was too much.

Although, I'd witnessed it countless times. Not necessarily in the females, but definitely in the males. They were insatiable, their drives overwhelming and unstoppable.

Yet I'd been the one to come multiple times. Not Edon. He'd only orgasmed once down my throat earlier, then faked a second.

Silas groaned as Edon positioned himself behind him, the two of them joining in a way I couldn't see but felt beneath their weight.

"Fuck," Silas whispered, his head dropping to my neck. As the sound that followed wasn't one of agony, I assumed Edon had used some form of lubricant. But he certainly wasn't gentle. He drove in hard, Silas receiving him with a grunt, his own cock pistoning into me at the same time.

I marveled at the intimate dance, the way our bodies locked together in such a unique fashion that guaranteed all our pleasure.

Edon's words replayed in my mind.

And soon, little mate, it'll be you in the middle.

"Ohhh," I moaned out loud, the idea of it heating me from head to toe.

Because yes. Yes, I wanted to experience that. And if the expression on Silas's face was anything to go by, I'd enjoy it immensely. He kissed me again, unleashing all his emotions with his tongue and forcing me to swallow each one.

Edon chose our pace, somehow angling himself in a way that didn't crush Silas into me even as he gave in to his more violent urges. Growls, groans, and words of approval spiraled between the three of us.

So different from what I'd observed in the past.

This wasn't about dominance—not entirely, anyway—but about mutual gratification. Edon whispered his lips across Silas's neck, his gaze capturing and holding mine. I reached up to brush my knuckles across his cheek, then returned Silas's kiss and lost myself again in the rapture of the moment.

Silas groaned, the intensity seeming to rip him in two as Edon propelled us into a frenzy. I lifted my hips, touched them both, nipped at Silas, watched Edon's expressions, and felt the ball of liquid fire churning once more. Until I couldn't see or think or move.

And I was falling.

Falling over a cliff into dark, all-consuming waters of ecstasy.

I felt Silas stiffen, heard his sounds of approval as he followed me. His teeth punctured my neck. Or maybe it was Edon who bit me. I really couldn't tell, too overwhelmed and engrossed in my liquid heaven. But I *felt* Edon come, his roar one I was sure everyone in the territory heard. It vibrated through Silas and directly to my heart, shadowing me in a protective layer I accepted without thought.

Everything just felt so right.

Complete.

Whole.

I refused to fight. Refused to think.

Instead, I closed my eyes, drunk on the sensations floating through my body, the tingling of my limbs, and the overall satisfaction warming my insides.

This was a life I could enjoy. At least for a little while.

I allowed it to follow me into my dreams. To ease me into a state of being I'd never before felt.

A state of happiness.

Of peace.

Of harmony.

Of home.

CHAPTER 23

EDON

Luna slept peacefully beside me, her cheeks flushed, her hair tousled, and her lips swollen. Silas rested on her other side, his palm on her hip and his chest pressed up against her back.

Protection radiated from him, his eyes closed but his body alert.

I'd never spent much time with a human turned lycan. Most were too weak to survive. Silas, however, proved all the odds wrong. He thrived in his new form, already rivaling the strength of those three times his age. A natural-born enforcer, at least according to my instincts.

And he was mine.

Everyone in the pack assumed him to be a regular mutt without much skill. I wanted to keep it that way, at least for now. Not only would it give me a playing card for the right moment, but it would allow him to continue to grow and master his skills.

It also provided me with additional security for Luna.

Whatever was happening here between the three of us defied the natural order. Alphas mated other alphas. Yet somehow Silas had inserted himself in the bonds meant for Luna and me alone. I sensed his presence deep inside, his earlier bite a mark that claimed Luna as his even though I'd already identified her as mine.

And when I'd bitten him, something additional snapped into place beyond our sire bond.

I needed to go to my grandfather, to ask him what the hell was happening. Not just between the three of us, but with the pack in general.

Like how my father had framed Luna for Bianca's murder.

That shouldn't be possible.

"What about the vampire?" Silas asked softly, his eyes still closed but his mind clearly attuned to mine. It seemed he'd finally realized the bond went both ways. Or maybe I'd telegraphed loudly. Either way, he was awake and listening and thinking. "The vampire we found smelled only of pack, not a specific culprit. Did your father orchestrate that as well?"

Light blue irises flickered at me as he lazily lifted his lids, his expression one of serene comfort from our fuck fest over an hour ago.

When I told him I wanted to take his ass, he hadn't even flinched. His studies had included such activities, but I knew from his mind that I'd taken the most care I could with him despite my harsher thrusts. I'd actually made it enjoyable—something that had shocked us both.

Because the whole experience was new for me.

I'd fucked females in a variety of ways, but never a male, and I doubted I'd ever desire another in such a manner. However, Silas? Yeah, I intended to do that again. And again. And again.

And eventually, I'd take Luna, too.

"You'll need to warm her up a bit more before that can

happen," Silas mused, proving to be inside my head. His lips curled. "And what a fascinating place your head is."

I snorted. "I can block you." Mental walls were something my grandfather had taught me how to build. He said they would be necessary for when I gained access to the pack psyche—which would happen as a result of my ascension. No one would be able to just pop into my head, though. Not like Silas, anyway. Or Luna when we completed the bond. Those connections would always be unique.

"Maybe, but you won't," Silas replied, referring to my threat to block him.

"But I could."

He smiled. "Sure."

His arrogance should have irritated me. Instead, it merely amused me. Probably because I was much too relaxed to be annoyed. "Regarding the vampire, I think you're right," I said, returning to the topic I'd been mulling over before my brain fled downward to my dick.

"Did I tell you I smelled more the other day?" Silas asked, his brow furrowing. "Or I smelled something. It was before I caught Luna running. She distracted me from it."

"No, you didn't mention it." I frowned. "Where was it?"

"Out near the border, in the marsh."

Meaning it was in Clemente territory, just outside of where the elite members of our pack resided. There were hundreds of wolves within our borders, but only a handful of carefully selected lycans lived at headquarters. Everyone else resided outside of the marsh areas in run-down towns or other patches of wilderness. "Have you smelled them anywhere else?"

"Prior to the dead one? No. But I haven't been out there recently."

Luna began to stir between us, her lips parting on an adorable little protest that said her body wasn't ready to wake yet. Given the events of today, I wasn't surprised. She'd already recovered from the beating—mostly because the pack hadn't been given enough time to do any severe damage. But sexually, Silas and I had exhausted her.

Something I would not apologize for.

Not when she wore the results of our affection so fucking well.

We should run the borders in the morning, Silas said, switching to our link.

I need to see my grandfather first.

Jolene. He seemed to be pondering the name, having clearly recalled it from earlier. *Why haven't I seen him?*

He doesn't socialize with my father's circle often. However, he lives nearby. I'll introduce you soon.

Surprise sparked in Silas's gaze. He didn't comment out loud, but I sensed his quiet pleasure at the potential opportunity. Nothing we were doing here was considered normal. Me—the alpha heir—introducing a newbie mutt to a former pack alpha? Yeah, that didn't happen in our society.

Yet something told me my grandfather would more than approve of my breaking that unspoken rule.

Can you stay with Luna tomorrow while I visit with my grandfather? I asked.

Silas grinned at me. *A request instead of a task? I need to let you fuck me more often.*

I scoffed at that. *I don't need you to let me do anything. A simple demand and you'll go down on all fours like a good little wolf.*

He arched a brow. *Yeah? Now who's acting arrogant?*

I nearly laughed. *We both know it's true. Just as we both know you'll guard our* little moon *tomorrow.*

"She's *my* little moon," he whispered, his arm sliding around her possessively. "And your little mate."

"And what nicknames shall we give each other?" I wondered out loud, pitching my voice low so as not to disturb the sleeping beauty between us.

Alpha, he taunted.

Omega, I returned.

Not the most original of names. But then again, maybe we didn't need any.

"Maybe Luna and I can run the border tomorrow together, see what we can find, while you meet with Jolene," he suggested quietly, proving to me his worth as a potential enforcer.

Silas's ability to focus appealed to me, his mind sharp and on task even during intimate moments. I supposed he had to be constantly analyzing situations given everything he'd survived over the years.

"I could bring her up to speed," he added. "Help us all prepare for whatever trial is next."

I nodded. "Yes." We were approaching the upcoming full moon. Whatever task my father meant to throw at me next would be the harshest. Because he was running out of time to incapacitate me. So either it'd be something to take me out of the running, or—

"He's going to try to kill Luna," Silas finished for me.

Because I couldn't ascend without a mate.

And my father had made it pretty clear these last few days that he saw her as expendable.

"It's not going to happen," I said.

"I know," Silas agreed.

I held his gaze for a long moment, noted the possession flaring in his pupils, and nodded again. "I know," I repeated. "Because he'll have to get through both of us." Something my father would never anticipate.

Oh, he might try to take me down.

But Silas? He'd never even consider it.

And that would be his ultimate failure.

Get some sleep, Silas whispered. *You need it more than I do. I'll keep watch.*

It seemed odd to rely on another, having spent my entire existence looking out for myself at every turn. However, for once, I obeyed another, and allowed my eyes to close.

Because he was right—I needed rest.

Good night, Edon.

Good night, Silas.

CHAPTER 24

LUNA

Warm. I snuggled into the source of my happiness, content with the heat blanketing my skin. A chuckle graced the air, deep and low and deliciously amused, followed by a kiss against my forehead.

"You appear well rested, little moon," Silas mused, his hand drifting up and down my spine.

I stretched against him on a sigh. "Mm-hmm."

Light peeked in through the drapes, illuminating Silas's features as I opened my eyes. He grinned down at me, the picture of ease. "Good morning, beautiful." He glanced at the window, his smile growing. "Well, afternoon."

"What time is it?" I wondered out loud, searching for a clock.

"Time for lunch and a run," he replied, nuzzling my cheek. "Edon wants us to check the borders."

"For what?"

"Odd scents," he replied, sliding out from under me. "I'll explain over lunch."

I grabbed his nape and pulled him back to me for a

long, indulgent kiss. Mmm, he tasted like peppermint and smelled of soap. His wet hair confirmed he'd taken a shower while I slept, but he hadn't bothered to put on any clothes. Something my hands were very grateful for as I explored his warm, muscular torso.

Fuck food.

I wanted to lick and taste him instead.

My wolf came alive with the idea, her fur smoothing out beneath my skin as I gave in to the urge to sink my nails into his nape while my opposite hand slid downward.

Silas smiled against my mouth.

"Careful or Edon will be jealous," he warned as my touch went south to his growing arousal.

Firm. Hot. Smooth. Perfection.

"Where is he?" I wondered aloud, referring to the alpha male who had awoken all these forbidden ideas inside my head. If this was all just a way to prime me as his mate, it'd more than worked. Because I wanted more. *So much more.*

"Edon's meeting with his grandfather," Silas replied, stretching out on top of me. "He left an hour ago."

I ran my tongue across his lower lip, my legs parting around his shifting hips. "Does he know we're awake?"

"He does."

"Are you talking to him right now?" I asked, my damp folds embracing Silas's hard cock and sliding against him in invitation.

He groaned, his forehead falling to mine. "I am."

"Mmm." I kissed him again, sighing as he entered me slowly all the way to the hilt. I didn't even need foreplay, my body already strung tight just from waking up beside him. Which was insane after everything that happened last night, all the orgasms ripped from my body.

But wow. I was addicted now. And I refused to stop.

Silas kissed me deeply, his hips setting a lazy rhythm that teased my senses. I squeezed him with my walls and wrapped my legs around his waist to encourage him to go faster—*harder*—but he maintained the same pace. Almost as if he was trying to taunt me.

I scratched my nails down his back, eliciting a hiss from him. He bit my lower lip in reprimand, then smiled. "Eager, little moon."

"Fuck me."

"I am."

I nearly growled. "You're playing."

"Yes," he agreed. "But still technically fucking you." He punctuated the point by thrusting deep. My back bowed off the bed in response, earning me a chuckle from him.

"Does Edon know you're inside me?" I asked, grasping his shoulders as he repeated the motion.

"Yes." He nibbled my jaw and pressed a kiss to my throat. "He says to make you earn it." His tongue traced a path up to my ear, his teeth snagging on the lobe. "And to remind you that he has a task for us to complete."

"Tell him I don't follow orders well," I panted, tightening my thighs around Silas's waist.

"Oh, he knows," Silas replied, his words a whisper against my ear. "But he doesn't mind, darling Luna. Do you want to know why?"

The dark provocation in his tone sent a delicious shiver down my spine. "Yes," I admitted, swallowing.

"Because he enjoys sensual punishment." Silas pulled out abruptly, forcing my legs to unwind, and flipped me before I could even begin to react.

So fast.

So strong.

So—oh, dear wolf—mine.

He slammed back inside me so harshly that I screamed and then moaned beneath the onslaught of pleasure that followed. "*Fuck*," I breathed, shocked and incredibly *hot*.

"That's what you want, right?" He growled the words against the back of my neck, his body covering mine as he drove into me with far more force than he did last night. His wolf clearly craved dominance. And mine appeared to adore submission, something I would have claimed to be impossible just a week ago.

"Silas," I hissed, shaking beneath him, my body torn between torment and ecstasy. *This* was a punishment on its own, and one hell of a way to wake up.

"Edon says to tell you that he plans to take your ass later," he murmured, his words warm against my sensitive nape. "He wants you writhing and wet and begging between us. Which is why he's telling me to stop, Luna. To leave you panting and wanting. Should I listen, little moon? Or should I play rebel, too?"

He didn't pause but picked up the pace.

"Don't," I said, referring to his threat to halt. "Keep going." I didn't care at all that I sounded desperate, because I was. Shit, the way his cock hit my insides, I thought I might combust, and I would if he withdrew again. "Silas..." His name tumbled out of me on a moan, eliciting a deep sound of approval from him.

"Yeah, that's what I thought," he replied, threading his fingers through my hair and twisting my head back at an angle that nearly hurt. And kissed me. Hard. His dominance complete as he seated himself inside me over and over, his tongue matching the thrusts below.

Domineering, all-encompassing, addicting.

I no longer recognized myself.

Didn't understand who I was becoming.

But I lived for this moment alone.

The stirring ache tightening my insides, sending liquid lava through my veins, and shooting off stars behind my eyes.

My orgasm crested but didn't peak.

My legs quivered.

My breaths turned to gasps.

So, so close.

Right there.

"Ohh," I groaned, shattering on a wave of intensity that shook me to my very soul.

Silas followed on a snarl, his teeth sharp against my neck, puncturing in a bite neither of us should indulge in. And yet, I accepted it. My wolf bowed down, acknowledging the stronger male and preening from his claim.

It left me shaking beneath him, my body a mess of rapturous quakes and agonized bliss.

"Fuck." The word was a puff of air against my neck from Silas, his heavy mass trembling in time with mine.

I nearly laughed, the puzzle we'd created with our limbs one that would take some careful untangling. We'd come together in a frenzy, the wolves taking over in the last few moments and driving our coupling.

Just like last night.

Only slightly less overwhelming without Edon.

But still far more amazing than anything I could have expected.

What are we doing? I wanted to ask. Except Silas probably didn't know. Just as I doubted Edon did either.

This was uncharted territory.

Alphas were destined to mate other alphas. One male and one female. Not a trio. Yet that didn't feel right. Edon and Silas were too connected, too *something*. I couldn't identify exactly what, but the idea of taking one over the other felt wrong.

Maybe time would fix it.

Although, I doubted that.

If anything, time would only deepen this strange link between the three of us.

Silas twisted and yanked me into him, kissing me thoroughly while gathering me in his arms. "Time for a shower, little moon. We can play more later. With Edon."

I shivered as he stood and effortlessly lifted me with him. "Is he mad?"

He smiled. "Scared?"

"No."

"Neither am I." He carried me into the oversized marble bathroom and set me on the counter, his arms blocking me in as he gripped the stone on either side of my thighs. "But he's amused, not angry. He knew we'd defy him. And now he's eager to punish us both. So thanks for that."

I smirked. "Not my fault."

"Oh, it was entirely your fault. I was ready for lunch and a run, but now I have to shower again." He pushed away to turn on the water, then glanced over his shoulder. "Now get your ass in here so I can fuck you again before we eat."

"My fault, huh?" I repeated, laughing. "Seems you're just as *hungry* as I am."

"Or maybe I'm just making sure the experience is worth my while." He waggled his brows and gave me a playful smile that warmed my insides.

This was a new side of Silas, a relaxed one.

I rather liked it.

"Fucking, food, and a run," I contemplated aloud. "My

kind of day." Not that I had a lot of experience with the fucking part. But between Edon and Silas, I'd be well educated very, very soon.

I sort of expected Edon to come barging in at any moment and demand to join us, but he never did. Instead, he remained in mental contact with Silas throughout our shower and spurred us on with a few dark promises of what he intended to do to us later. By the time we finished, we were ready to go again, but Silas insisted on eating and going for a run.

Once he explained why, I agreed.

I made us a few quick sandwiches—to replenish our depleted energy reserves—and then led the way to the outside boundaries to see what my nose could detect.

We went in wolf form because it was faster, and my sense of smell improved on all fours.

Silas trailed behind me, his much bigger size impressive for a human turned lycan. *Mutt* seemed too degrading a term for him. And *newbie* was too soft.

Maybe *changeling* would work.

My nose twitched, drawing me from my musings. Silas joined me, his focus already following the direction of the scent. He must have sensed it before me.

Another sign of his abnormal strength as a changeling.

He took off toward the scent with me on his heels, the stench of death growing with each step as we hit the boundary crossing.

I half expected to find another dead body, like they had last week.

But there was nothing.

Silas did a circle, his muzzle in the air, and snorted.

We'd found the strongest point, but there was no sign of a vampire.

He took a few steps out into the field, then turned and went the other direction, only to snort again and look at me.

I shook out my coat, giving him a negative on tracking, and started along the boundary in the opposite direction. But the scent lessened until it disappeared, sending me back the other way to the same spot.

This doesn't make any sense.

I began the shift, which triggered Silas to follow. When he was standing before me in full human form—something that took him slightly longer than it did me—I repeated my words out loud. "Someone, somehow, is fucking with pack and vampire scents," I added.

"Like they did with yours at Bianca's death site." He glanced around, his palm holding the back of his neck. "And the body we found reeked of pack, not a single culprit."

"It has to be his father, or someone high up. But I don't know how they're doing it."

"Neither does Edon," he replied, his lips flat. "He was supposed to ask his grandfather about it. Hopefully, he's learning something useful, because he's been silent for about an hour now."

I frowned. "Silent?"

"Yeah."

"Is that normal?"

He lifted a shoulder. "Edon only talks to me when he has something to say, which is more often than not, but I imagine he's busy right now."

Fair enough. I studied the field and then the terrain back to the main camp and pinched my lips to the side. "Why would a vampire play this close to the heart of the clan territory? If we were near the Silvano or Lilith Region borders, I'd understand it. But we're several hundreds of miles from the closest vampire stronghold. Hanging out here is an invitation for trouble."

Vampires and lycans played nice for the Blood Alliance, but they weren't exactly allies. They merely split everything fifty-fifty and ruled in their own ways within the boundaries of international law. Beyond that, they were not required to be friends or business partners. Instead, the vampires tended to make business arrangements with their fellow undead, while lycans stuck to pack trades.

"It's odd," Silas agreed, walking along the border. "Let me show you where we found the body. Maybe you'll pick up on something we didn't."

Doubtful, but I agreed anyway.

We jogged in human form to the spot about two miles away, but the scents were all clear of death.

"Edon disposed of the remains," Silas explained.

"He did a good job, because I can't pick up even a trace of it."

Silas nodded. "Yeah. He made sure of that."

We hunted around and found nothing.

I finally shook my head. "Everything seems fine here. Normal, even."

"Yeah." He blew out a breath. "I guess we'll—"

His knees buckled beneath him, sending him crashing to the ground on an agonized cry that rang harshly in my ears.

"Silas!" I collapsed with him, my hands going to his shoulders as my eyes roamed over him, searching for the source of his pain. But he appeared unmarred, his skin as tan and taut as moments ago.

But he held his heart as if someone had shot him there and fell to his side, his legs tucking into the fetal position.

"*Fuck...*," he wheezed, tears leaking from the edges of his eyes. "Edon," he finally managed, his voice hoarse, his body shuddering violently. "Something's... wrong... with Edon..."

CHAPTER 25
SILAS

It took far too long to shake off the initial burn in my chest.

And then I was running on all fours.

My body ached, my ears vibrated from the intense beating of my heart, and my vision blurred. But I had to get to him, to help him, to save—

No! he shouted through my mind.

I ignored him, my instincts pushing me over the earth with Luna hot on my tail. Our paws raced in sequence, her lithe form a strong presence at my back as we hit the outskirts of the main village.

They'll kill you, Silas, Edon barked into my thoughts. *Stop!*

I shook him off, but something in that command made me trip just behind one of the lodges. Luna landed on top of me, winded and dazed from my misstep.

It's another trial, Edon said quickly. *If you or Luna interferes, they'll use it as an excuse to kill you both. This is about allies. I can't... have... allies.*

The way he broke off at the end had my heart racing

all over again. He'd clearly exerted significant effort into yelling at me. Which meant I needed to *hear* him.

"What is it?" Luna asked, already in human form again.

I forced myself to shift, my breaths coming in pants from the harsh run and forced swiftness with which I changed back and forth between wolf and man.

Edon's link wavered, his consciousness coming in and out.

"He doesn't want us to interfere," I whispered, swallowing. "Says it's a test about allies."

"What sort of...?" Luna glanced sharply at the trees, taking a defensive position at my side.

My brow furrowed, my senses on alert, seeking whatever had captured her interest. *There*, my wolf spotted. A slight flicker of movement in the trees.

Luna growled low, the sound far more ominous than anything I'd ever heard from her.

And the intruder responded with a chuckle. "Claudette certainly outdid herself," a deep voice said as a male with silver hair and dark eyes stepped silently onto the path. "And Edon is right, Silas. This is about allies. If you go to him right now, they'll expect you to join. Or worse, they'll see how long you can last."

"Until what?" I demanded. I didn't need to demand his identity. His resemblance to my sire told me his identity— Edon's grandfather.

"A strength test," Luna said, her voice hoarse.

"Yes," the old man confirmed.

"What the hell is a strength test?" I mean, I understood the gist of it by the name. "What does it entail?"

"They beat the alpha until he's unconscious, just to see how much he can take," Luna whispered.

The elderly lycan nodded. "And knowing my son, he'll add both of you to the mix, just for fun."

"To remove all of Edon's allies from the board," Luna added. "Perhaps permanently." She canted her head, her gaze astute. "You're Jolene."

The elderly male smiled. "No one has called me by that name in many moons, child. But yes, I am." He glanced sharply to his left, all traces of amusement dying. "You must go before they find you."

Luna followed his gaze, her face whitening. "They'll hunt me."

"Silas knows a place." He arched a brow at me. "Don't you?"

The cabin, I realized. "But what about Edon?"

"Don't let my looks fool you, boy." His grin was all teeth, resembling the wolf beneath the skin. "I'm still an alpha, and that's my grandson in there."

Howls from the heart of the village sounded, sending Luna back two paces. "They're coming."

"Go," Jolene urged. "I'll distract them."

He unbuttoned his shirt, revealing a torso that displayed his strength, and dropped his trousers to begin his shift.

Luna grabbed my arm before I could watch the transformation, power flooding the air.

Holy shit.

"Silas!" Luna hissed, tugging on me. "If they find me—"

Another howl sounded, this one far too close.

And it didn't come from Jolene.

I fell to my knees, transitioning as fast as my body allowed. But it wasn't quick enough. Three wolves stepped around the corner, their gazes hungry as they locked on Luna midshift. She snarled, her hackles rising, and then

Jolene stepped in front of her with a growl, his large size a startling sight.

His low growl forced the other wolves to heel, their gazes dropping from the clear alpha before them.

I stood captivated by the show of dominance.

This is Edon's future. What he's capable of even now.

And yet his pack was beating him to a pulp. To what? Test his endurance?

I could *feel* his agony through the bond, his pain a visceral force of nature that called to me to find him and help him. But I also felt his reluctance, the warning in his mind to stay away. To protect Luna at all costs. To let him endure this trial alone.

Because if we came for him, his father would beat us, too.

And unlike Edon, we wouldn't survive.

A nip to my ear forced my attention to the side where Luna stared at me with an imploring expression. Fear radiated from her, more howls assaulting the air as someone announced our position to the pack.

Living as a lycan was no better than being a human.

They were animals, thriving on the pain of others and demanding submission in the cruelest of ways.

Even the strongest among them was punished just for his position. Beat down by his brethren to prove his place at the top.

Why the fuck would anyone allow that?

For the same reason I fought in the Immortal Cup. Edon endured their bullshit to secure his place at the top, to ascend to the only position where he could effect change.

These tests went so far beyond his fate. This was about restructuring the Clemente Clan. And if Edon had to, he'd put that above everyone else in his life—including me and Luna.

That was why he needed us to run.

He couldn't protect us tonight. We were on our own. But he'd left me with the keys to our safety. Such a clever male, always one step ahead.

My heart warmed with a respect I never expected to feel, one that had me meeting Luna's gaze and tilting my head in a *follow me* gesture.

Her relief was palpable as I took off into the woods, my paws pounding over the earth in a pattern meant to confuse anyone following us. Because no way was I leading them to Edon's refuge.

Edon's approval sang in my blood, his mind filled with gratitude even as his anguish violated our link. *Don't let those bastards kill you,* I said.

It'll take more than a beating, Omega, he whispered, his mental voice disturbingly soft.

I mean it, Alpha. We're not done yet.

Amusement met my words, but he no longer spoke. He seemed to be reserving his energy. As long as I felt him, I wouldn't worry.

Over an hour later, I finally led us to the small cabin outside the borders. Luna panted heavily behind me, her eyes alight with life and wonder and awe. She'd obviously enjoyed the run, or perhaps the adrenaline born from the escape.

I shifted near the door and opened it for her. "It's not as nice as his main place, but it's comfortable."

Oddly, the familiar surroundings held a hint of nostalgia for me. I'd barely spent any time here, nor had it been long since my last visit. Yet so much had occurred over the last few days that it felt like ages since I last set foot in this place.

However, the kitchen was still well stocked, and all the amenities worked.

Luna ventured into the main bedroom, likely trailing Edon's scent, and came out a few minutes later wearing an old T-shirt. She tossed me a pair of shorts that I put on while she rummaged through the cupboards.

Then she stilled, her shoulders tightening.

"Luna?" I slowly walked up behind her, placing my palm against her back. She trembled beneath my touch and turned into me. Whatever excitement she'd felt from the run had died a swift death. Now she stood before me with a posture that radiated defeat.

"We ran," she whispered.

"Yes."

She swallowed, looking up at me. "We ran like cowards."

"No, we did what Edon wanted us to do." I palmed her cheek. "They would have hurt us, Luna."

"We could have fought," she argued. "But we didn't even try. Fuck, I didn't even think to try. I just... fled." She blinked. "I... What if...?"

I folded my arms around her, tucking her head beneath my chin. "It's not our time to fight." *Yet*, I added mentally. Because one day—a day I suspect would be soon—we would fight. But not tonight. "We helped Edon by not being there." At least that was what I gathered from the bond.

"But what if he's wrong?" She pulled back to stare up at me. "What if his father takes it too far?"

"Then we have to rely on Jolene to help him," I said, unnerved by the notion of relying on anyone other than myself.

"Can...?" She paused, her throat working. She cleared it twice before continuing. "Can you feel him?"

"Yes." My connection to Edon thrived even beneath the pain. "He's conserving his strength." A plan had formed in the alpha's mind, one I couldn't quite define. But I knew he was okay. "I think the wolves are searching for us." Because there appeared to be a lull in the trial, some sort of waiting game that Edon was using to his advantage to heal.

She straightened her spine, a flash of challenge overtaking the uncertainty in her gaze. "I'll fight them if they find us."

"They won't find us here." I was certain of it, not just because of my evasiveness on the run, but because I trusted Edon. He kept this place for a reason. A safe house for times when he needed to hide—and now was one of those times. "But we should prepare just in case."

She nodded, slipping free of my arms. "Traps."

"Traps?" I repeated.

Another nod. "Yes. We'll smell them, but if we set alarms out in the fields, we'll hear them, too. And it'll give us enough time to ready ourselves."

Sounded like a good use of our time. "Okay. I'll help."

"No." She glanced at me. "You need to gather medical supplies. Edon is going to need us to nurse him back to health. So keep in touch with him, then bring him here when he's ready. Meanwhile, I'll prep the grounds."

I nearly smiled at her bossiness, intrigued by the alpha female coming out to play. But an amused reply wouldn't be all that appropriate considering our situation. So I settled on saying, "Okay. I'll keep talking to him."

"Good." She seemed a little more herself now that she'd found a measure of control. "Tell him we're waiting for him."

"I will."

"And that we're not going down without a fight."

"He knows that, Luna."

"He doesn't," she replied, meeting my gaze. "But he will." Something appeared to snap inside her, a resolve of sorts, one she didn't quite have before. I hadn't noticed it was missing because I didn't know to look, but I caught it now.

She no longer wanted to run.

Luna had finally accepted her mate.

And she would do whatever she needed to do to keep him.

My heart panged a little at the realization, my place firmly on the outside of their strengthening bond. Alas, now wasn't the time to worry about myself or my irrational feelings.

I had a sire to save. And for whatever reason, he'd put me in charge of the well-being of his mate. I wouldn't let him or Luna down.

I know, he whispered, the words a stroke against my heart. *I'll see you soon.*

CHAPTER 26

LUNA

I kicked a pile of dirt and snorted as it sent dust flying everywhere. This vegetation was so different from my homeland. A lot warmer, for one. And dry.

Although, I suspected the latter was due to a lack of rain.

Not that I cared about the weather.

Or even about the lack of water.

No, my mind was on Edon and the fact that I had run. It'd been second nature, my terror at being thrown into a circle with him overriding my senses.

And turning me into a fucking coward.

I growled low in my throat. It wasn't like me to flee. I always fought. Even strutting into the damn mating ceremony, I'd fought in my own way.

But the notion of having my strength tested by Walter and his men had locked me up in a manner I wasn't accustomed to. Visions of how they assaulted me after I punched Bianca, and the comments and licentious desires voiced during the punishment ring… I shuddered again just thinking about it all.

Was it really any wonder I'd wanted to escape?

Hadn't that been my goal since Edon marked me as his?

Yet arriving at the safe house with Silas had awoken a whole new field of thought. I'd run to save myself, something a week ago I would have respected. But leaving Edon to suffer now felt wrong. I'd seen too much of the male beneath the alpha veneer and had heard the whisper of his true intentions in the way he spoke about the past and future.

He reminded me of Logan.

And I would never leave Logan behind.

Another snarl worked its way out of my muzzle, the sound far more ferocious than I felt.

Everything had changed so quickly. My initial thoughts of running to rogue territories where I could fend for myself were gone in an instant. And behind, I felt a connection to a male I was born to hate.

All my life, I'd been promised to a future alpha with two primary purposes in mind—to mate an alpha female and force her to carry his offspring.

End of discussion.

No choice.

My life over before it even began.

Yet Edon wasn't the male I expected. He didn't force me to do anything. Not really, anyway. He minded my wants and needs, didn't push me outside of my boundaries, and clearly valued my protection.

Hence, Silas.

Oh, but that added a whole new layer of complexity to this entire situation. Because I liked Silas just as much as I liked Edon, but in an entirely different manner.

Both were dominant. No question. They desired my submission and would do what they had to do to acquire it.

With Edon, I expected that. Silas, however, was a surprise. My alpha inclinations and purebred genetics should make it easy to best him. Yet, not only did he put up one hell of a fight against me but he also *won*.

And it wasn't a result of my weakness.

I could take on wolves twice my size.

No, Silas had a strength to him that few others possessed. And I suspected it was born of years and years of having to fight to survive. It marked him as similar, but different, to Edon.

Silas also had a softness to him that Edon lacked. He was slightly more intuitive and constantly analyzing his surroundings and choices. Edon, too, contemplated his actions, but he never wavered in a decision and his word was law. Rather than debate it, Silas seemed to cave, deferring to the stronger of the pair rather than trying to rebuke him.

The dynamic between them was intoxicating and hot as hell.

It left me wanting them both equally, unable to choose, and that stirred a whole world of problems. Because, eventually, whatever game Edon was playing would die. He'd told me from the beginning that none of his wolves would ever fuck me. Yet Silas had done so more than once now without consequence.

Sure, Edon had allowed it. Twice. But there was no way he'd continue to accept it. Unless he shared me to help tame his possessive instincts? It was frowned upon for alphas to display proprietorial tendencies. Maybe Edon was just preparing himself for future social requirements involving mate sharing?

I frowned.

No. This went deeper. I could feel it in my bones, and Edon didn't seem all that eager to comply with societal requirements. He'd kept the other wolves from touching me more than once now. Except for Silas, whom he appeared quite eager to have join our nest.

Maybe *too* eager.

What if Edon prefers Silas? I stopped in my tracks, the moon bright overhead. *Didn't Edon say Silas gave him the best head of his life?* I performed for him just last night, and he'd said nothing, had even faked a second orgasm down my throat.

Because I wasn't as good?

It'd been my second time—Silas being the first—so of course it wasn't as good.

I shivered. Competition always heated my blood, but in this case, it chilled me. Because I didn't want to compete with Silas for Edon's affection. If he were anyone else, hell yes, I'd fight to the end. But not Silas.

Shaking out my coat, I continued walking, needing a new train of thought. This had just gotten too deep and confusing. I should be concerned about Edon's well-being, wondering if he would even survive that death trap, not thinking about my sexual skills—or lack thereof—and comparing myself to Silas.

Selfish, I thought to myself. *And stupid.*

Just like running.

Ugh. Part of me wanted to sprint back to camp to find Edon, but I knew it would be a death sentence. He was likely too hurt at this point to fight, and it'd be me against a pack of bloodthirsty wolves.

Who were beating the shit out of their future leader.

Why was this even acceptable behavior?

So degrading and—

My ears twitched, the sound of a branch snapping alerting me to the presence of another. Someone strong. His aura blasted mine, something that, I realized a second too late, had been done on purpose to grab my attention.

Jolene stood about ten feet away holding an unconscious Edon in his arms.

I startled, shocked that he'd managed to get so close to me in human form without my noticing. But then again, he was an alpha male for a reason. And he'd lived a very, very long life.

"He's breathing, but barely," he said, his voice grim. "Walter was going to kill him."

Had I been in human form, my lips would have parted. Murdering an alpha heir wasn't unheard of, but it was rare. Most alphas didn't want to give up their place to their offspring, yet our circle of life required it.

Walter must have thought he could just make another male. Given the mental state of his current mate, however, I suspected that would be impossible. Unless he found another alpha female to fuck.

Someone like… me. My eyes rounded. Oh. Fuck. No.

The expression on Jolene's face suggested he'd just read my mind. "Come," he demanded. "He needs the kind of healing only a mate can provide."

Claudette had spoken of this, the rare connection between lycans where strength could be given and borrowed for healing. I suspected Edon tapped into it the other night to help me after Walter and his men had beat me.

And now he needed the same from me.

No. He required a whole hell of a lot more.

Which is why he didn't want us at the ring, I realized as I followed Jolene. *Edon knew he'd need me for this.*

However, I had to be willing. So it went far deeper than preserving his only vitality source. Edon relying on me to help him in a time of need required significant trust. I could so easily walk away now and let him die. But he'd put his faith in me not to. And somehow, knowing that only made me move faster.

I didn't want to prove him wrong.

I wanted to make him proud.

To assist in the only way I could.

By being his mate in every fashion of the word.

"They demanded he reveal your location," Jolene informed me as we approached the cabin. "But he refused. Walter claimed he'd chosen you over his loyalty to the pack, and they annihilated him for it." He shook his head, a low growl coming from his chest. "My son has twisted this clan into a pack of asinine heathens."

I snorted my agreement even while my heart skipped a beat. Oh, he'd hidden me from Walter to protect himself just as much as me. I understood that. But this was the third time he'd safeguarded me from the horror of his pack.

Silas met us at the door, aware of our approach, his expression grim as I shifted back into human form. He handed me the shirt I'd abandoned on the front stoop and looked at the male beside me. "Edon says to thank you for intervening."

Jolene looked surprised for half a beat before moving directly to Edon's bedroom. "You can still hear him." Not a question, but a statement.

"Yes," he confirmed, causing me to breathe a sigh of relief.

"Then he's not as bad as I feared," he said, laying Edon out on the bed.

"He's surviving on energy reserves." Silas swallowed. "I, uh, can feel it."

Jolene seemed impressed. "Your sire bond is unusually deep."

Silas cleared his throat. "Yeah. Maybe." He started toward the bathroom. "I prepared some supplies that will help. I'll grab them."

I shared a glance with Jolene. "It doesn't bother you?" he asked. "Whatever's happenin' between the two of them?"

"Why would it bother me?" I asked, not really in the mood to play this game or discuss relationships right now.

"Why indeed," he drawled, a twinkle of amusement in his gaze. "Well, I suspect you know what to do."

I nodded.

"Good." He intercepted Silas as he returned, taking the supplies and handing them to me. "Silas is gonna help me find a cot to sleep on for the night. You get to work on my boy."

Silas gave me a look as if to ask, *Are you okay?*

I nodded again. *I've got this.*

And I did.

There was no other choice. Either I nursed Edon back to life or I well and truly ran… for the rest of my days. Because bowing to Walter—assuming that was his plan— would never happen. I'd die first.

Silas and Jolene left me alone, their voices turning to a low murmur as Jolene explained what I needed to do. Normally, it would have shocked me to hear an alpha be so patient and willing to explain to a new lycan, yet it didn't. Oddly, it only solidified what I had to do.

Jolene had taught Edon to be the man he was today, and clearly the elderly wolf's principles were deeply instilled in the male I now claimed as my mate.

I brushed Edon's thick hair away from his bruised face and bent to brush my lips over his. "I'm here," I whispered. "Take whatever you need."

Closing my eyes, I focused on his scent and breathed

him in. Deep, luscious pulls filled with forest and male and underlined with a hint of spice that seemed to be all Edon.

I accepted him.

Acknowledged his claim.

And allowed him access to my wolf.

Nothing happened, the air cool, his exhales shallow.

I picked up one of the towels, already warm and damp, and used it to wipe the blood away from his mouth, his cheeks, his forehead, then kissed him again.

His lips tingled beneath mine but didn't move, his breath still weak.

I repeated the action with the towel, cleaning up his torso and arms, his strong thighs and calves. It took nearly an hour of wiping him down, swapping towels in the bathroom and moving him this way and that to wash him thoroughly. He'd still need a shower, but at least his wounds were accessible.

Using the ointment Silas prepped, I swabbed each gash and wrapped up the deepest of the wounds. Throughout each ministration, I ran my lips over him, kissing his jaw, his temple, his mouth, his neck, and allowed him to feel my consent in each touch.

We hadn't truly finalized our mating. That wouldn't happen until the next full moon. He'd only claimed me. But now I was claiming him, assenting to our relationship, and granting him access to my soul.

His wolf seemed to yawn beneath his skin, the beating leaving him depleted and alone, but I knew he sensed me, could feel him sniffing the connection with interest.

I stretched out beside him, my palm on his abdomen, my other hand propping up my head, and began humming to him. A haunting melody, one Claudette taught me long ago, but it always made me feel better.

His breathing had evened out, his healing well

underway, but he appeared to be reluctant to use me. "Edon," I whispered, sliding my palm up his torso to rest over his heart. "I know I ran, but I'm not weak. You can take what you need."

Still nothing.

Stubborn wolf.

But I felt his interest. I pictured him prowling around me, scenting me, his growl low and filled with intrigue. My wolf didn't move, her posture one of strength, not submission. He needed an equal right now. A female worthy of his needs.

This time his growl wasn't just in my head or a figment of my imagination, but a real sound—a broken one from his tormented throat.

I leaned into him, running my nose up his neck and pressed my mouth to his ear. "Are you intimidated?" I whispered. "Is that why you won't take what you need?" I nibbled on his lobe, then bit down hard enough to draw blood. "I'm not afraid of you, Alpha."

A snarl came from his chest, the wolf threatening to break free.

"Take what you want," I told him, my voice a low purr. "I'm here."

He fell silent again, the pacing resuming—at least in my mind.

I sighed against his neck. "This is going to be a very long night if you continue on like this."

No reply.

"Good thing I'm stubborn, too," I said, kissing his steady pulse. "A battle of wills it is."

CHAPTER 27
EDON

Glenn.

Barry.

Oscar.

George.

My father.

A growl warmed my chest, the sound a vow of retribution designated for those swimming in my mind. I had a very long list of lycans I wanted to kill.

They'd taken the strength trial too far.

And my father demanding the location of my mate? Yeah, that was the icing on the cake. I knew why he wanted her, and it had nothing to do with pack loyalty.

My mother was barren after all the trials she'd endured beneath his rule. She barely even opened her eyes anymore. Making a new heir would be impossible. But with Luna? Oh, he could create one.

Fucking monster.

I spent so many years of my life trying to gain his favor, only to fail. Well, that was done. I no longer craved his acceptance or advice. I would become the alpha I intended to be at the next full moon, and my poor excuse for a father would be the first lycan I banned. His cronies would be next.

My entire body ached, especially my rib cage where my bones slowly mended back together. They'd shattered my insides beneath thousands of kicks; it was honestly a wonder I'd survived.

No.

Not a wonder.

My grandfather had stepped in, threatening to go to the Blood Alliance about my father's behavior. Killing an heir unjustly was frowned upon, and my father couldn't use a strength exercise as an excuse. Not unless I tried to fight back, which I hadn't. I'd taken their beating, as the alpha ritual required, and he had chosen to take it too far.

Well, he and my fucking packmates who had far too eagerly participated.

Hence, my list.

Another growl vibrated my chest, my anger thriving through my veins. I wanted to smash their—

My senses piqued as someone responded to my sound of ire.

Not vocally, but with another growl. A sexier one.

Luna.

Her supple form was stretched out beside me, her palm a pleasant weight over my heart. It took significant effort to peel my eyes open, but I was thankful for trying because I found a gorgeous sight staring down at me—waves of brown hair tousled over one shoulder, head resting on her opposite hand, and honey-brown irises gazing at me with a fierceness that caused my breath to hitch.

"About fucking time," she said, causing my eyebrows to lift.

My lips parted on a reply that lacked sound. Not that it

mattered, though. Because her mouth settled over mine before I could even try again.

Shock coursed through me, followed swiftly by heat and intense longing.

Shit. Luna was kissing me. Eagerly. Dominantly. It took half a beat for me to register why she acted so impulsively. She wanted me to activate our mating link and absorb her strength.

Not happening.

I refused to use her in that manner. Nor did I need the boost. My energy reserves were healing me just fine.

But her company?

Yeah, now that I'd accept.

Except I couldn't move without flinching. Nor was my mouth working right.

She palmed my jaw, causing me to wince. "It's broken," she whispered, her nose nuzzling mine. "Let me help you, Edon. Please." Another kiss, this one followed by a nip to my lower lip when I didn't do as she requested. "Why are you fighting me?"

Oh, the ways I could answer that if my mouth worked. I would tell her: *You fought me first, sweetheart. Maybe I consider it foreplay. Delayed gratification, little mate.*

However, the truth of it was, I didn't want to hurt her. I also didn't know her true intent. While I appreciated her being here for me, I also knew it was her obligation—one society had demanded of her. And I refused to force her. Especially when I didn't need her strength to heal. Would it restore me to full health faster? Yes. But she deserved better than me sucking the life from her like some vampire.

Luna pulled back, her gaze shadowing over. "Why are you rejecting me?"

My eyes actually widened. *What?* This wasn't about rejection.

"Is it… I mean, do you…?" She bit her lip, glancing away, then back at me again with a sadness that hurt far more than my fractured rib cage. "Do you want me to get Silas?" she asked softly, her expression radiating an emotion I couldn't name. Not quite sadness, but definitely spasmed with pain. "I don't know if the sire bond can help, but if you prefer him, I'll understand. And I'll get him for you."

Where are you? I asked Silas through the bond.

Doing a perimeter check with Jolene before he goes to sleep, he replied. *Why? Is something wrong?*

Yeah. Luna seems to think I'd prefer you playing nursemaid instead of her. While I wouldn't mind Silas lying beside me now, I didn't exactly favor him over Luna. *Something tells me her touch will be a bit more tender and what I need right now.*

He snorted in my head. *You don't strike me as the kind of guy who enjoys tender, Edon.*

I wouldn't mind it from a certain female wolf, I thought, gazing up at her. *Except she seems pretty upset.*

Because she thinks you would prefer me there? He sounded as confused as I felt. *What did you say to her?*

Nothing. My jaw is broken.

Still? I could almost see him scratching his head. *Jolene said you would heal faster because of your mating bond with Luna.*

Yeah, only if I take energy from her, but I'm not.

Why the hell not?

Because I don't want to force her.

You don't want…? He started laughing, causing me to frown.

That wasn't meant to be funny, Omega.

Oh, but it's rich, Alpha, he returned. *You'll command me to fuck her, but you won't accept the bond she's offering now? Really?*

Seriously? We're going there again? You can't tell me you didn't enjoy—

"Edon?" Luna whispered, the earlier annoyance in her tone completely gone now and replaced by something akin to disappointment. "I know you probably can't speak, but can you at least nod?"

I lifted my chin an inch, testing my neck movement. It hurt like a son of a bitch, but it worked.

If you would let the woman in and absorb some of her strength, maybe it wouldn't hurt, Silas taunted in my head.

Fuck off.

I swore the jackass blew me kisses in reply, his amusement palpable. But the look on Luna's face ruined my inclination to smile.

"Do you want me to get Silas for you?" she asked softly.

I didn't nod.

Her brow furrowed. "I don't… I don't know what you want, Edon. I'm trying to help, but you don't want me. Clearly. So I'm going to get Silas, okay? Maybe you'll let him help, or, I don't know." She shook her head, but I saw it in her eyes before she shuttered them.

Rejection, I realized. *She thinks I'm rejecting our mating.*

Because you are rejecting it, Silas replied.

No, I'm not. I'm just not sucking on her life source, I thought back at him, irritated.

But does she know that?

Apparently not, I said, noting the way her lower lip wobbled before she sucked it in. *Ah, little mate…*

She'd been so strong, lying beside me, wanting me to take from her. The lack of blood on my skin told me she'd bathed me, too.

She's accepting her place by your side, Silas murmured. *I saw it in her earlier.*

And I felt it now.

Luna started to roll off the bed, causing me to reach

for her. Which ended in a grimace and a groan that had her looking back at me in alarm.

"Sorry, I didn't mean to hurt you more. I was just trying to, uh, move." She cringed. "You need some pain medicine or something."

No, what I needed was a brand-new body. One that I could use to kill my father and his idiotic cronies.

"Look, with you rejecting me, I obviously can't help you," she said, some of her spine seeming to return. "So I'm going to get up real fast and find Silas. Since you and he are, well, closer."

Shit. That wasn't it at all.

I growled because it seemed to be the only response I could make, and it caused her to freeze in place.

Then she narrowed her eyes at me. "Did you just growl at me?"

This time, I nodded.

"Why?" she demanded.

Because you just accused me of rejecting our mating bond, I thought at her.

Of course, it was Silas who replied. *Then maybe you should do whatever it is you need to do to accept her.*

You make it sound easy, Omega.

Because it is, Alpha.

I wanted to argue that point, but I couldn't. Because I'd clearly accepted the sire bond to him without hesitation. But Luna was a bit more complex. I'd already initiated our mating against her will. If I took from her now, it would finalize our destinies.

Of course, she didn't have a choice regardless. And neither, really, did I.

Luna released a noise of frustration. "You're a stubborn wolf, you know that?"

My lips threatened to twitch—which hurt and sort of ruined the moment.

Her eyes narrowed. "You're amused?"

My chin tilted in the affirmative, which only had her glowering more.

"Rejecting me entertains you?" She scoffed, the mood between us chilling in a heartbeat. "Wow. Okay. I get that I wasn't exactly favorable to our mateship in the beginning, but I thought last night changed things. Which was really naïve of me, and I see that now."

Whoa, hold on. That's not—

"God, you know, I was actually worried about you?" She laughed, but the sound was tinged with sadness. "Never mind. I'll leave you here to your *amusement*. Because hell if I'm going to sit and enjoy it with you at my own personal expense."

She rolled off the bed, leaving me snarling at her back.

How *dare* she run off when I had no voice to defend myself!

Get back here, I demanded.

But she couldn't hear me, nor did she adhere to the command radiating from my chest. She kept moving, her spine straight even as her dejection soured the air.

Alpha female through and through, refusing to allow others to see her pain. But her scent belied her bravado.

When she reached the door, something inside me snapped.

No way in hell was I allowing her to walk away from me like this.

She staggered beneath the weight of our sudden connection, her breath puffing out of her in a gasp as I dug my mental claws into her and coerced her to stay. My wolf didn't want to play; it wanted to dominate.

This female belonged to me.

And she thought I meant to reject her?

Fuck. That.

Every wall constructed between us came tumbling down as I yanked forcefully on the mating link—the connection that began to form the first time I bit her. Neither of us had explored the bond, mostly because it was more of a formality than a desire. But now? Now I wanted to know everything about it.

Because if she believed for one second that I didn't want her, she had another think coming.

You. Are. My. Mate. The words were from my mental wolf, a growl into her heart and mind at the same time as he circled her like prey. *You will not walk away from me.*

She turned and swallowed, her eyes wide. "I... I..."

Get back here, I told her. *Now.*

But she didn't. Instead, the impudent little female glared at me. "No. You were laughing at me, Edon. Just because you engaged the bond now does not mean I have to accept it."

And she did the unthinkable, her mind swiftly rebuilding the blocks I'd just knocked down.

It was bad enough that our bond wasn't complete and I only had a one-way ticket into her mind. With the connection open, I could push things at her—like words and feelings—and take whatever she willingly offered, but that was it.

And now she wanted to shove me out completely?

Not fucking happening.

I wasn't laughing at you, Luna, I said quickly, needing her to hear me before she finished reconstructing that wall of hers. *I was amused by you calling me stubborn. And I didn't reject our mating bond. I just didn't want to use you.*

She stilled, her lips curling downward. "Explain."

Rather than explain, I recapped the entire conversation

from my point of view. I even clued her in on my discussion with Silas by providing an overview. Once I finished, her frown no longer existed.

"That's the dumbest thing I've ever heard," she accused. "The whole point of a mating bond is to help each other, Edon. You're not the only one with reserves of strength, and frankly, I'm insulted that you don't think I can handle a little vampirism. I'm not an omega or beta wolf, but a born alpha. It's in my blood, you dick."

My eyebrows rose. *Careful, little mate. You might be alpha born, but I'm still your alpha.*

"Are you?" she taunted. "Because all I see is a broken wolf who has refused to do what he needs to do under some misguided attempt to protect his female. A female, mind you, who can more than hold her own." Those beautiful eyes narrowed once more. "How would you feel if I rejected your strength? If I assumed you to be too weak to help me?"

That's not—

"No, that's *exactly* what this is, so don't try to play it another way. You don't think I'm strong enough to help you." She folded her arms, my shirt hitting her at her thighs. It was a very sexy look on her. Not that this was the time to consider it. "Why did you mate me, Edon? To make pups? To fuck your progeny? What purpose do I serve for you if you don't find my strength worthy to suit an alpha?"

My blood heated at her accusations, my heart racing in my chest. *Get. Over. Here.*

"No."

Now who is being stubborn? I asked, irritated as fuck. *You want to prove you're strong enough? Then march that sweet ass back to this bed and lie down.*

"I don't have to lie—" She gripped the wall for support

as her knees buckled beneath my wolf's hungry demand. One pull on her reserves had my rib cage sighing in relief and the rest of me begging for more, but I only meant for it to be a demonstration, not an actual solution.

Yet, now I didn't want to stop.

Now, Luna, I demanded, holding off on my desire to take more from her. *Unless you're suddenly too scared?*

An unflattering noise came from her throat, one that told me exactly how she felt about that. "I fucking hate you," she said as she moved toward the bed.

Liar, I whispered.

She scoffed but stretched out beside me again. "This doesn't mean I forgive you."

I indulged myself in another taste of her vitality, my wolf stretching in contentment beneath her beautiful warmth. She sighed beside me, her pleasure heating our link and encouraging me to take more. So I did, allowing her energy to tingle through my veins, down my limbs, into my bones, and to my very soul.

Fuck, but it was arousing and incredibly intimate. Like my own personal pain-relieving drug, only in a feminine, supple form with curves for days.

I needed to get hurt more often if this was my reward.

"Don't you dare," she said, either because I spoke those words through the bond or she picked them up, I wasn't sure.

Thank you, little mate, I murmured, meaning it.

She said nothing for a while, her focus on the ceiling, but eventually, she rolled onto her side to face me. "You're welcome."

CHAPTER 28
LUNA

My body tingled from Edon's intrusion. Not in a bad way, but a good one, leaving me a little breathless beside him. And needy.

He remained utterly still, his eyes closed as if in slumber, but I felt his alertness. Our bond wasn't yet complete, but I felt it lingering, the call from his wolf to mine to finish our link at the next full moon.

All it would take was a single bite—of my teeth into his skin.

Not all alphas required it, their initial claim enough to force a female into the mating link. But I knew Edon wanted more, could hear it now that he'd opened the gate and allowed me inside.

Every part of him was free for me to explore, while my own emotions and thoughts remained locked up behind a wall of steel that he couldn't access without the completion of our bond.

But his mind was now mine, and what a fascinating place to be.

I could sense Silas there, his sire bond strong and thriving.

I also picked up notes of his confused feelings, how he desired us both on a painfully equal level. Edon questioned it, wondering how to make it work, and my overreaction only added to his overall confusion.

He thought I was jealous of Silas. And maybe, to an extent, I was, but not entirely. When I thought he preferred his progeny, I felt left out more than anything else. Worthless, too, as if my entire purpose to him was soiled and wrong.

Then he'd explained his intentions.

Such a waste of time and energy.

In roughly thirty minutes, his body appeared healed— at least on the outside—because of our link. *So take that, stubborn wolf. Thinking I couldn't handle it, or didn't want to help. Idiot.*

His lips curled. "I may not be able to hear you, Luna, but I can sense your emotions." His voice sounded clear, his throat and jaw fully mended. And when he glanced at me, I noticed the lack of swelling in his facial features, his handsome face completely unmarred. "You're feeling smug."

"With good reason." I lifted my head onto my palm while remaining on my side and facing him without touching. "How are you feeling, Edon?"

"Relaxed." He rotated his head on the pillow, his eyes holding mine. "Warm."

We stared at each other like that for a long moment, peace floating between us. Everything just felt so right. The way my vitality hummed through my veins to his in effortless silence, lulling us into a state of perpetual tranquility.

"Kiss me," he whispered.

Not a request so much as a demand.

He was an alpha, after all.

I smiled. "You want me? Come get me."

His pupils flared with interest. "You going to make me run, little mate?"

I nearly laughed. "Another day, maybe. Right now, I'll settle for you shifting off your back." Seemed like a good place to start since he hadn't moved in what felt like hours.

"Are you doubting my ability to fuck you, Luna?" he asked, one eyebrow lifting. "Because I assure you, that won't be a problem."

"Who said anything about fucking? All you wanted was a kiss."

"If you're going to make me work for it, then I'll return the favor in kind." He moved before I could reply, his big body stationary one second and on top of me the next.

A breath pushed from my lungs in surprise not only at his show of strength but also at the speed with which he reacted. "*Fuck*," I breathed.

"Yeah, that's the idea," he murmured, his hips settling between my splayed thighs. "Now kiss me, little mate."

His lips were a hairsbreadth from mine, his body radiating heat and bathing me in a sea of lust I couldn't deny.

So I didn't.

I kissed him. Not sweetly, not quietly, but passionately, and adored the growl he gave me in return. It rumbled from his chest to mine, a possessive sound that immediately soaked my inner thighs in my readiness.

My wolf submitted on instinct, the much stronger alpha taking control of my mouth with his tongue. I moaned, the wanton rush of lust flooding my every thought.

I was so lost to him.

To his touch.

To his presence.

To his very existence.

The forced fate I'd dwelled on most of my life gave way to a fervor unlike anything I could have anticipated.

I wanted Edon. *Badly*.

And I allowed him to feel that by pressing my aching heat into his hard shaft. He groaned, the sound coming from deep in his abdomen and exciting my need. "Edon," I whispered, arching into him again.

"I thought you just wanted a kiss," he teased, nipping my lower lip and kissing a path to my ear. "Aren't you worried I can't perform?"

"The throbbing cock pressing into my pussy says you'll be just fine," I replied, swallowing thickly.

"Mmm, I don't know." He licked the column of my neck, tasting the perspiration dotting my skin and leaving me shaking beneath him. "Maybe you should be on top, little mate."

I shuddered, the image of mounting him in my own way destroying my ability to think or respond.

Because yes. *Fuck* yes. I wanted that more than I wanted to breathe.

And somehow he knew.

He rolled onto his back, taking me with him, his hands on my hips. I straddled him on impulse, keeping my sex against his, my body trembling with unrestrained desire.

"Take me," he encouraged, his fingers tugging on the shirt I still wore. "But remove this. I want to watch every move as you fuck me, Luna. Every moan, every bounce, every pant will be mine."

Oh, dear wolf, he's going to destroy me.

I slowly removed his old shirt from my body, tossing it to the floor below, and licked my lips. His predatory grin had me quivering, the promise in his gaze one I intended to fulfill.

"Scared?" he taunted.

"Terrified," I whispered. It wasn't a lie. Because this feeling stirring in my chest? Yeah, that scared me. But I couldn't stop myself from lifting and taking him inside me, from rocking my hips against his and growling his name low and long from my throat.

This was a gift.

One I cherished more than he would ever know.

The offering of freedom, to express my alpha instincts and take what I wanted from the strong male below.

Most females in my position were never offered such an experience, the males preferring to dominate in every form of the word. But Edon remained still, his body strung tight with the effort of allowing another to dictate the pace and ride him.

A tear slipped from the edge of my eye, one he caught with his thumb before wrapping his palm around the back of my neck and bringing me down for a knowing kiss. Maybe he did understand the gravity of what he offered, which only endeared him to me more.

"Edon," I whispered.

"Shh." He licked the seam of my mouth. "Devour me, little mate. Make me yours."

And I did; with every lick, nip, and kiss, I claimed him. *Mine.* The only thing I didn't do was bite—an act I would save for the next full moon, when it truly counted.

My stomach burned, my thighs shaking.

An orgasm hovered on the horizon, the kind that would demolish my ability to think and, likely, my inclination to breathe.

But I chased it anyway, rising and falling onto him,

driving him deeper, and moaning every time my clit rubbed him the right way.

Oh, how I needed more.

I picked up the pace, sweat dripping from us both, but it wasn't enough. I whimpered, collapsing against him, my lips kissing his jaw. My body convulsed almost painfully, the hint of rapture so close yet so far.

Edon threaded his fingers through my hair, bringing me back for a kiss, his opposite hand flattening on my lower back. His bottom half bucked into mine, causing me to gasp against his mouth. Fuck, not even full strength and the man could move.

I caved to his prowess, luxuriating in his skill.

Being on top provided me with the confidence associated with control, but with each stroke upward, he redefined the meaning of *alpha*. So much poise, so much power, so much *perfection*.

One of his palms remained on the back of my head while the other slid from my spine to my side and then to my stomach and downward.

The rough pad of his finger flicked my swollen nub, exactly how I needed it, and sent me cascading over the falls into a whirlpool of ecstasy. His name careened from my mouth, only to be swallowed by his as he caressed me through the intense waves of pleasure. Each one rippled over me, driving me to the edge of the earth and back again. I panted, whined, gasped, each noise consumed by Edon as his tongue fucked my mouth with expert skill.

I barely noticed my back hitting the mattress, or the male driving into the apex between my thighs.

All I could think was, *This is heaven.* With Edon blanketing me in his primal heat, I never wanted to move again. Except my hips still rose to meet his thrusts, my limbs vibrating beneath the onslaught of increased pressure in my lower abdomen, as another spiral of oblivion overwhelmed my senses and covered me in goose bumps.

Fuck...

It wasn't even my orgasm that had hit me, but Edon's. He'd left the link open, showering me in his sensations and pulling me into the euphoric black hole with him. And shit, it was hot. Sensual. Amazing.

He gave me everything.

His excitement.

His dominance.

His overwhelming urge to take me all over again as soon as he finished shaking.

His craving for darker pleasures.

I shivered, intrigued by the ideas flooding his thoughts—ideas he didn't hide from me. He wanted to take me in every way, mark me as his so no one else could touch me.

Except Silas.

I saw him in those fantasies, too. Edon liked the three of us together. No, he more than liked it. He *yearned* for it. Even now I could sense him communicating to Silas, but I couldn't hear them. Their link remained separate from the one I shared with Edon. However, I sensed Silas humming words into the alpha's thoughts—words Edon seemed to be returning.

"What is he saying?" I asked, my thighs still pillowing Edon's waist.

"That he wants to sleep on the couch," Edon replied, his lips against my neck. He lifted onto his elbows, his gaze warm as he studied my face. "He seems to think you'll be uncomfortable if he joins us, so he's ignoring my command."

Part of me wanted to grin at the latter part of that

sentence, but the former captivated my interest. "Why would I be uncomfortable?"

"You tell me, little mate." He combed his fingers through my hair. "Are you okay with Silas joining us?"

"What would you do if I said no?" I wondered out loud. "Would you deny him?"

He swallowed, his eyes flicking to the headboard before slowly returning to my face. "If it is the desire of my mate, yes. I think I would have to."

My eyebrows actually rose. "You would choose me over him?" For some reason, that didn't elate me the way I had expected it to. Actually, it had the opposite impact. "You can't do that to Silas."

He chuckled. "I didn't say I wanted to, Luna. I won't lie to you. I want him as badly as I want you, but your comfort is important to me. Just as it is to him. If you don't desire him in our bed, then he wouldn't want to join us. Which leaves me little choice but to respect both of your wishes."

I blinked. "You're not at all who I expected you to be."

"Considering you were anticipating a male like my father or your father, I'm going to take that as a compliment." He drew his thumb along my jaw, his eyes tracing the movement. "What should I tell Silas?"

"To get his ass in here," I replied without hesitation. "Why the hell would he sleep on the couch?"

His lips curled. "It's as if you can read my mind, darling Luna. Because I said the exact same thing to him." He kissed me deeply, his cock slowly sliding from my body. "Mmm, fucking you might be my new favorite activity, but Silas needs some relief."

"I'm fine," he replied from the side of the room, his lithe form leaning against the doorjamb in a pair of jeans. Water beaded across his naked torso, his hair damp from what I assumed was a recent shower. He must have taken one after his run of the perimeter.

"Prove it," Edon murmured, slipping off of me to the side. He gathered my body against him, spooning me with his chest to my back so we both faced the entryway. Edon lifted himself onto his elbow while his opposite palm ran over my stomach and downward to the evidence of our fucking. "Come here, Silas."

The other male narrowed his gaze but walked into the room and shut the door with his heel. He must have said something to Edon, because the alpha chuckled behind me. The vibration coupled with the finger gliding through my folds had my throat drying too much for me to speak.

Not that I knew what to say.

A moan seemed more appropriate, especially with the way Silas's gaze tracked Edon's movements. He gripped my thigh and guided my limb backward to rest over his legs, thereby spreading me wide for Silas's view.

"Doesn't she have a gorgeous pussy?" the alpha asked softly, his lips near my ear as his hand returned to my center.

Silas visibly swallowed. "Yes."

"But you're *fine*, right?" Edon dipped two fingers into me, penetrating me deep. "Take off your jeans, Silas. Show us how *fine* you are."

His glower deepened, those blue eyes darkening to a midnight-blue shade as he unbuttoned and unzipped his pants.

Both males were equally endowed and beautiful in their own rights, but Silas's shaft was slimmer and longer, while Edon's was thicker and almost harsher. Somehow, both cocks were appropriate to each man.

And I found myself thirsting for them both despite having just gotten off with Edon inside me.

Silas kicked his jeans off to the side, his hands on his hips. "Satisfied?"

"Me? Very." Edon circled my clit with his thumb, his entire hand seeming to explore the dampness between my thighs. "But you look uncomfortable, Silas. Maybe we can help with that. Unless you're still *fine*."

I squirmed as Silas knelt on the bed, his heat and presence an aphrodisiac to my senses. *Yes, please*, my wolf whispered.

"Lie down beside Luna," Edon instructed him, the authority in his voice leaving no room for argument. It was as if he hadn't just survived a near-life-threatening beating at all, like he wasn't still in the process of healing. Although, I felt him pulling on my reserves, just a little, to foster his recovery. He might be in charge again, but he wasn't at full strength. He was just an alpha with a hell of a lot of ego.

For good reason, I thought, smiling as Silas lay down beside me. "Hi," I whispered.

"Hi," he replied, giving me a much softer look than the one he'd given Edon. I sighed as he leaned in to kiss me, his lips soft and warm and coaxing against mine. Never rushed, just all Silas—tasting and mesmerizing.

Edon removed his touch, eliciting a whimper from me that Silas overpowered on a growl.

"*Fuck*, Edon," he groaned, arching in a way that removed his mouth from mine.

And I could see why.

Edon had grabbed Silas's shaft and was stroking him— using the combined juices of our arousal for lubrication.

That was why he'd touched me so completely, to coat his palm in the aftermath of our lovemaking and paint Silas's cock with it.

My thighs tensed, heat pooling in my lower abdomen.

Because wow, that was hot. And Silas seemed to approve as well, his eyes closing on a guttural sound as Edon twisted his grip over the head.

Who knew watching a male jack off another man could be so damn arousing?

Or maybe it was just watching these two interact, while sandwiched in the middle, that turned my blood to boiling lava.

Didn't matter.

I was lost to the moment, my eyes glued to Edon's hand and the rhythm he set. Not harsh or fast, but firm and knowing. Silas's muscles tensed, his abdomen a riddle of ridges I wanted to explore with my tongue.

"He's close, little mate," Edon murmured against my ear. "Do you want to slide down so he can come in your mouth? Or should I let him come all over your sweet cunt and have him lick you clean?"

Silas responded with an unintelligible noise, his eyes fluttering as his body began to convulse.

"Hmm, seems he decided for you." Edon nibbled my neck, his warmth a blanket against my back as Silas erupted against my folds, coating me in his seed. "Isn't he beautiful?"

I nodded. "Yes." He truly was, with his golden hair falling in waves to his ears, his neck straining from his tensed jaw, and his athletic form bulging with strength.

But it was the growl coming from him I adored most of all. So primal and masculine and utterly fascinating. Mmm, I wanted to hear him do that against my ear.

His eyelids lifted to reveal gorgeous blue irises, slightly unfocused from pleasure. "Fuck, Luna, keep looking at me like that and I'll come again."

Edon chuckled, his lips caressing my throat. "I think you should clean her up first. With your tongue."

Silas shuddered, then leaned in to brush his mouth against mine, his palm falling to my hip. "Did we make a mess, little moon?" He nuzzled my nose, his breath hot against my parted lips. "Do you want me to lick it all up? Or should I massage it into your flesh and mark you as ours?"

Bold words.

But they were met with approval from the male behind me. I *felt* it through our mating bond. He liked Silas laying claim to me. Just as he enjoyed sharing us both.

"Tell him what you want," Edon encouraged, his voice deep. "Tell *us* how to serve you, little mate."

He kissed my neck while Silas took my mouth, leaving me unable to reply between them. Not that I knew what I desired. I couldn't choose. I wanted both.

And when I finally had an opportunity to voice that out loud, both males chuckled. Edon's palm dipped between my legs, his fingers sliding through my folds and mixing our arousals together as one, then brought his hand up for both Silas and me to lick.

No words were exchanged.

Just feelings.

Our bodies moving as one—a joining of instinct alone.

I lost track of who touched whom, whose mouth belonged to whom, and just indulged in the sensations. All the while, I felt Edon's gentle tug against my strength, his body still healing despite his outward prowess.

And eventually, after much petting and pleasure, the three of us fell into a slumber.

Where I dreamt of a future about a trio of wolves who lived happily ever after.

Only to be eaten alive by society's rules…

CHAPTER 29
SILAS
A LITTLE OVER TWO WEEKS LATER...

The guests are arriving, I told Edon as I observed from the perimeter.

Car after car traveled down the gravel path toward the heart of the Clemente Clan territory. Inside were a mix of elite wolves and vampires, all here to witness tonight's full-moon ceremony.

Electricity danced across my fur coat, every part of me vigilant.

Tonight was Walter's last chance to stop Edon's ascension.

And the last two and a half weeks had been far too quiet for my liking.

His father had to be planning something because no way did he just give up after the strength test. Not after everything he'd pulled. Instead, he'd left the three of us on high alert waiting for an attack that never came.

Which meant we were all exhausted.

Something I suspected was the point.

Anything out of the ordinary? Edon asked.

Other than the fact that I'm the only one guarding the perimeter right now? Not really, no.

Edon was silent for a long moment before saying, *They're up to something.*

I know. Because last month, there were twenty of us on perimeter duty. Tonight? None. I wasn't even technically assigned to be out here. But my loyalty to Edon and Luna put me right where I needed to be.

We have an hour before we begin. I want you nearby when it all starts.

I'll be there. The confirmation really wasn't necessary, and neither was his demand, but they added to the formality of today.

We'd fallen into a dangerous rhythm these last few weeks, one where I'd begun to hold a much more powerful place in Edon's life. Tonight, however, he had reverted me to my place as his progeny.

No, actually, that wasn't quite right. I'd played the part of progeny at last month's full-moon ceremony. No one had spoken to me or acknowledged me, apart from my old friend Rae, whom I'd secretly spoken to during the opening reception. And Edon had treated me as if I didn't exist.

Nothing about tonight compared to my last experience.

Because I had Edon in my head. In my blood. In my very soul.

He'd also put me on protection duty not just for him but for Luna, too.

So no, this was nothing like the first ritual.

I had much more to lose this time.

And yet, I would be losing everything tonight regardless. Because Luna and Edon were about to finalize their mating bond. Once Luna bit him beneath the moon, he would become hers irrevocably, thereby sealing the connection he created a month ago.

Leaving me on the outside looking in.

Again.

My tail twitched, my ears flattening. Part of me wanted to celebrate with them, while the other part of me felt incredibly alone. I knew this was all meant to be temporary, but the last few weeks had been among the best of my life. Which was saying something beneath the shroud of stress.

I enjoyed being with Luna and Edon. A lot. And not just in a sexual sense. They just felt right, like they could be my home.

Which was crazy.

I had no home.

Only temporary beds.

I just happened to favor the one I'd slept in last night most of all. With Luna's head on my shoulder and Edon's arm around her waist, it'd been heaven. Only, I'd awoken this morning to reality shining down on me in the face of a coming moon.

Edon had provided a temporary distraction by having Luna go down on me while he fucked her from behind. He hadn't taken her ass yet—neither of us had—but I knew he would soon. After learning about her lack of real experience, he decided to ease her into it with my help. And while I loved being involved, something told me I wouldn't be there for the eventual climax.

Just an instinct.

A whisper of fate.

In the shape of a full-blown orb over my head.

I gazed up at it, my nose twitching at the growing stench of the undead descending upon our property.

Rather than brooding, I should be checking the other boundaries, searching for anything untoward.

Luna and Edon were counting on me, and I refused to let them down.

The problem was, I had no idea what to look for. With all these foreign scents and the heightening energy in—

My instincts flared, the distinct sound of a branch snapping to my left drawing my focus. One of the vehicles had stopped, pulling to the side of the road while all the others had continued onward. It left only me and the unknown entity inside alone on the perimeter.

Something that couldn't be a coincidence.

My suspicions were confirmed the second the door opened and a male in a black suit stepped onto the gravel path.

Dark eyes flashed beneath the pale moon, zeroing in on my location within the trees. "Silas," the royal vampire said, his voice easily carrying to my ears.

I shivered.

That he recognized me in wolf form after only one previous meeting spoke of his intense power. Not that I ever doubted it.

Kylan was notorious, after all.

Violent. Ruthless. Cruel.

And mated to one of my only friends.

He stepped aside, holding the door to his black car open, and arched a brow. Apparently, he considered that an invitation. Rae popped her head out with a frown. "Where is he?" she asked.

My lips curled. I missed that voice. Hell, I missed *her*.

And Willow.

We used to be so close, but it felt like a lifetime ago. A memory consisting of false dreams and hopes that were all slaughtered by the reality we now resided in.

Kylan nodded up in my direction. "He's playing in wolf form at the moment. Shall we bark at him? Maybe that'll encourage him to move faster."

I snorted. *Asshole.*

Excuse me? Edon replied.

That was meant for Kylan, not you.

Kylan? he repeated. *As in the most lethal vampire in the world?*

I shifted while saying, *The very one. He's summoning me.*

What? His concern radiated through our link as I looked around for the pants I'd purposely carried here in case I needed to be in human form. Although, this wasn't one of the scenarios I'd originally anticipated. Not that I minded.

It's fine. I told him about how Kylan arranged for Rae and me to speak during the last full moon, and felt Edon's shock through our link.

For once, the alpha was speechless. Good thing, too. I only had enough room to handle one dominant personality, and I needed all of my focus to approach the royal standing by the car.

He wore a suit—something that I assumed was standard issue for all vampires. While his relaxed position against the car appeared unthreatening, I knew better.

Rae peered out at me as I approached, her beautiful face lighting up in relief. She practically leapt out of the car and directly into my arms. If it bothered the royal, he didn't show it. He merely observed with a stoic expression, his boredom palpable.

"You're okay," Rae whispered, her hands running over my bare arms like a mother checking her child. She checked every inch of my torso as if needing to convince herself that I wasn't hurt.

I chuckled. "You've gotten rather handsy, Rae. That

professor from our socialization course would be so thrilled."

She startled, then laughed. "Hey, I aced that course."

"With my help," I reminded her.

"Yeah, yeah." She scoffed, then smiled. "I've missed you."

"Likewise." I hugged her again, this time without all the petting, and sighed against her hair. "It's good to see you." I had no idea how much I needed this embrace—how much I longed for my friend—until she arrived.

Emotions welled up inside me.

Abandonment.

Confusion.

Loyalty.

Adoration.

Loneliness.

"What's wrong?" Rae whispered, pulling back to study my face. She palmed my cheek, her gaze flickering between my eyes. "What have they done to you?"

"Might I suggest we return to the car?" Kylan said, his focus on the empty road ahead. "I would rather we not draw undue attention."

A soft beam of light appeared on the tail end of those words, indicating another approaching vehicle.

Rae slid back inside first.

Kylan gestured for me to follow.

My neck hummed with awareness as I adhered to his unspoken command, then my blood chilled as he joined us inside the stretched-out car. There were two benches—Rae and Kylan took one, while I took the seat across from them.

A tap on the roof sent the car into drive, navigating us toward the heart of the territory.

"Arriving with you is going to inspire questions," I noted dryly.

I must have telegraphed that to Edon, because he immediately replied with, *Oh, I have several for you.*

Later, I replied. *For when I'm not sitting across from a royal vampire.*

Apprehensiveness tingled through the bond, Edon's worry for my safety a warmth I rather liked.

I promise I'm fine, I told him. *Focus on Luna and the ceremony.*

"Are you talking to your new alpha?" Kylan asked, interest coloring his features as he wrapped an arm around Rae's shoulders. His fingers danced over the strap of her red dress—a color that matched her striking auburn hair.

I met his knowing gaze and decided lying to him would not go over well. "Yes. I am."

He nodded, his approval palpable. "That's an intriguing development. It's not common for an alpha to care about his progeny. At least, not anymore."

"What do you mean?" Rae interjected.

"In the old society, alphas took exquisite care of their made lycans. But in today's world, those in power are no longer expected to care for the young. And lycans, especially, prefer to create offspring through fucking rather than gifting immortality to an adult mortal."

He spoke with such stoicism, as if his words meant nothing at all. And maybe they didn't—*to him*. But they meant everything to me.

"Edon's not common," I said, realizing the error in my statement the second it left my lips. "What I mean is, he's a decent alpha. And he was checking in with me on security." Not exactly a lie. It just happened to be my personal security he was worried about more than the perimeter.

Kylan smirked. "Sure." His gaze glittered beneath the dim light overhead. "He seems to be taking excellent care of you. Based on your increased muscle mass and general health, I mean."

I swallowed. His astuteness and candor unnerved me. And I didn't know how to respond.

Fortunately, Rae did. "Shouldn't he look healthier? He's a lycan now."

"Most don't survive the turning these days," Kylan replied, his eyes not leaving mine. "Nor are they cared for afterward."

She snorted. "Why am I not surprised?"

Kylan grinned down at her—finally giving me a reprieve—and stroked her pulse with his thumb. "Because you're learning, Raelyn." He kissed her before she could reply, the move a strike that had my hands curling into fists.

Too fast.

Too harsh.

And fuck, I didn't want to smell my friend's responding arousal. But I was trapped in this very small space while he devoured her as if I wasn't seated across from them.

She squirmed, a protest sliding from her lips as he kissed a path down her neck and slid his fangs into her flesh. "Kylan…" His name came out on a chastising groan that had me swallowing across from them.

I'd seen Rae fake pleasure countless times in class.

This wasn't fake. At all.

My stomach churned, my heart skipping a beat. This was not how I wanted to see my childhood friend. Ever.

You have a lot of explaining to do, Edon growled into my head.

Yeah, I suspected I did. Although, it wasn't like my past came up much in conversation. He was more focused on the present and future, not my years at the university.

Kylan released Rae with a dark chuckle, leaving her winded and gazing up at him in confusion. "That should buy you about twenty minutes of privacy," he said, nuzzling her chin before nipping her bottom lip.

"Wh-what?" she asked, her chest heaving as she blinked several times.

He focused on me, his hand going to the door beside me. "Twenty minutes, Silas. Then I'm coming back for my consort. Be advised, allowing her to stay in a confined space with another male isn't something I enjoy. I suggest you not give me any reason to be even more uncomfortable. Understand?"

The car rolled to a stop beside yet another royal vampire—Jace. And beside him was a dark-haired female wearing what appeared to be a lingerie-style gown.

"Silence does not appease me, Silas," Kylan pressed. "Shall I repeat my concerns?"

"She's one of my best friends," I bit back, my irritation getting the best of me. "Your Highness," I added, hoping to temper my statement at least a little.

He grinned. "Edon looks good on you, young wolf. As does Luna." He twisted the handle before I could reply, then glanced back at Rae. "Pull yourself back together and meet me outside." The chill in his tone whipped through the car, but he winked at her before stepping out into the night. He slammed the door behind him and pulled a handkerchief from his pocket to dab his mouth before addressing the royal standing outside. "She's a work in progress."

"I see that," Jace replied, his lips going to the neck of the beauty beside him. "As is Juliet. Isn't that right, sweetheart?"

She didn't lift her eyes from her shoes but nodded stiffly. "Yes, Your Highness."

"Does her presence here mean Darius is nearby?" Kylan asked as the pair began walking.

"Yes, he's mingling with Luka and Mira somewhere."

"Ah, of course he is," Kylan murmured, his voice still strong in my ears despite his growing distance.

One perk of being a wolf? Fantastic hearing.

Just as I could hear Rae's heart beating a mile a minute in her chest. "Are you all right?" I asked.

She swallowed and nodded. "Yeah. Just. Yeah." She cleared her throat. "He's just... Kylan."

"And he's treating you okay?" I looked pointedly at the wound on her neck. "Because that looks like it hurts."

She laughed. "Trust me, it doesn't. He just got me all hot and, well, anyway. Biting is fine. It was his way of giving me a cover story for my absence so we could talk, and we're wasting time. How are you really?"

"I could ask you the same question. That's one hell of a cover story, Rae."

"As I said, he's Kylan. The only thing he's guilty of is making me crave more, which, I suspect, was the point. He's a territorial asshole like that, and you're sort of a button for him."

"Me?" I almost laughed. "A button? How?"

"He knows we used to, you know, for class. And for a while, he used your fate over my head because he thought I loved you as more than a friend."

My eyebrows shot up. "*What?*"

"It's neither here nor there, and you're deflecting," she accused. "Talk to me, Silas. What's going on?"

I blew out a breath and rubbed my palm over my face, shaking my head. "There's not enough time for me to tell you everything."

"So summarize it."

"It's really nothing. I'm just glad to see you, Rae. That's all."

Her icy blue eyes narrowed. "I can smell your lie. I can also smell Edon and Luna on you."

"Really?" My brow furrowed. *Since when could vampires scent lies?* "I thought baby vampires could hardly sense anything at all. And how do you know it's Edon and Luna?"

"Because my link to Kylan isn't, uh, typical."

I knew the circumstances surrounding her turning weren't exactly normal, but I thought that had more to do with politics than with the physical change. "How so?"

"We're not talking about me right now, Silas. We're talking about you. Why do you smell like the alpha heir and his new mate? And what's with the morose energy you were oozing earlier? It's not like you."

Ah, typical Rae, refusing to let me off easy. I sighed again. Deflecting her questions would only make her more suspicious and fight harder for an answer. And I didn't have the energy to fend her off. Besides, if I could talk to anyone, it was Rae. She knew me better than most, with the exception of maybe Willow.

My heart gave a pang at the memory of our lost friend. She was either already dead or wishing for death. I preferred to think of her as the former; it was less painful than the alternative.

Giving my head another shake, I met Rae's gaze and told her a short version of everything that had happened since my turning. If anything, it would be nice to have another ally on our side, someone to keep an eye on the surroundings and maybe clue me in on anything her new vampiric senses picked up on.

She remained eerily still while I spoke, her expression giving nothing away even as I explained my recent sleeping arrangements—with two alphas. I didn't give her specifics, but she read between the lines.

And I ended with a summary of Walter's exploits.

That reddened her cheeks. "What a dick," she said.

I laughed out loud. "Oh, Rae, I've missed your version of a filter."

"What? He sounds like an ass."

"You're not wrong," I admitted. "But it's left us all a little on edge for tonight."

She nodded thoughtfully. "And you're not on edge at all about the fact that the two wolves you've fallen for are mating each other—without you."

I blinked. "That's not, I mean, I care about them, sure, but they're supposed to be together. Whatever is happening with me is temporary."

"What you described doesn't sound all that temporary to me." She cocked her head. "I'm pretty sure Kylan would tell you it's downright uncommon."

"Same could be said about a harem member being turned into a vampire consort."

"Touché, but again, we're talking about you, not me." Some of her fiery personality surfaced with that comment. "You can admit to me how you feel, Silas. I won't judge you."

"I'm not afraid of you judging me, Rae. It's just a fact of life I have to accept. Edon and Luna are alpha mates. That doesn't involve me at all."

"Except you were roaming the perimeter and searching for threats—to protect them."

"As is my job as his progeny."

"And their lover," she added. "Don't discount what you are just because there's not a proper term for it." Her smile was sad. "I might be a vampire now, but I still know you, Silas. You've always been amazing at hiding your feelings.

That small slip in your facade tells me just how exhausted you are. You never slip."

I allowed my head to fall back onto the headrest behind me, my throat tightening. "It's been an enlightening few weeks, Rae."

"Months," she corrected. "And I agree."

"It was all bullshit," I continued, allowing some of my anger to slip free. "All of it. The grandeur, the promises of immortality—it was all *bullshit*." Fuck, how many people did I kill in the Immortal Cup? Six? And the problem was, I would have killed them all for the future I thought waited for me on the other side. People I knew. And how messed up was that? "It makes me so angry, Rae. So fucking angry."

She reached across to grab my hand and gave it a squeeze. "I know how you feel."

"Do you?" I asked, laughing humorously. "I suppose you do. Kylan, huh?"

Her lips quirked up. "He's not as bad as you think."

I snorted. "That wound on your neck says otherwise."

"Don't worry. I'll bite him back later."

"How does that work?" I wondered out loud. "You're both vampires. Don't you need human blood?"

Some of her amusement faded into a secretive expression. "Like I said, my turning wasn't exactly common."

I opened my mouth to press that comment, when an approaching scent tickled my nose. *Death.* Not the same perfume Kylan and Rae wore, but one similar to the putrid stench I kept picking up near the borders over the last month.

Except we were nowhere near the border now.

No, we were in the heart of Clemente Clan territory.

I glanced out the windows, searching for the source,

everything falling silent in the car. Rae must have picked up on my alertness, because she didn't say anything but instead glanced around, too.

"Vampires," she whispered. "A lot of them."

"Yeah," I agreed, searching the darkness with my wolf vision.

The door flew open, causing me to scramble back as Kylan appeared. "Come, Raelyn." He held out a hand. "Now."

She didn't hesitate, a palpable energy shifting between them.

"Warn your alpha heir, Silas," Kylan said, his voice laced with command. "A war is coming your way. And it seems the Silvano Clan is out for blood."

CHAPTER 30
LUNA

A FEW MINUTES EARLIER…

Everything felt wrong. The moon. The air. This ridiculous dress my mother brought me to wear. The way Edon wouldn't stop pacing. The hairs dancing along the back of my neck.

The fact that Silas isn't here… I swallowed, my eyes closing. *He should be here with us.*

No one could hear me but myself, and yet I knew Edon felt the same, could hear my thought echoing in his own.

Since opening the link between us a few weeks ago, neither of us had sought to close it. If anything, he'd only widened the entrance, allowing me unfettered access to his mind at all times. It was Edon's method of establishing trust, something I very much appreciated because I never had to guess at his intentions.

Annoyance radiated off him in waves, coupled with concern and a slight hint of fear.

Not for us, but for Silas.

Rae—the infamous harem member turned vampire— was apparently an old friend of his. Something he'd failed to mention to me and Edon.

Which had me questioning how much Silas trusted us.

A ridiculous thought, really. I knew how he felt, could sense it in his every touch. And Edon could *sense* his emotions.

No, it wasn't about trust at all. Silas just hadn't mentioned it, or really much about his past. We were all so focused on the present, on what Walter would do next.

I opened my eyes to find Edon watching me, his expression sheltered. "Almost time," he said softly.

"I know." The moon's energy slithered across my skin, making me thankful Edon chose this location to prepare. We were very alone here on his grandfather's private porch, hiding us from the flurry of activity in town. Jolene had gone on ahead saying he wanted to have a word with an old friend. We suspected he meant a member of the quiet resistance, but we were too concerned with our own fates to press it.

Edon cupped my cheek, his opposite hand falling to my hip, where his thumb stroked the silk fabric of my gown. "After tonight, we can begin anew."

I leaned into his touch. "Yes." I just wish I knew what that would entail. Everything had seemed so right these last few weeks with Edon and Silas, but tonight would change everything. The foreboding nature of it weighed against my spine, leaving me unnerved.

"You feel it, too," he whispered. "That something's missing."

"Silas," I said.

He nodded. "Yeah."

"He should be here."

Another nod. "Do you want me to call him?"

"I don't know." Would it make it better? Or would it feel like goodbye? Because I wasn't ready for that. Somehow, in some way, that wolf had gotten under my skin nearly as deeply as Edon had. Almost as if that bite he'd bestowed upon me was a claiming. Except I knew that was impossible. Only bites beneath the full moon ended in a mating.

Edon brushed a kiss against my lips before pressing his forehead to mine. "This isn't the end, little mate."

"Then why does it feel that way?" I asked, swallowing. "Why do I feel like everything's about to change?"

He sighed, his minty breath mingling with mine. "Because it is. But that doesn't mean it's an end so much as a new beginning."

"Without Silas."

"We don't know that."

"No. I think we both know exactly that," I argued, pulling back to stare up at him. "My bite will connect us irrevocably. Forever. It'll override your sire bond."

"But not delete it."

True. "It'll supersede it," I clarified. "Which isn't fair to Silas."

On that, he didn't have an argument. I saw it in his gaze.

"Forcing him to remain with us will be cruel," I added, swallowing. "You know that as well as I do. He'll never be an equal."

"He was never meant to be our equal, Luna." He lifted his touch from my hip to my cheek, cradling my face between his palms. "We're alphas. We're meant to mate. Silas…" He trailed off, his expression pained.

"He's not an omega," I whispered.

"I know."

"But he's not an alpha either," I admitted, my stomach churning. "Staying with him… Edon, it'll hurt him."

"I know," he repeated, his gaze falling.

"I don't want to hurt him."

He pressed his lips to mine again, this time the kiss lingering as if he needed a moment to gather his thoughts. But as he met my gaze once more, I knew what he planned to say.

We need to let him go.

It's for his own good.

Even if it kills us to do it.

However, none of those comments left his mouth. Instead, he froze, his hands going rigid against my skin.

And then I smelled it.

The rancid stench of death. Everywhere.

I couldn't look over his shoulder to survey our surroundings because he held me too tightly. Yet I *felt* the incoming wave of power.

This was more than a few royal vampires and their sovereigns.

An army approached.

Edon shoved me through the door of his grandfather's home, causing me to stumble into a nearby chair on a curse. And then he was shifting.

Snarls ripped from Edon's mouth as he charged toward the tree line that led to the main camp, leaving a command behind in my skull. *Stay*.

Fuck that, I thought back at him. Not that he could hear me. Not that anyone could hear anything over the sound of war in the backyard.

I took off after him, my gown disappearing in my wake as I called to my wolf.

My paws sprinted over the earth, my senses heightening with each growing second.

So many vampires. Rage. Blood. The need for a fight.

It shivered down my spine, stirring a pool of dread in my lower belly.

This was the final test—the one Walter had set up for

Edon to fail. I felt it in every bone of my being, knew what he desired.

My mate's death.

Not on my watch, I thought, pushing myself faster than ever before as I followed Edon's trail.

War cries littered the air, followed by howls.

I paused on the outskirts, my eyes going wide at the onslaught of chaos.

Hundreds of vampires had encircled the camp, their attack imminent.

Walter stood in the middle of them, squaring off against their leader—Silvano—an old-as-fuck vampire known for his temper.

Shit...

"I've sanctioned no such activities," Walter growled, his words echoing off the surrounding lodges. Wolves paced around him, but they were well outnumbered by the army of undead.

Edon joined him, walking into the circle on two legs while pulling up a pair of jeans he'd retrieved from somewhere. I crept up to the side of one of the houses to watch, my coat shivering beneath the wave of violent energy stirring in the air.

"What the fuck is going on?" Edon demanded.

"Silvano thinks we've been hunting and slaying vampires on our land," Walter said, folding his arms. "Something we all know I'd never sanction."

Oh, shit...

This all tied back to the first trial.

The one with the dead vampire body.

The body Edon had disposed of.

"I see." Silvano gestured for two of his suit-clad vampires to step forward, one of whom held a bag. He dumped the contents onto the lawn—a collection of heads.

"These say otherwise, Walter. Go ahead, take a whiff. They reek of your mutts."

My ears flattened, shock coursing through my system.

Edon merely folded his arms, mimicking his father's stance. "Then we have a problem in our clan, one I'll solve as soon as I ascend."

His father snorted a laugh. "How quaint." He turned to his son, eyes narrowing. "And so very coincidental."

"Took the words right out of my mouth," Edon replied, not looking the least bit ruffled. "If I didn't know better, I'd say this is all part of your fucked-up alpha trials. Well, you're too late, old man. I'm ready and I'm ascending, with or without your approval."

"So, what? You orchestrated all this to belittle my legacy? To taint my reputation?"

Edon's lips twitched. "We both know I don't have the support in this clan to pull off something like that."

"Oh, no?" Walter feigned surprise. "Maybe we should put that theory to the test." He glanced around while Silvano observed in stoic silence, his vampires all poised and ready for battle. One signal from him and chaos would begin, but he held off.

Because this was all for show.

The realization hit me as soon as Walter asked, "Who among you had a hand in this?" He glanced around, his gaze astute. "My guess is my son promised you something in return for framing me in this madness. That'll be hard for him to accomplish if he doesn't ascend this year. I implore you to step forward with the truth now, or risk an uncertain future, as my son has."

Bastard.

He planned all of this.

And that thought was confirmed as two males gingerly slunk forward, eyes averted.

"Forgive us, sir," one of them said, his voice low. "But E-Edon said it was sanctioned, that w-we were paying back a debt."

"H-he claimed it was done with Si-Silvano's approval," the other whispered.

Silence fell.

A hum of anger stroked my fur.

And then Edon laughed. "I can't believe you've let him manipulate you this way." He shook his head, still grinning. "You're both imbeciles."

Walter was an expert in the art of faking astonishment. "You just couldn't ascend normally, could you? Had to try to tarnish my reputation in the process." He shook his head, sighing. Then met Silvano's gaze. "He's been trouble from the beginning, but I've tried. It's hard, though, when his mother is so completely useless."

The female in question was nowhere to be seen.

But the words ignited a flame in Edon's gaze. "And why is she useless?" he demanded. "Oh, right, because you've broken her." He snorted and looked to Silvano. "I've neither sanctioned nor plotted against your territory in any way. What the hell would I have to gain from it?"

"A great deal," Walter argued. "Framing me and tarnishing my reputation would only prove to the pack that I was unfit to lead, and allow you to become their savior. Something we both know you very much need, as you're not all that respected by your peers."

He opened his hands for the wolves around him, most of whom snorted in agreement.

Walter sighed, the sound dramatic as he refocused on Silvano. "Tell me how to make this up to you, old friend. Tell me what you want."

"My death, I presume," Edon drawled. "Fascinating. I

mean, you've been trying to accomplish that throughout the trials. Right?"

He pressed a palm to his chest. "Me? All I've done is try to make you stronger." He again looked to the pack for approval, which they of course gave because they were all fucking sheep.

"Is that why you framed my mate for murder?" Edon asked. "Why you took it upon yourself to punish her—in an attempt to gang-rape her? Why you beat me to within an inch of my life in your so-called strength test?" He smiled. "Sure, *Dad*. I'm certain that was all done for my benefit."

"You've grown too close to her, and that mutt of yours, to think clearly, son. It's something I warned you against." He sounded so contrite and sad that I almost wanted to applaud him for the act.

The problem was, it seemed everyone around him believed this bullshit.

Several alphas had joined the ring, watching from the sidelines, including my parents. And a handful of royal vampires, too. They all wore matching expressions of indifference. But I sensed their acceptance.

They were going to let Walter kill his son.

To make it up to Silvano and—

"There's only one problem with your accusation," a deep voice said from behind the masses, startling me. Silas pushed through the ring in a pair of jeans and stepped up to his sire's side. The lack of surprise in Edon's features was either a result of anticipating Silas's arrival or very good acting.

"I was the one who found the dead vampire body," Silas said, eliciting a few expressions of surprise from the circle. "And those two idiots were right on my tail. When I reached out to Edon, he was just as shocked by the corpse as I was."

Walter snorted. "That proves nothing. You're just a mutt without any standing in this community."

Silas smiled. "And yet, it's my sire you're accusing. As I have access to his mind, I'd argue my input is worthwhile in this discussion."

"While I'd argue it's inadmissible due to influence," Walter replied without missing a beat. "Just as his bitch of a mate would be deemed worthless in this trial. Yet, I don't see her here trying to defend you, Edon. How interesting."

"You'd like that, wouldn't you?" Edon said, his lips thinning. "Because then you could claim her beneath the moon as your own. After my death, of course."

"Well, I'll need a new heir. Might as well use the only alpha female in the territory who can deliver the kind of son I require." Walter shrugged. "Although, I'll have to break her in a little. Since you've failed so spectacularly."

My blood chilled.

Over my dead body, I thought, a growl threatening my throat. But I swallowed it before I let it slip.

"You can try," Edon replied, canting his head to the side. "Something tells me it'll be harder than you think."

Silas snorted. "More like impossible." He folded his arms. "You know, I am curious about something."

Walter arched a brow. "And I should care why?"

Silas lifted a shoulder. "Because you're the alpha incumbent. I'm one of your wolves. Oh, and your son is my sire."

Brave words, I thought, my tail twitching.

But that wasn't it at all.

He was stalling.

I just didn't know why.

"None of those are reasons for me to acknowledge or

even listen to a mutt." Walter focused on his son. "What on earth have you been doing with this trash to give him such confidence?"

Edon's smile was wolfish. "Bonding."

"This has all been mildly entertaining," Silvano interjected. "Alas, I'm no longer amused by this family quarrel. Clemente Clan crossed the borders without permission and murdered several of my brethren. I seek retribution for the lives lost, of which I count twelve. An alpha heir is only one. I require eleven more."

"Don't you find it odd that you were able to cross the boundaries so easily with this many vampires?" Silas asked, his tone remarkably calm considering he was addressing a royal vampire. That he held the male's gaze spoke volumes. "I was the only one patrolling tonight, while there were almost two dozen of us on the last full moon. Seems a bit, I don't know, arranged?"

"Are you suggesting I'm working with Walter? To have my own men killed?" Silvano asked, his white eyebrow meeting his equally white hairline.

"I'm suggesting your arrival was anticipated. And also, Edon doesn't yet have the authority to command the wolves to leave the borders." Silas's arms fell to his sides. "Make of that what you will."

A setup.

Which I already figured out.

But now I wondered if Walter and Silvano were working together, if perhaps the vampire knew all along that the alpha wanted to remain in charge.

Maybe he had a few minions to sacrifice.

Wouldn't be unheard of to discard a few immortals in such a way—made the paperwork easier.

What if they had an agreement drawn up among themselves? Walter helped Silvano get rid of a few unruly vampires while Silvano helped Walter maintain his position. As they shared a boundary, it would be within their best interests to remain loyal to each other.

"That is intriguing," Kylan agreed from the sidelines.

"Yes," Jace concurred beside him. "I wondered why the wolves weren't on the border. Care to elaborate, Walter?"

The alpha chuckled. "Well, we were supposed to be having a ceremony tonight. I suspect my wolves were interested in observing."

"You had one last month and relegated many of them to border patrol," Silas said. "Including me."

"Because you're a mutt unworthy of attending," Walter growled, his veneer slipping slightly. "You're lucky we even let you into the heart of the territory—something I'll be rectifying quickly once this mess is over."

"But that still doesn't explain the others," Jace pressed. "Why force them to guard one ritual but not another?"

"Tonight's a bigger ceremony with the ascension of their new alpha," Walter replied, his gaze narrowing at the royal. "What are you really accusing me of, Jace?"

"Me?" He touched his chest, his dark brows lifting. "Nothing. I'm merely curious, old friend."

Typical politics. No one meant what they were saying, and yet everyone was tossing around accusations—in silence.

"Regardless of who allowed what, I am owed my retribution," Silvano declared, his voice ringing through the night.

Simple words.

Followed by a gesture of his hand that had my heart dropping to my stomach.

A shot rang through the air, piercing my ears and shooting my pulse into overdrive.

It wasn't sanctioned.

The discussion wasn't done.

But Silvano had clearly decided to finish it, with Edon as the target.

A scream rent the air, telling me the bullet was silver—a lycan's one nemesis other than time. And to my absolute horror, I watched as Silas fell.

He'd leapt in front of the gun, the barrel still pointed at Edon.

Chaos erupted in the wake of the gunfire, starting with Edon lunging at the attacker and twisting the man's head at an angle it would take several days to return from. While Silas writhed in the middle of the field, blood pooling from his wound.

I shrieked, my shift reverting on instinct and forcing me to run to him on two legs.

But someone else reached him first. A vampire in a suit. His name not registering. My mind fracturing beneath the insanity of the moment.

I tried to chase him, to call after Silas, but cement arms clamped down around my waist, yanking me backward.

"There you are," a deep voice said against my ear.

I shivered, the menacing energy coupled with the feel of his chest against my back twisted my heart. "Walter," I breathed.

"I prefer *sir*," he replied. "But we'll work on that, little slut. We'll be working on a lot of things."

CHAPTER 31
EDON

Silas! I roared, my body twisting this way and that as I fought blow after blow from the vampires descending upon the field. *You better not fucking die on me, Silas. Or I swear, I will crawl into the afterlife just to beat you myself.*

No reply.

Fuck!

I told him not to intervene.

I told him to stay put.

I told him not to speak.

Did he listen to me at all? No. And how the fuck did he move so damn fast? I hadn't even seen the gun, but I heard it just before the bullet sailed into Silas's chest. Now I had no idea where he even went or who took him. He just disappeared before I had a chance to react.

My fist met the face of another bloodsucker, my instinct to shift overwhelming my thoughts. But I couldn't afford the few seconds required to take on my beast form. There were too many damn vampires and not enough lycans fighting.

I growled, snapping my elbow back into another

assailant and my knee into the asshole in front of me. He collapsed on a grunt, his weapon falling to the ground. I snatched it up in a flash and used the dagger to slice the throat of the male behind me.

Then moved on to the next.

All the while calling to Silas.

Without a reply.

I could feel his life energy seeping from this plane, the silver taking him from me far too soon. And all I could feel was rage.

Walter would pay for this.

All his fucking cronies, too.

A howl parted my lips as I demanded the pack to assemble, to fight, and to my surprise, several answered the call.

About. Fucking. Time.

And those who hid? Well, they'd be first on my cull list. Because no way was I letting an army of vampires take me down.

Not today.

Not for something I didn't do.

My father disappeared, leaving me to fend for myself. *Coward.* Silvano stayed, but not to fight. He merely supervised, as if enjoying the carnage.

Killing vampires took a lot of effort.

Lycans were easier, as we lacked the immortal gene. But that didn't make us weak. I proved that by taking down three more of his men while he observed in stoic silence.

Where the hell was my grandfather? He could put an end to this madness.

And Luna… I'd felt her moments ago. Where had she run off to?

A smack against my side had me focusing on the idiot who'd just thought to strike me. I put him down with a fist to his chin before whirling on the vampire approaching behind me.

They were all so young, maybe a hundred years at best.

Which meant Silvano had brought his D-team to the fight.

Poor choice. But hey, it worked in my favor, so I wasn't about to complain.

Silas, I tried again.

Static. Quiet. Nothing.

My heart ached, my soul crying out at the injustice of his fall. Why had he jumped before that bullet? How—

Stars flickered behind my eyes as something hard slammed into the back of my skull. I blinked, shook my head, and danced around to fight, but my vision began to bleed into spots of light.

No. I wasn't giving up. Not yet. Not when… *What is that?* The sharp cry echoed in my ears, kick-starting my heart. *Luna!*

CHAPTER 32
LUNA

"Fuck you," I snarled, my arms straining as I tried futilely to loosen Walter's hold. He'd yanked me behind one of the houses, one hand encircling my neck while the opposite held both of my wrists.

"As soon as Edon dies, I'll grant your wish," he growled, his lips far too close to my neck for my liking.

His goal wasn't lost on me. My ties to Edon would die with him, allowing Walter to stake his claim beneath the moon.

And then I'd be well and truly fucked. Both figuratively and literally.

Not going to happen.

I kicked back against him, and he responded by shoving me into the log exterior of the home, causing me to cry out in pain. Because *fuck,* that hurt.

My father stood close by with a look of disgust on his face. Not at Walter, no. But at *me.*

And my mother—her eyes shone with tears.

Logan, however, appeared ready to commit murder.

He'd already tried to intervene once, which resulted in the black eye now blossoming on his handsome face.

Our father was a fucking dick.

But my brother appeared ready to try again. His hands fisted at his sides, his blue eyes locking on mine as he tried to convey some sort of plan. He looked pointedly at my wrists gripped tightly behind my back. And then he cocked his chin sharply.

I didn't understand his goal until he charged forward— his focus on Walter. I jerked my hands just as he crashed into the shocked alpha behind me, thereby breaking his grip.

However, the one on my neck squeezed harshly.

I hacked, my airway crushing beneath his grip, but was suddenly freed as Logan slammed a fist into Walter's jaw.

My father roared in fury, charging forward, only to be slammed off his path by my mother. "Run!" she shouted at me. Just before my father yanked her to the ground on a yelp.

I didn't want to listen.

I didn't want to run.

But I wasn't about to let their rebellion be all for nothing.

My legs took off, my body aching from the places Walter had manhandled me. If I could hide until sunrise, I'd be safe for another month. I just had to get away, to—

A hand clamped over my mouth, yanking me backward into a hard body that smelled of death. Another arm clamped around my middle as I tried to fight, furious that I'd escaped only to fall captive yet again.

What the fuck?!

I'm not this woman.

I am not weak.

Let me go!

I fought with everything I owned, earning me a curse and a grunt from my new captor. And then he slammed me harshly into an ungiving surface.

Another damn house.

I growled, fed up with being manhandled and treated like a damsel. This wasn't—

He spun me around, his forearm at my throat, and piercing blue eyes met mine. The color of ice. "I'm all for a feisty wolf, darling, but right now, we need your help to understand something."

My lips parted. *Jace.*

And who the hell was *we?*

He pushed me through the door of the home and shut it behind him with a kick. "We don't have a lot of time, so I suggest you be a good little wolf and play along."

"I told you, it's too soon," another male said, his stance casual as he leaned against the wall. "We need more time before we show our cards."

"So we let Edon die and try to start over?" Jolene replied, hands in his pockets. "Can't guarantee I'll be alive long enough to see it through, gentlemen. I've given that boy everything I've got, and he's exactly what we need in this region."

"And what about Silvano?" the dark-haired vampire asked, his tone as nonchalant as his pose. "It's going to raise a hell of a lot of questions, especially so soon after what happened to Robyn."

"That wasn't even related," a fourth voice put in with a sardonic snort. *Luka.*

Shit. What had Jace just pulled me into the middle of?

"Whether it was or wasn't isn't the point. All this unrest is going to alarm Lilith." The dark-haired one pushed off the wall. "I'm not discounting the fact that you've put a lot of effort into this, Jolene. I'm merely pointing out the paperwork that will be involved should we intervene. It may set us back years, as we'll be forced to maintain a low profile."

"If we don't intervene, we lose two clans," Jace replied softly. "Which sets us back several decades."

"Two?" Luka asked.

"Logan just assaulted Walter." Jace looked at me. "To save his sister."

I swallowed. Was this where he wanted my input? Because I didn't know what to say.

"Well, shit." Luka rubbed a hand down his face, shaking his head. "Niko isn't going to like that."

"No, I suspect not." Jace was still looking at me. "Tell us about your relationship with Edon and Silas."

My eyebrows rose. "Excuse me?"

"You're fucking them both. Is it because Edon's making you?" His flat tone didn't match the severity of his question.

"Fuck you," I growled. "And fuck your assumption."

His lips quirked upward. "Oh, Claudette has raised you perfectly, I see." He glanced at Luka. "There's hope for your precious daughter yet if Logan's anything like this one."

"Considering he just attacked Walter, I'll say he's a perfect candidate."

Jace lifted a shoulder. "True." His focus locked on me again. "Your relationship with Edon and Silas isn't accepted by current social conditions. How do you feel about that?"

"Like my relationship with Edon and Silas is none of your damn business," I replied flatly. "What the hell is this? There's a war going on outside, and you're all gossiping with me about who I'm fucking? Talking about my brother like he's some pawn in your game of chess? Fuck that. You're wasting my time." I took a step, only to find the dark-haired male suddenly at my back.

Power vibrated off him in waves, causing goose bumps to flare across my limbs and reminding me that I was very much naked in a room full of dominant males.

Not good.

Especially considering Jace's penchant to play with wolves.

I swallowed. "Look, Edon's innocent. He didn't attack Silvano's vampires or issue any sort of edict telling his wolves to go on the hunt. His father just wants to maintain his power." I looked imploringly at Jolene. "Tell them."

"They already know, sweetheart," he replied, sliding off his jacket and handing it to me. "They're trying to figure out if they should intervene."

"Well, if you ask me, I say you should," a new voice declared as Kylan entered from the back of the house. "I mean, what's a revolution without a little kickoff party?"

The only indication that they were surprised by his appearance was the slight stiffening in Luka's shoulders.

"You know, I missed my invitation to the party," Kylan drawled, his expression one of stark amusement. "But I've sensed your intentions for some time now. What are we all waiting for? I vote we take out Silvano. He's one of the reasons we're all in this mess. I promise he won't be missed by those who count."

Silence met his statement.

But the tick in Jace's jaw said the male had struck a nerve.

"I can do it," Kylan continued. "I mean, I already have a knack for pissing off Lilith. Maybe she'll put me wherever she hid Cam."

All the males exchanged a glance.

"Oh, come on. I can't be the only one who suspects he's still alive." He looked at Luka. "His Erosita lives with your clan, right?" He sighed at their continued silence. "I see. Well. If my services are requested for whatever the fuck this is, you know where to find me."

Jace stopped him with a hand on his shoulder, their gazes locking in a long, silent duel while the cries of wolves and vampires bled through the night air outside.

My chest ached for them all, especially Edon. The only thing that kept me upright was the strength radiating through his mating bond.

He was alive and fighting and mourning Silas.

Whom he couldn't feel anymore.

A tear slipped from the edge of my eye, my nails grasping my jacket even tighter around myself. "We can't just stand here," I whispered. "I don't know why you're all standing around debating a timeline when you could be helping. But I do know this: not intervening when you can just makes you all a bunch of cowards." I looked pointedly at Jolene. "Your grandson is fighting for his life out there. I'm going to join him with or without your help."

I thrust my elbow backward, expecting to strike the dark-haired one, but only met air. He stood by the door with an amused expression. "We should introduce her to Juliet," he said, glancing at Jace. "See if we can't instill some of that feisty energy."

"Trust me, D. Mira is already working on it," Luka put in.

D smiled. "Brilliant." And then he opened the door. "After you, little wolf."

Little wolf.

Little mate.

Little moon.

I was really, *really* tired of everyone calling me *little*.

I was not short.

I was not weak.

I just happened to be less muscled and tinier than the others around me. But I possessed an alpha bloodline for a reason. And they were all about to find out why.

CHAPTER 33

EDON

RED.

Everything around me was stained in *red*. The vampires. The wolves. Silvano and his fucking smirk. The moon. The grass. The male trying to bite me.

All. Fucking. Red.

I couldn't hear Silas. I couldn't find Luna. I couldn't focus on anything other than the assholes who kept trying to take me down.

I would not fall. Not like this. Not until I knew Silas's and Luna's fates.

A growl ripped from my throat as I took down yet another bloodsucker. They just kept *coming*. Fortunately, it seemed most of them were without weapons.

So what happened to the gun? I wondered for the thousandth time. Someone had one. Yet he'd fled, leaving only vampires with knives in his wake.

Which led me to believe it wasn't a vampire who tried to shoot me, but a wolf.

How did Silas know?

No. No time for that now. I'd analyze later.

Silvano. He was the key to ending this all. If I could just fucking get close enough to incapacitate him, his minions would—

Shit!

A sharp edge struck my rib cage, sending me to my knees and rolling away from the source as fire licked through my veins.

Another damn knife.

Better than a gun.

I whirled on the ground, ignoring the pain shooting up my side, and lashed out at my attacker. Only, the air fled my lungs and refused to replenish.

He punctured my lung.

Okay, so worse than a scrape.

A cringe rendered me useless for half a second—long enough for my assailant to jump on top of me and aim the blade at my throat.

I caught his wrist, twisting it, but spots danced before my vision, leaving me woozy. He pressed down, his strength matching mine because of his superior position.

Sadism radiated from the male's face, contorting his lips into a wicked sneer.

Not good. Not good at all.

I grasped his throat with my opposite hand while trying to break his wrist with my other palm. Anything to deter him from placing that deadly weapon at my neck once more.

But he inched closer.

And closer.

Until a ball of white knocked him off me with a violent snarl.

Luna.

Relief flooded me at the sight of her svelte form destroying the vampire's face while he screamed in agony, his knife long forgotten. I grabbed it, then gave myself a second to recover before jumping to my feet. It hurt like a son of a bitch, but newfound adrenaline surged inside me.

My mate was alive.

She was here.

And the woman fought like a damn goddess.

She took down two more vampires with her jaws alone, ripping out their throats before returning to my side, her sleek coat painted in blood.

Gorgeous.

If we weren't in the middle of a fight for our lives, I would have grabbed her, forced her to turn, and fucked her on this very field.

But I had another horde of vampires appearing from the tree line as if Silvano had a whole army of reserves just waiting to attack. He must have deployed them in waves. It explained why he hadn't acted sooner during my argument with Walter.

What are your real intentions? I wondered. Because he wouldn't waste this many resources just to take me down for an old friend. This had to be a double cross, a way to weaken the Clemente Clan and take more land.

And my idiot of a father had fallen for it by opening the borders.

Come right in.

Destroy my wolves.

As long as I keep my throne, I don't care.

When I survived this insanity, my father would pay.

With my lungs barely recovered—thanks to my lycan healing—more vampires poured onto the grounds, their orders clear. *Kill on sight.*

The newcomers were refreshed.

I was not.

My wolf ached to come out to play, but there wasn't

time. I twirled the knives in my hands—ones I'd stolen from the vampires who came before them.

"Welcome to the Clemente Clan," I greeted them, narrowing my eyes. "Allow me to properly introduce myself."

Luna growled and acquainted them with her teeth while I carved my initials into their skin.

I was mid-design on Vampire Three when a hush fell over the crowd. And all the bloodsuckers collectively fell to their knees.

My eyes tracked across the field to the cause.

Kylan.

He stood casually in the middle of the bloody field wearing a pristine suit. And unceremoniously dropped Silvano's head on the ground.

"I'm sorry. Did I interrupt?" he asked, his tone nonchalant as he wiped his hand off with a handkerchief.

"I think you destroyed their fun," Jace replied as he joined him.

"Pity." Kylan folded the soiled fabric and returned it to his pocket, then took in the crowd. "Well, I see our societal laws are working splendidly. Would someone like to call Lilith? I'm sure she'll be thrilled."

Silence.

Of course no one wanted to report this to the Blood Alliance.

Luna shifted beside me, her pale skin glowing with blood as she stood proud at my side. I brushed my lips along her neck, then skimmed my nose across her cheek, taking in her alluring scent. "Thank you," I whispered.

"You're my mate," she replied softly, her gaze finding mine. "Silas?"

I shook my head, my heart stuttering in my chest. *I can't sense him,* I admitted into her mind. *I can't sense him at all.*

And it left me feeling so fucking empty.

Hurt.

Lost.

Alone.

Guilty.

Luna cupped my cheek and kissed me tenderly, even as her eyes filled with tears. "You're not—"

"Where's Walter?" Jace demanded, shattering our moment.

I pressed my forehead to hers briefly, allowing myself the second of grief before righting my spine and focusing on the royal. It was on the tip of my tongue to claim my place as alpha when my father's gruff voice sounded from behind one of the lodges.

"Here." The asshole appeared with a handful of alphas, including Luna's father. All of them appeared pissed off, but my gaze was for the bastard leading them.

It was still a full moon.

And I had a hell of a lot of aggression to work out.

For myself.

For Luna.

For Silas.

"Fight me," I demanded before anyone else could speak. Politics be damned, I wanted this bullshit done. "End this once and for all."

His resulting laugh lacked humor. "Now isn't the time for your antics, boy."

I smiled. "On the contrary, now is the perfect fucking time. We're all here, right? It's still a full moon. My birthright defines tonight as my ascension. And I'm calling it. You want to keep your place as clan alpha? Earn it and fight me for it. Maybe you'll even have a leg up since I've been out here battling with the clan while you tucked your tail and ran."

A few of the exhausted wolves around me snorted their disgust, but for once, it was directed at my father and not me.

I tossed my blades onto the ground beside two of the kneeling vampires and stepped forward. "Fight. Me." I allowed the demand to permeate my growl, vibrating the field around us. "Or bow and acknowledge me as your alpha."

My father bristled. "I don't have to do or acknowledge anything."

"Actually, you do," my grandfather interjected. He strolled up to the field with Luka beside him, the two males standing at equal height. Energy radiated off them, denoting their bloodlines. But it was my grandfather who seemed to be the more powerful of the duo. "It's the right of any alpha heir to challenge the alpha incumbent during any full-moon ritual after the heir's twenty-second birthday. Which, for Edon, occurred three months ago."

Several wolves murmured their agreement, including two of the alphas at Walter's side.

I cocked a brow. "Scared?"

My father spit at the ground, his eyes narrowing. "Of you?" He let out another of those humorless laughs. "Hardly."

"Good." Because I intended to destroy him and I wanted him aware of every fucking minute. "Wolf or man form?"

He seemed to consider—whether it was my question or his chances of talking his way out of this, I wasn't sure.

I didn't care.

I just wanted to annihilate him.

"I want a second," he declared, referring not to time but to his desire for a partner.

Whispers hushed through the crowd, the alpha's

demand not a common one. Usually, two wolves fought to the death—alone.

But I immediately understood why my father chose this route.

He didn't think I had anyone to fight at my side, and he was banking on it being a two-on-one fight.

Asshole.

His lips curled. "Unless there's no one you trust to stand at your side?" he taunted.

Luna bristled. "I'll fucking stand at his side."

Fuck. That wasn't going to work for me. If she tried to fight my father, I'd lose my focus. I trusted her, knew she could fight, but no way could I allow my father to touch a hair on her head.

And his responding grin said he knew. "Well, this should—"

"I'll fight with him," my grandfather announced.

Murmurs littered the night, all shocked at the pronouncement. Except my father merely chuckled. "We both know that's against the rules, Jolene."

Jolene. Never *Father.* Or *Dad.* Always *Jolene.*

"Some would say provoking a war in order to maintain power is also against the rules," my grandfather replied casually.

Disbelief colored the alpha incumbent's features. "Don't tell me you believe the bullshit my son is spouting about me."

"Unfortunately, there's no way to confirm or deny the cause, what with all the witnesses being dead and all." He glanced pointedly at Silvano's head on the ground before looking at Kylan—who shrugged—and then took in the carnage of slain lycans throughout the field. Barry and Glenn were among them.

How sad.

"Do you believe this?" My father glanced at Niko. "The old alpha is accusing me of orchestrating this carnage. All to deflect away from the rules that say a former alpha is not permitted to play in the challenge ring. At least, not as a second."

"And here I thought you would welcome the chance to fight me," my grandfather drawled. "A shame you're such a coward."

I smirked. The old man knew how to play with words—a talent I'd picked up from him.

"Unlike you, Jolene, I merely wish to follow the rules, and as Luna spoke up first, I'm going to allow the bitch to serve as his second instead." His smile was all teeth. "Unless she's backing down from the challenge?"

I grimaced, knowing full well she wouldn't.

But a deeper voice responded instead. One that halted my heart.

"As his progeny, I volunteer to be his second."

CHAPTER 34
SILAS

The crowd parted around me, expressions of surprise on their faces.

Yeah, look all you want, pansy asses, I thought as I moved with Rae at my side. I was in a bit of a mood, thanks to the silver bullet that nearly pierced my heart.

When Rae told me what was happening, I hadn't even needed to think about my decision. Edon needed a second, and I was the only one he could trust apart from Luna. And while she could more than hold her own, I knew she'd also serve as a distraction. His protective instincts would require him to intervene, thereby skewing his focus.

With me, he should be able to do his thing. I hoped, anyway.

Jolene gave me a subtle nod from across the courtyard as I caught his eye. Rae had mentioned he was stalling, and Kylan told her it was because of me. They wanted me to fight at Edon's side. I didn't need their support, but I appreciated the vote of confidence.

The royal in question intercepted me, his midnight

irises dropping to my chest and noting the dry blood and healed wound. He smirked.

You're welcome, his eyes seemed to say, leaving me uneasy. I didn't want to owe him a debt, but I did. Except it wasn't like I'd asked for his help. He was the one who sliced his wrist open and forced me to drink from him.

He held out an arm for Rae. "Consort."

"Sire," she returned, settling into his side.

"Good luck, wolf," he murmured, moving out of my way.

Luck. Yeah. Seemed a bit frivolous.

Because I didn't need it.

His blood had left me feeling oddly energetic. Revitalized. All of my senses were heightened, as if I'd been reborn as something decidedly other. I could *hear* Edon's heart beating despite him being several yards away.

Fuck, I could hear *everyone*.

"Silas," Luna breathed, tears shining brightly in the depths of her eyes.

That look erased my thoughts and sent me walking swiftly in her direction. I caught her as she threw her arms around my neck. Edon met my gaze over her shoulder, his dark gaze sparkling with a multitude of questions.

Likely because he couldn't access my mind.

We'd have to figure out why later.

For now, he needed to get his head in the game and not worry about things we had no control over.

"Surprise isn't a good look on you, Alpha," I said, a warning lacing my tone. "I much prefer you enraged and craving vengeance." If we were going to fight his father, I needed his focus.

"You're okay," Luna whispered, not receiving the same memo.

And the broken quality in her words derailed me once more.

Fuck propriety. These idiots can wait another minute.

I cupped Luna's cheek and kissed her softly while ignoring the sounds of surprise rising from the crowd. She shivered against me, her arms winding around my neck. "You were shot." Her words were so soft I doubted anyone other than me and Edon heard her, even with their enhanced hearing. "With silver," she added.

"I healed." I brushed my lips over hers once more before pressing my mouth to her ear. "I'll explain later, little moon. I promise."

She nodded, her throat bobbing. "Right. Yeah." She seemed to be remembering our surroundings, a mask falling over her features. "Right," she repeated.

Edon stood motionless beside us, his ears picking up every word, his expression still rimmed with queries.

"You ready to ascend?" I asked him as I released Luna with a final kiss to her temple.

He looked me over, his gaze pausing on my chest and roaming downward before returning to my face. "Can you fight?"

I smiled. "I'm not bleeding, am I?"

"You look remarkably well healed for someone shot with silver," he apprised, narrowing his eyes. "Do I want to know how that's possible?"

"Not right now, no." I flicked my gaze to his father and squared my shoulders. "As I said, I volunteer as his second."

Walter chuckled, the sound cruel. "I think you've been *volunteering* to serve my son in more ways than one lately." He glanced at Jolene. "I suppose triads do run in the family, right?"

Triads? That wasn't a term I'd heard before, but I could guess at what it meant.

"Well, I accept your choice, Edon," Walter continued, his voice a low drawl. "I'll just take a piece out of Luna after I win."

Edon grinned. "So confident."

"I am," he replied. "Because I pick Niko as my second."

Gasps littered the courtyard, echoing off the surrounding lodges and trees. Edon and I shared a glance.

"That has to be against the rules," Luna said, taking the words right out of my mouth. "If Edon can't fight with Jolene, you can't fight with the alpha of another clan."

"Your daughter's manners are severely lacking," Walter informed Niko conversationally. "I'm starting to question how you raised your children in Ernest Clan."

Niko snorted. "Trust me, I'll be having a long chat with Claudette when I return." He glowered at Luna. "And the rules state Walter can pick anyone tied to his pack, of which I am, thanks to your union with his son. It may not be a common choice, but it's an acceptable one. As I have an heir who is almost of age, I am eligible to compete. Not that it matters, as I have no intention of losing."

Walter chuckled. "Neither do I."

"You're forgetting a key detail—the alpha heir must accept your terms," Jolene said. "And as they are ridiculous, I suggest—"

"Oh, I accept," Edon announced. "I was just waiting for the two of them to finish showboating." He sounded so poised and at ease by the prospect of taking down two alphas. No, not just alphas. But two *experienced* alphas.

With me by his side.

A newbie.

An omega.

"Are you sure about this?" I asked him softly. Because I sure as fuck wasn't. One of the other wolves in the clan? Yeah, sure. But another alpha? That was an entirely different situation.

"Definitely," he replied.

"Edon," Luna whispered, her hand circling his arm. "You don't know my father like I do. This isn't a good idea."

"Have some faith." He kissed her on the cheek and stepped forward. "What form do you choose, Walter?"

His choice of using his father's first name wasn't lost on me. He was detaching himself from family obligations and preparing himself for what had to be done.

He was readying himself for the inevitable kill.

"Wolf," his father replied, his eyes on me. "That won't be a problem for your new progeny, will it?"

Ass, I thought. He knew I'd be weaker in my animal form since it was all still so new to me.

But of course, Edon didn't take that into account. He merely said, "Wolf it is. I just need a minute with my second and we can begin."

"Sure," his father agreed, sounding smug.

Edon turned to me, his palm finding my nape as he tugged me close. "Why can't I hear you?" he demanded, the words a whisper meant for my ears alone. Luna didn't even seem to pick up on the question, because her brow furrowed as if she couldn't figure out what he was doing.

"I don't know," I admitted. "But I think it's related to Kylan."

"Kylan?"

"Yeah." I pitched my voice even lower, ensuring that absolutely no one—not even Luna—overheard. "He gave me his blood."

Edon's eyebrows shot up. "*What?*"

"What is it?" Luna asked, her concern palpable. "What are you two talking about?"

Edon held my gaze for a long moment, then released me and bent to speak directly into her ear. Despite the soft tenor, I heard every word—thanks to my enhanced senses. "Silas drank Kylan's blood."

She gasped, her pupils widening. "That's—"

"Forbidden," Edon finished for her. "Yes."

"It's not like the royal gave me a choice," I said through my teeth, my gaze slipping to the vampire in question. He winked at me from his position near the edge, completely unperturbed. "Why is it forbidden?"

"Because it enhances your senses and strengths," Edon whispered. "Which happens to be perfect for our current situation, apart from Kylan's energy blocking my access to your mind."

Luna frowned. "Walter must not realize Silas was shot."

"And I see no point to educate him otherwise," Edon replied, glancing at his father. "He more than earned a little surprise, don't you think?"

I rolled my shoulders, my neck popping along the way. "Yeah. I'd say he does."

He glanced down at my jeans and then back up. "Those mine?"

"Yeah."

"Good." He gripped my neck again and yanked me forward until our chests touched. "His blood might be running through your system right now, but you're still fucking mine. You feel me?"

His mouth sealed over mine, making it impossible to reply.

Holy. Fuck.

Edon was claiming me.

In front of the entire fucking pack.

And not just as his progeny.

The sheer possession in his kiss left me breathless and kick-started my heart.

Until a growl from his father halted the moment.

Edon ended our embrace with a nip to my lower lip, his dark eyes glowing with intent. "This isn't over."

"I know."

"No holding back, Omega."

"Right back at you, Alpha."

"Then let's kick some ass." He grabbed Luna and kissed her tenderly before spinning her into my arms. "That wasn't goodbye, little mate. Just a promise."

"I know," she breathed, her focus sliding from him to me. "You'll protect each other."

"Always," I vowed, bending my head to run my lips over her freshly kissed ones. "Be prepared to run should anything happen," I breathed against her ear.

I released her before she could reply and moved to Edon's side.

Walter stood scowling at his son from several yards away. "You disgust me."

"Good," he replied. "That means I'm doing something right."

His father opened his mouth to speak again, only to be cut off by Jace. "I'm growing bored by all the chitchat. Are you going to fight? Or shall I go have a drink and come back later?"

Walter chuckled. "Always so eager to watch wolves rip each other apart, aren't you, old friend?"

"I do enjoy a little blood, yes," the vampire drawled. "Maybe I'll sample some of your wolves when this is all done."

Walter shrugged. "You're my guest."

"Only for the moment," Edon put in. "Soon he'll be my guest, and there will be no sampling of anything without consent."

Walter shook his head. "I should have killed you when you were a pup."

Edon grinned. "Stop stalling, old man. Let's finish this."

"Gladly." Walter shrugged out of his jacket and shirt, revealing a muscular torso dotted in fine brown hairs. Niko followed suit, his body slightly less broad but equally lean and athletic.

"We need a strategy," I whispered.

"We have one." Edon popped the button on his jeans, sliding down the zipper. "Kill."

Yeah, excellent strategy, I thought, removing my pants. *Really glad I asked.*

I don't see the problem, wolf. Did you not assassinate the majority of your opponents during the Immortal Cup?

I jerked upright, my gaze honing in on Kylan. He studiously ignored me, his gaze on Rae. *Get out of my head.*

He tsked. *Now, now. I'm only here to help, then I'll release you back to your alpha.*

I don't want your help, I snarled, kicking my jeans away from my feet and calling my inner wolf.

If you die, Raelyn will be upset. Therefore, you will tolerate my assistance and strength just as you accepted my blood.

Had my lips not been in the process of elongating into a snout, I would have cursed. Kylan wanted to help? Fine. *Just don't distract me.*

On the contrary, wolf. I intend to guide you. Walter thinks you're weak in your animal form; it's why he chose it. And now that he's seen his son's affection for you, he's going to use both to his advantage by having Niko attack Edon while Walter tries to kill you. It's a classic move, one that he'll hope to use to distract his son and thereby weaken you both.

Thanks for the tip, I thought at him and shook out my coat.

That wasn't my tip, Silas. My suggestion is you hold your own against Walter until Edon is done with Niko.

Hold my own against a three-hundred-year-old alpha. Got it.

Three hundred twenty-two, but that's just semantics. Use my blood. I gave you more than enough. It's powerful. Don't waste it.

If I knew how to use it, I would.

Instinct, wolf. Follow your instincts.

Jolene stepped into the field, his expression stoic as he took in the four wolves in the courtyard. "Give them a wide berth," he advised, sending the crowd backward to create a giant ring—one that reminded me of a much larger version of the punishment circle.

Edon sat beside me, his wolf form slightly bigger than mine. He seemed perfectly at ease, as though we hadn't signed up to fight to the death.

Niko and Walter paced in expectation, their sizes rivaling Edon's.

Leaving me as the smallest.

The omega.

Great.

With that spirit, you'll die in two minutes, Kylan chastised. *And that will upset my consort. You do not want that to happen, Silas. Trust me.*

Threats don't really work in this situation, I informed him.

Did you really survive all this torment just to die at the hand of an alpha you loathe? he countered. *Because that would be a damn shame.*

It's not like I want to die.

Yeah? How about you prove it, wolf? Think about what that sadistic ass is going to do to your precious Luna. Think about what he's already done. Channel it and use my strength. Don't make me regret lending it to you.

His commentary overrode whatever Jolene was saying. Something about the parameters, which I summed up to be a fight to the death or until someone submitted.

As I was standing in a ring with three alpha males, I highly doubted the latter would occur.

Jolene listed a few ritual rules, stating no one from the audience could interfere—which caused Kylan to snort into my head—and reiterated the terms Edon agreed to with Walter.

"Whoever wins claims Clemente Clan as his own. If the alpha incumbent of Ernest Clan falls, his successor takes charge. Are there any objections before we begin?"

Silence.

"Then I hereby declare this challenge valid. You may be—"

Walter lunged, and I reacted by dodging to my left. *Fuck!* I didn't realize we would immediately start. The damn alpha hadn't even waited for Jolene to finish. And if the snarls I heard to my right were anything to go by, Niko hadn't either.

A whirl of white fur raced past me just before Walter charged again.

I dodged him, eliciting a growl from him and several gasps from the crowd. Why it shocked them, I had no idea. Nor did I have time to consider it as my attacker leapt toward me.

Another skip away, followed by a roll and a prance to the side, had him snarling furiously.

Apparently, he wasn't a fan of my playing hard to get.

Too bad for him.

Because I wasn't about to stop.

All I had going for me was speed and agility. If he

caught me, I was fucked. My strength didn't match his, and we both knew it. That was why he kept trying to catch me and why I kept just out of reach.

Shock permeated the air, followed by the pungent stench of fear.

I couldn't look to find out what caused it, my gaze firmly on the raging alpha coming after my tail.

His claws swiped a little too close for comfort as I danced just out of reach again.

If Kylan was talking, I didn't hear him, one hundred percent of my focus on the field and my opponent. I just needed to—

Something smacked into my back, sending me flying over the earth and directly into Walter's path. He slammed into me at full force, his claws ripping through my side in a sharp stab of agony.

Fuck!

Fight! a voice demanded. I didn't know whom it belonged to and didn't hang around to find out.

I struck out at Walter with one of my paws, faster and harder than ever before, and grunted when I hit solid fur. Fighting in animal form was new to me, something I had no experience with, so I gave myself over to my wolf and let him drive my motions.

Snap.

Swipe.

Duck.

Roll.

So fast.

Repeat.

Pain sliced up my back, nails digging into my flesh as I bit down on a mouthful of white fluff. And skin. Oh, yeah. I tasted blood. A lot of it. And I wanted *more*.

Walter was bigger and stronger, but I had speed on my

side and I used it to my advantage, returning his strikes with a vengeance. Yet it still wasn't enough. He had me pinned, his teeth searching for purchase against my throat.

I refused to yield, scrunching my shoulders and protecting my neck while squirming beneath him and seeking for a weakness. Anything to shove him off me, to—

Cheers sailed into the night, and suddenly Walter was gone. Edon pinned him, their forms evenly matched, and then they began to spar over the ground in a whirl of bloody fur I couldn't track.

I heaved a breath, climbed to my paws, and shook out my coat. Niko's headless form lay on the ground a few yards away, his wolf form having melted back into his human one upon death.

Edon won.

Not yet, a voice replied. *And he's wounded. So stop fucking around and go help him.*

I didn't think; I acted, running after the blur of white and knocking into Walter's side. He yelped as Edon caught his limb, his teeth shredding the leg to the bone and crushing it beneath his jaws.

I bit Walter's flank, forcing him to heel as Edon switched to the opposite thigh and bit down.

Only, Walter didn't want to stay still.

The bastard bellowed from his throat and rolled with a force I didn't expect, crushing me beneath him and leaving Edon somehow on top. Canines met my throat, pushing downward into my windpipe, crushing the vital—

Edon ripped him off me with a growl and clamped down on Walter's neck.

The sounds that came from them both would haunt me for eternity.

And yet, I couldn't stop watching, fascinated by the sight of Walter *bleeding*. I wanted to lap it up in victory, to bathe in his torment, but the damn wolf slammed a paw on the ground, causing Edon to freeze.

I didn't understand at first.

I thought something was wrong.

And then it registered.

Walter. Had. Fucking. Yielded.

Oh, hell no! That bastard deserved his death and worse, not to be let off and allowed to live.

But Edon stepped away, his lips curled to reveal his razor-sharp teeth as he watched Walter shift back into his human form with two very broken legs. He collapsed into the fetal position, like a fucking baby, and shivered.

"It's a fight to the death or until one of them yields," Jolene announced, his voice grim. "The Clemente Clan alpha incumbent has yielded."

Insults littered the air from all sides.

"At least Niko died with honor," one said.

"All for a sorry excuse for an alpha," another added.

"Pathetic."

"Weak."

"Kill him. He's not worthy of life."

Edon returned to his human form, a variety of gashes and deep wounds marring his athletic form, and stood. He narrowed his gaze at the male quivering on the ground. "Submit," he growled. "Call me your alpha."

Walter trembled, his shoulders shaking, but his lips remained closed.

Edon grabbed his nape and yanked him around to shout into his face. "Submit!"

"Y-you're the alpha," he whispered.

"Not good enough, old man." Edon tossed him back onto the ground. "Not. Fucking. Good. Enough." He kicked him in the side, causing Walter to cry out in pain. "I want to hear it from your fucking lips, you old piece of shit.

I want every fucking confession, too. Or I'll end you right now, right here."

Walter's resulting grin was bloody and malicious. "You don't have the balls to kill me, kid."

Edon's eyebrows rose. "No?" He glanced at me and then to Luna. "We all know you didn't kill Bianca, that my father somehow placed your scent all around the scene of the crime. How badly do you want to hear his admission?"

"It's not needed," Jolene said, stepping onto the field with a sword. "Your father's been tapping into the pack psyche. I've suspected it for years, and tonight confirmed it. He compelled his own wolves to ignite a war and then hid like a coward while they all fought for their lives." He shook his head and glanced down at the pathetic male on the ground. "You've literally driven yourself mad, just like I once advised would happen if you abused the power of being alpha."

"Fuck you," Walter spat, interrupting my mental reply. "You know nothing of true power. You're just a weak old man too afraid to do what's necessary to keep the pack alive."

"And it took me far too long to realize you felt that way, my son," he replied, handing Edon the sword. "I warned you the pack psyche isn't a place to meddle, but you've been playing in the minds of your wolves for too long."

Pack psyche, I thought, frowning. Luna mentioned that once, but I didn't really understand it. *Is it like a hive mind?*

Yes, Kylan replied. *I'm not a wolf, but from what I understand, the pack psyche is a mental plane of existence that can only be reached by the alpha of a clan. It gives him the ability to check in with every member under his protection, to monitor them, and to reach out as needed. Similar to your sire link to Edon, only it requires a significant amount of focus to intrude, while your bond is far more natural.*

From Edon's expression, he already understood all of this. He gave a humorless laugh and shook his head. "Fuck, I should have known. Of course you invaded the pack psyche. I never even considered that as a cause, but it makes so much sense. You turned everyone in this pack against me for your own gain—through brainwashing. And used them all—*their scents*—to frame others for crimes you committed."

Like the vampire, I translated, understanding. *That's why it smelled like pack. But how did he taint Bianca's body with Luna's scent?*

By altering the senses of those at the scene, Kylan replied. *Best guess, anyway. I assume her body was removed immediately?*

I honestly didn't know. But it was likely.

Walter snorted. "Trust me, the brainwashing wasn't required." He spit out a mouthful of blood and glowered up at his son. "Everyone knows you're a pathetic excuse for an alpha. They'll never follow you."

"Not the ones you kept close, no," Jolene interjected. "But you're forgetting all the other wolves who reside within our boundaries. Wolves who you've kept out of the inner circle. Wolves you denied for far too long. Wolves you've left to starve."

"They weren't worthy of my resources," Walter replied. "And they seem to be doing fine on their own."

"Because I guided them," Jolene growled. "I ensured they survived long enough for Edon's new reign."

Edon twirled the sword, his gaze narrowing. "Which begins now."

Walter began to speak, but Edon didn't give him a chance.

The blade sliced through the air so fast I almost missed the beautiful connection to Walter's stocky neck. Which would have been a shame because seeing him beheaded was one of the most magnificent sights of my existence.

Almost as good as watching his head roll across the ground to the chorus of gasps.

Luna stepped forward and spit on the old man's corpse. "Bastard."

I would have smiled, but that would have looked more like a snarl in my current form.

"I'd say that's a fair judgment," Jace announced conversationally. "I mean, the man did provoke a war with Silvano through his antics."

"Oh, they were working together," Kylan replied. "Did I fail to mention that when I dropped his head on the ground? My bad."

"A royal and an alpha leading their people to unnecessary harm?" another mused, causing conversation to boom through the air and leaving me with an insane headache of noise.

All to be ended by a screech of sound that came from an unknown source near the lodges.

Such agony and pain, and holy Goddess…

Lilith.

CHAPTER 35
EDON

Lilith entered the circle of death with wide green eyes, her stiletto heels sinking into the earth and her pristine blonde hair frizzing from the heat. This was not her terrain and it showed.

She took in the dead bodies of Niko and Walter, the sword in my hand, and then the field of death around us. Some of the vampires and lycans were beginning to stir, their supernatural genetics allowing them to heal—at least the ones who still had heads.

Only silver to the heart or a beheading could keep a wolf down indefinitely.

Which reminded me… *What happened to the gun used against Silas? And who fired it?*

None of the other vampires had fought with silver, telling me they were trying to minimize the damage. A fact that further proved my father and Silvano had been working together.

Except the attack went far beyond the means necessary to stage a coup.

So what had Silvano wanted to gain, exactly? He couldn't take over the territory if it still thrived with wolves, and as only a handful were truly dead, he stood no chance in owning Clemente Clan.

"Why?" Lilith demanded, her eyes on Silvano's head. "Who took his life?"

"I did," Kylan replied, his stance relaxed. "It was the only way to stop the fighting. Once I held his extinguished life in my hands, his vampires fell to my control. And I commanded them to cease their violent nonsense."

Lilith gaped at him. Then glanced around again, taking in their audience—wolves, vampires, royals, alphas, mates. She shook her head as if to clear it, her face far more pale than usual beneath the moon.

There were over a hundred gathered in this field. Most of whom were naked and covered in blood.

She studied Walter's remains, then narrowed her gaze at me. "I assume you're now in charge here?"

"Unofficially," I replied, straightening my spine. "We never had a chance to finish the rituals given the unexpected attack led by Silvano."

While I was technically the Clemente Alpha now, I hadn't ascended properly, so I didn't have access to the pack psyche yet. However, that wouldn't stop me from handling any challenges thrown my way. I might not have the mental power, but I did possess the physical means to stand my ground.

"Find us a meeting location, preferably out of the mud," she said, her voice ringing with an authority that ruffled the fur of my inner wolf. "I want all royals and alphas in attendance to report at once for an emergency council meeting."

Of course she did.

"Meanwhile, everyone else—clean yourselves up. We

are not animals," she seethed, turning on her heel before I could correct that statement. I had no idea where she thought she was going. Maybe back to her car, or just to the gravel road to clean off her ruined shoes.

"We can use the main lodge," I called after her and added some directions for her to follow.

She didn't acknowledge me but did turn the way I suggested. With a shake of my head, I turned to address my wolves.

"Gather the dead," I instructed. "We'll mourn them properly tomorrow. Move anyone who is healing and not yet awake to a safe location." I took in the still vampires, then focused on Kylan, as he'd claimed to be in charge of them now. "Silvano's vampires are welcome to collect their dead however they desire. My wolves won't interfere." I added that last part with a sharp glance toward the lycans in question. "We are at peace."

"For now," a vampire put in, his dark hair blending into the night. He approached Kylan, his casual attire of jeans and a T-shirt vastly different from all the royals in attendance. And were those tattoos peeking out beneath the hem, on his bicep? How strange. He almost appeared more wolfish than vampy.

"I will not bow to you," he announced flatly, his focus on Kylan.

"An unwise decision, but one I can respect," the royal replied. "*For now.*"

"As Silvano's oldest vampire on site, I will attend the council meeting in representation of his lands," the male added, ignoring the lingering threat in Kylan's tone. These two clearly had a history of some kind.

"Of course. We look forward to your explanation of what happened here." Kylan grinned. "I'm sure it's quite a tale." He pointedly turned his back on the ballsy vamp and addressed the crowd. "You heard Lilith—clean yourselves up. And if anyone draws a weapon or instigates another fight in our absence, I will dispense with you as I did Silvano."

A shudder seemed to traverse the crowd, Kylan's reputation for cruelty working strongly in his favor. No one wanted to go against the supposedly mad royal.

Not even me.

And his blood ran through my progeny's system.

Fuck.

I turned to Luna, my palm finding her nape as I tugged her in for a kiss that she reciprocated on a sigh. "Stay close to Silas. I don't know how this is going to go."

She nodded and cupped my cheek. "We'll be waiting for you."

"I know," I whispered, running my tongue across her bottom lip. "You owe me a bite, little mate." Something I would request right now—while we still had a full moon above our heads—if I couldn't feel everyone's eyes on me. Alas, duty called.

It was time to play alpha.

I released Luna with another brush of my mouth against hers, then grabbed Silas and captured his lips with my own.

Shock rippled through his body like it had the last time I kissed him, as if he couldn't believe I was showing him affection in front of everyone. We would be discussing that later because if he thought I meant to hide this, he had another think coming. I wanted them both, and fuck anyone who thought ill of me for it.

"Guard Luna," I told him.

"With my life," he vowed.

I let go of him and found my grandfather's gaze across the yard. There was a wistfulness to it that I didn't understand, but pride lurked in its depths. "I'll help out here while you tend to Lilith," he said, the words traveling across the space with ease, thanks to my wolf hearing.

I nodded. "Thank you."

"Just doing my job," he replied, grinning. "Take Logan with you. He'll represent Ernest Clan."

I frowned and looked around. "Where is he?" I hadn't seen him at all, not even during the fight.

My grandfather nodded his chin toward one of the cabins. Logan stood beside it with his arm around a badly beaten Cora. Luna followed the line of sight with a gasp and took off toward her mother, with Silas hot on her tail.

Fucking Niko.

If he were still alive, I'd kill him again. Because those blemishes on the alpha female's form had the dead alpha's mark all over them.

Logan released her to Luna, one of his eyes badly bruised and screwed shut—likely from his father's fist. Had he tried to join the fight to help Clemente Clan? And his father stopped him?

No, it had to be something worse for Cora to be given such a beating.

"We stood up to Walter when he tried to take Luna," Logan explained, sensing my confusion.

My eyebrows rose. "Walter *what*?"

"It doesn't matter," Luna said, her arm around Cora's waist. "He's dead. They are all dead. Go to the council; we'll be here when you get back." Alpha female underlined those words, causing my lips to twitch. Luna wore her dominance with pride, and I very much approved.

"Yes, ma'am," I replied, winking at her.

Silas snorted. "So you'll bow to her command, but not to mine."

"She's an alpha. You're just an omega." It was more of a taunt than the truth.

Another snort. "An omega who fought by your side in a death ring. For which you're welcome, by the way."

I clasped his shoulder and gave it a squeeze. "Yeah, you're right. You'll make a fine enforcer." Logan's brows lifted in surprise. He knew what that term meant, as did everyone standing close enough to hear. "Keep everyone in line while I'm gone."

I didn't wait for him to reply to my orders and instead led the way toward the main lodge with Logan at my side. We stopped by one of the cabins so I could grab a pair of jeans—they were a bit tight, but worked—and continued on in silence.

Everyone was waiting for us when we arrived, Lilith's expression holding a touch of impatience that I ignored as I settled into a position against the wall.

I knew there were a lot of alphas and royals in attendance tonight, but there hadn't been a chance for me to take stock of who was actually here. Most were among the usual crowd.

Claude, Lajos, Cormac, Jace—all vampires with a penchant for playing with lycans.

Kylan was the only uncommon attendee. His arrival last month had surprised me. All the royals were invited to these events, but only a handful usually appeared, and Kylan was notorious for keeping to himself. Now that I knew about his connection to Silas—whatever that was— his appearance made sense.

The ballsy vamp stood in Silvano's place with his arms crossed. Something about him struck me as not right. Power lurked beneath his skin—a power he seemed to be hiding. When he caught me staring, he arched a dark brow in challenge.

Yeah, I didn't want to fuck with him. He struck me as much harder and harsher than Silvano. Like he was used to handling wolves in addition to vampires.

No, thanks.

As for the lycan portion of the council, we had all our neighbors on this side of the globe, as well as a few from the areas surrounding Ernest Clan. All wolves enjoyed a good ascension, as it was part of our pack nature.

Luka from Majestic Clan.

Brandt from Calgary Clan.

Vlad from Vladik Clan.

Miko from Maykel Clan.

Dimka from Kostenka Clan.

All varying ages of leadership, but averaging around two hundred years or so. Which meant the majority were long-standing friends of my father, something that would likely hurt me after my ascension.

Oh well.

Those who opposed could kiss my fluffy ass.

"Now that we're all here, we can begin," Lilith announced, her focus on me—a subtle chastisement for making her wait. As if I would apologize for organizing my clan before attending a political meeting. My wolves would always come first.

Lilith launched into a diatribe about her disappointment in the council for not acting sooner, how only one of them had bothered to call for her, and how fortunate it was that she was already en route when she received that call.

A bunch of stately bullshit. What would she have done? Clapped her freshly manicured hands together and screeched for everyone to halt?

Yeah, that would have been a lovely sight.

She asked for an explanation of how it all began,

which Vlad provided as an observing party. When he reached the part about accusations of Silvano and Walter orchestrating the battle, all eyes fell to the ballsy vamp.

"What do you have to say about this, Ryder?" Lilith demanded.

He lifted a shoulder. "Sounds like classic Silvano to me. That asshole only ever thought of himself." He paused before adding, "May he rest in peace."

Lilith clearly did not appreciate that response. Her eyes narrowed. "That's all you have to say?"

"You act as though I knew what was happening," he replied. "A bunch of vampires passed through my lands on their way to the border, and I followed because it piqued my curiosity. I didn't even play in the mess. I'm only standing here as a result of my age and birthright. From what I observed, Silvano orchestrated one hell of an attack with the expectation of taking over Clemente Clan afterward. Best guess, he agreed to Walter's terms with the intention of double-crossing the alpha. Didn't work in either of their favors, though."

For once, the esteemed Goddess appeared speechless.

Okay, I might like this Ryder guy.

"But if I were you, I'd seek out Catalina," he added, his tone as bored as his stance. "She ran off after shooting the Clemente Clan's newest addition with silver. I guess she didn't want to face the consequences of that with the new alpha since he was her original target."

Kylan smirked. "Good thing Jace knocked her out and tied her up in one of the lodges."

"Seemed strange she was in such a hurry to flee when her brethren were all so eager to fight," Jace put in conversationally.

"Indeed," Kylan agreed. "Shall we fetch her for you, my lady?"

"As if I trust you not to kill her without a trial," Lilith seethed.

Kylan's brows rose. "I wasn't aware I required a trial under such situations. Would you have preferred we allowed them to continue fighting like animals?" He cocked his head to the side. "Or do we need to discuss the requirements dictated by our bloodlines? Because last I checked, I'm the oldest of vampire kind, and I would say that affords me a semblance of responsibility. But maybe I'm wrong. Perhaps I need a larger title to assert such power."

Several members of the council shared glances at the very clear challenge issued by Kylan. Everyone knew his birthright superseded Lilith's, but he never laid claim to her position. Likely because he didn't desire the headache that came from being in charge and preferred maintaining his own territory.

But his actions of late seemed to be pushing some of her boundaries.

Testing the waters.

Subtle provocations to her place at the top of the hierarchy.

"I want to talk to Catalina," she replied, her head held high, her gaze on Kylan alone. "All of you"—she glanced around quickly before focusing on the royal again—"will remain here while I investigate this mess and determine a proper recourse."

"You want us to stay in the Clemente Clan lands?" That came from Brandt. "For how long?"

"For as long as it takes me to make a decision," she snapped.

"I'm not some dog you can command, vampire queen," Dimka drawled. "We have responsibilities back home."

She narrowed her gaze at the ash-blond alpha. "You will stay until I give you permission to leave. Unless you'd prefer we relocate to Lilith City?"

Several of the alphas bristled at the threat. None of us wanted to go to the heart of vampire territory. Especially not *her* territory.

"Five days," Luka suggested. "We'll agree to remain here for five days while you investigate. That should be more than enough time, and it's a blink of an eye for most of us."

"Most of ye evidence will be washed away with'na week," Cormac agreed, his voice heavily accented. Scottish, I thought, if my geography of the old lands was right. "I cannae agree to longer, lass."

Several concurred with nods and words of assent, leaving Lilith no choice but to cave to their demands. "Fine. I will begin immediately."

I nearly scoffed. As if she would have waited a few hours.

"Jace, come with me. And, Edon? Make appropriate accommodations," she demanded. "Oh, and congratulations on your ascension." The latter was nearly a sneer, but she tacked on a polite smile before exiting the room with a flourish.

"I'll stay at Walter's," Jace said as he passed me. "Your mother and I are old acquaintances."

It was on the tip of my tongue to argue, but he left before I could comment.

And then everyone else in the room started adding their own accommodation requirements at once.

Shit. It's going to be a long damn week.

"Welcome to leadership, kid," Kylan said, clapping me on the shoulder.

Yeah. A great fucking welcome.

CHAPTER 36
LUNA

"You went to university together?" My eyes widened. "Wow. What are the odds?"

Silas and Rae shared a look. "Not great," they both replied at the same time.

I nodded, pretending to understand. These two clearly had a history together, one that left me feeling a little miffed because *I* wanted to be the one Silas shared glances like that with. But we were nowhere near that level despite our time together, and I had no way of knowing if we would ever reach that place.

If Kylan shared my jealousy, he didn't show it. He lounged beside Rae on Edon's couch, his arm stretched out along the back and his fingertips idly brushing the woman's shoulder. Silas sat catty-corner in a chair, while I relaxed on the ottoman next to him.

My mother and Logan were making up one of the guest rooms for themselves. Apparently, Rae and Kylan would be taking the area I'd originally claimed for myself, leaving me firmly in Edon's quarters until these new living arrangements were over.

Not that I minded.

I just hoped Silas would join us, too.

I cleared my throat. "When did you say Edon would be back?" I asked Kylan.

From what I understood, Edon was busy finding sleeping arrangements for all of our apparent guests. Most of the royals and alphas had only intended to attend the ceremony and return to their jets, but the Goddess demanded everyone stay until she sorted through the mess Edon's father had created.

"I didn't," Kylan replied. "He seemed hell-bent on removing Jace and Darius from Walter's home, a fight I really don't think he'll win. So it may be a while."

"Why would he care?" Silas asked.

"Because Jace has a penchant for seducing wolves, and there's a broken one living in that home who means a great deal to young Edon," Kylan explained, his lips curling. "Little does he realize, the two share quite a history."

"He won't hurt her," my mother said softly as she entered the room, her gaze downcast.

So utterly submissive for an alpha female. But at least she wasn't near catatonic like Edon's mom. No, mine actually stood up for herself on occasion. Like tonight.

And now she would never have to fend for herself again, unless my brother bargained her to another alpha. She was still young and pretty enough for others to show interest, at least in making her a concubine. However, I didn't see Logan ever agreeing to a deal, not if his protective stance beside her was anything to go by.

"I never said he would, Cora," Kylan replied. "I merely stated his penchant and their history."

My mother's lips twitched. "History is something Jace has with many."

I narrowed my gaze, but Edon stalked inside before I

could question her. He took one look at the living area and growled.

"Hi to you, too," Silas greeted, grinning.

"It's been a long fucking night." Edon went straight to the kitchen and came back with a beer that he rolled across his forehead. "I don't recall inviting you over, Kylan."

"That's all right, young alpha. I took it upon myself to do that for you," he replied.

Edon grunted. "I'm too exhausted to argue."

Kylan grinned. "No, I imagine the others put you through the wringer well enough." He stood and held out a hand to Rae. "Shall we retire and allow his triad to soothe him?"

Triad. Silas and I had asked Jolene to explain what that meant earlier tonight while we were cleaning up the courtyard. He'd answered vaguely about it being a rare relationship between three lycans, before being called away to help reset the shoulder of a recovering wolf. We didn't see him again after that.

"Why does everyone keep talking about triads?" Logan asked, his brow furrowing.

"Because your sister is in the heart of a blossoming one," Kylan replied as he pulled Rae up beside him. "Current society frowns upon them because it's an unbreakable bond that supersedes any and all other relationships within a pack, but denying fate is like trying to challenge a royal vampire—a very bad idea." He brushed his lips against Rae's mouth and smiled. "Unless you're Raelyn. Then you can challenge a royal vampire all you like."

She narrowed her gaze. "You're just trying to seduce me."

"Is it working?"

"Maybe." She nipped at his jaw, some unspoken

message passing between their gazes—one that had Kylan grinning and tugging her out of the room on a whisper of sound.

"He's changed," my mother said, her brow furrowing as she studied the empty hallway in their wake.

Logan ignored her, his blue irises flitting from me to Silas to Edon and back to me again. "Wait… The three of you are…?" His eyes narrowed at Edon. "You're *sharing* my sister with *him?*"

Edon caught my brother's fist before it came near his face and shoved him backward. "I've had a really long fucking night, Logan. We'll do this tomorrow."

Silas jumped off the chair and intercepted Logan as he went for Edon again. "Back off."

"It's fine," I interjected, standing up and joining Silas. "*I'm* fine."

Logan blinked. "This is messed up." He ran his fingers through his hair and blew out a breath. "Fuck, this entire night is fucking messed up."

"No shit," Edon muttered. "And the week isn't going to be any better."

Logan shook his head and turned away from us without a word, leaving us for the bedroom down the hall.

"I'll talk to him," my mother whispered, reaching out to squeeze my hand. "Once he realizes Claudette's history in her own triad with Jolene, he'll come around."

"*What?*" I gaped at her. "What history with Claudette?"

She frowned. "You mean he hasn't mentioned it?"

"No," all three of us said in unison.

"Explain," Edon added in his alpha tone.

"Oh, I don't think it's my place," my mother said, taking a step back. "Maybe you should talk to your grandfather about it. I didn't realize… I just thought…" Another step away from us. "Ask Jolene."

She fled on those words, causing my forehead to crinkle.

Edon muttered a curse and cracked open his beer. "Fuck it. Fuck it all. I'm done trying to solve puzzles tonight. I just want to escape for, like, an hour and not fucking think."

Silas glanced down at me before turning to face Edon. "We can help with that."

I smiled, rotating as well. "Yeah. We can totally help with that." Silas and I had showered together earlier while everyone else was cleaning off and changing.

But Edon was still filthy.

Bloody.

And wearing a pair of jeans that clearly didn't fit.

I tugged on the button, loosening the waistline. "Come with us, Alpha."

Silas took the beer from Edon, saying, "Yeah, come with us, Alpha," and led the way.

"I earned that," Edon grumbled, his cheeks flushing.

"And you'll be drinking it," Silas replied with a glance over his shoulder. "You said you didn't want to think. So let us do it for you." He held open the door to the master bedroom. "Trust us."

I moved past Edon and Silas and tugged my shirt over my head, letting it flutter to the floor. Then batted my eyes back at them. "I'll be in the shower while you two work this out."

Their growls followed me into the bathroom, where I lost my jeans and turned on the water.

Silas and I hadn't spoken much during our shower earlier, just helped each other wash off and kissed a few times before joining the others in the living area. It hadn't felt right without Edon. Like we were missing a piece of ourselves. It was one of those mutually understood things that didn't require words. A feeling I noted in Silas's gaze likely as easily as he did in mine.

And as he entered the bathroom now, I knew he understood and shared my intent.

He set the bottle down, pulled off his shirt and jeans, and smiled as Edon kicked off his own pants.

With a jerk of his head, Silas indicated where he wanted Edon to go.

The alpha's jaw ticked—unaccustomed to following orders—but he eventually caved and joined me beneath the warm spray.

I rewarded him by wrapping my arms around his neck and kissing him.

His hands fell to my hips as he pinned me against the wall, his arousal growing against my stomach and shooting heat into my veins. Silas joined us and stepped up behind the alpha, his palms sliding over Edon's back.

Soap—crisp and clean—tickled my nose and told me what he was doing.

Cleaning the alpha.

While I distracted him with my tongue.

Mmm, Edon could kiss so damn well. So dominant and overpowering and utterly perfect. I moaned, arching into him and allowing him to deepen our embrace while Silas worked on Edon's legs, ass, and arms.

Soon it would be my turn to soap down the front of him while they fucked each other's mouths, and just the idea of it had my thighs clenching with unsuppressed need.

Edon growled at whatever Silas did to his backside and ripped his lips away from mine to kiss his progeny into submission. From the way their mouths dueled, it seemed to be a battle for dominance—a mesmerizing one.

I loved when they embraced.

It was so primal and hot and arousing. The way Edon reached around to grip Silas by the neck set my blood on fire.

I took the soap from Silas's palm to run it over the alpha's abdomen, lathering across every inch of his torso before moving down to grip his straining cock. His chest vibrated in response, the thick member pulsing in my hand as I slid my grip lower to cup his balls.

"*Fuck,*" he breathed.

"Mmm, that's the idea," Silas replied, his lips trailing a path down Edon's neck to his shoulder.

It was almost always me or Silas in the middle, never Edon, and we were all enjoying the change. Even the alpha, who seemed a bit flustered by his progeny seizing control.

Silas captured my gaze and gestured downward with his chin, telling me what to do.

I smiled and slid down the wall to my knees before Edon, the water trickling over his abdomen to his thick thighs and washing the suds away. "Allow me to distract you, Alpha," I said, staring up at him. "Please."

His head fell back on a groan, the thick bulb jutting out toward my lips in implied welcome. I licked him, loving the salty essence on the tip, and then took him deep into my mouth. Silas kissed him again, making Edon jerk violently against my tongue.

My thighs clenched, my need growing by the second as they devoured each other.

Edon's fingers threaded through my hair, his opposite palm still holding Silas's nape as he guided him down and around to join me on the ground.

"My turn, little moon," Silas murmured, taking over.

His cheeks hollowed as he sucked the alpha's cock to the back of his throat and visibly swallowed.

Edon's forearm slammed into the wall to better brace himself, his opposite hand shifting between my head and Silas's as we rotated his shaft between our mouths. His moans turned to a dark, guttural sound that caused a gush of heat to slick down between my thighs.

Such a sexy fucking noise.

I wanted to hear it again.

I wanted to *feel* it against my pussy as he lapped me clean.

I wanted him to growl like that into my ear while he fucked me to completion.

I must have whimpered, because his fingers were suddenly in my hair, yanking me up off the ground and into him. In seconds, he had me pinned against the tile wall, his dick deep inside me on a single thrust and my thighs wrapped around his waist.

"Edon," I breathed, arching into him.

And then my mouth was occupied.

Not by Edon, but by Silas, his tongue hot and penetrating and so fucking addicting. I held on to Edon with one arm and wrapped my other around Silas, my claws digging into his scalp.

Someone palmed my breast.

Edon.

Another tweaked my opposite nipple.

Silas.

His lips descended to lick the peak while Edon claimed my mouth.

Thought escaped me, replaced firmly by feelings and sensation. A hot palm met my ass, the finger sliding through the crease to find my other hole. I didn't jerk or cringe, used to this game of Edon's, the preparation he continued to bestow upon my body.

Two digits slid inside, the double penetration eliciting a low whine from my mouth. Not because it hurt, but because I wanted *more.*

He must have known, because he added a third, which sent me whirling over the edge into an explosive climax I hadn't even felt coming. I screamed, my walls clamping down around him on both sides and forcing him to join me in oblivion.

Silas's head fell to my shoulder, his pants mingling with ours. Edon slid out of me, his grip trading with his progeny.

And then I was full again, this time with Silas's long, hard perfection.

My head hit the tiles, my body sore and tingling and way too tight, and yet burning all over again. Edon was there, his mouth on my neck, his palm returning to my ass. Silas drove into me sharply, his movements urgent, causing Edon's knuckles to slam into the wall. But that didn't stop him from gliding those fingers back inside and scissoring them in a way that made me squirm.

"Come, Omega," Edon growled. "Come so we can lick her clean together."

Oh, fuck…

My body shook, my limbs tightening.

Everything seemed to center in my lower abdomen.

So. Damn. Constricting.

Silas seemed to go deeper, searching for that spot I loved, and hit it with the force I needed to shatter all over again.

Black.

That was all I could see.

Pure. Bliss.

They'd literally fucked me into another realm of being, a blank state, my mind just completely shutting off.

And I didn't care, too blitzed out to breathe. But I felt them licking me clean, heard Silas chuckle as he retrieved the beer and told Edon to drink the liquid as he poured it over me. And drink he did.

Every single drop.

His tongue memorizing my flesh.

His mouth trailing kisses over my body as they laid me in the cloud of Edon's bed.

Both of them nurturing me, worshiping me, loving me.

I sighed and nuzzled into one of their chests while the other spooned me from behind.

Heaven, I decided. *This is my heaven.* And I refused to let anyone force me to leave.

CHAPTER 37
SILAS

"It's surreal to see you like this," I said as I found Rae curled up on the couch with a steaming mug of what smelled like chocolate. Kylan stood in the kitchen with Luna, the two of them conversing softly about breakfast.

Okay. *That* was even more surreal.

At least the bastard was out of my head. It only took two fucking days.

I just want to make sure we're on the same page, he kept saying. *And I may need to use you to protect my Raelyn.*

It did not escape me that the only reason he saved my life was to appease his consort. That if we weren't old friends, he would have let me die without a second thought. So having him in my head for so long really sucked. Especially as he kept reminding me that he could make me his puppet.

I don't care much for him either, Edon muttered into my head.

I was so happy to have him back that I didn't even bother to remark on him reading my mind without permission. Instead, I asked, *Where are you?*

Checking up on my mother.

Again?

Jace is living at her house, he growled.

I frowned. *I thought you said they were just playing chess?*

During his visit yesterday, he'd found the two of them on the porch engaged in a serious game. It had unnerved the alpha so much that he'd returned with a bewildered expression, stating he'd never seen his mother so lively. Which, I supposed, was saying a lot since all she was doing was sitting in a chair while moving game pieces around on a chessboard.

Edon grumbled something incoherent back at me, causing me to chuckle. It sounded a lot like, *Fucking royal bloodsucking jackhole.*

Try not to get killed by that royal jackhole, yeah?

The alpha's responding snort vibrated in my head. *I brought Logan with me. We can take him.*

Uh-huh, I thought back at him, collapsing in the recliner chair beside Rae. *Glad you two are getting along now.* It'd been tense at first, but Luna's continued promise that she was fine seemed to appease her brother a bit. Although, that didn't stop him from having a stern word with me and Edon about what would happen should we hurt her. As if we'd ever let that happen.

"Edon?" Rae asked, a smile in her light blue eyes.

"Yeah." I ran my fingers through my hair—it was getting shaggy again. "He's really not happy about Jace staying with Aurora."

"Jace has a way of maintaining a reputation without actually fulfilling it," Kylan said cryptically as he joined Rae on the couch.

"Hmm, that sounds oddly familiar," Rae replied, tapping her chin thoughtfully. "No idea why…"

Kylan nipped her pulse and nuzzled her neck, the

gesture inexplicably playful. And so not what I would ever expect from someone so notoriously known for his sadism. "Mmm, seems there are many playing with reputations lately," he murmured against her throat. "Such as the wolves approaching the door."

I picked up on the scent a second after he said it, but it was Luna who went sprinting toward the foyer. She threw open the door. "Where the hell have you been?" she demanded. "I have questions for you."

Jolene chuckled. "Hello, darling. I assume Cora's been talking?" He stepped into the house with Luka at his back, his astute gaze roaming over the living area. "Where's my grandson?"

"Checking up on Aurora," I said, standing. "He's not keen on Jace staying with her."

Luka grunted. "Good luck to Edon. Jace is a force of nature."

"You mated Claudette?" Luna interjected, her entire focus on Jolene. "And never thought to tell us about it?"

He narrowed his gaze at her. "Careful with your tone, young lady. I'll be needin' a long nap before we go muckin' through my past. Not that it's any of your business, mind."

She popped her hands onto her hips, undeterred. "You being in a triad with my mentor isn't any of my business? Fascinating. I'd say it's pretty pertinent, don't you, Silas?"

Oh, I knew better than to disagree with my little moon. "I think he owes us an explanation of what a triad is and how it applies to our situation, yeah. But I also think we should wait until Edon is here to hear it."

The latter earned me a brief grin from Jolene. "We should probably discuss what Luka and I have overheard first, but I think we should wait for my grandson. Tell him to come back and to bring Jace and Darius with him."

"Does this mean I finally get to play?" Kylan drawled,

cocking his head to the side. "Or are we still pretending I don't know what you all are up to?"

Luka narrowed his blue eyes at the royal. "For the record, I voted against bringing you on board."

"On board what?" Luna asked.

"But Jace and Darius seem to think you could be an ally," Luka continued, ignoring my little moon.

"In what?" I demanded, not pleased to see her dismissed so callously.

Luka looked me up and down, taking my measure. I hadn't actually met the alpha male yet, but I knew of him. Leader of the Majestic Clan, mated to Mira, and overall not all that memorable. "You must have a mighty big sack to stand up to a two-hundred-year-old alpha, boy."

"Told you he was special," Jolene drawled, clapping me on the shoulder. "Luna, too. Their little triad is going to prove invaluable." He glanced around. "Logan, too, wherever he's run off to. At least according to my Claudette."

"Still want to know what the hell you all are talking about," Luna replied, a low growl permeating her tone. "And more information about this *triad* everyone keeps mentioning."

Kylan sighed. "It's a rare relationship bond between three lycans. You, Silas, and Edon are clearly in a triad. Why is this so difficult and cryptic?"

"Because a ritual must be performed to solidify it," Jolene replied. "But I'm not sayin' more until the others are here. Meanwhile, I'll be makin' myself some coffee."

Your grandfather is being cryptic and rude to Luna, I growled. *Okay, not rude. But he won't explain the triad until you're back, and he wants you to bring Jace and Darius with you.*

"Tell him to bring Aurora, too. It'd be good to see her." That came from Luka.

I relayed the message to Edon.

What am I, a fucking errand boy? he demanded.

Guess that makes me a glorified messenger, I replied.

Edon snorted. *I'll sort my granddad out when I get there. Give Luna a kiss for me.*

Will do.

With tongue, he added.

I smiled. *The tasks you assign me are so cumbersome.* I grabbed Luna on her way to the kitchen and tugged her into me, my lips capturing hers before she had a chance to speak. "That's from Edon," I whispered after a moment. "And this is from me." I deepened the embrace, leaving her breathless and panting in my arms while everyone observed.

Mine, I thought at them, my instinct to protect her overwhelming. Maybe because there were too many dominant males in the house. Or just because I felt like it. Either way, I claimed her with a nip and caught her resulting grin with my tongue.

Ours, Edon corrected.

Ours, I agreed. *Hurry back.*

CHAPTER 38

EDON

Too many fucking visitors in my house, I thought as I settled into my favorite chair. The couch beside me was littered with vampires—Jace, Darius, Kylan, and Rae. Darius's blood virgin, Juliet, sat primly in a chair pulled in from the kitchen area.

Luka was on the ottoman.

Jolene took my other recliner.

Logan lounged on the floor.

Cora, Mira, and my mother were in the dining room, drinking tea. Which was a really weird experience since my mom never left her house willingly to socialize. I couldn't even remember the last time she lifted her head, let alone spoke.

Yet Walter's death seemed to have loosened her up just a little, or maybe it was the royal she seemed so fond of. She had actually kissed Jace on the cheek before taking a seat across from Mira.

Like, what the fuck was that about?

Focus, Silas chastised. He stood behind me with his

arms folded across the top cushion of my recliner, while Luna snuggled in beside me.

You're lucky I'm distracted, I told him as I kissed the top of my little mate's head.

And yet, you being distracted is what I'm trying to fix, he drawled.

I snorted and looked up at him. *Tired of being the omega? Want to play in the alpha's shoes?*

What I want are answers, he replied flatly.

Well, I couldn't argue with him there. "Where have you been?" I asked my grandfather. "We tried to find you."

"Luna mentioned that," he replied conversationally. "I was with Luka, eavesdropping on Lilith's interrogation of Catalina."

As far as excuses went, that was a good one.

"At the airfield?" Lilith had refused to stay in Clemente Clan headquarters, stating her private jet would suffice. And she'd taken Silvano's sovereign with her.

"Yeah. It wasn't easy," he replied, scowling.

I imagined not. There weren't many trees out there.

Huh. Who knew my grandfather still had it in him to play spy? I knew he was revered in his day as one of the strongest alphas of his time, but his age showed. Most lycans lived to be around six to seven hundred years old, and he was pushing the upper end of that range.

"And?" Kylan prompted, sounding bored. "What did the good sovereign have to say about her royal's behavior?"

"That he had tasked her with taking out Edon and Walter in a double cross." Luka lifted his ankle to rest on his opposite knee. "Catalina also confirmed that Silvano was using Walter to take care of some unruly vampires. He handed them off to the Clemente Clan for disposal."

Meaning the wolves shredded the bloodsuckers apart. "And my father had agreed to it." I didn't phrase it as a question but as a statement. Walter was an even bigger asshole than I gave him credit for.

"From what Catalina confirmed, yes. The lycans made a sport of it, like the moon chase, only hunting down crippled vampires instead." My grandfather sounded sickened by the admission.

"That explains all the scents without the bodies," Silas put in, referring to the stench he kept picking up on near the headquarters' perimeter.

I nodded. "Yeah, it does. So why double-cross Walter?" I rarely used my father's given name, but it felt more natural now. As if he no longer deserved the endearment of *dad*.

"Catalina said Silvano's goal was to gain more territory, especially around the old border between Texas and Louisiana. Where the blood farms and breeding camps are housed in this region," Luka said.

"He thought by weakening the pack, he could expand," Jace clarified. "And as the blood farms and breeding camps carry financial incentives, he could benefit from taking that over from the Clemente Clan."

"And charge our wolves a higher rate to procreate," I translated. "Something the clan would be willing to pay if they lost their leadership and needed to start over." I didn't know what kind of blood types the camps housed at the moment, but if there were traces of alpha in any of the humans, they'd be fucked nearly to death to create a new lineage.

You can create alpha lines from humans? Silas asked.

Yeah. I suspect you have traces of it, I admitted. *It's all about dominant tendencies, something I'd say you carry in spades.* Which was why I intended to make him my enforcer.

So an alpha doesn't need to be lycan born? He sounded

confused. I couldn't really blame him. Genetics was complicated.

If a lycan sires a child with a mortal, then turns that mortal into a lycan during the pregnancy, the child will be born a lycan.

That sounds too easy, he said, looking down at me.

I met his gaze as I replied, *There's a ninety-nine percent fatality rate. The transition while a female is pregnant is typically lethal to the mother and the child. Only the strongest of mortals survive.*

Ah, and the strongest are usually alphas, he translated.

Not usually, but always. Most humans are killed in the process. "Which explains why he wanted the breeding camps. Brilliant bastard," I marveled out loud, interrupting whatever Jace had been saying to Kylan.

They both looked at me with arched eyebrows, obviously not pleased with my interruption, and desiring an explanation.

I cleared my throat. "I was just explaining the alpha creation process to Silas."

"Between lycans and humans," Silas clarified. "I didn't know that was how it worked. At the camps, I mean."

"Depends on the goal of the breeder," Jace said, his focus on me. "And what conclusion did you draw, Edon?"

"If Silvano destroyed the alpha bloodline in Clemente Clan, the lycans left behind would have been desperate to create a new ruling family. Which would either require involvement from other clans—an unlikely choice given how few alpha females remain in our world—or they would try the breeding farms."

"And pay top price for each host," my grandfather added. "That's the motive Luka and I determined as well." Pride lit his gaze as he added that last line—the emotion directed at me, not himself.

"What about Lilith?" I wondered out loud. "Has she drawn the same conclusion?"

Both of the alphas shook their heads. "She called in Ryder," my grandfather replied. "Seems to think he knows more than he's sayin'."

"I'm certain he does," Kylan replied, amused. "But it won't be about Silvano."

"Who is Ryder?" I asked. "He's not part of Silvano's hierarchy. Or I would have met him." Yet the other day in the field was the first time I'd ever seen the vampire. Age and power had wafted off him like a dark cloud, and he hadn't fought at all. "Why is he even here?"

"He lives near the camps," Luka explained. "On the Silvano side. He keeps to himself, refuses to play the political game, and only came along 'cause Silvano walked the army through his property."

"Yeah, he was asking Lilith to excuse him, saying he only volunteered to represent Silvano for the initial meeting and had no intention of staying." My grandfather snorted. "She refused, of course. Said with Catalina in custody, she needed an elder around to keep all Silvano's vamps in line."

Kylan smirked. "Bet he's thrilled he volunteered."

"Do you think he knew what Silvano intended?" I asked. "Was he working with him?"

Kylan laughed outright. "Hell no. He hated that bastard."

"Silvano marched the vampires through Ryder's lands," Luka said.

"I'm sure he did," Kylan replied. "It was the best way to provoke the old recluse to come out and play, and Ryder fell for it."

"But why provoke him at all?" I wondered aloud. "Why bring him into it?"

"Maybe to act as a scapegoat, should he need it. Or because it was the easiest route." Kylan shrugged. "Regardless, I'm certain Ryder isn't involved. He might be old and senile, but he's not suicidal."

"I'm inclined to agree with Kylan that Ryder would never work with Silvano on this." Jace's tone rang with confidence. "But that's the real problem. The question remains: How will Lilith react to the news?"

"You mean, will she punish me for taking Silvano's life?" Kylan grinned. "She can try."

Jace smirked. "She can, yes. Meanwhile, Edon and Logan should be all right, as Walter was the one who accepted the challenge and requested to fight with Niko at his side. No major hiccups, but I imagine she'll be watching them closely as a result."

"It was all within pack law," I added. "She can't fault us for following it." But Kylan, yeah, he might have an issue or two.

"Indeed." Darius scratched the dark scruff dotting his jaw. "Still, I think we all need to lie low for a few months while the dust settles. Too many upsets so close together is going to put the alliance on edge, and we can't afford to be noticed."

"Killing Silvano to stop the vampires and wolves from killing each other is hardly going to be seen as a revolutionary move," Kylan pointed out. "I'm the mad royal, remember? I do crazy shit all the time." He punctuated that with a kiss against Rae's neck. "Right, consort?"

She just shook her head, but the hum of energy between them suggested she was in his head. *How fascinating.* I wasn't aware vampire sires could communicate like that with their progeny. I always thought it was a wolf thing.

He turned her after he made her his Erosita, Silas explained softly. *She told me it altered her transformation.*

Fascinating, I repeated.

"It's true. All the rebellious acts of late have somehow involved Kylan. If anyone is at risk of censure, it's him." Luka glanced at the royal. "Which is why I didn't want to bring you on board. You're a danger to our plans."

"Are you suggesting I might tattle on you all to save myself?" Kylan asked, his lips curling. "What happened to good old-fashioned trust, wolf? Can't you smell my loyalty?"

I snorted at that. "You smell old and powerful to me." Just like Jace and Darius. They were at least two or three thousand years old.

Logan grunted. "They smell old to me, too. But I'd like to know what all this revolution shit is about while we're on the topic."

Jace smiled. "You're sitting in the middle of it."

And so began an hour-long conversation about those who sought to take down the Blood Alliance Council.

Four of the founding members were in this room—Jace, Darius, Luka, and Jolene. But there were several others across the globe, all living in quiet and waiting for their cue to rise up. It was something they hadn't planned to do for several more years, perhaps even decades, but events over the last two months had escalated their timeline.

This week, in particular, punted them way into the future.

Because Logan and I were groomed with a purpose—to lead our clans toward rebellion. However, it had to be subtle. Little things like getting rid of the moon chase might not be noticed, especially as it only happened a few times a year.

Another would be to allow relationships to form, to encourage matings rather than degrade them.

It just had to be quiet. Unnoticeable by the other packs.

"With Silvano out of the picture, we might have an opportunity," Darius put in. "Jaxon is one of the oldest in the territory."

"But not in a leadership position," Jace replied.

"Neither was I." Darius grinned. "Yet, here we are."

"Because of my place at the top." The royal winked at Darius's blood virgin. "It's nice to see your eyes, sweetheart."

She blushed but didn't drop her gaze. Clearly, she was in on all of this, because from what I understood, blood virgins were bred to be submissive to a fault. Yet she seemed rather confident and poised beside Darius, as if she had every right to sit in this circle.

And maybe she did.

"How many other young lycans are being trained for your rebellion?" Luna asked, her eyes on Luka. "Your daughter? For Logan?"

His expression darkened. "Just because Niko decided to retire early does not mean my daughter is to be wed next month."

Well, that wasn't at all what Luna had asked. But it seemed to be a sore subject for the alpha lycan.

"So my pack is to go without leadership until you decide she's ready?" Logan asked, his eyebrow inching upward. "You know I can't ascend without a mate."

"It's a topic we'll continue to discuss," Jolene put in with a sharp look at Luka. "And to answer your question, Luna, there are a handful of mentors in place to help guide the mentalities of younger lycans, yes. However, you, Edon, and Logan were our primary objectives for this wave. As we mentioned earlier, we thought we had more time. But it seems our pawns are falling into place earlier than anticipated."

"Much earlier," Darius agreed. "We'll need to reevaluate several avenues, but it seems others have opened up for us to navigate."

"You're welcome," Kylan interjected.

Darius ignored him. "I think it would be wise for Edon to engage in his triad, as it will set an immediate relationship precedent for the pack. Just as I would advise Luka to reconsider his stance on his daughter's nuptials. Ernest Clan will require unity to rebuild, and Logan can't do that alone."

Luka growled, but I jumped in before he could reply. "You know what would be wise? For someone to explain what the fuck a triad is before asking me to do it," I suggested, not so politely.

All eyes fell to my grandfather.

He sighed in resignation. "It's what I had with your grandmama and Claudette."

Luna stiffened beside me. "And what does that mean, exactly?" she demanded.

"Yeah, what she said," Logan agreed.

I didn't comment since I wondered the same thing.

But I was the one my grandfather addressed. "The three of us were very much a unit, similar to the one you, Silas, and Luna are forming." Sadness swirled in the depths of his dark eyes. "Your grandmama was the alpha female and Claudette was a human turned lycan. During my initial alpha rituals, I turned her, then claimed Yazmine beneath the moon a few weeks later."

As was the custom for an alpha ascension.

I understood that.

"And?" I prompted.

"And unlike your pairing to Luna, Yazmine was mine by choice. Meaning we went into our initial claiming with love already in our hearts. As you know, the male bites first. Then the female bites during the next full moon. But something happened between me and Claudette in the interim, and that something spread to my Yazy. We didn't understand it at first; the physical connection was just incredibly intense."

Sounds familiar, I thought.

"And by the next full moon, the three of us were too engaged for Yazmine and me to go through with our pairing alone. We invited Claudette to join us and performed a triad bonding instead, much to the surprise of our pack. Then we lived together as a trio for nearly five hundred years, three hundred of which I ruled Clemente Clan. We didn't split until the new world order, and to this day, I believe that split is what killed my Yazy." He swallowed, his eyes falling. "Triads are not meant to be separated."

"What he's telling you is a warning," my mother added softly from the living area, her voice surprising us all. "You can't enter a triad lightly. All three of you have to be committed and be prepared to fight for it."

CHAPTER 39
LUNA

Two days later and Lilith still hadn't reconvened the council. Apparently, she wasn't in a hurry to deliver a verdict.

Which left wolves and vampires all over Clemente Clan headquarters.

And specifically, in Edon's house.

I stretched my legs, limbering up for a much-needed run as Silas joined me outside. "Human or wolf?" he asked.

"Human." Because I wanted to talk to him about all this triad business. We'd avoided the Jolene bombshell for long enough. While I could sense how Edon felt, I had no idea what Silas thought about it all.

Fucking around temporarily as a trio was fine.

Committing to one for eternity? Yeah, entirely different scenario. Even if it broke my heart to see Silas go, I'd let him if that was what he wanted.

And therein lies the problem—I can't read him. Just as he can't read me.

Supposedly, that problem would be fixed if we

accepted each other under the next full moon, but I wasn't willing to do that until I knew he desired the same things I did.

"Human it is." He left to slip on a pair of socks and shoes and returned without a shirt. Something my eyes more than appreciated. "Ready?"

"Yep."

He grinned. "Lead the way."

"You just want to check out my ass," I said, taking off at a jog for the tree line.

"Those shorts are awfully short, little moon. Can't blame me for admiring the view."

I snorted and picked up the pace because I could. "You just saw me naked, like, an hour ago." He'd joined me in the shower not to fool around but for company. Which was nice. I liked the way he washed my hair.

Of course, I'd need another thorough cleansing after this run.

Maybe Edon would be back by then and the three of us could have some fun. I supposed it depended on how Edon's chat with his grandfather went. They were reviewing the list of packmates Jolene recommended for promotion to headquarters. Apparently, he'd been keeping tabs on everyone over the last ten years, preparing for the moment his grandson ascended.

A slap to my ass had me jumping a step. "Hey!"

"I thought we were going for a run. This is more like a lazy stroll."

I glanced over my shoulder at the cocky male. "You want to race, newbie?"

"What happened to *big wolf*?" he teased, referring to that day in the kitchen.

"You haven't earned it yet," I tossed back at him. "Beat me to the creek and maybe I'll reconsider."

I took off at full speed, not giving him a chance to reply or react. His chuckle followed me, the sound far too close for my comfort. So I pushed myself harder, my inner wolf growling in jealousy of my two legs. She wanted to be free to run, to smell the trees, and to feel the air currents against her coat.

Later, I promised.

I wanted to talk to Silas in our clothes because I didn't trust myself to engage him naked. We'd end up in a pile of limbs. Especially after an adrenaline-filled sprint through the woods.

His shoulder brushed mine, his long legs carrying him faster.

On four paws, I held my own because of my experience. But it seemed he had me beat in human form.

With every inch he put between us, I grew more and more agitated.

And equally aroused.

Because the man was sleek, lean muscle streaking through the trees and dodging branches like a professional. I wanted to lick that trail of sweat beading down his spine, nip the back of his neck, and pin him to the ground.

Only to have him wrestling me beneath him, something I knew he would do. And then he'd slide right into my waiting heat.

This is why we're wearing clothes.

Except my tank top suddenly felt sticky and far too heavy.

My shorts were too thick.

My shoes suffocating.

I wanted to *breathe*.

No.

I had to talk to him first, and we were almost to the

creek—the same spot in which I'd played with Edon all those weeks ago. So much had changed since then.

A revolution? Who would have ever thought that was possible? But hell yes, I was in. Edon and Silas, too. The question was, would we fight together as a triad or as friendly packmates?

Silas reached the water's edge first, his triumphant smile drawing me to him all the more. It took serious effort not to jump him and wrap my legs around his waist. But I stopped just barely at his side, hands on my hips as I panted in much-needed breath.

He'd pushed me to my limit. I could still go another few miles, but damn. My legs felt a little like jelly.

"Did I earn my nickname?" he asked, much less winded than me. Something told me he could have gone harder, and would have, had it been Edon racing him.

I would need to work harder to keep up with those two. *Lucky male genetics.*

Silas cupped my cheek and brushed his mouth against mine. "I prefer *sweets* to *big wolf.*"

"Yeah?" I licked his lower lip. "What if I prefer *big wolf?*"

"You could nickname me *furball* and I'd still answer to you, Luna," he whispered, kissing me again.

And damn, he tasted so good. Like sex and wolf and man all wrapped up in a Silas package. Mmm, but I needed to talk to him first. That was the whole—*oh, that feels good*—point of this—

I arched into him, groaning as his tongue did something decidedly wicked with mine.

Hello, hardness, I thought, feeling his excitement beneath his jeans. He must have enjoyed that run as much as I did, even though we only went a mile or so.

His palm wrapped around the back of my neck, his

opposite hand falling to my hip, and he devoured me with his mouth.

We kissed a little in the shower, but it was more nips and fun. Silas had meant to play then. Now? Yeah, now he seemed hungry. No, *starved.* And I was his next meal.

"Silas," I breathed, my pulse racing as it always did when he touched me. "I want—" His tongue silenced me and scattered my thoughts.

I shivered, my wolf bowing to his.

Hmm, no, I need… "Triad," I managed to force out, the word sounding much sultrier than I anticipated.

But it caught his attention. "Triad?" he repeated, pulling back just far enough to stare down at me with his blown-out pupils.

Oh, dear moon, the hunger in his gaze…

Focus! I chastised myself.

I cleared my throat, trying to remember what I wanted to say. But I couldn't. Not with him so near, his blue irises hypnotizing me, his full lips taunting me for another kiss. I wanted him, and not just physically. I wanted *Silas.* All of him.

"I want the triad," I whispered. "I want to be with you. With Edon. With *us.* I want to hear your mind. To know your soul. To touch your heart. I want to know what it would be like to be loved by you. To love you in return. To be your mate, your everything. To connect all three of us. Forever. But I won't make you, even if it's all I can think about, all I've ever truly wanted for myself in this life. Because you have a right to choose. And I would never take that away from you."

"Hey, hey," he said softly, his thumb brushing away the tears that had fallen unknowingly from my eyes.

Goddess, I was crying.

But the thought of him not wanting me in return broke something inside me.

I hadn't realized just how important this was to me until this second, this very breath. If he rejected me, rejected *us*, I… I wouldn't be able to breathe right again.

I already love him, I realized. *I already love them both.*

I pressed my hand to my mouth, shock riveting my system. How had I let this happen? Or was there never a choice?

My wolf submitted to them both on instinct.

She *knew* her mates even when my human half didn't.

"Luna," Silas murmured, his thumb stroking over my cheekbone again. "Sweet little moon, look at me."

I had let my gaze drop without realizing it, my mortification at falling so deeply threatening to destroy me.

"I-I can't," I admitted. Not a response to the command to look at him, but to the very real heartache ripping me apart. Never in my life had I felt like this, so terrified by the potential of someone's response.

I hated not being able to sense him or his thoughts. *How does he feel?*

It would be so easy to assume, but forever was a long time. This relationship circumvented so many of society's standards. Nothing about being a triad was considered typical. None of us truly understood what it meant beyond what Jolene had said.

But I wanted it so badly that my chest ached with the emptiness of incompletion. It hurt to breathe, bringing more tears to my eyes.

This wasn't about him rejecting us but about us denying the bond.

Now that I'd allowed myself to consider the triad, I could sense what the incompletion was doing to me. "I feel so empty, Silas."

"I know. I feel it, too," he whispered, his lips against my forehead. "It's agony without you inside me, little moon. Edon's there—I feel him every day—but you… I miss you even when you're standing right in front of me. I want that connection to you, too. That bond, to call you truly mine, to claim you both. I already do in my heart, Luna. You're already mine."

I swallowed, my eyes glassing over again. "You do?"

"Every day," he promised. "You're my little moon. My Luna. On the next full moon, I'll prove it to the world. To you and Edon both. I wouldn't be anywhere else."

I grabbed him and kissed him, my tears falling between us as I let all my inhibitions go. All my doubts. All my fears. Everything. I gave him all I had, kissing him until I couldn't even breathe and not stopping to refill my lungs.

He owned me.

Edon, too.

My neck prickled with awareness, a familiar warmth approaching from behind. How he found us, how he *knew*, I didn't care. Because as I felt Edon's lips on my shoulder, I collapsed, allowing both males to cradle me between them.

"I want it, too," he whispered into my ear. "I've wanted you both since the beginning. You're mine, little mate. And Silas is mine, too."

My clothes disappeared into a pile on the rocks. Silas's following suit. And Edon had arrived naked, likely in his wolf form.

I turned in his arms, kissing him as I did Silas, pouring all my emotions, my *heart*, into my tongue as it stroked against his. *I love you,* I thought at him. *I love you so much it hurts.*

He couldn't hear me, our mating bond incomplete.

And it sliced me wide open.

I didn't want to wait until the full moon, but we didn't have a choice.

Four more weeks... I'd have to survive all that time without him hearing me, without connecting to Silas.

"Don't cry, little mate." Edon licked the tear from my cheek. "We'll fix this soon."

"I want you to hear me," I said. "I want you both to *hear* me."

"Then scream for us, sweetheart," Edon said. "Scream for everyone to hear, to tell the world who owns you."

Silas nibbled my shoulder, his hot body pressed to my back. "Let us take care of you. Let us show you how we feel about you, how we feel about each other. Join us together, Luna. Mate us both. At the same time."

I shuddered, my heart slamming against my lungs. "Yes." I swallowed. "Yes."

If we couldn't have each other mentally, then we would do this physically.

Both of them inside me at once.

Sensing everything I had to offer.

"Yes," I said for a third time, my head falling back against Silas's chest as Edon licked up the column of my throat. His palm pressed into my abdomen, sliding downward to the ache between my legs.

"So wet," he hissed, his fingers slipping easily inside.

I moaned, my hips rising up against his touch, begging him to go deeper.

But he had something else in mind.

He removed his hand, then guided it around to my backside. Silas shifted to allow him room to move, but I felt his cock pressed into the alpha's wrist.

Heat slithered through my veins, lighting my body on fire as Edon penetrated my puckered hole.

Silas yanked my head back for a kiss, distracting me

with his tongue. But the pressure built inside me as Edon worked to lubricate both sides, readying me to take them both.

It would destroy me.

Cripple my ability to think of anyone but them.

And I was okay with that. Because Silas and Edon made me feel whole. They were my pack, my past, present, and future, and I would only ever desire them.

"She's ready," Edon whispered seconds, or maybe minutes, later. I didn't know, my body strung too tight with anticipation to comprehend time.

He captured my mouth, his tongue fucking me thoroughly as he guided the three of us to the ground. Leaves pillowed my bare legs, pleasing my inner wolf immensely. Silas lay on his back beside me, his handsome features melting my heart. "Hop on, little moon," he invited.

His arousal beckoned me with a pulse that made my pussy clench in expectation. *Yes, please.* I crawled over him, straddling his hips and wrapping his shaft in my damp folds.

"*Fuck...*" He grabbed my hips, shifting me to where he wanted me—with his head at my entrance. "Slide down."

I did.

Because that demand? It demolished my ability to rebel, to fight, to do anything other than accept. My lower abdomen quivered, the feel of his thick, hot length inside me a growing addiction in my blood. I seated myself on him, locking us so deeply that he groaned in approval.

Edon grabbed my hip, his teeth skimming my shoulder. "Bend down and kiss him, little mate."

My heart fluttered, my wolf preening beneath the alpha's command.

I leaned into Silas, embracing him with my mouth and sighing as he wrapped his palm around my nape.

Mine, he was saying.

Yours, I agreed.

This was what I needed, our bodies connecting and confirming we belonged together. "More," I begged, no, *ordered*. It wasn't a request but a requirement. I needed *more*.

Edon stroked down my spine, eliciting goose bumps in his wake. It left me feeling light and cherished. More gentle touches, his tongue gliding along my lower back as he gripped my ass and spread me wide.

I half expected to feel his mouth *there*. Instead, he shifted, and something much harder and larger pressed against my opening.

I swallowed, suddenly unsure.

But a nip from Silas reminded me of my task, his lips moving beneath mine. Wicked. Smooth. Perfection. Urging me to return his kiss. And I did, losing myself to him as an intense pressure began to fill me from behind.

Slowly.

Carefully.

In and out, one inch at a time.

It hurt.

Yet it also did all sorts of sinful things to my insides.

I groaned into Silas's mouth, my lower half throbbing in both pain and pleasure, the two males joining with me in a way that left me spellbound.

"How do you feel, Luna?" Edon asked, his breath slightly more labored than before, as if he were pacing himself in this task.

"Hot," I whispered, swallowing. "*Full*."

He chuckled. "Not full yet, little mate." He thrust in a little more, causing me to both flinch and moan.

"I can feel you," Silas said, his jaw clenching. "Fuck, I can *feel* you."

"Wait until I start to move," Edon replied, his hands running up and down my sides. "Just a little more, Luna. Almost there."

Something unintelligible left my mouth as he forced me to take him to the hilt.

Something that sounded a lot like a growl mingled with a scream.

Something that was reminiscent of his name and a curse.

He dropped his head to my back as he allowed me to adjust to them both. I couldn't move, pinned between two strong males, their hands and lips tracing along my skin as they each praised me for taking them both. For accepting our bond. For allowing us to join so completely.

And that was exactly how I felt—*complete*.

These were my two mates. My males. My lovers. My future.

"Fuck me," I said, needing to feel them move. "I need you to *fuck* me."

Silas chuckled, his lips ghosting over my cheek. "You heard the woman, Edon."

"Still topping from the bottom," he mused out loud.

"As if you would have it any other way," Silas replied.

"I wouldn't." Edon slid almost all the way out of me and rammed back in, causing me to cry out.

Fuck.

I expected that to hurt. It didn't. Instead, it left me winded in the best way. "*Please*," I said, unsure of what I wanted to beg for more. Another thrust? Harder? Softer? Faster? I just felt so full. So absolute. So alive.

His hips snapped into mine again. "Is this what you

want, little mate?" he asked against my ear. "To feel me taking your virgin ass and making it mine?"

Silas arched beneath me, his cock pulsing inside me. "Again," he breathed.

Edon complied, leaving me breathless and *hot* between them. I was wrapped up in delicious masculine muscles all moving in time with my body, sealing me in a cocoon of feral sex.

Both of them found a rhythm, one I tried to maintain, but each pump left me seeing stars. I'd never felt so utterly dominated. Completely mastered. Owned. Yet worshiped.

They were kissing me, touching me, making sure I loved it every bit as much as they did. And that care alone sent me cascading into a well of oblivion so deep that I fought to resurface.

A pinch to my clit brought me back, teeth against my neck, a palm squeezing my breast, and a stark demand to "Come again."

Edon. He wanted my pleasure, to split me in half for everyone to hear.

And my body craved to give it to him.

Both males moved sharply, in and out, hitting me in places I never knew were orgasmic points. It left me shaking between them, my pleasure mounting again, only this time was far more intense. Liquid lava poured through my system, culminating in my lower belly, threatening to burst.

"Edon," I whimpered. "Silas." I didn't know whom to beg, whom to cry out to, but as the fire escalated inside, I began to sweat. To vibrate. To scream.

It was ripping me in two. Half of me claimed by Silas, the other half by Edon. And their names poured from my mouth, just as they desired.

"Fucking beautiful," Edon praised, his cock so deep in

my ass that I couldn't move, could only convulse as pleasure continued to ripple through me.

"Perfection," Silas agreed, his back bowing off the ground as he came inside me on a roar that echoed off the trees and blasted my senses apart.

Edon followed us both, his seed pumping deep inside me as if to find Silas's essence.

A sudden peace settled over me.

Joined.

We were finally together. All three of us, in mind, body, and spirit.

With Silas beneath me and Edon at my back, we were finally mated in a harmony of bliss.

Mine, my wolf whispered. *These males are mine.*

Just as I was theirs.

We didn't need a ceremony to complete us.

We were already complete.

As one.

The ritual next month would just be a formality. Because I felt it in my blood that our souls were already bound. Promised for eternity.

A triad.

Forever.

CHAPTER 40
EDON

Lilith paced the main lodge room, her gown fluttering around her in a ridiculous wave of red. She looked ready to attend a damn ball, not address an agitated crowd of alphas and royals.

Tonight was her deadline of five days since the incident. And she'd waited until the very last second to call her "emergency council meeting." Talk about a power trip.

I folded my arms and leaned against the wall, watching as she paced the wooden floor in her five-inch stilettos. One would think this bitch would be eager to run on back home. Alas, no.

"I have reviewed the evidence," she announced, pausing in the center beneath the brightest light. It gave her pale hair an ugly yellow glow. Fitting for her personality, it seemed.

It's starting, I told Silas. He was back at my house with Rae, Luna, Darius, and Juliet.

If something happened tonight, they were under strict orders to run to Jace Region. But I suspected the escape act wouldn't be needed. Lilith would have brought an army with her if that were the case, and yet only two minions stood off to the side—both young vampires Kylan and Jace could take out with a second's notice.

This revolutionary team was certainly proving handy.

Lilith cleared her throat and stared down Kylan. "I cannot allow a precedent to be set where royals or alphas decide to take the life of another just to soothe a situation. We're immortals. There are ways to incapacitate us without ending a life."

The royal smiled. "Duly noted. I'll remember that going forward."

"Why didn't you just shoot him? Or break his neck? Why remove his head?" she demanded.

"Because I didn't like the prick," Kylan replied. "And he put my life in danger by instigating a war. Why are we not analyzing his guilt, Lilith? How many lives were lost unnecessarily due to his meddling?"

"How do you know he's guilty?" she countered.

"Is it not obvious?" he asked, his eyebrows rising. "I thought you concluded your evidence research. If you've not ascertained that Silvano double-crossed Walter with the intent of hurting Clemente Clan for his own financial gain, then perhaps you need another five days in that fancy jet of yours."

That royal had balls. Big ones.

And Lilith appeared ready to murder him for it. Blood stained her porcelain cheeks, painting her skin in a cherry-red tone. "You ascertained all that before killing him?"

He narrowed his gaze. "I am over five thousand years old, Lilith. Nearly twice your age. That's granted me experience unlike anything you could ever fathom. And a double cross such as Silvano's is not an uncommon occurrence throughout my very long history. So yes, *young one*, I did. And I delivered the justice he deserved."

He took a step forward, his height advantage clear as he looked down at her.

"My only regret is not taking the wolf's head, too, as he certainly deserved it for plotting such a ludicrous political move. Had it been me, I would have been much slyer about it. But again, that kind of knowledge comes with experience. Something I have in spades."

She swallowed but didn't otherwise move. "Are you threatening me, Kylan?"

"No, sweetheart," he replied, smiling. "Why on earth would I desire your seat at the top? I live with enough targets on my back."

Silence fell over the room.

The sound of hearts beating echoing off the walls.

Everyone waited for her verdict and Kylan's reaction.

Your friend Rae might be one of the bravest people I've ever met, I murmured to Silas.

Why?

Because she lives with Kylan. That royal is fucking terrifying. He didn't appear fazed at all, his stance intimidating yet relaxed at the same time.

Something told me he would have no problem winning a fight against Lilith. Especially with this crowd. She might have a few supporters in attendance, but there were also several against her.

Except we couldn't go after her yet. I'd asked, and Jace explained that they needed her alive because she was the only one in existence who could help them find Cam, the former vampire king. He was believed to be dead. His *Erosita*—who lived with Majestic Clan, apparently— proved otherwise. Because if Cam was dead, she would be, too.

I'd absorbed all that information with a shocked expression.

Silas, however, had just shrugged and said, *"Nothing in this world is what it seems."*

If only we could all be that laid-back and accepting about it.

"No additions to your harem," Lilith declared. "No Blood Day attendance. No social outings of any kind. You are hereby confined to Kylan Region until I say otherwise. Is that understood?"

"Is this supposed to be my punishment?" he asked, cocking his head. "Sounds like a vacation."

"Then I'll consider adding blood rationings to the list," she seethed. "Get back in line or I *will* threaten your position at the top as royal."

His lips curled. "You could try. But I wouldn't recommend it."

Her jaw ticked as he stepped back to his place in our makeshift circle.

It'd been part of our plan for him to take control of the show, and he'd acted splendidly. I just hoped he didn't end up with any repercussions from it. But at least all the spotlight would remain on him as a potential rebel, and not on any of us.

"Edon and Logan are granted permission to ascend," she continued with a flourish, pointedly turning her back on Kylan. "Edon acted within his right of the challenge, and I see no reason for him to be punished. Logan was an innocent bystander whom I'm grateful to have coming of age. Unfortunately, he cannot ascend for eleven more moons, which poses a leadership problem in his clan."

"I have a suggestion," Luka cut in. "If I may."

She waved a hand. "I'm all ears, Alpha."

He cleared his throat and stepped forward. "After Edon's ascension, send Jolene to Ernest Clan to act as a leader while Logan completes his final year of training.

The former alpha may be old, but he's still a force of nature. As was evidenced the other night when he took on the ceremonial role for Edon's challenge. I feel he would be more than fit to administer the alpha trials next year."

She considered him for a long moment. "Are there any objections to the notion?" she asked, addressing the other alphas in the room. Her gaze fell on me. "Edon?"

"I agree with Luka's suggestion. Jolene might be old, but he's still an alpha." I purposely used his given name, not my endearment for him. The more detached she believed me to be, the more likely she would agree. As much as I would miss him, I knew this was his desire—to return to his Claudette.

"And I have no objections either," Logan added. "There are no elder alphas in my clan, and I would be grateful for the leadership of one so experienced."

A few others nodded in agreement, no one speaking out about the clearly obvious path.

"Very well," Lilith said. "Edon, please advise Jolene of his new placement after we finish here."

"I will," I agreed. Not that I had a choice. She may have used the word *please*, but she meant it as an order.

She nodded. "The last item for us to handle is Silvano Region. Sovereign Catalina confessed to her involvement in his nefarious plans to instigate a war for the benefit of gaining land." She glanced at Kylan, a subtle edge to her tone. "Which means I can't trust his political choices in that region and need to conduct a full investigation personally. So I will temporarily be taking over as the royal of the territory until an appropriate candidate can be found."

"Or you could allow me to serve temporarily and save yourself multiple trips," Ryder drawled, causing several heads to turn his way. "I mean, I meet all the royal qualifications, and I already live in the region. Seems a more suitable answer."

Well, that's unexpected.

What is? Silas replied.

Ryder just volunteered to be the temporary royal of Silvano Region. And from the look on Lilith's face, she was *not* happy about it.

"You were offered a royalship a century ago and turned it down," she snapped, her temper showing. "Why now?"

"Because you said it would only be temporary." He smiled. "Temporary royalty, I'll accept. Permanent royalty? In this new world? No."

She bristled. "You are not suitable to lead."

"Why?" he countered. "Because I turned down your precious offer a century ago?" he snorted. "We both know I'm more than qualified, Lilith. And if I wanted to, I could demand the position permanently."

We could have heard a pin drop—it was that silent.

The other royals in the room seemed to be in agreement, their gazes riveted on Lilith, waiting for her decision.

But Ryder wasn't done.

"I've *chosen* to mind my own business, but Silvano changed that when he led an army of idiots through my yard. I don't know what he's been teaching vampires in his region, or why. What I do know is they need a makeover, one only I can provide." He arched a brow. "Unless you're doubting my sanity, too?"

Kylan smirked.

Ryder did not.

"We both know Texas isn't your playground, Lil," Ryder added. "Let me wrangle 'em up for you, teach 'em a lesson, while you find a fitting candidate to take my place.

Although, as payment, I want freedom to go back to not giving a fuck and minding my own business. Understood?"

Damn, he was giving Kylan stiff competition in the balls department. Because fuck. He'd just essentially commanded her decision, acting as though she'd already agreed.

And maybe she had.

Because she just kept staring at him, visibly speechless.

"Seems a sound arrangement, lass," Cormac said. "He's worthy and offering. Cannae get better than that, if ye ask me."

Lajos nodded. "It will take time to find a suitable candidate, Lilith. Managing both territories in the interim would be a hefty task. Give it to Ryder; just keep the bastard on a leash."

Ryder snorted. "Keep your bedroom fetishes out of this discussion, Lajos."

Lilith raised her hand between them before Lajos could reply. "Enough." She lowered her arm and pressed an index finger to her temple to massage it. "Fine. Ryder can take over as *temporary* royal. Until I come up with a better solution."

Shit. She caved. I expected her to fight harder or outright deny him, but she suddenly appeared too exhausted to care.

Darius says it's a smart political move, Silas replied. *Ryder could claim royalty at any time and demand a territory. She really isn't in a place to deny him.*

Really?

That's what Darius says.

Huh. Vampire politics was fucked up.

"I think that covers everything, then," Lilith continued. "The entire council will convene in Lilith City in two months' time. We will no longer be convening annually, but quarterly." She looked around the room, searching for an objection.

"Is that a social occasion I am not to attend?" Kylan asked, reminding me of an unruly child raising a petulant question.

It raised a smirk from Ryder across the room. "We could only be so lucky."

"*All* council members are to attend," Lilith replied, her tone laced with command. "Even Robyn."

All the good humor fled from Kylan's features. "It's as if you're daring me to kill another royal, Lilith."

She narrowed her gaze. "Given your recent track record, Kylan, I wouldn't recommend it."

"Why, darling, that almost sounds like a challenge," he murmured. "I assume we're all free to leave?"

Her jaw clenched. "Yes. You may go," she replied with a very tight smile.

"Excellent." He turned with a flourish, leaving without so much as a glance back.

Several followed but paused to thank me for my hospitality on their way out. A few even congratulated me, commenting that they would return for my official ascension. Jace was among the latter. Luka, too. Apparently, we would be having a party again in a little less than a month. Awesome.

Fortunately, Lilith said she wouldn't be able to make it.

Feigning my disappointment had not been easy.

Even Logan seemed to struggle as he waited beside me.

The rumble of cars starting outside was a welcome sound, causing me to sigh as the last of the council members disappeared, leaving me alone with Logan. We had a few matters to tend to, what with my grandfather moving to his territory.

"How would you feel about me bringing Claudette with me?" Logan asked. "To your ascension, I mean."

"I think my granddad would like that," I said, smiling. "Do you mind if I hold on to him for a few weeks? To sort out the chaos in Clemente Clan?"

He had sat through one of the meetings with my grandfather where we reviewed all the pack members, their skill sets, locations, and potential for advancement. So Logan knew what kind of shitstorm Walter had left for me to clean up.

"Yeah, I can manage for a few weeks without him." He smiled. "It'll give me a chance to sort a few members out on my own."

My own lips quirked up. "I hear that." There were several assholes around here I couldn't wait to remove. I clapped him on the back. "Keep in touch, yeah?"

"Pretty sure that's a given," he drawled. "Gotta make sure you don't hurt my big sister."

I laughed as we exited the lodge. "Trust me. Your sister can handle herself."

Pride lit up his blue eyes. "Yeah. She can."

I'm coming home, I told Silas. *Get Luna naked.*

Already a work in progress, he replied in a breathy tone. *We started as soon as the vampires left.*

I wouldn't have it any other way.

CHAPTER 41
LUNA

This was much different from my first mating ceremony.

For one, I didn't want to ruin it.

And for another, I wanted the alpha to smell my recent sexual experience for an entirely different reason.

The look in Edon's eyes as he kissed a path down my body before the pack made my efforts worth it. And as he met the apex between my thighs, he growled in hunger at scenting Silas's recent marking.

If the alpha sniffed around the back, he'd smell himself.

But he didn't.

Instead, he grinned and bit me where he originally did just over two months ago, reclaiming me for all to see. Only this time, Silas knelt and bit my opposite thigh.

I swallowed, the heat of their joint embrace lighting an ember inside me that refused to cool. If they didn't get up here quickly, I'd join them on the ground.

But slowly they stood, their matching grins so very wolfish.

"Do you accept us as your mates?" Edon asked, his eyes darker than midnight and yet glistening from the full moon above.

"I do." I wrapped my palm around the back of his neck and kissed him, then repeated the gesture with Silas. And knelt before them.

I ran my nose up and down their thighs, breathing in their rich masculine scents. These two virile males were all mine. For eternity. Mmm. The things we would do together. But first I had to claim them properly beneath the moon, in front of our peers and the pack, and all our ancestors above.

My teeth sank into Silas first, our connection snapping into place with a force that stole the breath from my lungs. All his emotions, his thoughts, his senses became mine. Just as he inherited the same from me, our link permanent and amazing and filling a void deep inside me.

Oh, but I needed Edon, too.

I wasted no time in biting him.

He groaned into my mind, two months of partial fulfillment slamming into me at once. Fuck, his desire to mate was potent. The happiness that followed nearly knocked me to the ground. And the overwhelming sense of love that flourished inside him, it melted my heart.

I jumped up into his arms, capturing his lips with mine and devoured him. Silas growled, his fingers threading in my hair as he tugged me away and covered my mouth with his own.

Mates, I breathed.

Yes, they replied in unison.

We kissed for so long that our audience grew restless. They wanted more. The three of us were naked, our arousal evident. But we weren't done yet.

Edon needed to establish a mating link to Silas and vice

versa. It would go deeper than their sire-progeny bond and firmly solidify our triad.

After another long kiss with Edon, the males released me to focus on each other. "Before I do this, I have an announcement to make," my alpha mate said, his voice gruff and sexy as fuck. I loved his dominant tone. It was the one that made me go to my knees, but as I heard what he wanted to say in his mind, I didn't follow my instinct.

Instead, I smiled.

Yes, I told him. Not that he needed my approval, but I gave it nonetheless.

He gazed out at the crowd, his focus falling on several members of our clan—all new additions to headquarters after some careful selections these past few weeks. Such a different vibe from my first arrival. These lycans were curious, if a little wary. However, Edon would lead them into a new way of life, while Silas and I would help in any way he needed.

"It's very rare for a human turned lycan to survive. Even rarer for him to exude much strength in his new form. That said, I've noticed uncanny will and prowess in my progeny. So much so that I suspect he's of a rare alpha bloodline. Which would explain Luna's and my attraction to him." He paused to smile at Silas, a light hum telling me they were talking mind to mind.

Soon the three of us would possess that trait.

No walls.

No hiding.

All open intensity and love.

"So why am I telling you all this?" Edon continued, his amusement palpable from whatever Silas had said. Probably a comment about why Edon and I were enamored with him.

The only thing attractive about my blood is the way it fills my cock when you both want to fuck, Silas murmured into my mind. *That's what I told him.*

I bit my lip to keep from laughing and gave him a come-hither look instead. It earned me a low growl through our new connection.

Stop flirting, Edon chastised softly. *I'm making an important announcement.*

Out loud he said, "I'm telling you all this because I'm promoting Silas to the position of enforcer within the pack."

A wave of shock settled over the pack.

Followed by a clap.

Jolene stood, his eyes glittering with satisfaction, his hands loud as he applauded. And soon the others joined in, their focus and respect landing on Silas.

All signs of amusement had fled, his expression one of open astonishment. "Enforcer?"

"Consider it your new—official—nickname," Edon murmured, smiling as the sound of approval heightened. "You earned it."

I don't even know what it means, Silas whispered.

It means you're his right-hand man, I explained. *If Edon ever steps away on business, you're the acting alpha. It's extremely rare. Most alphas don't name an enforcer because it suggests he believes you're a contender for his position at the top. That you could be the Alpha of Clemente Clan.*

Silas gaped at Edon. "You can't be serious."

"You know I never do anything without purpose," he replied, wrapping his palm around the back of Silas's neck. "And now it's time to make you truly ours." He knelt while holding his new enforcer's gaze, adoration and esteem radiating from his expression. "Will you have us, Silas?"

"Yes." It came out choked, so he cleared his throat and

said it again. "Yes." He reached for my hand, holding me close.

And Edon struck.

I shuddered, feeling the connections snapping, the energy sizzling between the three of us as the triad called for Silas to finish it.

The men switched places, Edon's arm sliding around my lower back as Silas knelt before us and kissed the alpha's lower abdomen. A taunting promise lit his blue gaze, sending a tremor through me for an entirely different reason.

Such a tease, I heard Edon chastise.

That I could sense him talking to Silas confirmed how close we were to completion. I whimpered, needing it to be done, to finalize our destiny.

I love you both, Silas murmured. *To the moon and back.*

To the moon and back, Edon agreed.

For eternity, I added.

Electricity wrapped around the three of us as Silas bit down, finishing the ritual.

Power snapped into place.

Voices.

Feelings.

Sensations.

Love.

All of it at once, leaving me overflowing with life—*three* lives.

I sighed, collapsing into the arms of my males, our lips all over each other at once. Not for sex. But for adoration. Worship. A vow for forever.

I barely registered the clapping, too caught up in the new connection to focus on much else. Silas's mouth whispered over mine. Edon caressed my neck. They were both in my head, but the alpha was louder.

Time to ascend, little mate, he murmured. *Join me?*

He didn't mean in the actual ascension—a female couldn't be alpha of a clan—but in the ceremony. *I wouldn't miss it.*

Enforcer? he asked.

I go where you go, Silas replied. *Always.*

You'll both be the ones who keep me grounded, he said softly. *There are trying times ahead.*

And we'll be with you every step of the way, I vowed.

Every step, Silas echoed.

I know, he whispered.

And he really did. I felt that surety radiating through him.

Just as I sensed his love.

Our love.

There might be a revolution brewing on the horizon, one that had the potential to end in disaster. But I wasn't scared. In fact, I welcomed anyone to try to take us down. Because as a unit, we were unstoppable.

Touch one of us, and we'll end you.

We're the Clemente Clan triad.

Tread carefully.

We bite.

Epilogue

"Beautiful ascension," Jace praised with a glance up at the moon.

"Thanks," I replied. "But it was Edon who ascended." And he was standing about ten yards to the right talking to Luka.

"Oh, I know. But I have something for you, wolf." Jace handed me an envelope. "It's from Kylan. As you know, he couldn't attend due to Lilith's little grounding punishment."

I frowned at the item. "He wrote me a letter?"

Jace shrugged. "Said it had information you would want. I didn't read it, so I have no idea what he meant."

"I see. Well, thanks."

He nodded and turned, then paused and rotated back around. "What does Edon plan to do with Walter's leftover harem? I assume he won't be using the slave girls in Aurora's basement?"

"I wasn't aware there were any," I replied, frowning. Edon and I had never discussed it. In fact, I'd never actually seen Walter's harem. I sort of assumed he'd killed them all.

Jace smiled. "Then Aurora did as I suggested. Clever girl."

"Which was what?"

"Ah, a gentleman doesn't kiss and tell, new wolf." He winked. "Consider that a lesson."

The royal wandered off with his hands in his pockets and a kick in his step, leaving me torn between demanding an explanation and reading the letter.

She gave them to Luka, Edon murmured. *There were only three, as Walter had a penchant for fucking his harem to death. It seems my mother tried to help the remaining females by feeding them when my poor excuse for a father wasn't looking.*

I grimaced. *That doesn't surprise me. But why didn't you say anything?* It seemed like something he'd mention.

Because I only just found out. The pack psyche is filled with information. Apparently, my grandfather helped her.

He's a lot scrappier than he lets on, I replied, eyeing the older male in the crowd.

He had an arm around a much smaller woman, her hair as white as his. But the way he held her reminded me of how I embraced my Luna. She stood beside them, the stars in her eyes. Happiness radiated from her, causing me to smile. *She really is beautiful, isn't she?*

Yeah, she is, Edon agreed softly. *Our little mate.*

Our little moon, I mused back at him.

You know I can hear you both, right? Luna put in. *Open connection now, boys. Behave.*

Never, Edon growled.

I could already see that fucking later would be fun. All of us in each other's heads? Yeah, that would be hot. Too bad we had another hour of mingling to do first. At least we were clothed again, because if I had to watch Edon and Luna prance around naked all night, I wouldn't last another five minutes.

So needy, Edon teased.

Says the male who is growing harder by the second, I tossed back at him as I opened the envelope. Might as well distract myself for a moment with Kylan's letter. I couldn't imagine what he had to say unless it was regarding Rae.

I unfolded the note, my eyes roaming over the words in a quick sweep that brought my heart to my throat.

Oh, fuck…

Willow.

Young Wolf,

My consort requested I send you my findings on an old friend. To fulfill her wishes, I'm drafting this correspondence.

After finally locating your friend's camp destination, I stumbled upon some troubling news. It seems she escaped four weeks ago and has yet to be found. Which leads me to believe she's now in Silvano Region. If only she'd chosen the opposite direction to run, you'd have her in your custody now, as she was being held in Clemente Clan's breeding camp.

I'll continue my search. However, for now, I've reached a dead end. Let's hope your friend has a fire similar to yours and my consort's. She'll need it to survive.

Regards,
—K

P.S. Congratulations on the triad.

The Blood Alliance World Continues with *Rebel Bitten…*

Once upon a time, humankind ruled the world while lycans and vampires lived in secret.

This is no longer that time.

Willow

They're chasing me, even into my dreams.

And when I awake, I see *him*. Striking black eyes with a hint of the devil inside. He's my savior and my worst nightmare combined.

Because he owns me.
He found me.
He saved me.

But I don't want to be owned. I want to be free. Even if it kills me.

Ryder

I needed a diversion, a plaything, something to distract me from this perpetual boredom. And she appeared as if the Almighty above had heard my prayers.

Or, more accurately, the devil.

Because I'm not a good man. Humanity died inside me long ago. It was what I needed to survive.

But she's such a pretty little thing. I think I'll keep her and make her mine. At least for a little while. Humans are so fragile, after all.

Welcome to Ryder Region.
It may not be mine yet, but it will be soon.
For I haven't lived this long by playing nice.
I prefer to bite.

USA Today Bestselling Author Lexi C. Foss loves to play in dark worlds, especially the ones that bite. She lives in North Carolina with her husband and their furry children. When not writing, she's busy crossing items off her travel bucket list, or chasing eclipses around the globe. She's quirky, consumes way too much coffee, and loves to swim.

Want access to the most up-to-date information for all of Lexi's books? Sign-up for her newsletter here.

Lexi also likes to hang out with readers on Facebook in her exclusive readers group - Join Here.

Where To Find Lexi:
www.LexiCFoss.com